D1210317

Angus Donald was born in 1965 and educated at Marlborough College and Edinburgh University. He has worked as a fruit-picker in Greece, a waiter in New York and as an anthropologist studying magic and witchcraft in Indonesia. For the past fifteen years, he has been a journalist in Hong Kong, India, Afghanistan and London. He is married to Mary, with whom he has a baby daughter, and he now writes full time from home in Tonbridge, Kent.

Also by Angus Donald

Outlaw
Holy Warrior

KING'S
MAN

ANGUS DONALD

sphere

SPHERE

First published in Great Britain in 2011 by Sphere

Copyright © Angus Donald 2011

The moral right of the author has been asserted.

*All characters and events in this publication, other
than those clearly in the public domain, are fictitious
and any resemblance to real persons,
living or dead, is purely coincidental.*

All rights reserved.
No part of this publication may be reproduced, stored in a retrieval
system, or transmitted, in any form or by any means, without
the prior permission in writing of the publisher, nor be otherwise
circulated in any form of binding or cover other than that in which
it is published and without a similar condition
including this condition being imposed on the subsequent purchaser.

A CIP catalogue record for this book
is available from the British Library.

Hardback ISBN 978-1-84744-491-2
Trade paperback ISBN 978-1-84744-483-7

Typeset in Bembo by
Palimpsest Book Production Limited, Falkirk, Stirlingshire
Printed and bound in Great Britain by
Clays Ltd, St Ives plc

Sphere
An imprint of
Little, Brown Book Group
100 Victoria Embankment
London EC4Y 0DY

An Hachette Company
www.hachette.co.uk

www.littlebrown.co.uk

For my darling daughter Emma,
with oceans of love

Nottingham Castle, March 1194

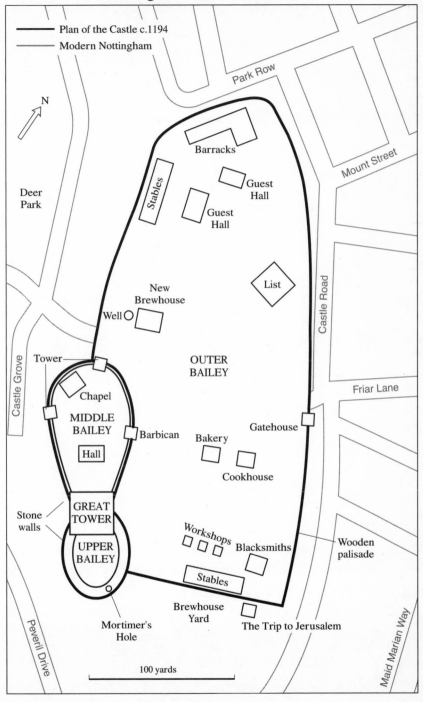

Part One

Chapter One

I can hear the sound of singing floating across the courtyard from the big barn, thin and faint yet warmly comforting, like the last wisps of a happy dream to a man waking from deep slumber. I have left the remnants of the wedding party to their pleasures, leaving the bride Marie and her new husband Osric and dozens of their friends and neighbours to carouse long into the dark night. I have provided ale and wine, more than they could ever drink at half a dozen nuptials, and I slaughtered two of my sheep and a great sow, and all three carcasses spent the afternoon roasting over slow fires in the courtyard so that there might be plenty of meat for the newly joined couple and all their boozy well-wishers. But I slipped away from the throng when the serious drinking began and the wine-flushed carollers began to loosen their belts; I did not wish to be asked to perform alongside them. My voice is a little weaker, as is natural, now that I have reached almost sixty years of age, but I am still proud of my talent as a *trouvère*,

3

a maker of fine music, and I husband my delicate throat-cords and do not choose to bellow like a cow in calf for the amusement of country-wedding drunks – I who have traded verses with a king, and held noble lords and prelates across Christendom spellbound with my skill.

But, in truth, there is another quiet reason why I have withdrawn here to my private chamber at the end of the great hall of Westbury, where, with a freshly sharpened quill and new-made oak gall ink, I am committing these words to parchment – I do not like Osric, the bridegroom.

There: I have admitted it. It is difficult to say exactly why I do not like him: he is a plain, ordinary man, round in the belly and with a pointed, peering, mole-like face and short chubby arms, and he will, I believe, make my widowed daughter-in-law Marie a good husband. He came here to Westbury a year ago as my bailiff, and he has rendered me good service in that office, ensuring that the manor – the only one I now hold – is well ordered and shows a little silver in profit every year. But I do not trust him; there is a slyness about him that repels me. His manner is furtive. I believe, in my secret heart, that he covets my position as lord of this manor, and sometimes I see him looking at me, as we eat together as a family at the long table in the hall, and I detect a glint of hatred in his tiny underground eye. It may be nothing but the foolish fancies of an old man, but I do not think so – I believe that despite my kindness to him, and the fact that I have allowed him to marry my son Rob's widow, Osric would like to see me hurried into my grave and himself sitting at the head of this long table, fawned on by my servants and addressed in this hall as 'my lord'.

I will go further: I believe that he means to kill me.

4

Pshaw! What nonsense, you will say to yourself. The old grey-beard's wits are plainly as addled as a year-old goose egg. And it is true that I am well furnished with years, and that I sometimes forget the names of these dullards around me today, and dwell too much on the bright days of the past. But I know about betrayal: in my time, I have betrayed those who placed their trust in me. And I see the look of a traitor, a God-damned Judas, in Osric's face. To strike a telling blow, one must be close to the man you are to play false; and Osric is now as close to me as ever he can be.

My death would not, of course, immediately make him the lord of this manor; if I were to die, the manor would pass to my heir, my nine-year-old grandson and namesake Alan, who is away now in Yorkshire learning the skills of a knight – learning how to fight on horseback and on foot, and how to dance and sing and make verses, how to speak and write in Latin, to play chess and serve elegantly at table and innumerable other gentlemanly skills.

But a child lord is weak, and easy to control: his mother Marie would have legal authority over him, just as Osric, now her husband, would have authority over her. Who is to say what Osric might do then? The boy might have a fatal 'accident' or be imprisoned for years in some dark place while Osric makes free with the bounty of the manor. Who can say?

I have read over the words that I have just written and it might seem to a reader that I am afraid of Osric, like a coward – but I am not craven and I have shown my courage on more occasions than I care to remember. But I have decided not to strike the words out but to let the sentiments above stand, for I have made a promise that in this record of my life, this record that I now scratch out with an ageing hand, I will tell the truth, and always the truth. I do perhaps fear Osric a little; at least, I am distrustful of his intentions, and wary. And I cannot sleep at night for thinking about him and what he might do to me and those whom I love. But I can do nothing; I cannot kill him out of hand on a mere suspicion, and I cannot drive the husband of my daughter-in-law away from this manor; Marie would never allow it – and who would oversee the smooth running of Westbury? No, I must endure, and watch and be always on my guard.

And I must get along with my story now, while the hall is empty and quiet, for this tale is not about Osric's darkling ambitions, nor about Marie – nor even about little Alan, the delight of my remaining years – it is about myself, and the adventures that I had in the time of good King Richard, whom we called the Lionheart, when I was a young man, full of green sap, strong in body and mind, fearful of almost nothing save the wrath of my lord, Robert Odo, the Earl of Locksley – who was better known to the common people of England as Robin Hood – a savage warrior, a lawless thief, a Church-condemned heretic and, may Almighty God forgive me, for many long years, my good and true friend.

The sentry was young, a boy of no more than sixteen or seventeen summers, but he was quite old enough to die. I watched him as he walked up and down the dark rutted track that led north from my position, up to the brow of the hill; and I noted that his air in these, his last precious moments on this Earth, was one of resentful boredom. He had been on duty for perhaps an hour, I reckoned, judging by the position of the moon: I had seen him slouch up from the camp about midnight, yawning and stretching, and grudgingly take over from an older man, a squat warrior who clapped him hard on the shoulder with joy at his relief and hurried off to his warm blankets in one of the scores of tents that littered the field below the muddy track and made up the enemy encampment before Kirkton.

The young sentry was not due to be relieved for another two hours but by then, God willing, he would be dead. I could make out his young face in the faint moonlight, a pale patch in the darkness, as he trudged towards me down the track; as he came closer I could see that he was ill-favoured, with a thin, well-pimpled visage: he looked like a sulky boy making his reluctant way to church when he would rather be at play.

Moodily he booted a stone out of his path and it skittered alarmingly near to where I was lying, in total darkness and black-clad from head to toe, face thickly smeared with greasy mud, in the lee of an old stone wall that ran at right angles to the track. For a panicky moment, I thought he would follow the stone's path straight towards me, coming off the track for another kick at the pebble that had landed only a few feet from my hiding place. If he had done that, he would have seen me for sure, or sensed me somehow, and I'd have had to launch myself at him, from the front, in full view, and try to drop him before he could make a sound. That would have been difficult. To be truthful, it would have been nigh on impossible, as I was tethered by a rope around my waist to a large, heavy, oozing sack. I tried not to think about its grisly contents.

As I pressed my shoulder against the rough stone of the wall, my hands by my sides, barely breathing, my fingertips brushed the handle of the dagger in my boot. It was my only weapon: a long, very thin, stabbing blade, triangular in section, with a strong steel crosspiece and a black wooden handle; the kind of weapon known as a misericorde, for it was used to grant the mercy of death to knights badly wounded in battle, the *coup de grâce*. The impoverished Italian knight who sold it to me called it a stiletto, a little stake, and though he took my silver needfully, he looked at me somewhat warily, too. For this was no weapon for honourable battle; this was a weapon for black murder in the dark of night, a tool for silent killing.

The sentry boy mooched on past my wall without even glancing into the darkness at its base where I was concealed and I suppressed a shiver while I fumbled with the knotted rope at my waist, finally freeing myself of my gruesome burden. My black clothes were soaking wet – after a brisk shower of rain around midnight, my tunic and hose had sucked up moisture from the damp ground like a sponge as I had crawled inch by inch through the wet grass to my ambush spot, dragging the heavy sack behind me. It had taken me nearly two hours to work myself into this position, propelling myself forward on toes and fingertips, staying low in the darkest folds of this sheep pasture, down over the brow of the hill, across a hundred yards of naked field and up to the relative concealment of the drystone wall. I had moved, most of the time, when the sentries, first the squat older man, and now this boy, were facing the other way, as they marched up to the top of the lane, took a cursory glance around and marched back down again. It was like some lethal game of Grandmother's Footsteps, although I could take no enjoyment in it. When the sentry was looking towards me, I buried my face in the wet turf and stayed absolutely still, trusting my ears to tell me if I was discovered. It was important, I had been told, never to stare directly at his face – men have an instinct for when they are being watched and some are more gifted than others at spotting a face in the darkness.

But I could certainly feel the heat of someone's gaze upon me – I was being watched myself just then, but not by this stripling soldier tramping the road before me. My friend Hanno, formerly a celebrated hunter from the inky forests of Bavaria, and now the chief scout for our small band of warrior-pilgrims, was lodged in a tree just below the skyline some two hundred yards away, his body wrapped cunningly around the trunk and branches like a serpent so as to appear part of the wood in the darkness. I knew he was watching me and I hoped that my approach had met with his approval. He had taught me everything he knew about stealthy movement on the long journey home from the Holy Land – in daylight and darkness, in forest, mountain and desert – and what he knew was considerable. He'd also personally tutored me, painstakingly, over many months, in the art of the silent kill. And he had suggested that I take on this deadly task as a test of my new skills. Everyone in our ragged band seemed to think it was a good idea, except me. So here I was: wet, cold, lying in a sheepshit-dotted pasture in the middle of the night, face blackened with mud, waiting for the right moment to slaughter an unsuspecting child.

I heard the boy reach the end of his tramp at the bottom of the track, cough, spit, and turn to begin his journey slowly back up the hill. He was out of my line of sight but audibly coming ever closer to the wall. He passed me and then suddenly stopped a few yards further up the track. Had he seen me? Surely he must hear my heart banging like a great drum in my chest? But no, he had merely paused to stare dully at the fingernail of moon that adorned the sky, trying to guess the hour. He did look so very young, I thought, although a part of me knew he was only perhaps a year or two junior to me. He switched the long spear he held from one shoulder to the other and with his free right hand he scratched at the inflamed spots on his cheek. He was close enough now, no more than two long paces away; close enough for me to strike, now that I was free of the drag of the sodden sack. And when he turned away to resume his march I told myself I would rise up and strike him down. I tensed my body, flexed my toes, hand on the dagger handle, waiting for him to move. I searched the surrounding area, eyes narrowed and roving slowly lest the slightest flash of white eyeball should attract attention; no one was stirring, the camp was silent as a stone at that hour. It was all clear. The moment he turned away, I'd be up and on him like a creeping farmyard cat on a sun-dulled dove.

But the boy remained still, half-turned towards me, and he continued to gaze like a simpleton at the moon, now picking at something stubborn inside his nose. *Turn away, turn away, you dolt,* I shrieked inside my head. *Turn away and let this deed be done.* But he stood like one of the marble statues I had seen on my Mediterranean travels, and continued to stare upwards at the star-sprinkled sky and to mine away inside his nostril.

My body was beginning to shake, not just from the cold and the wet: my pent-up muscles were demanding violent action. I wanted to move while I still had the courage to commit this murder – for foul murder it was; although the black surcoat he wore, with its blood-red chevrons across the chest, marked him as my enemy. Nevertheless, I knew in my heart that this cold killing was no better than a shameful piece of butchery, an execution – and I did not relish its accomplishment. He would not be the first man or boy that I had killed, no, not by a long summer's day. I had killed before many times in my young life, in battle and out of it – but this felt different. And wrong. It was not only my friend Hanno who was watching me from on high; I felt that God Himself was looking down on my actions. And the Lord of Hosts was telling my conscience loud and clear that this was a mortal sin.

I knew that Robin would laugh if he could read my thoughts before this kill: he would think me soft, womanish. He would shrug and half-smile, if I were to voice my doubts about murdering this boy. And I knew exactly what he would say if he were by my side: 'It is necessary, Alan,' he would whisper, and then he would take the misericorde from my hand and do the deed himself – quickly, efficiently, without a moment's pause. And never lose a wink of sleep afterwards.

Finally the boy stopped gawping at the moon, turned his back to me and took a first reluctant step up the path. I swallowed, blinked, and forced myself to rise as silently as I could from my dark corner, leaving the heavy sack in the shadows, but pulling the dagger from my boot as I did so. I kept my mind almost blank, thinking only, *Now I will do this, now I will do that*. And I took the first unsteady step, my foot squelching loudly in a patch of mud. I checked myself and stumbled slightly on wobbly legs, but my victim heard nothing. Suddenly my courage rose in me like a pot of water boiling over: I took three fast running steps and threw myself at his back; my left hand snaking around his head to clamp over mouth and nose and prevent him making a sound as my chest thumped into his spine. He fell forward, slamming into the turf bank at the side of the muddy track with jolting force, with me on top of him, the impact of our landing nearly causing me to drop the dagger. Nearly – but drop it I did not. He squirmed wildly under me but I got the blade of the misericorde into the right position on the back of his neck, in the hollow at the base of his skull, the thin point resting between the mail links of his coif, and shoved once, upwards, very hard, sending the eight-inch triangular blade up through the mail rings, splitting them apart, through skin, muscle, spinal cord and deep into his soft brain. I twisted the misericorde left and right, like a man scrambling a pot of buttered eggs with a spoon. His body gave one more frightful spasm under mine, as every muscle in his body twitched and then relaxed, and I felt him soiling himself in a loud farting rush of fluid, but then, God and all His holy saints be praised, he moved no more.

My panting breath was sawing in my throat, my hand was crushed between his face and the turf; my heart was beating as if it would burst out of my chest – and I wanted desperately to vomit, to piss, to void my own bowels. I could feel tears burning the backs of my eyelids, and it was only by using a great deal of force on myself that I fought back these unmanly urges. I turned my head and looked over my shoulder at the sleeping camp. All was quiet. So far, it seemed, no one had noticed anything. But for the limp, shit-drizzled corpse lying under me, it might never have happened.

I tugged my jelly-slick blade from his lolling head, plunged it into the turf to clean it, wiped it on my sleeve and shoved it back into the leather sheath in my left boot. I saw that in his death spasm he had bitten into the meat of the middle finger on my left hand, but I could feel no pain in that moment as I bound the finger tightly, quickly, with a scrap of linen torn from my undershirt. Then I pulled his corpse off the road and, with some difficulty, stripped the black-and-red surcoat from his dead weight and pulled it over my own sodden black clothes. I took off his helmet and gathered up his spear and sword and set them to one side. Then I recovered the bag from the lee of the stone wall and, peeling back the moist sacking, I pulled out a massive sticky lozenge of meat and bone, about a foot and a half long, complete with pointed ears and white, still eyeballs; it was the severed head of a wild moorland pony, cut from the neck below the animal's square jawline, and very nearly drained of blood. I looked round anxiously at the sleeping camp; there was still nothing stirring.

Using the boy's own sword, I hacked off his young head as neatly as I could, a difficult job in the dark with a long unwieldy blade, sawing and slicing through spine, windpipe and the muscles and tendons of his neck as quietly as possible. The sword was a cheap one, blunt, notched and with the wooden handle loose and rattling on the tang. It was not neatly done, and I was terrified that the wet sounds of my cack-handed butchery could be heard in the camp, but finally I finished my grisly work and, trying my best to avoid bloodying my clothes, I propped the headless corpse in a sitting position in the ditch by the side of the track and balanced the wild horse's head on the trunk, between the shoulders, where the boy's would have been. I secured the beast's head in place with the thin muddy rope that had been attached to the sack; tied it over the equine crown in front of the ears and round under the boy's armpits, then sat back and surveyed my handiwork with a shiver of satisfaction. It looked truly gruesome; eerie and unnatural – a man's body with a long horse's head atop. The boy's own sightless poll I grasped by its lank hair and hurled as far as I could, away into the darkness. It might be recovered, eventually, but the terrifying animal-headed corpse would still do its work on the men who discovered it.

I made the sign of the cross over my gory confection to keep his spirit quiet, mumbled an apologetic prayer to St Michael, the sword-wielding archangel and patron saint of battle, and gathered up my victim's helmet, sword-belt and spear. Then I began to trudge up the muddy track. My whole body was shaking, every step I took was unsteady, and suddenly the pain in my bitten hand came roaring out of nowhere like an angry bear. I switched the spear to my other hand and fought the reeling giddiness in my head. My victim had been slightly shorter than me, even before I hacked off his pimply head, and a shade thinner, but I calculated that on that dark night, from a distance of a hundred yards or so, if I walked in his tracks, I could pass as his double before an unsuspicious eye. I finally won control of my body and mind and banished the thoughts of the infernal deed I had just done; I slumped my shoulders a little and tried to emulate his resentful slack-kneed slouching as I walked away from his mutilated cadaver.

As I reached the brow of the hill, and paused, pretending to scour the area with my eyes like a dutiful sentry, I heard the mournful call of a barn owl hooting three times from the tree on the ridge away to my right. And for the first time in hours, I cracked a smile.

Hanno.

It was the signal, a message as warming to my heart as a hug from a loving mother.

If I had heard the sour barking screech of a mating vixen,

the message would have been: *Run for your life, the kill has been discovered. Run.*

But Hanno's skilful imitation of a hunting owl was telling me that, for the moment, I was safe. And in that moment, I loved him for it.

I could imagine his ugly round face, his stubbled, badly shaven head and wide grin, and hear his harsh foreign-accented words of praise at my completion of an unpleasant, difficult, bloody task, and I turned towards the tree where I knew he was concealed, a mere hundred and fifty yards away now that I was at the top of the track, and had to resist the urge to raise my hand to him in salute. Instead, I turned on my heel and, walking boldly, even jauntily, surcoat swishing around my shins, spear casually on my left shoulder, I made my way downhill, away from the muddy road, away from my friend Hanno, and plunged into the heart of the enemy encampment.

I walked with purpose, quietly but never stealthily, through the sleeping tents of my enemies, with what I hoped was a nonchalant grin fixed to my face – though it was, of course, too dark to see my expression. A few campfires were still smouldering between the tents, and a handful of men-at-arms dozed beside them wrapped in blankets, or sat slumped over jugs of ale. The September night still retained a little of the warmth of summer, but most of the men had retired to the large, low, saggy woollen tents that were dotted over almost all the surface of the open field.

Somewhere in the sleeping camp, I knew, was a friend and comrade, a strange middle-aged Norman woman named Elise. She had attached herself to our company on the way to the

Holy Land, and had become the leader of the women who had joined our marching column. A healer of no little skill, she had undoubtedly saved many a life on the long journey to Outremer and back, tending the hurts of battle. Some whispered that she had other, darker skills and could read the future, but while I had found that her prophecies for the most part seemed to come true, they were always vague enough to be interpreted in several ways.

My master had sent Elise into the camp two days previously, to read the soldiers' palms, tell wondrous and bone-chilling fireside tales – and to deliberately sow a particular fear among the enemy's ranks. I hoped that she was safe: had she been captured and found to be a spy, she would have faced a slow and painful death.

I had half-overheard Robin give her orders the day before she left us to wander in the guise of a travelling seller of trinkets into the camp – to be honest, I had been hanging around him hoping to persuade him that I was not the right man for the task of dealing with the sentry; but I had the impression he knew this and was avoiding a conversation with me.

'Elise, you are sure that you can do this; that you wish to do this?' Robin said, fixing her with his strange silver eyes, his handsome face concerned and kindly. They were equals in height, but she was as thin as a straw, clad in a long shapeless dark dress that had once been green, her lined face topped with a mass of white fluffy hair. She looked like nothing so much as a giant seeding dandelion.

'Oh yes, Master Robin, I can do this. It is but a small thing to spin a few tales at a campfire.'

'And you know which tales you are to spin?' asked my master.

'Yes, yes, I know,' she said impatiently, 'the spirits of dead men are trapped inside the wild ponies hereabouts, and horse-headed monsters patrol the night stealing men's souls for the Devil . . . Wooooooah! Hooooagh!' She made a series of loud eerie noises in the back of her throat and waggled her fingers in the air like a madwoman. It should have been ridiculous, comical even, but on that warm September afternoon I felt my blood chill a little. 'Don't you worry, master, they will all have nightmares,' this odd woman continued. 'And don't you concern yourself about me, sir; no harm will come to me. I have seen the shape of the future in a bubbling cauldron of blood soup, and all will be well; you shall have your victory, sir. Mark my words. A great victory after a night of fire and mortal fear.'

Robin embraced her, and promised that she would be well rewarded for the risks she was taking. 'Serving you, my lord, is reward enough,' said this strange creature calmly in her French-accented tones. 'Your fame will last for more than a thousand years,' Elise continued; her eyes seemed to have glazed over, and she clearly had at least one foot sunk in the swamp of madness. 'And those who serve you, they too will be remembered: John, Tuck, Alan, even my poor dead husband Will – they shall not be forgotten. So, I say again: the reward of serving you is enough: it is a path to immortality.' And she gave a short, high-pitched laugh that was uncomfortably close to a cackle.

He had that wondrous ability, did Robin, of commanding love in the people around him, no matter what he did. And I was not immune myself – I had witnessed Robin committing the most appalling crimes, yet I was still his faithful hound.

17

Hearing her half-crazed declaration of loyalty nipped at my conscience and I slunk away from Robin without raising the subject of the sentry's death. I could not bear to be seen to be less courageous, or less loyal to Robin, than a bone-skinny, half-crazed wise woman.

I avoided the firelight as I walked through the enemy camp that dark night, circling around behind the tents whenever possible, and kept on sauntering downhill, roughly south-west, heading towards the dark, looming bulk of Kirkton Castle, Robin's high seat overlooking the Locksley Valley. Although my master was lord of Sheffield, Ecclesfield, Grimesthorpe and Greasbrough, and dozens of smaller manors scattered all over the north of England, Kirkton Castle was his home. It was also the home of Robin's wife, Marie-Anne, the Countess of Locksley, and she was even now inside its walls, besieged by the very men whose sleeping forms I was passing, whose snores and farts I could now hear. However, with God's help, and Robin's cunning, the castle would not be under siege for much longer.

The camp of the besieger, Sir Ralph Murdac, erstwhile High Sheriff of Nottinghamshire, Derbyshire and the Royal Forests, was laid out in the shape of a crescent moon, well out of bow shot, about three hundred and fifty yards to the north-east of Kirkton. Some of Robin's men, including myself, had watched it from concealment up on the high hills for four days and nights: we knew that it contained more than three hundred armed men in total – mostly spearmen, but with a handful of crossbowmen and about eighty cavalry – and that its strength easily overmatched our small force.

Robin had left England two and a half years ago to take part in the Great Pilgrimage to the Holy Land with a small, well-trained army of archers, spearmen and cavalry, but battle, disease and the fleshpots of the Levant had thinned our ranks so that when we landed at Dover ten days ago, seasick, sore and wet through from a rough Channel crossing, we had only thirty men-at-arms capable of straddling a horse, and a score or so of Robin's surviving archers. But though we were a ragged lot, battered by much hard travel and the loss of many comrades, the fires of war in the Holy Land and the brutal journey home had tempered us like the finest steel, so that we believed ourselves to be the equal of any company twice our strength. Yet for all that we were hardened by battle, and confident in our abilities, we could not face a force such as the one Sir Ralph Murdac had mustered here – six times the size of ours – in honest, open battle and expect to be victorious.

Murdac was a loathsome man, a short, dark Norman lordling with the Christian kindness of an angry adder and the trustworthiness of a rabid rat. While he had been High Sheriff – before King Richard came to the throne – my master had been a very successful thief and outlaw, the famous Robin Hood of song and tale, no less, and he had humiliated this sheriff in many ways, robbing and killing his servants without the least compunction. They had long hated each other but had clashed in full battle only once before, more than three years ago at the manor of Linden Lea, north of Nottingham. On that occasion, after two days of the most appalling carnage, Robin had emerged the victor – but only by the skin of his teeth. Murdac had fled the country, avoiding the righteous wrath of King Richard, who wished to interview his sheriff about a vast quantity of missing tax silver, and the little shit-weasel had then taken refuge in Scotland, staying with powerful relatives. But when Richard departed his realm to undertake the Great Pilgrimage across the seas, Murdac had emerged from his Scottish bolthole and taken service with Prince John, King Richard's treacherous younger brother. Now protected by John, Sir Ralph Murdac had offered a huge bounty in silver for Robin's head, and at least one man to my knowledge had died trying to claim it.

Apart from his bitter enmity with my master, I, too, had cause to hate Ralph Murdac: when I was nine years of age, his men-at-arms had burst into our peasant cottage before dawn, ripped my father from his bed and, after falsely accusing him of theft, had hanged him from an oak tree in the centre of the village. Four years later, the same Ralph Murdac had threatened to cut off my right hand when I was caught stealing a pie in Nottingham market; and later still he had had me cruelly tortured in a dungeon at Winchester in an attempt to get information about Robin. If I ever had the chance, I would kill him in a heartbeat, with a great deal of pleasure: he was less than a clump of rotting duckweed in my eyes, and the world would be a better place with his filthy presence expunged from it.

By the grace of God, and the kindness of Robin, I had risen in rank since the days when I was a poor fatherless village boy, forced to thieve to fill my belly. I was now Alan of Westbury, lord of a small manor in Nottinghamshire that had been granted to me by the Earl of Locksley. This gift was something for which I would be forever grateful. I had been a nobody, a starving cutpurse, but now I had a place among men of honour, among noble warriors, not only as a holy pilgrim newly returned from Outremer, but as the holder of half a knight's fee of land. I had made the impossible, almost unthinkable leap from humble peasant to horse-borne lord of the manor; and I had Robin to thank for it.

I tried my best to repay my debt to Robin by loyal service in war and in peace, and by giving him the gift of my music. For now, as well as being one of his captains, a leader of his ragtag troops, I was Robin's *trouvère*, his personal musician. I hummed a snatch of music softly under my breath as I walked through the camp of my mortal enemy, striding as confidently as I could manage and trying not to trip over the guy ropes in the darkness.

My eye was drawn to a large tent in the centre of the field; in the rare splashes of firelight I could just make out that it was a gaudy, striped affair, black and blood-red. My footsteps seemed to take me towards it of their own volition, and as I drew closer I saw a short figure dressed in dark clothes standing outside the entrance to the pavilion by the remains of a large campfire. By the dying flickers of the campfire's flames I could see that it was Murdac himself, apparently standing alone, and examining a jewel-encrusted box; turning the object over and over in his hands so that the precious stones shot out gorgeous bright gleams of reflected firelight.

My feet took me closer and closer to his hateful shape. Surely this was an opportunity sent by God: Murdac alone, in the darkness, facing away from me. I paused, just a dozen yards from the little man, and the spear seemed to leap off my shoulder and level itself. I can do this, I told myself; if I can kill an innocent sentry-boy, I can scrub this shit-stain from the world. I would have no qualms at all about sending *his* stinking soul to the Devil.

I clutched the spear more tightly and was just about to sprint forward and slam the sharp point deep into Murdac's kidneys, when the little bastard bent down and gathered a handful of dry twigs from a wood pile at his feet and threw them on the fire. And, as the kindling caught, the flames licked higher and revealed the presence of two other figures on the far side of the fire. I stopped dead and stood as still as a rock, spear extended in front of me, silently uttering a prayer of thanks to St Michael that I was still cloaked by the night, invisible to those who stood in the widening pool of firelight.

I could not see them clearly in the dancing flames, but I could make out their distinctive shapes in the gloom: a tall man on the left, taller than me by half a head, and I am six foot high in my bare feet; but, while I am broad in the shoulder, deep in the chest and well muscled in the arms from long hours practising with a heavy sword, he was thin, painfully thin, like a man who has survived a long famine or a terrible disease.

His height and thinness were accentuated by his shadowy companion's extraordinary shape: he was a huge bald man, and I swear on Our Lord Jesus Christ that he was as broad as he was high; a round mass, neckless, squat and lumped with muscle, like an ogre from a children's tale. They looked like a stick and a ball standing side by side.

Then Ralph Murdac spoke, and his familiar high-pitched French whine set my teeth on edge: 'Thank my lord prince for his noble gift,' he said, and he slightly raised the jewelled box, 'and tell him that I will attend his royal court in less than a month; the moment that I have concluded matters here.'

'My lord,' the squat ogre rumbled in French, and his voice sounded like the grinding together of two enormous rocks, 'His

22

Highness has requested your presence on the morrow; he has had bad news from abroad and desires your counsel. He was most insistent that you should attend him.'

'I will attend him as soon as I am able,' snapped Murdac crossly. 'But I must have my son. I must reclaim my son from this nest of bandits. Surely His Royal Highness will understand . . .'

The two men said nothing, but the ogre gave a mountainous shrug, and they both turned away at the same time and disappeared into the great tent.

I wanted to be gone; the knowledge that I had very nearly thrown my life away in an ill-considered, suicidal attack raised goose bumps on my whole body. I had missed certain death by a heartbeat. Those two grotesque men would have shouted a warning to Murdac before I could even get within spear-range, and I would then have likely missed my mark and been hunted through the camp like a lone rat in a pit full of blood-crazed terriers. I was Daniel in the lion's den, I told myself, and only by remembering this and putting aside any thoughts of revenge against Murdac would I live to see another dawn.

I walked quickly away from the great tent without being seen – regretfully leaving the silhouette of my enemy unharmed by the fire – and once again bent my steps towards the dark mass of castle on the southern skyline. There was a sentry on the far side of the camp, alert and patrolling his section of the perimeter with an unnatural keenness for the late hour. Leaving the encampment behind and walking the bare twenty yards of open turf towards him, I notched up my courage for a final pantomime. I marched straight up to the man, my right hand casually behind my back, and called to him abruptly, in my most officer-like tones: 'Hey you! What's the password? Come on, come on; don't tell me you've forgotten it.'

He looked at me strangely, noting the mud- and blood-smeared black surcoat, and the odd combination of my youth and my arrogance. Then, perhaps reassured by the direction I had come from, he said: 'I haven't forgotten it, sir: it's Magdalene. But I might well ask, sir, who are *you*?'

'I've been told to relieve you. That's all you need to know,' I said rudely. 'Sir Ralph's orders.'

He nodded, but still seemed a little uncertain. The hand behind my back gripped the handle of the misericorde tightly; in a couple of moments he was going to feel its point in his heart if he didn't accept my explanation. I stared at him challengingly, straight in the eye. But finally he seemed to be convinced by my high-handedness and he shrugged and pushed past me, heading back towards the encampment. I watched him until he disappeared into the crowd of dark tents and finally relaxed, breathed out a huge lungful of air, and slid the slim blade back into my boot.

I had used up a lot of my nerves in this one night, and I noticed that my hands were trembling slightly, but I still had one obstacle to overcome: the walls of Kirkton Castle itself.

In the event, getting into the castle was simpler than I had expected. I merely walked away from the mass of tents, through a wide empty expanse of silent sheep pasture and towards the looming black bulk of Kirkton. When I was fifty yards away, a torch sprang to light on the battlements and, in response to it, I shouted: 'Hello, Kirkton! I'm a friend. Hello! Don't shoot. I come from Robin. I come from Lord Locksley.'

An arrow slashed past my ear and buried itself in the ground

24

a dozen yards behind me, and I lifted both arms in the air and shouted again: 'Hello, Kirkton. I come from the Earl of Locksley; let me in for the love of God.'

Another arrow hissed past and I heard a deep, Welsh-accented voice, a voice I knew well but had not heard for more than two years, shouting, 'Stop shooting, you *ynfytyn*, stop wasting arrows.' And then, much louder: 'Who is out there? Come forward and name yourself.'

'Tuck, it's me – Alan. Get that idiot to stop trying to spit me like a bloody capon. Don't you recognize me, you great tub of pork dripping? It's Alan Dale. It's me.'

'God bless my soul!' said the Welsh voice. 'Alan Dale, back from the Holy Land, back from the dead. Miracles and wonders will never cease.' And a rich, golden-brown belly laugh rolled out towards me through the darkness.

Chapter Two

They hauled me up over the wooden battlements on a loop of rope in less time than it takes to skin a rabbit – my old friend Tuck and a burly but shame-faced archer on guard duty called Gwen, whom I knew only slightly. The front gate was barred tight shut, Tuck told me in a low tone, and awakening the gate-guard to explain why the main portal needed to be opened would have taken too much time and caused far too much fuss. I was so pleased to see my stout friend that I hardly minded at all that I had trodden in a month-old corpse – my foot sinking into its rotten guts almost up to the boot top – that lay in the ditch below the palisade, while I was waiting for the loop to be thrown down.

Tuck had hardly changed at all in the time I had known him; he had the same cheerful round face, creased from half a lifetime of smiles, the same bulbous nose, reddish-brown hair, now dusted with a little grey, but still cut in the tonsure. While he was no longer a monk, as he had been when I first met him, he was still a member of the clergy: now the personal chaplain to Marie-Anne, Countess of Locksley. His new rank did not seem to have changed his attire. His brown monk's habit was perhaps more worn and stained, and he seemed to have lost a small amount of weight – but apart from that he was exactly the same strong, broad, confident man that I had left behind at Kirkton when Robin and I rode out of its gates for the Holy Land more than two years ago.

The castle, too, was wonderfully familiar, even in the darkness. And as Tuck, leaving Gwen still mumbling apologies to continue his sentry duty, led me down from the walkway that ran all the way around the inside of the wooden battlements, down into the bailey courtyard of the castle, and over into the great hall, he chatted away happily as if we had parted just the week before. I was only half listening to him, my head being filled with such emotions after my bloody adventures that night; and I was further fuddled by the joyful sense of homecoming that almost overwhelmed me as I looked around at my master's stronghold in the darkness.

'. . . and we are pretty much down to our last barrel of flour,' Tuck said. 'The water and ale are holding out, of course, but then I've been rationing from the beginning of the siege . . .'

Murdac's men, I gathered from Tuck's happy prattle, had arrived a month ago, unheralded, and had immediately launched an attack on the castle. But the garrison of forty men that Robin had left behind to protect his wife and child had been supplemented by a force of another two score men-at-arms who owed allegiance to William of Edwinstowe, Robin's elder brother.

The combined force inside Kirkton had managed to fight off two determined assaults and then Murdac's forces, bloodied but unbeaten, had set up camp in the fields around the castle and seemed to be attempting to starve the inhabitants of Kirkton into submission.

'Lord Edwinstowe is here?' I asked Tuck.

'He is now snoring like summer thunder through yonder door,' my friend replied, nodding at the entrance to the solar at the end of the great hall, Robin and Marie-Anne's private chamber.

'And Marie-Anne?' I asked Tuck, incredulous.

'She has taken up residence in the tower. It's the safest place for her if the enemy ever gets into the castle. She is in good health and quite comfortable, she tells me, and it allows her to keep an eye on the stores, which we have stockpiled there. Her little boy Hugh's in fine fettle, too.'

'Robin's brother William threw Marie-Anne out of her own bed, in her own castle . . .' I was beginning to feel the stirrings of rage at this insult to my master's lady, who was now forced to sleep in the motte, the stout square wooden tower that loomed over the bailey. It was the castle's last line of defence, and a powerful two-storey fortification, situated on a great mound of earth, which a handful of good men could hold against many enemies if the bailey was overrun, but it was a rough-and-ready structure, built with an eye on military strength, not comfort, and it was no place for a gently born lady to reside.

'Peace, Alan, be at peace,' said Tuck. 'Lord Edwinstowe is the master of this castle – for the time being. Doubtless things will change now that Robin has returned. It was right that he should have the master's chamber. He saved us, you know; without his men-at-arms we would have been overrun when Murdac attacked. It is true that the siege has been quiet for a while now – bar the odd exchange of arrows and insults – but it would not do for him to be offended. It is his men who keep the enemy beyond our walls.'

I could see his point, yet a part of me still wished to kick open the door of Marie-Anne's chamber and drag the sleeping baron out into the courtyard. But I said nothing and merely shot a hot glare at the solar door.

'You're different, Alan,' said Tuck. 'You've changed since I last saw you; become harder, more wrathful. But never mind all that, tell me, how was the Holy Land, was it wonderful? Did you pray at the Church of the Holy Sepulchre? Did you feel the living presence of Our Lord and Saviour Jesus Christ?' Tuck's eyes were shining; he had wanted badly to join us on the Great Pilgrimage and it was only out of a strong sense of loyalty to Robin that he had remained in Kirkton to watch over Marie-Anne. I was glad that he had stayed; whatever he said about William of Edwinstowe, I knew that it had been Tuck who kept my lady safe in Robin's absence.

'It was . . . hard. Very tiring; exhausting and bloody, and many good men died for nothing . . . But I will tell you all about it later,' I told Tuck.

'Of course,' he said, bowing his head in acquiescence. 'We have more urgent matters to attend to. Where is Robin now? What are his plans?'

So while Tuck bustled about and fetched me a mug of ale and a plate of bread and salty ham, I told him of Robin's plans for lifting the siege. When I had finished explaining how a small force could defeat a much larger army, and exactly what Robin wished us to do to help him accomplish this, Tuck sat back, his mouth slightly open, and said with genuine awe in his voice: 'That man has the Devil in his marrow bones. It is an excellent plan, Alan, and it might even work, but it is not a scheme that could ever have been devised by a good Christian. I pray for his soul, I truly do, for I fear that in the next world Robin will burn for eternity.'

He ran over the details once again with me, but my tiredness was overcoming me like a sickness. It was nearly dawn and I could barely keep my eyes open when, finally, Tuck said: 'So this will all take place at midnight tonight?'

I nodded, yawning.

'Well, God have mercy on their souls. But you must rest, Alan.' And he lent me an old blanket and guided me over to a pile of greasy furs at the side of the hall, where only moments later I slid down into grateful slumber.

I awoke in broad daylight, with a vision of loveliness, a blonde angel standing over me. Her behaviour, though, was far from angelic. She was booting me none too gently in the ribs with a dainty kidskin slipper and crying: 'Alan, Alan, get up. I've been waiting ages for you to wake. This is no time to be a slug-a-bed – get up! I want to talk to you. I've got so much to tell you!'

As I knuckled the sleep from my eyes, I saw that it was Goody, more properly Godifa, Marie-Anne's ward and an old friend from my days as an outlaw. She must have been nearly fifteen, I calculated swiftly, an age when many country maids would have already been betrothed, even married with children, and she was a rare beauty: fine gold hair, tied in twin plaits, framed a sweet oval face with a small, short nose, and a healthy blush of pink in the cheek. Her eyes were the violet-blue of a thistle in bloom, and her loveliness almost took my breath away. I realized I was gawping at her, trying to find words of greeting and failing.

'Stop flapping your mouth at me like a freshly caught fish and come and have some breakfast,' she said. 'I want to hear everything, absolutely everything about your adventures in the Holy Land. Is it true that the Saracens are cannibals? I've been told that they eat the raw flesh of the Christian children that they capture . . .'

I silenced her foolish questions and salved my own inexplicable speechlessness with an embrace. For a moment, when I put my big clumsy arms around her, she melted into my body, before struggling away and crying, 'Oh, Alan, you smell – in fact, you stink! You stink of blood, sweat and worse, and . . . Oh, you smell of men. You must have a bath immediately . . .'

I was suddenly aware of the clothes I stood in, still stiff and creased from having been soaked and then slept in; my face was crusted with dried mud and, looking down at my fingers, I saw that they were still spattered with the young sentry's dried blood. When I pushed a dirty hand through it, I could feel that my cropped blond hair was standing in stiff spikes on my crown.

'I have travelled three thousand weary miles to get here, suffering untold hardship and danger in foreign lands, not to mention killing a man and sneaking through the enemy's camp last night – I think it would be strange if I came out of all that smelling of rose water!'

I was stung, just a little, to have this gorgeous, sense-strumming girl complaining of my soldierly odour. Although I knew I did not look my best, I wanted to be treated as a returning hero, a victorious warrior, not a malodorous vagabond.

'Anyway, I have no time to waste splashing about like a silly little girl in soapy suds and hot water; I must speak to Lord Edwinstowe without delay.'

It was Goody's turn to pretend to be offended. 'Do only little girls wash? Very well, sir, I shall inform His Lordship that a certain uncouth and very smelly soldier-boy requires his company immediately.' And she stuck her tongue out at me and swept away. But for the mocking tongue, she would have appeared quite the grand, well-born lady, and I realized that she had changed in more than just her looks.

I fetched my own breakfast from the kitchens, and spent half an hour idling in the bailey courtyard chewing on a dry crust and looking about me in the September sunshine like a yokel at a county fair. It was hard to believe, given the placid yet bustling air of the place, that outside the wooden walls of the bailey were hundreds of enemies intent on our destruction. But the bailey was rather full, I noticed; I assumed that all the people in the surrounding villages and smallholdings had been gathered into the castle to keep them safe from Murdac's pillaging men-at-arms. I was wondering if any of the peasant men here could fight worth a damn when I noticed two boys scuffling in a ring of their cheering fellows. One was short and dark, about ten or eleven, the other tall, an adolescent, almost a man. The match looked so uneven that I was sure the small, dark boy would be badly injured. And it crossed my mind to intervene, give the taller boy a cuff or two and send him on his way. Instead, to my surprise, after ducking a couple of haymakers from the tall one, the dark boy grabbed his opponent's right arm as it flashed past his head, tucked his right shoulder into the tall boy's right armpit, pulled down, hunched over and hurled him on to the packed mud of the courtyard floor. The tall adolescent was as surprised as I was. And while the little dark lad pulled the dazed fellow back to his feet – I could see that it was not a serious fight, mere playful rough-housing – I saw Tuck making his way into the throng of chattering boys and shooing them towards a stable-shed that had been converted into a schoolhouse. As the flock of boys passed me, I called out to Tuck and beckoned him over.

'Who is that short dark boy?' I asked my friend. 'And by what witchcraft did he learn to tumble taller fellows in the dust like that?'

Tuck beamed with almost paternal pride and shouted to the boy: 'Thomas, Thomas, come here – I want to introduce you to somebody.' And when the dark lad obediently trotted over, Tuck said to him: 'This, my boy, is Alan of Westbury, *trouvère* to the Earl of Locksley, newly returned from battling the Saracens in the Holy Land.'

The boy stared directly at me, his charcoal-black eyes a match with his dark hair. He had an air of tremendous assurance about him; not arrogance, just the look of someone who has found his place in the world and who will concede it to nobody. He appeared unusually solid – brown and strong, like a pillar of seasoned oak; it was an unnerving quality in one so young. 'I am honoured to make your acquaintance,' he said gravely. Then he added: 'Sir, may I ask, are you Alan Dale the swordsman?'

I nodded, struck by his total self-assurance. He was interrogating me! 'I have occasionally been called that,' I admitted.

'Then might I ask a great boon?' this extraordinary boy continued. 'Would you condescend to exchange a few passes with me one day, and perhaps show me something of your prowess? I wish to learn how to fight, and I have been told that you are one of the best men with a blade in England.'

'It seems that you already know how to fight,' I said, inclining my head at the tall boy he had recently bested, who was now limping into the makeshift schoolhouse.

He shrugged: 'That was just boyish nonsense, merely a kind of wrestling that I am attempting to devise; I wish to learn to fight like a proper soldier.'

His air of cool maturity was so pronounced that it was almost laughable. I was looking at a boy who could not be much more than eleven, and yet he spoke like a man in his prime. But, in truth, I sensed he would be a difficult fellow to laugh at; his stance, his stare, his whole being demanded that he be taken seriously.

'If we survive this coming battle against Ralph Murdac's men, I will gladly exchange a few passes with you, assuming you still wish to do so – but on one condition,' I said, matching his solemn tone.

'Sir?' he said inquiringly.

'That you teach me the trick with which you tumbled the taller boy.' I smiled at him. 'Fellow warriors should teach each other their skills, don't you think? That way we all learn to be better men.'

He was taken aback by my words, I could see, but to his credit he hardly showed it; it was almost as if he were used to being addressed as an equal by full-grown men-at-arms. 'Thank you, sir,' he said gravely. 'I shall look forward to that day.' And he bowed deeply from the waist and, turning, jogged off towards the school shed.

I turned to Tuck: 'What an extraordinary lad! Wherever did you find him?'

'That, my friend, is Thomas ap Lloyd,' said Tuck. 'Does the name seem familiar?'

I just looked at him blankly.

'He's the son of Lloyd ap Gruffyd. Surely you remember him?'

I had no recollection of anyone by that name.

Tuck laughed at me, but the sound was coloured with a strange sadness. 'Have you killed so many, Alan, that their names no longer mean anything to you?' he said. 'Oh, Alan, we must look to your soul before too long. I fear the blood of so many slaughtered men may have stained it permanently.' And he walked away, shaking his head gently, making for the schoolhouse, which was now packed with chattering youths and children of both sexes.

And then I knew who the boy's father was: the Welsh archer who had tried to kill Robin before we left for Outremer. Hoping to claim Murdac's bounty, he had crept into Robin's chamber one night and found me asleep there, waiting to deliver a message to my master. Mistaking me for Robin, the bowman attacked. After a short, terrifying fight in the darkness, I had killed the fellow. The boy, I recalled, this Thomas ap Lloyd whom I had just met, had subsequently been taken into the castle for his own protection. There was a strange logic in this act of Christian kindness, and I felt Tuck's influence: 'The sins of the father must not be visited on the son,' the former

35

monk had once quoted to me, and I saw that he had put his principle into action.

But a chilling thought hit me, carried into my mind on the back of the last: would the son one day feel the need to seek revenge for his father's death? If he did, I would, reluctantly, have to cut him down. I knew in my heart that, young as Thomas was, I could and would do the deed – if, as Robin would have put it, it was necessary.

What was I turning into? Would I become like my master, the most cold-hearted, ruthless killer I had ever encountered? I shivered, though the day was quite warm.

My dark reverie was interrupted by a soft, sweet voice I knew well crying: 'Alan! Oh, Alan, welcome home. It is wonderful to see you!'

It was my friend and hostess, Marie-Anne, Countess of Locksley. I bowed low before her with a bent knee and an elegant waft of my hand, my black mood instantly lifted by her lovely guileless smile.

She took me by both upper arms, hugged me briefly, and then stared into my eyes. 'How is he? Is he well?' she said earnestly.

'Robin is quite well,' I said, 'and he bade me to offer you a tender kiss, a soft embrace and all the love in his heart.'

I was lying, of course. Robin had bid me say no such thing, and he would hate that I was putting my words in his mouth, but I was very fond of Marie-Anne and I could see that she required reassurance about Robin's affections. Who was I to deny her comfort in this matter? There was a dark shadow that lay between Robin and this beautiful lady before me; and while I could not banish it, I could at least make her feel happy for a while.

'He is coming tonight,' I said. 'And he will flush this rabble of Murdac's away from your walls with fire and steel.'

'I knew he would come,' she said, her eyes glinting with moisture. 'Even in the darkest days, I knew he would come. Has he changed at all? Did he say anything about . . . about . . . his family?' She stumbled to a halt. I knew what she was referring to – her baby son Hugh – but I chose to misinterpret her words.

'He told me that I must speak to his brother Lord Edwinstowe as soon as possible, my lady. Would you be so good as to lead me to him?'

Marie-Anne leant forward and wrinkled her nose. Then she said briskly: 'Of course, but I think before you are taken into His Lordship's presence, you should change into a costume that more befits a noble warrior of Christ, one who has made the Great Pilgrimage to the Holy Land. And perhaps, before that, you might like to have a wash . . .'

And so within a quarter of an hour, I was seated in the bathhouse in a steaming wooden tub, with my modesty covered by a sheet, while serving maids poured flagons of hot water around my pink and soapy torso. It felt wonderful. Marie-Anne was as good as her word and after my hot bath she saw to it that I was dressed in clean under-drawers, new green hose, a fine linen chemise and a grey woollen tunic. On top of that I wore a thick cloak of fine green wool with a gold-thread-embroidered border, and a new sword from the armoury was strapped around my waist. I felt a good deal better to be clean, it must be admitted, and to be garbed once again as the Lord of Westbury filled my heart with a deep, quiet satisfaction.

William, Lord Edwinstowe, was seated in a wide, brightly

painted chair at the head of Robin's hall, dressed in a long flowing purple robe, his shoulder-length curled brown hair held in place by a circlet of gold. I was brought into his presence by a servant and, after I had made my bow, the baron and I stared at each other for a while without speaking. He had the resemblance of Robin, I saw, but with a thinner face and harsh lines cut down either side of his mouth. His eyes were brown, however, rather than Robin's extraordinary silvery-grey and, although he was seated, I could see that he was a shade taller than my master. When he eventually spoke, his voice too was different: higher, not so musical as my Earl's honey tones.

'So you have come to me from Robert of Locksley,' he said. 'And where is he now, may I ask?'

'He is close, sir,' I said, 'in the hills to the north, well hidden, but he is watching the castle as we speak.'

'So my little brother hides and watches, while I defend *his* castle from *his* enemies?' His tone contained more than a touch of sneer, and I felt the beginnings of a blush of rage on my cheek. I knew, however, that I must keep my temper: I could not afford to offend the man. Robin's plan depended on his goodwill and he must be encouraged to act as Robin desired for the plan to succeed.

'My lord will attack Murdac's camp tonight,' I said calmly, 'with all his men, at midnight.'

'Will he now?' said William. 'And how many men does he have left at his beck and call, I wonder? I heard there was much slaughter in Outremer, that the Great Pilgrimage was a failure, and the long, difficult journey home . . . well, such distance bleeds away men like good liquor leaking from a pricked wine sack.'

'He has half a hundred doughty men-at-arms yet,' I said, gritting my teeth. The man was infuriating.

'Fifty is far too few to attack Sir Ralph Murdac,' William pronounced. 'The fellow has three, maybe four hundred soldiers out there. If it had not been for my aid, they would have overrun this castle weeks ago.'

'And Robin is most grateful. He also has a scheme, a clever trick, that he believes will sap the courage of the enemy and cause their legs to turn to jelly, their spines to water. With your help, he believes . . .'

'With my help, you say? Yes, undoubtedly he wants my help. When did he *not* need my help! Even as a child he needed my aid, and then when he was cast out from all decent society and became an accursed footpad, running around Sherwood playing his silly games, I offered him my help then, too . . .'

I was beginning, despite myself, to get very angry with this baron, this lounging, purple-clad blockhead before me. Fearing that my anger would show in my eyes, I looked away and caught sight of Tuck standing by the wall of the hall. Beside him, watching me, were two enormous wolfhounds, giant beasts named Gog and Magog for their terrible destructive abilities in battle. One of the beasts yawned, a huge jaw-cracking gape that showed every one of his spear-blade teeth.

And my anger faded a little. Even the dogs found this man a pompous bore, I thought, and smiled inside.

'. . . tricks and schemes, schemes and tricks, that is what my little brother has been relying on since he was a stripling. If I had a shilling for every time . . .'

I interrupted him then: 'My lord,' I said, aiming for humility and missing by a good English mile, 'the Earl of Locksley requests that when he attacks the camp at midnight tonight, you will sally forth with all the forces at your command and help him to sweep these enemies before us. He trusts you will come to his aid once again in this matter. Your help is vital to the success of his carefully laid plans.'

'Can't be done, it simply can't be done,' said William grumpily. 'He has too few men – fifty, and the handful of men in here, against the whole of Murdac's force. He'll be crushed. We'll all be killed. No. It's arrant madness. No, no, what we must do is wait. Wait here for reinforcements. I have sent letters to many of my friends begging them to come; and come they will, too, in vast numbers. And the King – our noble Richard – must return soon to his kingdom, and he'll set things a-right. No, young man, you must return to your impetuous master and bid him to be cautious; bid him to wait till the time is ripe.'

I could see why Robin was not close to his brother: the man was deliberately obstructive, long-winded and – most surprisingly for a knight, a nobleman of Norman lineage – he appeared to be supremely cautious, even a little timid.

'My lord,' I said, as slowly and clearly as I could, 'the Earl will attack at midnight tonight. I cannot return to him and, even if I could, he would not change his plans. You must support him tonight. You must.'

'Must? You impertinent puppy! You do not tell me what I must or must not do! I am the master in this castle and you – you are dismissed. But I tell you one thing before you leave my presence: I will not risk my life and the lives of my men in this foolish venture. Now get out of my sight! Go!'

And so with a heavy heart, I went. I had failed my master.

Because of my stupidity, the crassness of my appeal to Edwinstowe, there was a very good chance that Robin's assault would fail and all my friends, facing overwhelming odds, would be cut down in the darkness. Because of me.

Chapter Three

The first hint that the attack was beginning came in the form of a spark of firelight, high on the brow of the hill; a red blinking eye in the darkness. Then came another, and another. They began to move – and grow. And the night air was ripped apart by a series of screaming wails, a clutch of different notes but blending together in a strange and disturbing way, an unearthly devilish sound that seemed to rise up from the very bowels of Hell itself. Even I, who knew the source of this weird, howling music, and had heard it several times before, was struck by its power to bring horror to the night. I had first heard the sound at the battle of Arsuf on the road to Jaffa in the Holy Land, where it presaged an attack by the fearsome cavalry of Saladin. It was the sound of Turkish trumpets, of massed clarions and shrieking fifes, of booming gongs and clashing cymbals and ear-scalding whistles; an infernal din designed to strike terror into any Christian heart – even when played rather poorly by a gaggle of Yorkshire villagers recruited specially for the task by their newly returned lord.

When I heard that hellish din, I was standing on the walkway behind the palisade on the north-eastern side of Kirkton Castle. I was in full war gear, which had been supplied by Marie-Anne: conical helmet with a nose piece, kite-shaped shield and long spear, a sword at my waist, the misericorde in my boot; knee-length chain-mail hauberk to protect my body over a big padded jacket known as a gambeson or aketon, leather gauntlets on my hands and stout boots sewn with strips of steel to guard my ankles and shins.

Within a few heartbeats, the first shouts of alarm were sounding from Murdac's camp. And out of the darkness, down the gently rolling hill, the spots of flickering orange light grew and took shape and revealed themselves. Out of the black night thundered three wild moorland ponies, eyes rolling in terror, shrill neighs torturing the darkness, hooves madly churning the damp turf – and the source of their terror was firmly harnessed to them: for behind each wild pony was a wooden cart, piled high with wood and straw and soused with oil and pig fat, and burning like the infernos of the Devil's own demesne.

The noise from the camp in the field below me was enough by now to wake the dead from their slumbers. But above the yells, and the hellish music, I thought I could make out a lone woman's voice, with a slight Norman-French accent, shouting in English over and over again: 'It is the horse-demons, the steeds of Satan – run, run. They are coming; the horse-demons are coming to steal your souls.'

The wild horses, maddened by the fiery carts they could not

escape, charged straight down the hill into Murdac's camp sowing destruction in their flaming wakes. They charged into the outskirts of the camp, trampling tents and crushing half-sleeping men beneath their hooves and the wheels of the heavy wooden carts. Many tents and shelters of the men-at-arms were burning by now; flags and pavilions set alight, pyramids of stacked spears collapsed and snapped like twigs beneath the wheels. The camp was humming like a kicked ants' nest, half-dressed men running hither and yon, screaming in rage and fear and confusion. And the lone Frenchwoman's voice continued to shout: 'The horses of the Devil are coming; the steeds of Satan; they are coming for your souls,' adding her mad shrieks to the bounding chaos. And the wild, eerie Saracen music wailed, boomed and screeched on, its hideous sounds adding eldritch notes of terror to the night.

Then the arrows began to hiss out of the darkness.

Men silhouetted by the leaping firelight were spitted like red deer by unseen skilful hands as they stumbled out of their shelters, barely armed, fuddled by sleep, confused by the noise, the blaze and the hot winds of panic. One man appeared to be more in control of himself, a captain no doubt, but as he barked orders to the men running about his tent, three arrows smacked into him in less than half a heartbeat. I knew that Robin's archers, scattered around the perimeter of the camp and shielded only by darkness, had orders to shoot down first any who appeared to be in command. And there were few who were still in possession of their faculties on this night of chaos and cacophony, as the archers plucked the lives of Murdac's men from this world one by one.

The wild horses with their fiery burdens were in the centre

of the camp now, galloping in screaming terror, and as I watched, the wheel of a cart struck a large iron cooking pot and careered over, spilling its flaming, roaring load over a swathe of the camp and starting a dozen fresh fires. The arrows whizzed through the darkness, thumping home into the bodies of terrified running men who had nowhere to hide. One brave figure appeared out of the darkness and shot dead a maddened pony, which was galloping past him, with a single, well-aimed crossbow bolt to the head. But while the poor horse stumbled and died, and the cart tumbled forward and tipped its burning load over the convulsing animal's dying body, the crossbowman was in turn skewered through the neck by a yard-long arrow that flickered out of the darkness to leave him choking on his knees in a circle of burning straw and roasting horse blood.

A high, clear trumpet blast, easily heard even over the noise of the blaring Saracen horns, dragged my eyes up to the north, where a mass of strange cavalry had appeared. The heavily armed, mounted men, about thirty of them, seemed huge and menacing, draped as they were in long, dark cowled cloaks that swept over the horses' rumps and swirled down by their boots. Their long sharp spears pricked the fire-lit night, and their painted shields portrayed a crude red figure of a horse, daubed in dried blood on a white background; but their faces – or the place where their faces should have been – were the most dreadful sight of all. Each man, though mounted on a steed, appeared himself to have the long head of a horse, with pointed ears, white eyes, and blood-red flaring nostrils. Even I felt a twinge of dread, and I knew full well that it was merely Robin's men, masked with rolled discs of sheepskin, ears and eye holes cut out and the mask painted to look like the muzzle of a hellish beast. They appeared to be Satan's steeds indeed, come to carry away men's souls.

The devilish horsemen charged. The spear points descended to the horizontal as one and this steel-tipped mass came on like a great black thunder cloud, surging down the slope in a shallow V-shaped formation to bring death and destruction into the camp.

'Alan, Alan, come on! Come on! It is time,' shouted a voice below me. And I looked down to see Tuck, flanked by his two enormous dogs, Gog and Magog, holding the reins of a horse meant for me. It was time: and if Edwinstowe and his men refused to join us, there were still more than a few stout men-at-arms who owed their loyalty only to Robin and who would ride out with us this night to heap more terror on the enemies of their lord.

The gates were thrown open and we burst out of them in a pack, perhaps a dozen of us mounted, with myself in the lead, and a score of men on foot: Robin's spearmen and bowmen, left behind while he was on the Great Pilgrimage, supplemented with a handful of the braver or perhaps just more loyal men from the surrounding lands. Led by Father Tuck, the foot soldiers ran behind the cavalry, screaming their war cries, each man wielding a long spear or short sword from the castle armoury. I noticed with admiration and a little trepidation, looking over my shoulder, that the lad Thomas had armed himself with a kindling axe and had joined the other local men running behind the horsemen. I had no time to tell him to return to the hall as we surged out into the night towards the enemy.

We horsemen cantered out of the gate which lay at the south-east of the castle and turned left, spurring ahead of the infantry to hurtle into the southern section of Murdac's camp. My chest was thrumming with the black thrill of battle, the unparalleled feeling of having a well-trained horse between my legs, a stout shield on my arm and a long spear couched under my right elbow. I knew that our chances were slim, but I felt little fear that weird, wild night. We were riding to the charge; and battle, with all its mad-flecked, God-cursed, sky-soaring joy, was upon us.

A terrified picket, a sentry in red and black, turned to run back into the camp when he saw us coming out of the night: a mob of galloping horsemen screaming like devils and heading straight for him. As he turned to run, a grey and reddish blur streaked past me, one of Tuck's enormous battle-trained wolf-hounds. The animal leapt at the running man, his giant jaws opening and snapping shut, crunching deep into the meat of his right leg, and then they were both rolling on the dark turf, a tangle of grey fur and flapping black surcoat, appalling screams for mercy and bone-grinding growls. And then I was past them, and there were sleep-shackled enemies blundering from between the tents to my front, only half visible in the blackness. I lined up the horse and galloped straight at a man-at-arms who was struggling into a leather-backed mail shirt, his arms up above his head, his face covered by the hauberk, and I screamed 'Westbury!' as I drove my right arm forward and plunged the lance-tip deep into his unprotected doughy belly.

He dropped immediately and seemed to curl like a snake around my spear. But I managed to twist my wrist and pull the point free of the man's guts as I thundered past. I had only just levelled the spear again when I found I was facing another enemy, a mounted man-at-arms in a boiled-leather cuirasse and helmet, screaming hate and waving a heavy mace at me. I rose in the saddle and my lance jerked forward and punched through the stiff leather and into his chest, the blood-smeared point given its enormous killing power by my galloping horse. He was a dead man before he was even within range to strike a blow. Releasing my spear, leaving it bobbing madly from his torso, his blood greasing the front of his cuirasse, I hauled out my sword. I could hear battle-charged shouts behind me as our assorted footmen tore into the south end of the camp, hacking and howling, stamping and stabbing at their foes, wiping out all in their path like a wave of human fury crashing on to a beach. Leaving them to their bloody business, I was intent on reaching the centre of the sweep of tents where I knew Murdac's shelter to be. I longed to face him, to take my sword to him in the joyous carnage of battle, and send him to Hell where he belonged. But as I urged the horse forward, slicing my sword down into the neck of a passing man-at-arms and batting a terrified crossbowman out of my path with the flat of the blade, I could see that Robin's plan was already working. Scores of men-at-arms in black and red were streaming from the camp and away eastwards into the darkness, some crying out loud to God in their terror, others saving their breath to make good their escape.

I guided my horse round the side of a broad, low tent and came face to face with a terrifying apparition: a giant man on a huge horse, a black monstrous shape lit only by splashes of firelight but seeming to loom over me. He had a great double-headed axe in one enormous fist, and I could see that it was dripping with fresh blood, and the head on those giant shoulders was that of a massive stallion, its nostrils seemingly breathing fire. I could not help myself but I reined back in alarm, and then the apparition used his free left hand to lift the sheepskin horse mask from his face and reveal the grinning, sweaty visage and yellow matted locks of John Nailor, Robin's right-hand man and my good friend.

'Boo!' he said, as if playing a hiding game with a child.

I managed a shaky smile at my old comrade. And Little John said: 'God's dangling gonads, Alan, don't tell me *your* bowels were loosened by all this mummery!'

I shook my head and lied through my teeth: 'Of course not, but the trick seems to have worked on Murdac's men. The bastards are all running away.'

'Not all of them, Alan,' said Little John. And he nodded to the east where a group of a dozen men-at-arms on foot were being pushed into line by a grizzled sergeant to form a forlorn-looking and very thin shield wall. 'This little fight's not over yet, Alan. Come on! There's more sport to be had.'

He pulled the terrifying horse mask back down over his face and we turned our mounts together, put back our spurs and charged, knee to knee, axe and sword swinging, myself screaming 'Westbury! Westbury!' and Little John making a hideous keening noise deep in his throat. We charged like madmen, or creatures from some terrible nightmare, straight at the thin wall of a dozen frightened soldiers who were cowering behind their kite-shaped shields. And the formation shattered like a clay cup dropped on a stone floor as they ran for their lives, scattering into the darkness. I managed to land only a glancing blow on to the helmet of one fleeing man before he scurried under an upturned cart, safely away from my searching blade. I let him live; reining in, panting, to survey the night and catch my breath.

49

Little John had been wrong. The battle was, to all intents and purposes, over, and as I turned to speak to him I saw that he too had disappeared into the night. I was alone, and just ahead of me was Sir Ralph Murdac's black-and-red striped tent, now with a circle of pine-pitch torches burning around it. I walked my horse over towards the circle of light; praying fervently to St Michael that I should be lucky enough to find the little Norman rat still in his foul nest.

Murdac was not there, but Robin was. My master was un-horsed, the sheepskin mask hanging by a cord around his neck, a great war bow in his hands, an arrow nocked, the hempen string drawn back to his ear. He was aiming across my path, away from the light and into the darkness; my head turned and my eye naturally followed his aim. A small dark figure was racing a midnight-black horse away from the camp as fast as possible, its pounding legs snapping guy ropes and tumbling tents in his wake. And I knew in my bones that it was Murdac. A heartbeat later my master released the bowstring and sent a yard of ash, tipped with a needle-like bodkin point, flashing away into the darkness. The arrow struck Murdac. I saw the strike, high in his back on the left-hand side; it was a superb shot, one that only Robin and a handful of other men in the world could have made. The bobbing target was more than a hundred yards away by then, the range increasing with every moment as horse and rider surged towards safety. Murdac's black-and-red surcoat could only be seen intermittently that dark night, when the horse and rider passed through a patch of firelight; it was a nigh-on impossible feat to hit the target, and yet Robin had made it. But it was not a lethal strike; I saw Murdac lurch forward in the saddle with the heavy impact of the shaft in his back. But he did not fall and moments later he was still in the saddle, swaying wildly, but remaining defiantly a-horse, and passing swiftly beyond view down the dale towards the River Locksley as the dark curtains of night closed behind him.

I heard Robin curse softly under his breath as I leapt off my mount to greet him and congratulate him on his stunning victory.

'I meant to kill him, Alan,' said my master after we had clasped right arms in greeting. 'I meant to kill him for sure this time, and I honestly thought I had him, but once again it seems that I have failed.'

'He may yet die from his wound,' I said, smiling at him with affection. 'Perhaps God intends for him to suffer a slow and hideously painful death, when the wound goes black and the pus runs thick and begins to smell of month-old rancid mutton . . .'

'You're just trying to cheer me up,' said Robin with a wry laugh. 'Or possibly make me feel peckish. Either way, thank you, Alan. No, I missed my mark with Murdac, and we shall have to deal with him again on some other occasion. Now, we have other matters to attend to; come, we'd better make sure these bastards are all dead, captured or gone from here.'

Robin turned away and was calling for his horse when William, Lord Edwinstowe, with a score of mounted men-at-arms behind him, trotted into the circle of torchlight around Murdac's pavilion. I knew that Edwinstowe's men had not charged with us when we rushed out of the castle gate to support Robin's attack, and none of them carried the marks of battle – not a scratch nor a splash of blood on a single one of them.

51

But the cautious baron must have seen the way the battle was going, that Murdac's men were running, and come to the conclusion that he must join in if only for the sake of his knightly reputation. I realized then that, though he might be Robin's brother, I thoroughly despised him.

'Robert,' Edwinstowe said curtly, nodding at my master. 'William,' came the equally terse reply. Then Robin, by now mounted, walked his horse over to his brother. He smiled at him without much warmth, and said: 'I thank you for the great service you have rendered me over the past few weeks. I am in your debt.'

'Well, Brother, when I got wind of Ralph Murdac's plans to attack Kirkton, what else could I do but come here? I merely fulfilled my family duty,' said Edwinstowe. 'No more, no less. Duty to one's family is a sacred trust, and it must supersede all other . . . considerations.'

'And I am most grateful,' said Robin. 'I shall not forget what you have done for me here.'

Baron Edwinstowe half-smiled; he seemed pleased by Robin's thanks. 'It seems that I underestimated your battle plans. I must congratulate you on this scheme, this . . . ruse, and on your notable victory.' His gauntleted hand described an arc that took in the shattered, smouldering enemy camp, now empty of Murdac's men. Robin gave him a bright, gleaming smile. And for a moment the baron seemed to be about to say something more, but he merely nodded and then turned his horse and, leading his conroi of unmarked men-at-arms, he trotted back towards Kirkton Castle.

The prisoners looked tired and very frightened. Pale-faced and bound at the wrists and neck with stout ropes, a forlorn two dozen men, some lightly wounded – the very badly hurt had been mercifully dispatched to their Maker in the immediate aftermath of the battle – sat disconsolately with their backs to the wooden palisade, stripped nearly naked, and guarded by a handful of joyfully victorious archers, who were sharing flasks of mead and time-honoured army jokes. It was not long past dawn in the bailey courtyard of Kirkton Castle and Hanno was congratulating me on my kill the night before last. 'I am very pleased with you, Alan,' said my Bavarian friend, his round shaven head split with a grin to reveal his ragged assortment of broken grey teeth. 'It is a beautiful killing, ah yes. Very nice, very quiet, and very nearly perfect.'

My bitten finger throbbed from misuse, even though I had strapped it tightly before the battle last night. I looked at my friend a little sourly and I marvelled at his use of the word 'beautiful' for such a sordid piece of butchery.

'What do you mean, *nearly* perfect?' I said. 'I took him down without a sound.' I was feeling the melancholy humour I always felt after a bout of bloodletting, when the world seemed flat and grey, and my soul was heavy with regret at the men I had killed. My finger was paining me more than a little, too.

'Ah, Alan, do not mistake me,' said Hanno, all seriousness now. 'I am most proud of you – but next time you must take him while he stands, left hand and dagger together' – he mimed clamping a hand over an invisible victim's mouth and shoving the blade into the back of his skull at the same time – 'not use your weight to knock him to the ground, and *then* kill him while you both roll around like happy pigs fucking in the mud.'

'Well, *next time*, I'll try to do much better,' I said with a grimace. I was feeling slightly sick at the memory of that bloody murder in the black field. Hanno was a passionate advocate of perfection, endlessly harping on about it: the perfect ale, the perfect woman, the perfect sword blow. He also had no ear at all for when I was being sarcastic.

'This is the correct spirit, Alan,' said Hanno, nodding earnestly. 'Each time you perform a task, you must try to do it better than the last time – until it is perfect. I recall my first silent kill . . . oh, it is many years ago, in Bavaria. I am in the service of Leopold, Duke of Austria, a great and powerful man, and the orders come down to me from the renowned and most noble knight Fulk von Rittenburg . . .'

At that moment, I was spared having to hear a story I had heard a dozen times before by the arrival of Robin, still wearing the long dark cloak that had been part of his horse-demon costume the night before, accompanied by Little John and Marie-Anne and a nursemaid who was carrying a small, solemn-looking, slightly pudgy boy – he must have been about two and a half years of age, if my calculations were correct.

Robin stopped in front of the prisoners and quietly drew his sword. His face was as bleak as a full gibbet in mid-winter. Behind him I could see Marie-Anne looking strangely frightened and confused. John, on the other hand, looked unconcerned and he shot me a cheery wink.

'Get them on their feet,' Robin said curtly to the archer guards. And while the prisoners were roughly pulled into a standing position, Robin studied them, his eyes as coldly metallic as the naked blade in his hand.

'You came to this place and laid siege to my castle with your master, the coward who calls himself Sir Ralph Murdac, seeking to murder my servants and despoil my lands, while I

54

was away fighting for Christendom in the Holy Land. Is this not true?'

The bound men said nothing, shuffling their feet and staring at the packed-earth floor of the bailey. One fellow began to weep silently. Robin continued: 'And yet did not His Holiness Pope Celestine declare that a man's lands and estates are under the protection of Mother Church while he takes part in a holy pilgrimage? To attack such a man's property is to break the Truce of God, which is a grave sin, as despicable as attacking Church property itself, is it not?'

The men remained silent. Robin paused for a beat, and then went on: 'And so, by God's holy law, by the law of His Holiness the Pope, you all richly deserve death for your crimes outside these walls. Do you not?'

I was privately amused that my master, a man who I knew did not have the slightest allegiance to the Pope in Rome, or any high Christian churchman for that matter, should use this law as a justification, I assumed, for executing these men. *Get on with it*, I thought to myself. *If you have decided to kill them, get it done. Don't give them a long sermon to take with them to their graves.*

'But what angers me more than a cowardly attack on my lands while I was fighting the good fight in Outremer,' Robin continued, 'is that your master has cast suspicion on the honour of my lady wife, the Countess of Locksley.' Robin's gaze lashed the cowed men, many of whom were now mumbling prayers under their breath, convinced their time on Earth was nearly ended.

'The coward Murdac claims that Hugh here, my little *son*,' Robin emphasized the last word, 'is not truly my son, but his.'

55

For more than a year, I knew, Sir Ralph Murdac had been spreading the rumour that he had lain with Marie-Anne and got her with child. The rumours had reached us as far away as the Island of Sicily, and they had made Robin heartsick, and a figure of ridicule, the cuckolded husband – something Robin could not abide. Worse still, the rumours were true. Murdac had lain with Marie-Anne when she was his captive, during Robin's outlaw days, and although it was surely a forced coupling, the boy was undeniably his. I was shocked that Robin should speak publicly about these intensely private and shameful matters. Even I, one of his closest men, had never dared to speak of it to him. But it seemed he was now determined to make the subject an open one.

'Before the Virgin, does any man here support the liar Murdac's claim, and say that my boy Hugh is his whelp?'

The prisoners stared at the little boy sitting quietly in his nursemaid's arms. The boy stared back with his huge pale blue eyes from under a mop of jet hair. God forgive me for saying this, but he was the very image of Murdac, a miniature Sir Ralph – and every man here could see it. Still nobody said a word.

Fast as a cut snake, Robin lunged forward with his sword, sinking the blade a foot deep into the naked belly of the nearest prisoner, who screamed in pain and collapsed bleeding and whimpering to the floor, clutching his punctured midriff. Even though I believed that Robin meant to kill them all, I was as surprised as any man in that courtyard by the suddenness and callousness of his strike.

Robin held the sword up towards the morning sky, the unfortunate prisoner's bright blood trickling down the central channel of the blade towards the hilt. 'I will be answered,' my master said quietly, his voice ice-hard. 'And so I ask you again: Does any man here maintain Sir Ralph's claim that this is not my son?'

There was an immediate chorus of 'No, my lord!' and 'By my faith, he is your son, sir!' and similar answers from the prisoners. The man who had been stabbed gave a groaning cry, a little writhe and, mercifully, appeared to pass out from the pain.

But one of the standing prisoners took a half step forward. He was a handsome man, tall and proud. 'I will not lie,' he said, looking directly at Robin, matching his stare. 'I will not go before the face of God with a lie on my lips. He is not your son – you only need to look at him to see that. Clearly his true father—' Robin's sword flashed out and ripped through his throat, and he dropped to his knees, gouting blood between clutching fingers as his precious life-fluid cascaded down his white chest.

'Anyone else?' said Robin, as still and cold as a grave-stone.

Another loud chorus of 'No, my lord! He is surely your son!'

'You all deserve death for your actions over the past few weeks . . . but I am a merciful man,' said Robin. And behind him, I saw Little John explode in a loud coughing or choking fit, covering his mouth with one huge hand, his face glowing a bright rosy red as he struggled to regain his composure. My master gave John a stern flick of a glance, and twisted his mouth very slightly in rebuke, then he continued: 'I am a merciful man, unless I am crossed, and I may, I *may* now be moved to show mercy. If any man here will swear before God and the

Virgin, and all that he holds dear, that he will serve me, and my *son* Hugh, faithfully, all his days, with all his might and main, I shall grant him his miserable life. Is any man here prepared to take this solemn oath?'

A forest of hands shot up into the air, many tied to other men's – one particularly short man was jerked off his feet by the raised hands of two tall men on either side of him. And there was a clamour of voices declaring: 'I will, my lord, gladly, I will.' In fact, perhaps not very surprisingly, it seemed that the entire mass of prisoners was prepared to accept the offer of a life in faithful service to Robin.

As the prisoners were cut loose by the archers, each kneeling in turn to make the pledge of loyalty to Robin, placing their hands between his, I was struck by how clever my master had been. He had, at a stroke, recruited a score of trained men-at-arms, which he badly needed, who would now find it difficult, if not impossible, to return to Murdac's banner because they had publicly acknowledged that Hugh was Robin's son. He had weeded out, and swiftly dispatched, the one man who would never serve him, and had displayed a ruthless strength, and a generous clemency which, it was to be hoped, would bind these soldiers to him more strongly. But would these men, Sir Ralph Murdac's men, really remain loyal when the threat of imminent death had passed? I marked their faces and vowed that in future I would keep a wary eye on each and every one of them.

Chapter Four

During the next few weeks, Kirkton Castle enjoyed a period of peace and tranquillity that was a balm to the soul after our long wanderings. The early autumn weather was sunny and warm, and it seemed that my master Robin was pleased to be home once again with his wife Marie-Anne. Little Hugh toddled around the bailey, a cheerful, chubby little boy, who looked more and more like Sir Ralph Murdac with every passing day, although nobody was foolish enough to comment on it, and yet Robin seemed to have settled, at least in his mind, that the child was his, and he showed the infant a reserved fatherly kindness whenever their paths crossed.

In truth my master was a fully occupied man in these weeks following his return. After two and a half years of absence there was a great deal of administration of his estates to reconcile. Taxes and rents to collect, fences, sheep hurdles and bridges to mend, disputes to settle, and far-flung manors to visit, sometimes for the first time. I too had duties at my home and took leave of my master to return, briefly, to Westbury.

Robin had found a steward to run the manor for me, an elderly man, twig-thin, with steel-grey hair and a dry wit, called Baldwin – and I liked him from the first. I found when I visited that he had the place well in hand, running the manor fairly but firmly in my absence, ensuring that, after the tithes were paid to the Church, and taxes to the Crown, I had a small profit in silver and a surplus in grain. After checking his accounts, I found I had nothing to do there but ride about the lands trying to look lordly, spend the money he had gathered for me, and occasionally sit in judgement over the villagers in the manor court. Baldwin treated me with politeness and a small but satisfactory amount of deference, though he was of Norman stock, and he must have known that I was not born into the noble class. I was pleased to have such an amenable, competent man to run my lands.

There were a few empty, run-down cottages in the village of Westbury, and I gave them out to a handful of Robin's veterans who, through injury or advancing age or just a desire to settle down and be married, wished to give up the dangerous life of a man-at-arms and till my fields and put down roots somewhere. It might be advantageous, at some point in the future, I reasoned, to have half a dozen seasoned soldiers at hand, in the event of an emergency, a fire or an attack by enemies.

I could not remain long in Westbury, however, for Robin soon had me travelling the country delivering messages to his friends and allies, testing the mood of the land. So I spent most of my days in the autumn and early winter of that year – which

Tuck told me was eleven hundred and ninety-two years after Our Lord's birth – in the saddle, and my nights at castles or religious houses up and down the length of the country. It was tiring work but not lonely as I took Hanno with me as body-guard and companion. He had a fund of stories about his travels, telling me tales of black bears that lived in his native Bavarian forests, and the local witches, and ghouls and wicked elves who stole children away from their cradles . . .

Hanno had joined our company after the siege of Acre. King Richard had captured the strongly fortified port only a month after his arrival in the Holy Land, a feat that was much admired, even by his enemies. Acre had been under siege for nearly two years at that point, and was considered all but impregnable, but Richard's arrival with siege engines and massive re-inforcements had sealed its fate. I had been sick when the citadel fell; wounded and suffering from a mysterious malady that kept me in a feeble, dizzy condition for weeks. Hanno had also been wounded and we had been allowed to recover in the same quarter of Acre, the part controlled by the Knights Hospitaller, the healing monks who combined a deep love of Christ with a fearsome reputation as ruthless fighting men.

Hanno had been part of the German contingent in Outremer under Duke Leopold of Austria, but he had been left behind when his liege lord had departed for home after quarrelling badly with King Richard, the leader of the expedition. Our impetuous English monarch had kicked the Duke's banner from the walls of Acre when it had been hung beside his own and the standard of King Philip Augustus of France. He said that it was not fitting for the flag of a mere duke to hang beside that of kings. Actually, it was all about money, as it so often is in warfare – and peacetime, too, as Robin was fond of telling me. Or rather, plunder. By displaying his banner next to Richard's and Philip's, Leopold was claiming an equal share – one third – of all the loot from the captured city of Acre. And Richard wasn't going to allow this. From his point of view, Duke Leopold had failed to capture Acre after trying for so many months, whereas Richard had succeeded in a matter of weeks. The upshot was that, soon afterwards, Leopold quit the Great Pilgrimage, returning to Austria furious with King Richard and vowing to get his revenge.

Abandoned by his lord because he was too weak to be moved, Hanno had slowly recovered and then joined Robin's force of Sherwood outlaws turned soldiers. Despite the language barrier, which Hanno soon overcame, after a fashion – he had the curious habit of always speaking as if the event he was speaking about was happening at that very moment – as a hunter and warrior he fitted in well with Robin's gang of former deer-poachers and murderous brigands. And he seemed to adopt me, taking it upon himself to teach me everything he knew about stalking large prey – whether animal or human.

At the castles and great houses that I stayed in while travelling England on Robin's business that winter, I was usually obliged to entertain my audience in the evenings with music, mostly of my own composition, although sometimes other men's work, and I was pleased to notice that I had something of a growing reputation as a *trouvère*. At Pembroke Castle in South Wales, after hearing 'My Joy Summons Me' – a *canso* I had devised with King Richard the Lionheart himself in Sicily on the way to the Holy Land – the famous knight William the Marshal, now a great magnate and, in Richard's absence, one of the justiciars of England, even paid me the compliment of inviting me to leave Robin's service and join his household.

Though the Marshal promised me bright gold and the grants of several manors, I regretfully informed him that I could not leave my master after we had endured so much together on our travels out East. He was not pleased at being refused; plainly he was not used to it, and he had some difficulty in hiding his considerable irritation.

'Of course, I understand your loyalty to Locksley; I even applaud it,' said the Marshal grumpily. He was a giant, abrupt, grey-brown man of late middle years, with huge scarred hands, who was then perhaps the most renowned fighting man in the country. We were standing on the battlements of his newly completed stone tower at Pembroke watching a multitude of labourers and masons working like busy ants to construct a curtain wall below us. 'But you should know that your precious Earl is riding for a fall. It is well known that he is the King's man, but King Richard is far away in Outremer and who knows when he will return. Or indeed if he ever will.' The Marshal paused here and shot me a significant look before continuing.

'Locksley has enemies here in England, and I don't just mean that little weasel Murdac. Our noble Prince John looks askance at anyone who champions King Richard – it's plain as the nose on his face that he wants the throne for himself – and I have heard that certain very powerful elements in the Church are after your master's blood as well. A lot of people want to see Robert of Locksley brought down, young Alan. You should leave him while you have the opportunity. Come, throw in your lot with me, no one will speak ill of you for leaving

63

Locksley to join the greatest knight in Christendom.' He grinned at me to show that he was jesting about his fame and prowess, but in truth he was very proud of his reputation as a warrior. 'Seriously, Alan, my people tell me that Locksley is doomed. Too many powerful men want to see him humbled. Join me – your exquisite music will be properly rewarded and I can always use another first-class swordsman in my household.'

He was a good man, the Marshal, under his gruff soldierly exterior and for all his pride – and he meant well by me. Even so, I refused his offer. However, I was worried by what he had said. I knew, of course, that Prince John coveted the throne of England; part of Robin's secret orders from King Richard when my master left the Holy Land had been to keep an eye on brother John and thwart him in his manoeuvring to increase his power, if at all possible. But I was also concerned by the Marshal's mention of 'certain very powerful elements of the Church' being after his blood. Robin had long thumbed his nose at the clergy – in his outlaw days he made a particular point of robbing rich churchmen when they passed through his woodland domain – and now, it seemed, his chickens were coming home to roost.

Since the purpose of my mission, in addition to delivering my lord's messages, was to report anything that might concern him or his family, I scribbled a note to Robin on a scrap of old parchment and had Hanno gallop it immediately to Kirkton.

While I waited for Hanno to return with fresh orders, I tarried at Pembroke, watching the building work with no little awe at the vast sums of money being expended, playing music for the Marshal, practising my sword-and-shield work with his household knights, and flirting discreetly with Isabel, my middle-aged host's lovely young wife, who was more or less the same age as me. And at every opportunity I tried to find out more about the threat to Robin from the Church. More solid information came my way a few days later, and with it an unpleasant shock.

Hanno had returned to my side, bearing terse instructions from Robin for us to return home. I was not sorry to be leaving Pembroke for I had become slightly infatuated with Isabel, and only my considerable regard for the Marshal had prevented me from expressing my passionate feelings for her. It was better to be away from temptation, I told myself. As we were packing our traps in preparation for our departure, my host appeared with a request: he wanted me to give a special performance after supper that night for an honoured guest. I was bound to oblige him, as I had been enjoying his hospitality for weeks, and I was not unhappy to do so – I wanted to perform a love song I had written for Isabel, to give her something beautiful to remember me by.

The *canso* I had written for her was a rather sentimental one, based on an Arab tale I had heard in Outremer about an ordinary brown thrush and a gorgeous white rose. The knightly thrush is desperately in love with the rose but because of their differences in rank they can never be together. Furthermore, the white rose's soft petals are jealously protected by many cruel thorns. But the thrush, mad with love and scorning all danger, throws himself on to the rose, seeking just one brief kiss, and willingly spears himself to death on the sharp thorns. And ever afterwards, all roses shall be red as blood, to commemorate the sacrifice of the thrush who died for love.

You might think this mawkish, sentimental swill, but I may

say in all honesty that Isabel adored my *canso*, and by the looks she gave me afterwards I believe that I might well have been invited to enjoy the full sweetness of her petals had I remained. Instead, the next day Hanno and I rode away in the chill December dawn, and I never saw my white rose again. I think that, given the Marshal's fearsome reputation as a fighting man, it was for the best: he was not a man who would take being cuckolded lightly.

But I did have one encounter that night in Pembroke that was most significant to this tale. After I had performed my *canso*, and several other works, I was introduced to the Marshal's honoured guest. His name was Sir Aymeric de St Maur and he was an emissary of William de Newham, the Master of the Temple in London, the head of the English branch of the Order of the Poor Fellow-Soldiers of Christ and the Temple of Solomon – the renowned Knights Templar.

This Sir Aymeric, then, was a Templar, part of an elite order of fighting monks, famed all over the world for their piety and prowess. The Templars were the sword arm of Holy Mother Church, the sacred warriors of Our Lord Jesus Christ, answerable only to their Grand Master and His Holiness the Pope himself. The Templars had been in the forefront of battle in Outremer and, along with the Knights Hospitaller, they had earned great distinction there for their ruthless ferocity in war and total devotion to the Christian cause. They gave no quarter to their enemies in the Holy Land, and asked none. As a testament to their supreme efficacy as warriors, if ever a Templar soldier was captured by Saladin, he was immediately put to death. And these fighting monks looked on this death as a blessed martyrdom.

I had known several Templars in the past, in England and in the Holy Land, and I had always found them to be impressive men: Sir Aymeric de St Maur was no exception.

He was a tall, broad man in his thirties, straight-backed, with close-cropped black hair, and dressed in the pure white robe of the Templars with its red cross on the breast. He was noble of bearing, every inch a soldier, but his mouth seemed to indicate a certain cold cruelty that I did not care for. And when, after the musical supper, I was introduced to him by William the Marshal he immediately took a step back, almost as if fearful of me, and made the sign of the Cross in the air between us.

'You serve the Earl of Locksley?' he said in a curious tone of voice, half-uncertain, half-accusatory. 'The heretic? The demon-worshipper? It is hard to believe that one whose music is so clearly inspired by Heaven should serve one so steeped in foul practices.'

Despite the compliment, I bridled. 'I serve the Earl, and proudly, too. But he is no heretic. Perhaps he is not as attentive to his soul as he might be, and he perhaps should be more respectful of the Church, but he is certainly no Devil-worshipper.'

'Is that so?' asked this Templar, cocking an eyebrow. 'I heard a curious tale recently about the Earl of Locksley, who you admit is so inattentive of his immortal soul and disrespectful of Holy Mother Church; though perhaps the story is false . . .' He looked at me warily for a moment.

'Yes?' I snapped.

'I heard . . .' said the knight, and then he paused for a heartbeat. 'I heard that Robert of Locksley, when badly outnumbered by his enemies, summoned horse-demons from the very bowels of Hell to help him win a battle in Yorkshire against Prince John's liegeman Sir Ralph Murdac.'

He made the sign of the Cross again.

'It was just a trick,' I said hotly. 'A *ruse de guerre*. It was merely a few men in masks, and horse-drawn fire-carts and a little heathen music to put terror in the minds of his enemies. There were no black arts involved. I swear it. I swear by Almighty God, by the Virgin and all the saints, there was no devilry. He was just trying to frighten his enemies. And it worked very well, I may say.'

'Heathen music? Hmm, interesting. Ah well,' said this pig-headed Templar. 'If you say there was no devilment involved, I must believe you.' He clearly did not, and his voice had taken on a distant, chilly tone as if he had already made up his mind about me. 'Doubtless the truth will be fully revealed at the inquisition.'

'The inquisition?' I said, now utterly bewildered.

'Did you not know?' said this monkish knight, feigning surprise. 'Lord Locksley has been summoned to appear before an episcopal inquisition to be held by the Master of our Order to answer charges of heresy. Pope Celestine sanctioned it personally – and it will be rather a special occasion, I believe. As you must know, all the bishops in Christendom have been charged by His Holiness with suppressing heresy wherever they find it. Mostly it's a way of extirpating the southern heretics, those damned Cathars, but the Master has been granted a special dispensation by the Holy Father himself to investigate Robert, Earl of Locksley. And so your lord, if he has any respect for the Vicar of Christ, God's anointed representative on Earth, must attend a tribunal in London on St Polycarpus's Day on pain of excommunication and an interdict on all his lands.'

The Templar knight smiled at me grimly. 'If what you say is true, he should think of it as a welcome chance to clear his good name.'

I stumbled away from the conversation with Sir Aymeric de St Maur in a state of shock. St Polycarpus's Day was the twenty-third of February, about ten weeks hence. Did Robin know about this? He must do, which is why he was summoning Hanno and me to his side. Would he then present himself at the inquisition? It would be risky not to. Excommunication was one of the most serious sanctions that the Church could impose on mortal man: it meant that the sinner would no longer be considered part of the Christian communion; once excommunicated he was publicly excluded from the Church and became a sort of spiritual outlaw, unable to receive the Eucharist and therefore damned to eternal torment in Hell. But I also knew that Robin could not give two rotten apples for the Church's opinion of his soul. I'm not even sure that he believed that he had one. And he never willingly received the Eucharist anyway.

The interdict on his lands was more serious. It meant that no church services could be performed anywhere on his lands: no one could be married, no child baptized, and no dead man could be buried in a large part of South Yorkshire, and significant areas of Nottinghamshire, too. And this was worrying news. To make an enemy of the Church was no small thing. Children who died in infancy would go to Hell without baptism; corpses would pile up on the sides of the roads. All his tenants and villeins would be incensed with their lord over this, perhaps even to the point of rebellion, unless Robin could succeed in getting the interdict swiftly lifted.

But to attend this inquisition and be found guilty would be worse: the penalty for a man found guilty of a grave heresy was confiscation of all his lands and goods – and, in the most serious cases, death by burning at the stake.

Two days later, Hanno and I were in the buttery attached to the great hall at Kirkton Castle, refreshing ourselves with two large mugs of freshly brewed ale from the butts stored there. The alewife, a big-boned woman, was fond of Hanno for some reason, and was fussing around us pressing us to have a morsel of cheese and to make ourselves free with the ale cask. I had often noted Hanno's predilection for alewives – fat, thin, tall, short, he loved all women who brewed ale. This was no mystery, for I don't think I have ever met a man who was more fond of drinking ale. He cared nothing for wine or mead – ale was his drink, his liquid love, and he would touch no other.

As we drank deeply of the alewife's powerful brew, I reflected that I had been foolish to have been so concerned about my lord. When we arrived at Kirkton that morning, after many miles of hard riding, Robin had laughed – laughed out loud when I told him about the Templars and their specially sanctioned heresy inquisition on St Polycarpus's Day.

'I know all about that, Alan. I received a letter from the Master of the Temple himself inviting me to come and meekly put my head into his noose. I wrote back respectfully declining his invitation and suggesting – very politely – that he ask the huskier novices to refrain from buggering him for a few moments to allow him time to shove this inquisition up his fundament.'

I was shocked. I knew that Robin was fearless but to insult the Master of the Temple in such a crude way, a senior member of the most respected knightly order in the world . . .

'But have you not made it worse?' I asked. 'Will they not now come and attack you here, at Kirkton?'

'How could I make it worse? They have declared war against me personally, they are seeking to have me burnt alive at the stake – and it is not because they are concerned about some silly conjuring tricks in a petty Yorkshire skirmish or about the state of my immortal soul. Think, Alan. You know what this is really about . . .'

I knew exactly to what he referred: frankincense – the extremely lucrative trade in this incense, burnt in every major church in Christendom every day. This most precious commodity originated in southern Arabia and its trade had been a significant source of revenue for the Knights Templar and their associates in Outremer – until Robin had persuaded the Arabian frankincense merchants – none too gently, it has to be said – to trade with him instead. Robin's friend Reuben, a tough and clever Jew, had remained in Outremer when most of the rest of us had returned to England and he was responsible for continuing the commerce in frankincense, acting on Robin's behalf. And what lucrative trade! The little whitish-yellow crystals of frankincense, bought for pennies in the land of Al-Yaman at the foot of the Arabian peninsula, were worth more than their weight in gold in Europe. Reuben bought large quantities from the traders in Gaza for a modest amount of silver, and shipped the precious crumbs to Sicily where another of Robin's confederates sold them on to Italy and the rest of Europe.

I did not know the full details of the trade, but I had seen its results. When we had arrived at Dover several months ago, we had been raggedy, seasick and exhausted, but also very, very rich. We had carried with us on our long journey home – in conditions of strictest secrecy, of course – several large chests of silver, thousands of pounds' worth, which were now lodged in Robin's strongly built counting house in the bailey of Kirkton Castle. And that was not the full extent of Robin's fortune. Since we had returned from the East, two more shipments of silver had arrived at Kirkton with the compliments of Reuben and a letter assuring his friend that all was well in Gaza and that commerce was booming. The frankincense trade had made Robin a wealthy man and would continue to enrich him – unless the Master of the Knights Templar and His Holiness the Pope had their way.

This is what Robin was alluding to when he said that the Templars were not truly concerned with the state of his soul. They wanted to unseat him from his golden frankincense throne and recover the trade for themselves; doubtless His Holiness had been promised a fat slice of the pie as well.

'It is just an opening move in a long, complicated game,' Robin said. 'They think I am vulnerable to their threats of excommunication. I am not; I care not a clipped farthing for the pronouncements of faraway priests and popes. And interdiction? I can buy that off. Geoffrey, the Archbishop of York, would sell his sister for a chest of silver, let alone mumble a few words to lift some priestly malediction on my lands.'

What he said was true: Archbishop Geoffrey, King Richard's illegitimate older brother, was notoriously venal; he had been forced to take holy orders to make him ineligible for the throne and thereafter he seemed determined to make himself the richest prelate in England.

But, though I did feel a little reassured by Robin's words, as ever, I found his complete lack of respect for the institutions of the Church deeply unsettling.

'What about might? Will they not ride north and besiege us again?' I suggested. To my mind, Robin was too complacent. I did not think the famous fighting Templars were a force to be so easily ignored.

'How many Templar knights do you think there are in England at the moment, Alan?' asked Robin. 'A dozen? Perhaps a score of them? All their fighting men are out East: in Outremer, in Acre, in Jaffa or in Cyprus. They have too few knights here to start seriously throwing their weight around. And if they recruit common foot soldiers, well, I too have the silver to attract men-at-arms to my standard.'

This was true. And, in fact, Robin had already begun spending his frankincense hoard to this end. Apart from the twenty men whose lives he had spared after the battle outside the walls of Kirkton, Robin had arranged for a fresh contingent of fifty master archers to join him from Wales. Father Tuck, who had once been a bowman, had arranged for these men to join Robin's wolf banner. In addition there were three score of cavalrymen, recruited locally, that he was training in the lush green dales around the castle. Kirkton was once again bustling with soldiers, and I reflected that perhaps Robin was right: perhaps there was nothing the Templars could do but make impotent spiritual threats.

I was wrong.

Chapter Five

I watched from the south-facing battlements as the armed column approached Kirkton Castle, plodding up the steep muddy road from the river valley bottom. I had been gazing out over the drizzle-washed dales, taking a sharp breath of fresh air and trying to find a rhyme for 'damsel'. The column came on slowly, red-and-gold flags hanging limply above a dozen damp horsemen, watery winter sunlight occasionally breaking through the grey cloud cover and glinting off mail coats and spear points. Above the clop of hooves and the rumble of distant thunder, I could hear the steel accoutrements of battle chinking daintily. But these men in dripping hoods, their bodies slumped by tiredness, were not coming to war. Their approach was too slow, too open for them to be anything other than peaceful visitors of some kind, and, of course, there were too few of them.

Despite their damp clothes I could see that they were

travelling in some style – all their horses were big and well fed, their lanolin-impregnated woollen rain cloaks were of the finest quality: clearly this was the entourage of some wealthy noble or courtier. But it was a strange season to be abroad – during the cold, dour month of January many knightly folk preferred to remain at home and bide by a roaring fire rather than venture out into the elements. Whoever it was that had ordered this journey had urgent business with us.

When the damp and muddy horsemen finally arrived at the closed gates of Kirkton Castle, and announced their presence formally with the blast of a trumpet, I was astonished to recognize my old friend and one-time musical mentor Bernard de Sezanne at the head of the column. Bernard was the last person I expected to see braving the chill to pay a call on his friends. He hated to be far from a well-stocked buttery, a friendly young woman or two and a cosy hearth.

Christmas was weeks past, and we had kept the festive season tolerably well at Kirkton with much eating and drinking, and singing and laughter. I had fulfilled my promise to young Thomas, too, and had given him several lessons in the use of the sword. He was talented and I believed that one day he would be a fair swordsman, but he was still too small and weak to wield a blade with any skill – nevertheless he was fast, very fast indeed. He had, in turn, shown me how he had thrown the much bigger boy and explained to me his ideas about wrestling: 'I try to use the strength of the other man against him,' he told me gravely. And then he demonstrated how, with quickness and a judicious use of leverage, he used the momentum of his opponent to defeat him. When we grappled, he even managed to have me on my back in the dirt a couple of times

75

before I felt that my dignity had suffered enough for one day at the hands of a small boy.

The weather over the Christmas period had been mild but now we were in the middle of a cold spell, with bleak short days and little to cheer the soul, and with the prospect of spring still several months away. Kirkton was uneasy in itself, too. Unusual things had been occurring in the area; things which the local peasants, as ever, blamed on witchcraft: a calf had been born with two heads, an old man had drowned in his own well, and strange lights had been seen in the sky at night. In the alehouses of Locksley and in the surrounding villages it was whispered that the Hag of Hallamshire, a terrifying black-clad witch with a hideous visage straight from a nightmare, had returned to the area. She was said to steal babies and sacrifice them to the Devil and then feast on their blood. Several villeins from Locksley claimed to have seen the Hag out on the dales shouting curses in a strange tongue at the moon when they were returning home from the alehouse at midnight. I would normally have dismissed such talk as nothing more than the over-stoked imaginations of drunks, were it not for a weird message that the Norman fortune-teller Elise had given me.

Elise had been much praised for her role in the victory against Ralph Murdac's men, and Robin had given her a fine grey mare and a bag of silver as a reward for spreading terror so well among the besieging troops. She was now, despite her foreign and sometimes alarming ways, a popular figure at the castle: not only for the help she had given against Murdac but also because she had a rare skill as a healer, and several men and women of Kirkton owed their lives to her skill with herbs. On Robin's advice, she had paid a visit to another famous healer, wise woman, and some said witch, named Brigid, who was an old friend of Robin's and, it has to be admitted, of mine too.

Brigid, who lived in seclusion in a small hut deep in Sherwood Forest, thirty miles to the south of Kirkton, had healed my arm when I was bitten by a wolf a few years before; I still bore the scars – a row of pink dimples on my right arm. When Elise announced that she was planning to visit Brigid, I gave her a small bag of dried orange peel to give to Brigid as a present from me. The stick-hard brown skin of the fruit had travelled with me all the way from Spain where I had purchased it from an Arab doctor whom I'd consulted about a troublesome cough and running nose. The man had told me that by steeping the dried peel in boiling water and adding a little honey I might make a soothing liquor to combat my ailments. To be honest, I had not bothered to make the drink and my cold had cured itself, but the little leather sack had remained with me, untouched for many long months in my saddlebag. I thought that Brigid might find it both interesting and medicinally useful.

Elise was gone for a month over the Christmas period, but when she returned she took me to one side in the great hall and, after passing on Brigid's greetings and thanks for my gift, gave me some disquieting news.

'My sister-in-craft thanks you for the gift but bids you to beware,' said Elise. 'She has cast the runes and she tells me that you must avoid at all costs an ugly woman in black, who wishes you ill.'

'Is this another silly tale about the Hag?' I asked, a little alarmed in spite of myself.

'I know not,' said Elise. 'But my sister is a wise woman and I should not take her warnings lightly, were I you.'

Fine, I thought. *Fine. Beware a woman in black. Beware the Hag of Hallamshire.* I told myself that I was not frightened of witches. Well, only a little.

'Are you going to let us in then, or do you expect us to freeze to death out here?' Bernard shouted up at the wooden battlements. I stopped my day-dreaming and hurriedly gave the signal to the porters, who unbarred the huge wooden gates and swung them open to admit my friend; then I ran down the nearest set of steps to greet my old music teacher as he trotted into the bailey.

Bernard's nose was blue-red with cold, which matched the colours of his rich clothes. As I helped him down from his horse he pretended to be an old man, moving stiffly with many little grunts and sighs. 'A drink, Alan, a drink – and quickly, for the love of God. I would give my very soul for a sip of wine.' And so I led him into the hall, leaving the gate guards to succour the horses and men-at-arms of his escort, and installed him on a bench by the central fire that burned all day at that time of the year while a servant was dispatched to bring hot spiced wine for both of us.

'Welcome to Kirkton Castle, Bernard,' I said. 'And what brings you out in our bracing Yorkshire weather?'

Bernard waggled a limp hand in my face. 'Shhh, shhh, my boy, not now, not now. Let me get a little heat back into my tired old bones.'

Bernard was perhaps in his mid-thirties, but he loved to be dramatic and it pleased him to pretend to be an ancient grandfather, victim of gout and the rheumatics and every passing chill.

Fortunately, the servant returned soon afterwards with a

flagon of hot mulled wine. After two large restorative cups, Bernard finally deigned to speak to me.

'Ahhh, that's better,' he said, thrusting out his cup to be refilled. 'Alan, you are a gifted host, a man who knows when to be silent and merely pour the wine. I can feel life returning to my frozen limbs.' He peered at me closely. 'How is your music these days? Are you composing?'

I didn't have the chance to answer, for he continued: 'I hear things about you, Alan, in my travels about the world. Good things, mostly. I even heard someone attempting one of your *tensos* the other day, the one about the debate between King Arthur and the field mouse.' He hummed a snatch of my music. 'The fool made a complete hash of it, of course, and I had to show him how it should be done. But it is good that people are performing your works. I'm proud of you, Alan. You make a tired old man very happy.'

'You are not so old, Bernard. Come, tell me your news. What brings you here?'

'Bad news, Alan. Very bad. The worst kind. I have been dispatched by my royal lady, by Queen Eleanor of Aquitaine, may she live another thousand years, with an invitation for your master and mistress to join her at Westminster. Sent out into this freezing wasteland to seek you out, with scant thought for the chill it must cause in my old bones. But I'd better deliver my message to the great man himself. Where is the noble Earl of Locksley?' He looked about the hall in a comical manner, one hand shading his eyes, as if Robin might be hiding like a cutpurse in some dark corner.

'He's gone hunting today. He'll be back soon. What is this terrible news, then?' I said impatiently.

'You'll find out in good time. Doubtless His Lordship will tell you it all. But I will keep it till he returns. Give me some more wine, I beg you.'

And, infuriatingly, he refused to say another word on the subject until Robin returned an hour later, wet, happy and tired, with a brace of young fallow deer draped over his saddle as the grey winter day slid imperceptibly into the darkness of true night.

When Robin had washed and restored himself with wine and food, he summoned Bernard to his carved oak chair at the end of the hall to hear the news.

'I come from Queen Eleanor, esteemed mother of our good King Richard,' my old music teacher began, 'with news of the worst, the gravest kind, my lord.'

Robin nodded and made an impatient circling motion with his wrist and hand, urging the French *trouvère* to get to the point.

'Calamity has struck,' went on Bernard, clutching at his brow, 'disaster is upon us,' he said, and then he paused.

'Yes, yes, calamity, disaster, news of the worst kind. I understand. Get on with it, man,' Robin said with uncharacteristic shortness.

Bernard allowed himself to savour one more moment of drama, testing the patience of my master to the utmost before he said: 'Richard has been taken. Our noble King is in chains. He has been captured by evil men while he was making his way home to England.' Another pause. And I could see that Robin was now extremely annoyed.

'Who has him? By whom has he been captured?' asked Robin coldly, his face a mask. He was fingering his sword hilt and, I reckoned, was only three heartbeats away from freeing Bernard from the burden of his own head.

'By Duke Leopold of Austria! He is now languishing in chains at the mercy of his mortal enemy. In deepest, darkest Germany!'

It *was* appalling news. Disastrous. And I could forgive Bernard for making the most of its delivery. Peace and prosperity in England depended on Richard being alive. His acknowledged heir, his little nephew Arthur, Duke of Brittany, was a mere child of five, and the whole kingdom knew that his brother Prince John had his eye on the throne. If Richard were to be killed in Germany, England could well erupt into civil war with some of the barons supporting the legitimate heir, despite his extreme youth, and others making the practical decision to follow John, who was more likely to win a contest of military strength. Bloody chaos would follow: there were still grandfathers alive who could remember the dark days of the Anarchy, when King Stephen and the Empress Matilda vied for mastery of the country. It was a time of famine and fear, with marauding bands of soldiers roaming the land, burning cottages and crops, stealing stored food, raping maids and generally despoiling the territories of their enemies.

'This is going to be very, very costly,' said Robin.

I was deep in thoughts of the carnage of civil war, and it took me a few moments to grasp his meaning. And then it dawned. Richard was too valuable a captive to be killed out of hand, no matter how much Duke Leopold hated him. His royal person was worth a king's ransom. And England would have to pay it.

'Queen Eleanor commands your presence: she wishes you and the lady Marie-Anne to attend her at Westminster as soon as possible,' said Bernard, in the measured tones of a diplomat, far removed from his excited rendering of the fateful news about King Richard.

'She wants to discuss what's to be done, no doubt,' said Robin. 'All right, we'll come to Westminster. Yes, we need to make plans. We leave tomorrow at dawn.'

The next day, as a pale blue light washed over the hills to the east and rolled back the night, our company rode out of the great gate at Kirkton and took the road east towards Sheffield. As I trotted out of the portal, I looked back and saw the first pink fingers of daylight catching the pair of lumpen shapes on long poles either side of the gatehouse: the severed heads of two men-at-arms, impaled on long spears – former Murdac men who had turned deserter.

The men had stolen a few items, including a small bag of coins, and had dropped silently over the walls and headed south in the middle of the night on foot, presumably hoping to become outlaws or possibly rejoin Sir Ralph at Nottingham. When the theft and their disappearance had been noticed in the morning, Hanno was dispatched with half a dozen mounted archers to track them down and bring them home to face Robin's justice. The shaven-headed Bavarian had taken no more than half a day to catch them, trapping them in a wood near Chesterfield, and he reappeared that evening with two bodies slung over a couple of packhorses. One deserter had died in the mêlée; he was the lucky one. The other man Robin had hanged until he was partially dead, and then flogged with metal-tipped whips – the remaining former Murdac men-at-arms being detailed to perform the punishment – and finally, with his skin hanging off him in bloody strips, and the blood puddling around his feet, he was beheaded in front of a jeering crowd in the centre of the bailey. The heads of both deserters were then stuck on spears and mounted either side of the main gate as a terrible warning to anyone else who might think of betraying Robin.

As I looked back at the gruesome display, I shivered slightly, and not just from the cold of dawn. Their faces had been pecked by carrion crows over the past few weeks until they were barely recognizable as men at all. And yet they seemed to be silently cursing us, hating us, casting an evil spell over our departure from Kirkton.

Four days later, the city of London lay before us, a dirty smudge of smoke on the southern horizon. I fancied I could already smell the stink of twenty thousand busy folk all crammed into a few square miles. But, mercifully, we were not planning to enter its maze of twisting streets and cramped dirty houses amid the deafening babble of its thronging crowds. Instead, we turned off Watling Street, the great Roman artery that had taken us all the way from Coventry to the north-western edge of the capital city, and rode south through the sleepy hamlet of Charing, and past green fields and orchards along the side of the slow-rolling River Thames to a rich Benedictine abbey, inhabited by sixty learned monks, overshadowed by the high bulk of Westminster Hall, the huge palace of the kings of England.

We were a large company, more than fifty souls in all, well mounted and guarded by a score of Robin's men-at-arms and a dozen mounted archers. Robin, myself, Hanno and Tuck were in the vanguard, while Marie-Anne, Goody, little Hugh and a couple of nursemaids trundled along in the centre of the column, shielded from the elements by a covered wagon. As well as a strong force of soldiers, Robin had also brought cooks and bakers, farriers, maids, serving men and all the staff he would need to support his dignity as an earl while he was a guest of Queen Eleanor.

It had taken us four days to ride from Kirkton to Westminster, staying overnight at the castles of friends and allies, our pace much slowed by the wagons, and I was glad to be at our destination. My horse, a well-schooled grey gelding that I called Ghost, who had been with me all the way to Outremer and back, had picked up a stone in his right forehoof outside St Alban's, and though I had speedily removed it, he was still limping. Fearing that the frog of his hoof had been bruised, I longed for the shelter of a nice quiet stable where he could rest and I could take a proper look at the offending limb.

A little royal hospitality would have been most welcome too, and Queen Eleanor did not disappoint. When we had shed our damp, travel-stained clothes in the dormitory of the Abbey and changed into something more fitting for regal company, we were ushered across the road into the great high hall where we were received by the Queen herself. A feast had been prepared for us, and we gorged on baked swan, lamprey stew and roast boar, with sweet white bread, and refreshed ourselves with the delicious light red wine of Bordeaux, part of Eleanor's ancestral fiefdom. When the meal was done and we had sluiced the grease from our hands, Robin, Tuck and I were ushered into a private chamber off the side of the hall overlooking the river, along with a couple of the other guests:

Walter de Coutances and Hugh de Puiset, two of King Richard's most loyal supporters in England.

'Good of you to come so swiftly, Robert,' said the Queen in French, allowing Robin to stoop and kiss her heavily ringed hand. She had a wonderful voice, deep, rich and a little husky, that sent a delicious ripple down the spine of any man who heard her speak. 'I know you have your own troubles at present.'

'He is my King, Your Highness, in chains or out of them,' replied Robin gravely in the same language. 'He made me what I am, and I do not forget his kindness.'

Eleanor smiled at me. 'And if I remember rightly, you are Alan Dale, my scapegrace *trouvère* Bernard's old pupil. We met at Winchester, I recall, in rather dramatic circumstances.' And she favoured me with a nod and twinkle from her bright brown eyes. I was struck once more by how beautiful Eleanor was; she must have been nearly seventy but she remained slim and lithe and her skin was as unlined as a girl's. Her memory was still excellent, too. She was referring to a time three years ago when I had been publicly unmasked as an outlaw under her roof, a cuckoo in the nest, you might say, and had been unceremoniously slung into the deepest dungeon.

I merely bowed and mumbled: 'Your Highness, I'm honoured that you remember me . . .' and then trailed off, unsure whether or not it would be the proper thing to comment further on my former humiliation in Winchester.

Robin saved me from having to say more: 'My lady, would you be kind enough to share with us the latest information that you possess about King Richard,' he said.

'Yes, you are right, Robin – to business. Walter, what do we know so far?' said the Queen, looking over at the short, rather dumpy middle-aged churchman standing to her left.

Walter de Coutances might not have seemed very impressive, and his speaking voice was the dull, inflectionless monotone of a dusty scholar, but he was said to be the cleverest man in England, and he was surely one of the most powerful. He had been a vice-chancellor under the old King Henry, and then had been made Archbishop of Rouen by him. When old Henry died, Walter had invested Richard as Duke of Normandy and had helped to crown him King of England three years ago. I knew him by sight, as he had accompanied Richard on the Great Pilgrimage, but he had been sent back to England from Sicily to act for the King at home in his absence, and we had never actually spoken to each other.

Walter cleared his throat. 'The truth is that we do not know very much,' he began. 'We understand that Richard took ship from Outremer in October of last year and that, as most of Europe was closed to him, he attempted to travel in secret up to Saxony in eastern Germany, where he was sure of a friendly welcome from his brother-in-law Duke Henry. He landed, we think, somewhere to the east of Venice, near Aquileia on the Adriatic coast . . .'

As Walter continued in his dry voice, I reflected how unfortunate it was that Richard had made so many enemies among the powerful men of Europe while taking part in the Great Pilgrimage. As well as a falling out with King Philip of France and Duke Leopold of Austria, he had alienated Henry VI, the Holy Roman Emperor, Leopold's overlord and ruler of most of Italy, by making a treaty with Tancred of Sicily, a rich island that the Emperor coveted. With France and Italy barred to him, Richard had little choice but to take the long eastern route home. And this apparently had been his downfall.

'. . . he wanted to travel in secret,' Walter droned on, 'and so, unwisely as it turned out, the King dismissed all but a handful of his men, and travelled in disguise as a Templar knight, north from the Adriatic coast towards Saxony. He didn't get very far. It seems he was betrayed, or discovered somehow in a, um, a brothel – I fear His Highness has little talent for acting the part of a lesser mortal – and taken by Duke Leopold's men. At that point we lost track of him and as of now we have no idea where he is. Our spies have, however, intercepted a copy of a letter dated last month from the Emperor to King Philip of France boasting of Richard's capture.'

Walter rummaged in a stack of documents on the table in front of him and pulled out a curled parchment. He then began to read:

'Because our Imperial Majesty has no doubt that your Royal Highness will take pleasure in all those providences of God which exalt us and our Empire, we have thought it proper to inform you of what happened to Richard, King of England, the enemy of our Empire and the disturber of our Kingdom as he was crossing the seas on his way back to his dominions . . .'

The letter proceeded to recount what Walter had just told us about Richard's journey and ended:

'Our dearly beloved cousin Leopold, Duke of Austria, captured the king in a disreputable house near Vienna. He is now in our power. We know this news will bring you great happiness.'

'I'll wager it will!' exclaimed Hugh de Puiset, a small, shrill, bouncy man, who seemed rather too excitable to be a bishop.

'He must be the happiest man in Christendom! And you will note that there is no acknowledgement, no mention at all in the letter that the Germans are breaking the Truce of God that protects all Christian knights who fought in Outremer. We must complain to His Holiness the Pope at once: the person of a knight taking part in a holy pilgrimage, or returning from one, and all his lands and property are sacrosanct! This is an outrage! Both Emperor Henry and Duke Leopold must be excommunicated at once!'

I thought of the Templars' threat to Robin, and wondered how much an Emperor would care about being excommunicated; if Robin, a mere earl, could safely ignore it, was it much of a sanction for a great European monarch?

'Well, yes, of course,' said Walter slowly. 'Excommunication – certainly, we are already working on His Holiness to achieve that. But will that threat alone bring King Richard safely back to us? I very much doubt it.'

'The real problem is Philip of France,' said Robin. Everyone in the room stared at him. It seemed an odd thing to say. But Walter de Coutances was smiling and nodding at my master, who continued talking into the amazed silence: 'Both Henry and Leopold need silver, some would say they need it very badly. But King Philip's treasury is well stocked; what Philip wants is land. He wants Normandy – in truth, he wants all of King Richard's possessions on that side of the Channel. And this is his best chance to get it. Philip may well attempt to buy Richard from the Germans and then force our King to give up his lands across the sea.'

There was a pause while we digested Robin's words.

'Richard would never willingly cede any of his patrimony.

Not a single acre. Never, not while he draws breath,' said his mother stoutly.

'And what of Prince John?' asked Robin. 'If Richard were dead, would *he* cede Normandy to Philip in exchange for the English crown?'

There was an uncomfortable silence, which no one appeared to want to break. John, too, was the son of Eleanor, and no one wished to offend her with a candid expression of their opinion of him.

'Where is the Prince now, by the way?' said Robin. He seemed to want to make a point of some sort.

The silence in that royal chamber was like a physical presence; an uncanny emptiness of noise. Finally, Archbishop Walter let out a long sigh and said: 'He is in London at the moment, but we have information that he is making plans to pay a visit to Paris.'

'Ah,' said Robin.

Robin and Queen Eleanor and her counsellors met several times over the next few days, but feeling out of my depth surrounded by so many great and wise folk, and having little to contribute to the discussions, I begged Robin to excuse me from joining in their further deliberations. This left me kicking my heels in the echoing space of Westminster Hall, for Ghost was unable to put any weight on his lamed foot and I owned no other mount except an elderly mule, a pack animal unsuitable for riding. To counter my boredom, I set out to explore the area around Westminster – by boat.

I had made friends with a local waterman named Perkin, a snub-nosed, red-headed fellow of about my age who was the proud owner of a sixteen-foot skiff. I was not a good sailor and had unhappy memories of travelling by sea during the Great Pilgrimage, but being carried downstream on the current of the Thames was a wholly different and quite pleasurable experience. With Perkin manning the long steering oar, we would be wafted gently down around the bend in the river to the City of London. These journeys gave me a sense of serenity: alone on the water with my new friend, and nary a sound but the slap of waves against the sides of his skiff and the harsh cry of a seagull or perhaps the occasional friendly hail of a passing boatman, I felt all my cares slip away, washed downstream, along with Perkin and myself, by the grey-brown waters of the Thames. At that time, I found it a novel experience to see the city from the water, sweeping slowly past quays where merchants unloaded their wares, their cloths and spices, and crates of exotic fruit; floating gently past the high walls of grand townhouses, past markets with fishermen crying their catch of the day, right up to the half-built stone bridge where the current, squeezed between the tall arches, speeded up in the centre of the river and we were shot through the dark tunnel on a wave of green spume and laughter. I liked to look upwards at the vault of the bridge's arches, and the chapel dedicated to St Thomas à Becket in the centre of the structure, as we were swept under it, until Perkin quietly informed me that some of the wooden buildings that jutted out of the side of the bridge were privies and that I must be wary of falling ordure. We would return, Perkin and myself hauling on an oar each, up the calmer side of the river near the southern bank, where the bridge had yet to be completed, past the bustling Augustinian Priory of Southwark and the wide foul-smelling mud flats and miniature forests of bulrushes, and then the long pull round the bend on the side of the open heathland of Lambeth moor and finally back across the river to Westminster.

One day, I took Goody with us in Perkin's boat, thinking she might enjoy a day out away from the chattering women of the Queen's court.

It was a disaster.

My feelings for Goody were muddled at that time. Having known her since she was a child, I tended to forget that she was now a young woman, and found myself treating her with the rough friendliness and condescension due to a younger sister. On that misty February morning, when I took her down to Perkin's skiff and introduced her to the waterman, she seemed out of sorts, bad tempered and snappish, and I noticed that she had a very small spot on the end of her nose. Much later, it occurred to me that it might have been her time of the month. As I handed her into the boat she stumbled slightly and I had to catch her to stop her falling into the muddy shallows of the Thames. Accidentally, I swear on the bones of Christ, as I grabbed her body, I found myself clutching at her small hard breasts. When she was righted again, and safely on board, she slapped me, a hard stinging blow that left my head ringing. I was astounded, speechless. I had not meant to manhandle her in a lascivious way, I was merely trying to save her splashing into the filthy river water.

'You keep your rough soldier's hands to yourself, Alan Dale,' she said tartly as she sat down and arranged her skirts around her in the prow of the skiff. 'I've been warned about this sort of thing: men who come back from a war with only one thing on their minds. I don't know what strumpets you encountered

91

on your travels in the East, but you are in Christian lands now and here you may not so easily paw a lady for your pleasure.'

Perkin began laughing so hard he almost fell overboard. I flushed with sudden impotent rage and took my seat in the centre of the boat, silent, seething. At that moment, I could have happily picked her up and tossed her in the mud. Instead, I ground my teeth and looked out to the far Lambeth shore, pretending to study a heron that was flapping lazily along a stretch of marshland. I should have made a joke about it, or apologized, but instead we set off in an awkward, burning silence.

I had chosen a bad day for seeing the sights of London; as we glided along downstream, a low bank of fog began to roll in from the distant sea. Soon we could barely see beyond the end of the skiff, let alone make out the sights of the city, bar a few occasional glimpses through the drifting smoky grey mist.

'Keep a sharp eye out for other craft, master,' said Perkin to me. 'Many a good man has drowned after a careless collision mid-river.'

Seeking to make a joke, but also perhaps, in my heart of hearts, trying to take some revenge, I said: 'Those other boats won't have any difficulty in seeing us' – I grinned at Goody – 'not with that giant pimple glowing bright as a beacon on my lady's nose! Ha-ha!'

I was trying to lighten the atmosphere. To be honest, Goody had only a minuscule pink blemish, but I saw that my jesting remark had hit home – and hard. Goody gasped as if I had struck her, her hand flashed to her face to cover the spot, and to my astonishment she suddenly burst into tears, sobbing and snuffling and covering her face as the tears streamed down it.

Once again I was speechless – I had seen this very girl once stab a dangerous madman in the eye with a poniard; and in so doing save my life – how could she be crying over a silly jest from an old friend? I felt the immediate urge to go up to the prow and put my arm around her to comfort her, but I feared she would think I was making advances again. And so I did nothing. I merely said gruffly: 'Are you quite well, my lady? Is there anything I can do for your comfort?' At which she burst into a fresh bout of sobbing.

We continued downstream, with Goody quietly weeping, myself feeling wretched and useless and Perkin struck dumb with embarrassment at the antics of his two passengers. After a decent interval, I turned to Perkin, and said briskly: 'Well, we won't be able to see much today, waterman – shall we go back?' Then I looked to the prow, saying: 'Goody?' and she nodded but said nothing, her face tear-streaked, red and blotched.

We rowed back to Westminster with both Goody and me in abject misery. I could not wait to be out of the boat and away from my shame. What was the matter with the girl: was she ill? Why couldn't she tell me? As we tied up at the wharf, I offered my hand to Goody, to help her out of the boat, but she ignored my arm and jumped nimbly on to the wooden jetty and without another word, and without any sort of escort, she hurried away into the misty morning making for the haven of the women's quarters of Westminster Hall.

I was just turning to Perkin to pay him for the boat ride when, out of the corner of my eye, I saw two figures in the crowds by the wharf that triggered a half-memory. There, not twenty yards away, was a very tall, thin man, standing next to a huge, broad man. I knew them, but where had I seen them before? Before I could place them, the two men turned and melted away into the thick banks of river mist and I soon forgot their presence as I tried to make amends for my clumsiness towards Goody by overpaying Perkin.

Chapter Six

I was upset and angry with myself all that day for having made Goody cry – I was very fond of her after all. And, perhaps rashly, I accepted an invitation to go drinking with Bernard that evening. My old vielle teacher took me to a tavern by the river, under the sign of the Blue Boar, where, he said, the wine was expensive but the wenches were cheap. It was a dreary place, one big low room with greasy rushes on the floor and a fire burning in a walled central hearth. At a long counter against one wall, the owner manned barrels of wine and ale, serving us foaming flagons of greenish wine from Germany between wiping at the grime on a shelf of pewter mugs with a dirty rag. Two slatternly girls, full-breasted but clad in nothing more than grubby light chemises, flitted about the place, bringing our drinks to the table with a plate of stale bread, cold pork and pickles. But while I had no appetite for women or food, I drank with sincere conviction, aiming to find oblivion and wash away my feeling of shame with long draughts of the tavern-keeper's surprisingly good Rhenish wine.

Bernard was dressed in bright silks and was in fine form, cracking jokes, his nose glowing with wine, and telling me about a new work he was composing – I forget the details now, but he claimed it would set the noble houses of Europe ablaze with the exquisite beauty of his music and its wondrously clever rhymes. He insisted on singing a few snatches to me, rudely demanding silence from the two or three other drinkers in the tavern – strangers, of course, rough men by the look of them, who did not take kindly to being told to be quiet by some foppish drunk – while he sang, beating the tabletop with the palm of his hand to keep time. I conceded that it was a decent enough composition, but Bernard seemed disappointed in my response. He then began to tell me about his love affairs with the ladies of Queen Eleanor's court: they were many and very complicated.

It was clear to me, as my friend boasted and lied outrageously, that he was having the time of his life as Eleanor's *trouvère*. However, such was my black humour that I could respond to Bernard's bright chatter only with grunts and nods. Indeed, I must have been lamentable company, but he took it in good part. For a while I stopped listening entirely and stared around the dingy tavern, my eye eventually alighting on a big, dark-haired man who was muttering to himself and shooting evil glances our way as he stood drinking ale from a gallon pot in the corner.

I tore my gaze from the man, and turned back to Bernard to hear him say: '. . . and when the poor villein complained about the burdens of being a father and asked for compensation for his daughter's lost virginity, Prince John had him chained in his dungeon in a lead cope. As the heavy metal sheet was fitted around the man's neck and shoulders, and knowing that the cope would slowly crush him to death, Prince John said: "How's that for a father's burden!" Which was considered very witty by everyone – well, everyone except the poor man with a hundred pounds of lead round his neck!' Bernard laughed like a lunatic, slapping his knee and calling for another flagon of wine.

Eventually, realizing that even his funniest stories could not lift my spirits, my friend disappeared into a back room with one of the slatterns. I finished my wine and was just thinking of settling up with the owner and going to bed, when I looked up from my stool to find the big, dark-haired man looming over me, a thick oak cudgel held casually over one broad shoulder.

'I don't like you,' he said, and glowered at me. He had a rough southern accent, and was clearly very drunk. 'I don't like you at all, or your friend, or any of your kind,' he continued. 'Musicians, *trouvères* or whatever you call yourselves – you're nothing but pedlars of soppy ditties, mincing little sodomites, lickspittles to any lord who will listen to your Goddamned noise.'

The tavern-keeper called over from the ale tuns, where he was polishing a metal tankard: 'You behave yourself now, Tom. Leave the musical gentleman alone. We don't want any trouble here.'

The big man – Tom, apparently – ignored him.

'I don't like you . . .' he began again. But I had had more than enough.

'You know something? I don't think I care for you much either,' I said, looking up at him. 'So why don't you take yourself out of my face and go and find a pig to fuck – one that's not too choosy about its bed-mates.'

Tom leaned further over me, his huge bulk nearly blocking out the dim light in that grimy den. 'You listen to me you little poof—'

And I thought: *Yes, this will do. This is what I've wanted all night.*

My sword was with my other belongings at Westminster Hall, but my misericorde was snug in my boot. In fact, I had no need of either. I merely launched myself directly upwards, using all the power in my young legs, surging straight up with the force of a battering ram, the top of my skull smashing into his mouth with stunning force. Tom staggered back and, now standing, I went up on to the balls of my feet and whipped my forehead forward in a short, hard arc, crunching it into his nose in a second devastating headbutt. My poll smashed into his face like a boulder crushing a loaf of new bread. He stumbled away, spitting blood and teeth, a look of dazed incomprehension on his big ugly face, and I lashed out with my right boot, catching him squarely in the fork of his crotch. He doubled over, mooing in agony. Taking a step back, I swept up the stool I had been sitting on, swung hard and shattered the heavy wooden disc of the seat over the back of his head. Like a felled tree he toppled over slowly and crashed to the floor, landing in a senseless heap on the dirty rushes, bleeding quietly but copiously from a jagged split in the back of his scalp.

I looked up to find the tavern owner staring at me in amazement. Trying to control the shaking in my hands from my sudden surge of rage, I fished in the purse at my waist and threw a handful of coins on to the counter. 'That's for the wine – and the stool,' I said, making for the doorway. 'And you'd better give that great ox a drink of ale when he wakes.'

I had thought that a night of boozing and brawling might make me feel better about Goody – it did not. The next day I woke with an aching head and a deep sense of guilt. I hoped I had not killed Tom in the fight the night before. He did not deserve to die for being a drunken boor.

I mentioned the boating affair with Goody to Marie-Anne that day, hoping that as a woman she would know what I could do to make things right with my young friend.

'I would not trouble yourself too much about it,' said the Countess of Locksley, as we shared a cold supper in her chambers. I had been summoned to entertain her while Robin was ensconced with the Queen discussing King Richard's plight. Marie-Anne must have sensed that my heart wasn't in my music, for after I had picked my way through a few of her favourite *cansos*, she invited me to set down my vielle and bow and join her in her meal.

'Girls that age have a difficult time, stuck halfway between childhood and the full bloom of a woman,' she said. 'She ought to be married by now, really, and have babies to care for, but as she has neither land nor money, it is difficult for her to attract the right suitors.'

'But she is truly beautiful, she has a lovely face – surely there must be some men who are interested,' I said. Marie-Anne gave me a slantendicular look. 'You could always write her a song,' she said, 'if you wanted to make amends. I'm sure she would appreciate it, and it would be a fine way to tell her that you are sorry.'

I considered this. It was a good idea, I thought. 'I'll do it,' I said. 'But . . .' And at that moment the chamber door opened and a little bundle of raw energy on two pudgy legs came barrelling in, running straight up to Marie-Anne with a delighted cry of '*Maman!*', pursued by a red-faced nursemaid. 'I am so sorry for disturbing you, my lady,' she said breathlessly, 'but he got away from me while I was sorting out his clothes chest.'

'That's quite all right, Ysmay,' said Marie-Anne, scooping up little Hugh in her arms, smoothing his black hair and bestowing a kiss on his soft pale cheek. I rose from my stool and was about to make my excuses and leave when the Countess stopped me: 'Alan, do you think . . . when the weather is a little clearer . . . you could arrange for myself and Hugh to take a boat ride downriver with you? Not a grand outing, just a few of us. Perhaps you could ask your friend Perkin . . .'

I told her that it would be my pleasure to arrange it, bowed low and left the chamber.

The day I chose for Marie-Anne's boating expedition was bright and clear, and surprisingly warm – it was almost spring-like although we were still only halfway through February. Our party was made up of the Countess, little Hugh and his nurse-maid Ysmay, myself, Perkin and Tuck, who as Marie-Anne's personal chaplain had taken to carrying a wooden cross as tall as he was. The cross, as well as being the holy symbol and a badge of office, served as a walking staff to support my corpulent friend, who by now was well into middle age – though he did not like his juniors to remind him of the fact.

I had spoken to the Bishop of London, a kindly man named Richard FitzNeal, who was staying at Westminster in order to give counsel to the Queen at this time of crisis, asking on behalf of the Countess whether we might visit his manor of Fulham, a few miles upstream. The gardens there were said to be of surpassing beauty and I thought Marie-Anne might enjoy them. Bishop Richard was a wonderful old stick, past sixty years of age but still vigorous and very learned – his book about the administration of the kingdom was very highly regarded – and he was happy for us to enjoy his manor.

'Of course, my dear boy, of course,' he said. 'I shall send ahead and make sure everything is prepared for you when you arrive. Would the Countess not like to stay there for several days? I am busy here with the Queen, but if she would like a break from court life she would be very welcome to stay at Fulham, for weeks if she wants to; masses of room, nobody there but the servants . . .'

I assured the good bishop that we were merely going there for the day, this coming Thursday, but I was warmed by his generosity. I left him issuing orders to his clerks to have his people in Fulham prepare for our arrival with a lavish meal and the finest wines. Marie-Anne was very popular at Westminster; her beauty and charm – and, the more cynical might say, her close friendship with Queen Eleanor – made her someone that the entire Court seemed to adore. And even elderly bishops were not immune to her charms, it seemed.

The skiff was fully laden as Perkin shoved off and he and I took our places at the oars. The going was hard; moving the bulk of the fully laden boat against the current required a good deal of sweat and muscle power from my snub-nosed friend and me, but I was young and strong in those days and I did not mind that we were going upstream. It would make the afternoon all the sweeter when, full of the bishop's good food and drink, we would be able to glide back down to Westminster with the minimum of effort.

As I hauled on the long pinewood oar, I faced backwards, timing my stroke with Perkin, who was seated to my left. And it was Perkin who first alerted me to the small black ship. As we stroked our way slowly up the river, heading due south at that point, Perkin turned to me and, nodding at a dark, low form behind us, on our side, the western side of the river, but closer into the bank, he said quietly: 'That bugger is moving very strangely. Going too slow for a craft that size. Must have at least ten oarsmen, but it's moving no faster than we are.'

He was right; the small ship, a low, clinker-built vessel, its sides daubed with pitch, with a single mast but no sail hoisted, was being rowed by five men on each side and yet it seemed to move at the same pace as us. In fact, it might be said to be following us.

At first I was just idly curious, but after half an hour had passed, I began to be slightly alarmed. The river had turned west and we were now sticking close to the northern shore, but the black ship was still there behind us. And it was more conspicuous for the fact that, on that clear day, in that part of the river, there was very little traffic on the water.

I was certain now that the ship was following us, and no sooner was that thought born than the vessel began to move more speedily, coming up fast on the landward side. I cursed my decision not to engage a bigger boat for our jaunt that day, for in Perkin's small skiff there had been no room for extra bodies and the only fighting men on board were myself and Tuck, although I suspected that Perkin could handle himself in a tight situation, and I noticed that he wore an evil-looking long dagger at his belt.

I looked sideways at the waterman and it seemed that we both had the same thought simultaneously. Perkin muttered: 'River pirates; God damn their black souls!' I was too intent on pulling on my oar as powerfully as I could to reply. But for all our efforts we were losing the race.

The black ship was now almost level with us, positioning itself between our skiff and the north bank of the Thames, about a hundred paces away, where the little village of Chelsea was laid out on the shore, the wind blowing the smoke of dozens of cooking fires towards us. Crouched in the prow of the black ship I could see more than half a dozen armed men, rough-looking fellows armed with swords, clubs and spears, dressed in greasy furs and leather armour, but with no distinguishing badges to say whom they served. To a man, they were eyeing us hungrily. Perkin and I braced our feet against the skiff's ridged wooden bottom, and put our backs into the task of rowing. The river turned south at that point and we tried to cut straight across to the other side, to a marshy area where there was a village on an island known as Battersea.

The river was less than half a mile wide at this point and with God's help, and by rowing with all our might, I hoped we could make it to the wild swampy grassland on the southern shore where we could try to lose our pursuers or find a hiding place. We would have done it, too, but for one factor: the wind. It was blowing directly from the north and as we, in our little open rowing boat, headed south, the black ship hoisted

103

a grubby white sail and her oarsmen increased the pace and turned south to follow us.

They overhauled us rapidly, slicing swiftly through the water like a great dark fish. Even with Perkin and myself straining every muscle, there was no way we could escape. The happy chatter in the skiff had ceased, and all eyes were now on our pursuers.

'Who are those men?' asked Marie-Anne in a small but calm voice. She was clutching little Hugh to her bosom.

'I do not know, my lady, but I fear that they mean us harm.'

The black ship was by now no more than thirty yards away and still coming on apace, oars flashing in time, the sail bellying out. The southern shore was a good hundred and fifty yards away; indeed, we were smack in the middle of the river. There was no way that we could outrun the black ship and so I relinquished my oar to Perkin, stood up, made my way to the stern of the rocking boat, and drew my sword. I heard Tuck coming up behind me, and soon I felt his comforting bulk at my side. Perkin was holding his oar upright in both hands, breathing hard, the boat drifting gently with the current of the river. As the black ship approached, I looked at the half-dozen ruffians jostling each other in the prow: big, ugly bastards, all grinning at me. One man was actually licking his lips.

Tuck lifted his heavy wooden cross in his right hand, holding it out towards the black ship, as if to ward off evil. 'Who are you?' he boomed across the water. 'Why do you trouble good Christian folk as they go about their lawful business?'

'We come with an invitation for the Lady Marie-Anne and her son,' said a big, grey-bearded brute, armed with a rusty sword; he was the lip-licker. 'She is invited to spend a little time with some noble friends of ours. Hand her and her son over and we'll let you go in peace. That's a promise.'

'Lay a finger on her and I'll cut out your liver and feed it to the fish,' I said, as calmly as I could, though my heart was banging. 'That is my promise to you.'

I was very conscious of the fact that I wore no hauberk, just a light woollen tunic and hose, with my sword belt over the top. But I had a weapon in each hand, sword in my right, misericorde in my left, and I was determined to send some of these bastards to Hell before they got anywhere near my lady.

Behind me I heard Marie-Anne say, 'Alan, perhaps if we could just talk . . .' but there was no more time for words. The black ship surged forward under the power of her oarsmen, crashing into the side of our little boat and nearly capsizing it. Grappling hooks flew out, bit into the sides of our skiff, were pulled in and held fast. The grey-beard wasted no time; he leapt across from his prow, swinging his sword at my head. He landed with a crash on the stern seat of Perkin's skiff, and I ducked just in time as the blade hissed over my bare head. I came up and took a step forward; he was overbalanced from his swipe, and I punched the misericorde with a left-hand roundhouse blow into his side, crunching through ribs, the sharp triangular point raking deep into his lungs. He howled with pain and shock and I followed the first strike with a smash to his face with the pommel of my sword, mashing lips and teeth. He dropped his sword and toppled back into his own ship with a scream of rage, spitting blood, but I had no time to watch his progress. A spear was stabbed hard at my face and I leaned back and to the side, allowing the shaft to slide over my shoulder, then I chopped down with my sword into the arm of the spearman, almost severing his limb at the elbow.

Beside me, Tuck was swinging the heavy cross in wide sweeps. The crosspiece caught one of the pirates in the side of the face, crushing his eye and hurling him into the sea with a shrill bird-like cry. Another man bounded across from the black ship wielding a huge double-handed axe. Tuck caught the swing of the weapon in the crosspiece of his staff, but the blade sheared the tough wood in half, leaving the middle-aged monk with nothing more than a heavy stick in his hands. I leapt forward, keeping low to avoid a wild swing from the axeman, and sliced open his neck with my sword. As he died, he sprawled on to me, knocking me to the floor of the skiff. I pushed his gory corpse away, our legs tangled, and I watched with horror as more enemies jumped aboard and surrounded Marie-Anne and Hugh at the far end of the craft.

I saw Perkin bash a leaping man on the shoulder with his long clumsy oar, and then drop it, draw his dagger and plunge it into the belly of another man, but a pirate's swinging club found the back of his head and he dropped immediately, legs unstrung, into the bottom of the boat. There was a knot of men around Marie-Anne. A heavily bearded man punched her hard in the temple with his mailed fist, knocking her down to her knees, and I saw little Hugh being lifted screaming and kicking high above the fray in enemy hands, then passed above the heads of the knot of men around Ysmay, away and over to the black ship. I shouted a curse, struggled to my feet and lunged forward again, but my sword was checked by a tall boarder with a long moustache, and while I hacked and slashed desperately at him – he showing some unusual skill and checking my passage forwards – I realized that the rest of the pirates were leaving the skiff, many scratched and bleeding, cutting the grappling irons loose and leaping back into their own craft. I feinted low at the moustached man's groin with my sword, stepped forward, twisted a full circle inside his reach and slammed the misericorde into his left ear, backhand, hard, into his brain. The only pirates on board our little vessel now were corpses.

Already five yards of grey water separated us from the black ship, which was rapidly pulling away, our foes jeering at us and waving their weapons. I ducked as a spear was hurled at my head. When I straightened again, I saw that I was the only person still standing in our boat. Perkin was unconscious, lying in a bloody pool in the scuppers; Ysmay the nurse was gone – hacked apart while trying to protect her charge; her small severed hand lay on the rowing bench in a pool of black blood like a delicate white crab. Marie-Anne was slumped across the prow, but by the movement of her bosom she was clearly still breathing, praise God. Tuck had taken a sword thrust to the arm, which had cut deeply into the big muscles there. Only I was unscathed.

I looked after the fast-disappearing black ship and lifted my blood-clotted sword, pointing it threateningly towards them, silently hoping that one day God might allow me to have my vengeance on them. In return, one of the pirates lifted a small black-haired bundle, squealing with rage, short pudgy legs kicking in his fury. I could clearly see the blue kidskin shoes on his little feet. It was Hugh. I'd been responsible for the loss of my mistress's only son, the heir to the Earldom of Locksley.

And the thought hit me like a kick from an angry mule: now I'd have to break the news to Robin.

Chapter Seven

'You say you are sorry? *Sorry*? You took my wife and my son out on the river for a childish jaunt, away from the safety of Westminster Hall and our men, with no protection whatsoever. Not a single man-at-arms!' Robin's voice was an icy whip. 'And now, my wife has been beaten unconscious, her maidservant murdered, and my son kidnapped. And you stand there and say you are sorry.'

Robin's eyes glinted like a drawn knife in the darkness. And I wondered if he would kill me on the spot or devise appalling tortures to prolong the agony.

'There was no room on the boat for anyone else,' I mumbled. 'I thought we would be safe enough. No one knew where we were going . . .' I could not continue with my defence. I looked at Robin, at his pale expressionless face and blazing eyes, and I could find no more words. It was hopeless; I was entirely to blame for the loss of Hugh and I merely hoped my death would be swift.

'No one knew where you were going? Half of Westminster knew about your little trip; when you told the Bishop of London, you might as well have written out your itinerary and nailed it up on the Abbey door . . .'

Robin paused and took a big gulp of air. 'Just . . . Just get out – go! I don't even want to look at you.' He turned away, scrubbing his eyebrows with the heels of his palms.

I made a fast bow and backed away hurriedly, relief blossoming in my heart. At least I was still alive – for the moment.

Tuck was sympathetic when I told him how I had been publicly lambasted by my master. 'It's God's will, of course; it's always God's will,' said my tubby old friend as I was helping him to bandage his wounded arm in the infirmary of Westminster Abbey. 'In a sense, you could say it was not your fault at all – though I wouldn't suggest you say that to Robin just at the moment. God meant for little Hugh to be captured or He would not have allowed it to happen. It's as simple as that. And He meant for me to take this wound, otherwise it would not have happened.'

I envied Tuck his deep faith; he always seemed to be serene, putting his trust in the Lord and allowing the world to go whichever way God wished. Not that he was passive; he always did and said what he thought was right, quite fearlessly, but he was not perturbed when things went against him, or when someone else suffered a setback. He was totally convinced of the existence of a Divine plan, and while he might not know his part in it, he was content to surrender himself to the will of the Almighty.

My own faith had been rocked by the useless slaughter I had seen in the Holy Land, by the killing of good men for no good reason. I could not believe that a merciful God would allow such terrible things to happen. But he did. And while Tuck said it was all part of a plan, I sometimes wondered, in my most secret heart – and doubtless I shall be damned for these evil thoughts – whether God was truly much concerned with the fate of humanity. Perhaps it is the Devil that rules the Earth and God is unable, or too indifferent, to put a stop to his works.

Needless to say, I did not voice such heretical misgivings to Tuck. Instead I asked him to hear my confession, and received the comfort that only a well-worn ritual can bestow. We went to the Abbey church of St Peter and, kneeling beside him on the cold stone floor, I told him of all the folk I had killed in Outremer, in cold blood and in hot; and of the evil I had seen done, and of the evil things I had done. I told him, on my knees and humbly begging God's forgiveness, of a servant boy I had killed, and why I had done it; of a lovely Arab slave girl whom I had thought I loved, and with whom I had committed many carnal sins. Her name was Nur, and she had been the most beautiful girl I had ever seen. But my enemy, an evil man named Malbête, had taken her and, to punish me, he had cut off her nose and lips and ears and spoiled that transcendent beauty for ever. But perhaps my sin was greater than Malbête's, for I had told Nur that I loved her, I had promised that I would always love and protect her; and yet, and yet . . . It is still hard for me to admit this: when Malbête had hacked away her beauty, I found that I did not love her, that I could not love her as I had promised. And so she had left me, taking her poor disfigured face away to hide it from the world in shame.

Then I told Tuck about a good man, a noble knight, a friend

whom I had seen cut down by thieves – and how I had never taken revenge for him, never punished his murderer. For the murderer of this good man was Robin, my master.

And of all these sins Tuck absolved me, lifting a terrible weight from my heart, in the name of the Father, the Son and the Holy Ghost. Amen.

The next day at dusk, Robin summoned Tuck and myself to a private chamber leading off Westminster Hall. Though he was cool with me it seemed that Robin had overcome his fury of the day before. He was not alone: Queen Eleanor of Aquitaine was seated in a corner of the room on a vast throne, flanked by the loyal Archbishop of Rouen, Walter de Coutances, in a slightly smaller chair. There were two other churchmen in the room, shadowy figures in the white habits of Cistercian monks, standing silently against the far wall, and a handful of servants and clerks scurrying around with parchments and scrolls.

Robin got straight to the point. 'These two gentlemen are the abbots of the great Cistercian houses of Boxley and Robertsbridge; they are men of God; men of peace, not war,' he said, looking directly at Tuck and myself. 'The Queen has selected them to go to Germany to seek out King Richard and try to establish contact with him. Father Tuck was to have accompanied them on this difficult, and possibly dangerous journey, to act both as my representative and to offer a measure of physical protection against footpads, outlaws, wild men of the road and the like.'

Robin said this with a perfectly straight face. A few short years ago, two peace-loving abbots would have been exactly the sort of traveller that he would have preyed on should they have been so foolish as to venture into Sherwood Forest. I heard Queen Eleanor give an amused chuckle at Robin's words. I wisely kept silent.

'Since Father Tuck has been injured,' Robin continued, looking hard at me, 'and because you are to blame for his injuries, it has been decided that in three days' time you will accompany these venerable abbots to Germany and see to it that they come to no harm.' He fixed me with his cold silver-grey gaze. 'I am in deadly earnest, Alan: this mission is of the utmost importance to the kingdom. You must not take any risks with these good men's lives.'

I admit I was taken aback. I had expected some sort of punishment, but it seemed that instead of chastisement, I was to be sent on a journey. I was excited, quite elated in fact. It was an adventure: to go off across the world to seek out my King. Trying not to show my happiness, I made my way across to the two abbots and solemnly kissed the rings on their hands in respectful greeting.

They were a dour pair, both tall and slender, with greying hair shaved neatly in a circle at the crown in the clerical tonsure. Indeed, they were so alike in their looks, dress and demeanour that at first I took them to be brothers. They were not, of course, but over the next few weeks that I spent with them, they sometimes seemed as indistinguishable as twins.

As I made to leave, the Queen addressed me. 'When you find my son,' she said, in her haughty, smoky burr, ' – you will notice that I do not say "if" – *when* you find my son Richard, you will tell him that we in England will do everything we can to ensure his swift release. He must not despair; tell him to put his trust in God and . . . tell him that his mother will not fail him in his hour of need.'

She was perhaps the greatest lady in Christendom; during her long life she had reigned over lands stretching from the Pennines to the Pyrenees, been married to the two most powerful Christian monarchs, the kings of England and France, and controlled the fate of millions of souls, yet, in that moment, I saw her for what she truly was: a mother whose beloved son was at the mercy of his enemies.

The next day I spent mostly with Robin and Tuck, looking at very rough old charts of the rivers of Germany, Austria and the Holy Roman Empire, and discussing a host of schemes and plans. The two abbots joined us briefly, but they seemed to be ignorant of the area we would be travelling to and were under the impression that I was to be their guide. They were happy, it seemed, to put their trust in me – although I had never been to those parts before and was no more familiar with them than I was with the mountains of the moon – and, if I were to falter, in a higher power. 'God will steer us in the right direction,' said one with a pious smile; whether it was Boxley or Robertsbridge I could not say. I was already having difficulty telling them apart.

There was nothing for it but to recruit help; a man with genuine knowledge of the area and a perfect command of the local language, too: Hanno.

My round-headed friend was overjoyed to be joining me on this journey; it was a chance for him to revisit his homeland, and perhaps see something of his friends and family. And I was pleased to have him with us, for he was a master of most types of warfare and, though I did not doubt my own abilities in this arena, I was taking my role as protector of the abbots seriously and Hanno would be invaluable to have at my side in a fight. He joined me in Robin's quarters, and the three of us were discussing which religious houses we might safely stay at on our journey, when the door flew open and Marie-Anne came striding into the room. It was clear that she had been weeping, and there was an evil purple bruise on the side of her blotched face that was only partially covered by her white linen headdress. In one hand she was holding out a scroll of yellow parchment, sealed with wax and tied with a red ribbon, a letter. Her other hand was held out of sight behind her back.

'This came for you,' said Marie-Anne, thrusting the rolled parchment at Robin, her voice trembling with emotion, a mixture of rage, hope and fear.

'And with it came . . . this!' Marie-Anne pulled her hand from behind her: she was holding a tiny blue shoe, a shoe that I had last seen on the end of Hugh's foot as the black ship pulled swiftly away from us over the grey waters of the Thames.

I never read that letter, although its full import was made very clear to me that evening. On the surface it was another courteous invitation for Robin to present himself at the new Temple Church the next day – St Polycarpus's Day – to answer before the inquisition convened by the Order of the Temple the charges of heresy, demon-worship, blasphemy and other assorted acts of wickedness. There was no mention of little Hugh at all. And yet the real meaning was entirely clear. Either Robin submitted to the Templars' justice or his son and heir would die. The letter requested Robin to present himself, unarmed and with only two attendants, at the Templars' Gate at noon the next day. Robin's face was quite expressionless as he scanned the missive. I saw him look up at Marie-Anne and hand her the letter to read. Her face, in contrast, became white and worried, and she began to gnaw at her little finger as she looked at him, her big blue eyes beseeching. Robin hesitated for only a single heartbeat, and then he smiled. It was a bright, warm, comforting smile, a loving smile that made a solemn promise, and he opened his arms wide and she fell into them weeping, but this time with relief. They were enfolded in a tight embrace for a long time, the only sound that of muffled sobbing from Marie-Anne as she crushed her face against Robin's neck, while Hanno and I exchanged embarrassed glances.

'Well,' said Robin, finally releasing his Countess. 'It seems that I have underestimated these people. Alan, would you be kind enough to call for one of the Queen's messengers. I think we need to make the terms for the boy's release absolutely crystal clear.'

I knew in my heart what Robin was about to do. He was about to willingly put his head into a Templar noose to save the life of a little boy – a boy who was not even his true son. Whatever Robin had done in the past, whatever selfish sins he had committed, he was still willing to sacrifice his own life in an instant, to burn at the stake, a hideously painful and slow death, for love of his wife, for love of Marie-Anne and her bastard son Hugh, the progeny of an enemy.

I should not have been surprised by Robin's actions, as I knew him well by then and fully understood his outlook. He had explained it to me years before, quite soon after I had joined his group of outlaws. 'There are two kinds of people in the world, Alan,' he said, 'those inside my circle, whom

I love and serve and who love and serve me – and those outside it.'

At the time I merely thought he was giving me a warning, and I had nodded enthusiastically to show that I understood, but later I realized he was explaining his personal doctrine to me. Robin had continued: 'Those inside the circle are precious to me, and while they are faithful, I will always be loyal to them and do my utmost to protect them, even at the cost of my own life. Those outside this circle,' he shrugged, 'they are nothing.' The way he said it had sent a chill down my spine.

When I contemplate Robin's crimes, the acts of selfishness and cruelty that most appalled me, I try to remember that it was always people outside his charmed circle, or those who had betrayed him, who suffered by his actions. For those inside the circle, such as Marie-Anne, and little Hugh, and even myself, he would gladly die.

We rode east up the Strondway, the broad street leading towards London, in force: twenty mounted men-at-arms in full war gear, armed with sword, shield and spear, as well as Robin, Tuck, myself and Marie-Anne. Our route took us past the inn of the Bishop of Exeter, which was shut tight and locked, the bishop being away from town, through the raised wooden barrier of the Templar Bar and into Fleet Street. At the Temple Gate, we halted outside the round arch of the entrance while a standard bearer carrying Robin's personal flag, a black-and-grey wolf's head snarling from a white background, blew a trumpet to alert the occupants to our presence, although there was strictly no need, as I had already seen a man scurrying away into the Outer Court to inform his Templar masters that we had arrived. The sun was high, a pale coin in a grey February sky, and we waited without speaking, the only sound the occasional clop of a horse's hoof, a whinny or two and the gentle jingle of steel bridle parts as the horses shook their heads.

As we waited, I looked east up the muddy street, past various huts and dwellings, past an alehouse and a pie shop to a large open-fronted building on the north side of the road, where a fire was roaring under a large, smoke-blackened metal hood. As I watched, a huge muscular man with a mop of bright blond hair and what looked like a leather patch over one eye pulled a strip of metal from the fire and began to hammer at it on an anvil in front of the forge. The blacksmith was half a bow-shot away with his back to me, and yet, as I observed him knocking flakes of orange metal from the half-made sword blade with powerful strokes of his hammer, I had the strange feeling that I knew him from somewhere. But that, surely, was impossible – I knew almost nobody in London. Silently I willed him to turn and look at us, so that I might identify him, but he remained bent over the anvil, bashing away at the red-hot metal while turning it with a great pair of pincers. That in itself was slightly odd. Who would not stop work for a few moments and turn to gawp at a conroi of heavily armed cavalry a hundred yards away? Perhaps he was entirely intent on his work, I mused, or deaf from the constantly ringing blows of his hammer, as well as half-blinded.

My attention was soon diverted from the industrious blacksmith by the arrival at the gate of a Templar knight, accompanied by six tough-looking Templar sergeants dressed in black tunics over their hauberks and armed with swords and spears. I saw that the knight was Sir Aymeric de St Maur, the

117

man I had met in Pembroke Castle, who had called Robin a demon-worshipper. And in his mailed fist, gripped securely, was the arm of a squirming little boy.

I heard Marie-Anne give a sharp cry and out of the corner of my eye I saw her slip from the saddle and run over to Hugh. But before she could reach him and take him into her arms, Sir Aymeric raised a commanding hand, palm faced forward, that stopped her in her tracks. And I saw that one of the sergeants was now holding a knife to little Hugh's throat. 'Surrender yourself, unarmed,' said the knight, over Marie-Anne's head directly to Robin. But Robin was already moving, sliding off his horse with easy grace. My master lifted his arms wide to show he carried no weapon and advanced to the Temple Gate. I dismounted from Ghost as quickly as I could, and Tuck and I, both of us unarmed, went over to join Robin in the entrance to the Templar's court. Marie-Anne was fussing over little Hugh, kissing him and murmuring endearments, and she barely had time to cast her husband a grateful glance before Robin, Tuck and I were surrounded by the Templar men-at-arms and marched down the dark, narrow corridor and into the Outer Court.

As we tramped away from Marie-Anne and Hugh and Robin's well-armed troopers, I had the strongest impression that we were marching through the portals of Hell. Behind us, I heard the gate slam shut with a hollow boom.

The Outer Court of the New Temple compound was a large area with a packed-earth floor, with low wattle-and-daub buildings – a granary, a brewery, various storehouses, barracks and servants' quarters – dotted about here and there. To the south was a neatly kept orchard of apple and pear trees, extending down to a scatter of huts and a wooden wharf on the River Thames. We saw little of it, however, as we were almost immediately hustled to the left, heading east through a covered walkway along the side of the Grand Master's house and into the Temple Church itself. I had never been inside it before, and, in spite of my anxiety for Robin, I was struck by the grave beauty, even majesty, of the building. We passed through a heavy iron-bound door set in a round arch at its western end and into the main chamber. Some twenty paces across, filled with pale yellow sunlight and perfectly round, it was said to have been built in imitation of the Church of the Holy Sepulchre in Jerusalem, the site of the tomb of Christ, which, alas, despite my long sojourn in the Holy Land, I'd never had the good fortune to visit.

Six huge black pillars formed a ring at the centre of the space; these supported a circular upper storey. I peered up towards the domed roof, where six vast windows allowed the sparse February sunshine to pour in. On the ground floor, a couple of dozen men were milling around, talking quietly amongst themselves; many wore white surcoats with the red breast cross of Templar knights, others were clad in the more colourful attire of secular noblemen. A few men had already taken their places on the stone bench that ran around the outer wall. Over in the north-eastern quadrant of the church I caught sight of Richard FitzNeal, the silver-haired Bishop of London, looking worried as he took his seat.

Straight ahead of me, due east, was the chancel, a twenty-yard-long rectangular chamber, which extended off the circular main space and housed the altar and an enormous golden crucifix bearing the figure of Our Lord twisted in His Passion. Crossing myself, I muttered a quick prayer before we were ushered to our places on the stone bench, just to the right of the main door, by the font, in the southern quadrant. Robin sat in the middle, between Tuck and myself, and two Templar sergeants sat flanking Tuck and me. The other men-at-arms who had escorted us inside disposed themselves around the church and leaned on their spears, occasionally glancing over at our little group with narrow gaolers' eyes.

I gazed around at the church in awe, marvelling at the walls that glowed like precious jewels in the sunlight, decorated with vivid paintings of Jerusalem and King Solomon's Temple, and rich hangings of gold and blue and scarlet thread that depicted scenes from the Bible, and wondrous carvings of human faces set in carved arches around the inner wall, just above the stone benches – some grotesque, some kindly, some fearsome, some saintly – all seemingly waiting to witness the proceedings that were about to take place.

This was the beating heart of the English Order of the Temple, a chamber of purity and goodness and Christian strength, and I did not feel worthy to be inside such a place. I closed my eyes once again in prayer, beseeching God to give me strength through the coming trial; and asking that he might see fit to protect my master from the righteous wrath of these holy knights.

A fanfare of trumpets interrupted my devotions, and when I opened my eyes heralds were striding through the doorway to my left, their trumpets adorned with the red and gold of the royal standard. We were ordered to our feet by a gesture from the Templar sergeant, and into the church strode Prince

John himself, apparently deep in conversation with Sir William de Newham, the English Provincial Master of the Temple. Behind him came Sir Aymeric de St Maur, who was chatting to a companion; I realized with a heavy heart but no real sense of surprise that the Templar knight's companion was Sir Ralph Murdac.

The Master, William de Newham, took his seat at the eastern end of the round church in an imposing high-backed chair. He was a portly, irritable-looking, red-faced man with large eyes shot with blood, now flanked on either side by his two wardens, senior knights who acted as his officials. Together with the Master, these were the men who would pass judgement this day on the Earl of Locksley. The great wooden door was slammed shut, with one man-at-arms posted outside to see that we were not disturbed, and another, an inner guard, posted inside, his sword drawn in readiness, to be doubly sure that the proceedings of the inquisition would not be interrupted. Prince John was ushered to a position of honour on the opposite side of the church from Robin, Tuck and me – the north side – and on taking his seat he immediately began making a fuss, demanding cushions to ease the hardness of the stone bench. Sir Ralph Murdac, after lending his voice to the demand for more cushions, shouting at several of the Templar sergeants and urging them to be quick about bringing his master's comforts, finally settled himself and looked over to our side with a self-satisfied smirk on his face.

As always, when I looked on Ralph Murdac's features, I felt a surge of hatred in my guts. But that day it was particularly strong, and I worried for an instant that I might disgrace myself by vomiting my bile on the smooth, grey flagstone floor. Somehow I mastered my stomach and forced myself to make a careful study of my enemy. Apart from that glimpse in the firelight outside Kirkton Castle, I had not had the misfortune to look upon his loathsome features for several years. He was clean shaven and bareheaded, his black hair cut into a neat bowl shape – clearly he had had a barber visit him that day. His clothes were of fine black silk, well cut, expensive and cared for; his face was handsome, though his lips were faintly too red for my taste, giving him an air of petulance and secret vice. His light blue eyes, cold as frost, glittered as he stared straight back at me. I was struck, once again, at how similar he was to little Hugh, in looks at least; I could only pray that Hugh would not turn out to share the same blackness of heart. He was too far away for me to catch his scent, but I wondered if he still favoured that revolting lavender perfume which had always made me sneeze.

Then I noticed something that made a spark of joy leap in my heart: Murdac was holding one shoulder awkwardly, slightly higher than the other. At first I thought it was just a peculiar way of sitting, but then he moved, turning sideways to whisper something to his master, Prince John, and I realized what it was. He was crippled, a hunchback. Robin's arrow, fired into the darkness on that night of fire and blood outside Kirkton Castle, might not have killed the man, but it had certainly spoiled his posture.

I smiled broadly at Murdac now, meeting his gaze, looking pointedly at his high shoulder, grinning at him like a monkey. And I looked sideways at Robin, hoping he had noticed it too, but my master was staring serenely into the middle distance, humming softly to himself under his breath, as if he had not a care in the world. If things went badly for Robin, he was but a few short hours away from an agonizing, fiery end. But then I have never met a man who was calmer in the face of death.

It was Prince John who started the hearing, in his typically ungracious way. Giving a jerk of his dark-red curly head to the Master of the Temple, he waved one finger of his beringed right hand and croaked: 'Well, shall we get on with it, then? I don't wish to be here all day.'

The Master, who had been conferring earnestly with one of his wardens and a clerk brandishing a clutch of curling parchments, looked up, surprised to have his authority usurped in his own church.

To his credit, he resisted what had, in effect, been a royal command. 'In a moment, Your Highness,' he said, narrowing his eyes. 'Try to possess yourself with a just little more patience.' His tone had the slightest edge to it; a note of condescension, as if talking to an impetuous child.

As I watched Aymeric de St Maur rise from his seat in the southern part of the church, not far from us, and cross to the Master's chair, a thought struck me. I turned to Robin and asked: 'Where is the Queen? Where is the Lady Eleanor? Surely she should come to your aid?'

Robin turned to me and smiled – he looked as cool as a summer breeze. Almost without moving his lips, he said, very quietly: 'The Queen cannot come to my aid, Alan. She must stay aloof from this contest. She needs the English Templars to help her free Richard, or rather she needs their silver and their ability to arrange credit. We are all on our own here, Alan. Just play your part, and all will be well in the end.'

I must have looked uncertain, for he gave me a conspiratorial wink and muttered: 'Do not trouble yourself too much, Alan. Everything is going to be just fine. Tuck assures me that the Almighty has a master plan; God has it all worked out, apparently.' And he grinned at me, quite blasphemously, before saying: 'And have you noticed Murdac's crooked back?' I could only smile back at him, heartened by his less-than-Christian pleasure in an enemy's discomfort.

The Master of the Templars now rose to his feet, gave a brief signal to one of the sergeants, and led the whole church in a prayer asking God that the truth be uncovered and justice be done this day in His sacred house, before His eyes. Then the sergeant led Robin to the centre of the church, placing him in such a way that he stood directly before the Master but everyone in the round church would have a clear view of him.

The Master then held up a thick, curling piece of parchment and read aloud in Latin. It was a letter from His Holiness the Pope, adorned with the Papal seal, sanctioning this inquisition in the Temple Church in London on this day and naming the individual to be investigated as Robert Odo, Earl of Locksley. It was a long, dull document, which referred to a Papal Bull known as *Ad abolendam* that had been issued by Pope Lucius nearly ten years ago, urging the high churchmen of Christendom to actively seek out all heretics and those who sheltered or supported them, and bring them swiftly to justice.

His authority as an episcopal inquisitor thus established, the Master took his seat and the inquisition began.

'Do you Robert Odo, Earl of Locksley, believe in God the Father Almighty, maker of Heaven and Earth, and in his only son Jesus Christ our Saviour?' asked the Master in French, fixing Robin with his bloodshot eyes.

'I do,' said Robin gravely, in the same language. I knew that he was lying through his sinful teeth – but there was no other answer that he could make.

'And do you believe that the word of God was made flesh as Jesus Christ and that by his suffering and death on the Cross this sinful world was redeemed?'

'No question about it,' said Robin, his face a picture of Christian innocence.

'And do you believe that on the third day after He was crucified He rose again from the dead and ascended into Heaven, and now sits at the right hand of God the Father?'

'Absolutely . . . third day, right hand, all of that stuff,' said Robin, his eyes seeming to shine with conviction.

'And do you believe in the Holy Trinity of God the Father, God the Son and God the Holy Ghost? And that Mary was a virgin before and after the birth of her son Jesus Christ?'

'Oh, for God's sake, do get on with it!' Prince John's harsh voice cut through the recitation of a well-known and much-loved formula. Though the Master ignored his interruption, his high colour became a little more pronounced.

'I certainly do,' said Robin jauntily. 'I'm entirely sure Mary was a virgin, before *and* afterwards – oh, very much so.'

'And do you swear by Almighty God, by Jesus Christ, by the Virgin Mary and all the saints, at the peril of your immortal soul if you prove false, that you will only speak the truth this day?'

'Yes, indeed. I swear it; I swear it on my immortal soul,' said Robin confidently, but somehow still managing to sound impossibly sincere.

The Master seemed a little flustered by Robin's breezy tone. He looked back down at a roll of parchment in his hand: 'You stand accused of the grave crimes of heresy, of necromancy, of demon-worship, of blasphemy, of taking the Lord's name in vain . . .'

Robin interrupted him, talking over the Master's words: '. . . of picking my nose on a Sunday, of whistling in church, of stealing sweetmeats from children, of refusing to share my toys . . . My lords, these charges are completely absurd. They've been invented by enemies who seek . . .'

There had been several shocked chuckles from the secular knights seated around the church at Robin's lampooning of the Master's list of grave charges, but most people were too surprised by the turn of events to react.

The Master was not one of them. 'Silence!' he roared, furious that anyone should have the temerity to interrupt him. His cheeks were glowing a dangerous dark red. 'You are insolent, sir. You will not speak unless you are asked a direct question; if you interrupt me again I will have you gagged.'

Robin said nothing; he let out a long breath and stared into space above the Master's head, smiling faintly. His expression was once more beatifically serene. Just then, as the church fell silent after the Master's threat, Tuck let out an almighty fart, a resounding trumpet that seemed to last for several heartbeats and echo around the whole building.

'Silence!' screamed the Master. I noticed that his face was growing a deep purple and a vein seemed to be jumping in his forehead. 'Who did that? I demand to know who made that disgusting noise.'

'Forgive me, Master,' said Tuck. 'I had a little too much ale with my supper last night.' And once again, he let blow an enormous, foul-smelling eructation. 'I humbly beg your pardon.'

At least half the people in the church were laughing now. And the Master's face had turned an even nastier shade of puce. 'If I hear one more inappropriate . . . sound . . . of any kind . . . from anyone, I shall have that person removed from this court, bound, shackled and thrown in the crypt.'

It was obvious that the Master meant what he said: his face was still beetroot but, after a while, he had calmed himself enough to resume reading the charges from the parchment. It was a long list, but mostly seemed to consist of variations on the same theme – that Robin was a heretic, a godless Christ-denier, a worshipper of demons who conjured up foul spirits from the furthermost pit. When the Master had finished reading, he fixed Robin sternly with his gaze and said formally: 'Earl of Locksley, you now stand accused. What answer do you make to these charges?'

'They are all lies,' said Robin simply, in a level, reasonable voice that carried to every part of the church. 'They are lies invented by enemies who wish to see me destroyed. I deny all of these charges. Every single one.'

The Master stared at him for a few moments, as if expecting him to say more. Then he nodded once and said: 'Then we shall hear the evidence against you.'

Escorted to his seat by the Templar sergeant, my Lord of Locksley took his place next to me, stretched out his long legs and sat back, evidently completely at his ease.

Ralph Murdac was next to take the position at the centre of the church. He walked forward with as much dignity as he could, his left shoulder wedged up high by his ear, and stood in front of the Master and his two wardens and made a sacred vow that he would tell only the truth this day before this court.

'That man,' said Murdac, flinging out an accusing finger in Robin's direction, 'Robert Odo, the so-called Earl of Locksley, is so steeped in heresy and sin and blasphemy of the vilest kind that he besmirches this very church with his presence.'

I had half-forgotten his slithery, lisping tones, but it brought the hairs up on the back of my neck as I heard him speak about my lord in these terms.

'Well spoken, that man; quite true, quite true,' croaked Prince John loudly from his cushioned nest.

The Master fixed him with his blood-streaked eyes. 'My lord Prince, may I beseech you, keep your counsel until we have heard the evidence.'

There was no mention of binding, shackling and imprisonment in the crypt, but the Master was still clearly determined not to cede authority in his own court. Prince John merely grunted and waved a languid hand indicating that Sir Ralph Murdac should continue.

Murdac half-bowed and picked up his thread: 'When he was an outlaw, shunned by all decent law-abiding men and living wild in the woods like an animal, Robert Odo was known to practise the most disgusting diabolic acts in pursuit of a false religion, even going so far as to sacrifice live human beings to a bloodthirsty woodland demon. Since he has been foolishly allowed back into Christian society, his lands are renowned as a nest of witches and warlocks, of succubi, incubi and foul half-human creatures from the depths of Hell – ask any good man from the area of Kirkton, or Locksley or Sheffield itself and they will confirm that the Devil and his minions are abroad on many a dark night, in the shape of wild men with the heads of horses that breathe fire and can turn a man to stone with one look. A local witch, the Hag of Hallamshire – a hideously deformed crone who steals Christian babies to sacrifice for her dark arts – has been spotted many times in the area . . .'

'Yes, yes,' said the Master testily, 'there are rumours of witch-craft all over England. But this man is charged with heresy. Do you have any specific evidence of heresy?'

'I have seen these horse-demons, doubtless summoned by Locksley's incantations, with my very own eyes,' said Murdac proudly. 'I saw these foul creatures ride into battle in the company of the prisoner here before us.' Once again, Murdac threw out a finger at my master.

'Go on,' said the Master. There had been a ripple of interest in the church at Murdac's accusatory words. The Bishop of London, who happened to be directly in my line of sight, was frowning and looking seriously concerned.

'Last September, on the eve of the holy day of saints Cornelius and Cyprian, I was camped peaceably outside Kirkton Castle engaged in parley with the whorish Countess of Locksley for the return of my son from her custody' – I stole a sideways glance at Robin but his serene expression had hardly changed, although a little smile was playing around his mouth and, oddly, that chilled me more than any amount of ranting threats – 'when I was set upon by an army of fiends from Hell. First they caused barrow-loads of fire to fall from the Heavens, scorching my men to the bone, and then the Devil's cavalry, led by the heresiarch, the malevolent Robert of Locksley, appeared as if by magic. These steeds of Satan – giant men with the heads of stallions on fire-breathing mounts – came to ravage my camp and slaughter my men. It was only through Christ's mercy, and doubtless the intercession of saints Cornelius and Cyprian, that any of us escaped with our lives.'

'And you swear before God that you saw all this with your own eyes?' said the Master.

'On my honour,' said Murdac. 'And before Almighty God, I so swear.'

I heard Tuck give a loud disbelieving snort under his breath. Murdac stalked back to his place, evidently pleased by his performance.

'Well spoken, that man; well spoken,' came a royal croak from the northern quadrant of the church.

The Master whispered to one of his wardens, who made a note on a piece of parchment.

'Bring forth the accused,' the Master intoned. And when Robin had, once again, been brought into the centre of the circle he said: 'What have you to say about this matter of the horse demons?'

Robin took a deep breath and rolled his shoulders slowly. 'It is true . . .' he said, and paused, and there was a collective intake of breath around the church. 'It is true that Ralph Murdac was before my castle of Kirkton with many hundreds of armed men. Contrary to the laws of the Church and the edict of His Holiness the Pope, he was attacking my property as I was returning from the Holy Land after fighting in the name of Christendom to recover the land of Our Lord's birth.'

There was a murmur of approval around the church. Many of the men present had fought ferociously in the Holy Land, many had lost dear comrades there; in fact, one of the principal aims of the Templar knights was the defence of Outremer.

And the Church *did* promise protection to knights and their property while they were away on pilgrimage. Robin had scored a point, and everyone in the church knew it. I saw the Bishop of London begin to relax a little; he smiled over at us, nodding his silver head.

'When I returned from the Holy Land where Our Saviour Jesus Christ taught, much wearied by hard battle against the Saracens,' continued Robin, shoving home his point ruthlessly, 'I found Ralph Murdac besieging my castle. So many of my good men had fallen in the East in defence of Christ's teachings that I found myself left with a mere fifty Christian souls capable of giving battle to my enemies. Unless I wished to surrender my family and my lands to a cur who holds the Church's laws in contempt, I was therefore forced to resort to subterfuge, to use a low trick.

'This man's wild talk of fire-breathing horse-headed men is all nonsense, the babbling of a coward,' said Robin, indicating Murdac with a flick of his left hand, but not deigning to look at him. 'True, I rolled fire-carts into his camp; and true, my men wore sheepskin masks, painted to look like horses' heads, to frighten his craven men-at-arms, but there was no heresy involved, and it is ridiculous to imagine that demons were summoned. We prayed to Almighty God and his only son Jesus Christ to deliver us from our enemies and by His good grace – and the strength and prowess of my men – the enemy were defeated.'

Here Robin stopped, and the Master stared at him for a few heartbeats, waiting to hear more. 'Can you prove any of what you say?' the Templar leader said finally.

Robin beckoned to me. 'I call upon my loyal vassal Alan of

Westbury to bear witness to the truth of what I say. Alan took part in that action, and he is a good Christian soul who would never allow himself to become involved in anything that went against the teachings of the Church. Stand up, Alan. Come forward and speak.'

I walked as calmly as I could into the centre of the church; my legs felt soft and my belly fluttery, and I was conscious of the gaze of more than thirty pairs of noble eyes. But keeping my chin up, I stared straight at the Master, and said: 'What the Earl of Locksley says is Gospel true. There were no horse-demons summoned; it was merely a *ruse de guerre*, a trick to make the enemy fearful of us.'

There was a rustling sound from around the church and mutterings of approval. I could feel the opinion of those gathered there turning in our favour like a great tide. The men gathered here were warriors, first and foremost, and many of them had used a cunning ruse or two to achieve victory.

'Very well, you may both return to your seats,' said the Master.

As we walked back to our places in the south-western quarter of the church, Tuck was beaming at us. When we took our seats, he began to utter words of congratulation, but Robin cut him off. 'It's not over yet, Tuck,' my master whispered, 'not by a long march. That was merely the first clash of swords.'

'I call upon Sir Aymeric de St Maur to produce further evidence,' boomed the Master, and looking to my right, I saw that, as usual, Robin was correct.

The Templar knight was standing over a wretched creature: a man, half-naked and lying on his side, his arms bound behind his back, who had been beaten and misused in the most appalling fashion. Patches of his flesh were burnt, red raw and oozing from the hot irons – and I remembered with a shudder my own torture at the hands of Sir Ralph Murdac. But there was something else about him that troubled me even more: tattooed on the poor man's chest, easily visible thanks to his bound arms, was a symbol in the shape of the letter Y. I knew that sign, and I knew what it meant.

My mind leapt back to an awful night in Sherwood Forest nearly four years ago and a wretch no less terrified than this man now before me – a man who was tied to an ancient stone and butchered in a demonic ceremony as a sacrifice to a pagan god – a ceremony of worship to Cernunnos, a woodland deity, a figure that the Church regarded as a foul demon. Robin had played a leading part in the ceremony, and worshipping the demon Cernunnos must certainly be viewed as heresy of the vilest kind.

Sir Aymeric de St Maur dragged the wretch to the centre of the church by his hair. And the man lay there weeping, either with pain or fear, cowering on the floor before the Master. Every man in the room seemed to crane forward to get a better look at him.

'This villein is known as John,' began Aymeric, speaking, as we all had until this point, in French. 'He once belonged to the manor of Alfreton, but he killed a man and ran away from justice five years ago and took to living wild in Sherwood Forest. He became a beggar and a footpad – and a demon-worshipper, as is indicated by this mark on his chest.'

Aymeric pointed to the Y-shaped tattoo. Beside me, Robin sat up a little straighter and cocked his head to one side, observing the unfortunate villein with a speculative but still astoundingly untroubled eye.

'We had to use a good deal of persuasion on him,' said Aymeric, giving the prisoner a savage kick that caused the man to writhe on the floor, smearing the stone flags with his blood and burn fluids, 'but finally he confessed to his foul deeds. And he told us a very interesting story concerning the Earl of Locksley.'

There was absolute silence in the church, not a cough, not a shuffled foot.

Sir Aymeric continued, his voice echoing in the stillness: 'This man claims he participated in a diabolical ceremony at Easter four years ago in which a prisoner of war, a man-at-arms known as Piers in the service of Sir Ralph Murdac, then the High Sheriff of Nottinghamshire, was sacrificed to a demon called Cernunnos by a notorious local witch. During the ceremony, Robert Odo, who went by the name of Robin Hood in those days, fully took part in the bloody, heretical ritual. Indeed, he claimed that he had been possessed by the demon Cernunnos himself.'

There were gasps all around the church and every eye now fixed itself on Robin and our little group. I saw that the Bishop of London was shaking his silver head and chewing on one fingernail. He looked as if he were ready to burst into tears.

'Is this true?' asked the Master, addressing the wretch on the floor in English. 'You, villein, is what Sir Aymeric says true? Did you participate in a blood-thirsty heretical ceremony worshipping a false god, in which the Earl of Locksley also played a central part?'

The tattooed man gave a little moan of fear, and stammered: 'Oh yes, sir, please don't hurt me. It is true, every word of it. I swear before Almighty God, and Jesus, Joseph and Mary, and all the saints, please . . .'

134

'That's enough!' Aymeric reached down and cuffed the man violently around the head, and the poor wretch slumped to the floor and resumed his silent weeping.

'Take him away,' ordered the Master, switching back into French; and the poor man was dragged off and bundled down the steps to the crypt by two burly Templar sergeants.

'What response do you make to this accusation?' the Master asked Robin.

My lord rose to his feet. 'That man has clearly been tortured out of his wits and would say anything to ease his pains. By Church decree, by the decree of the Holy Father himself, his testimony has no validity in an inquisition,' he said briskly. 'By Church law, a tortured man's testimony is not acceptable. Am I not correct, Master?'

The Master conferred with his two wardens. There was much rustling of parchments and consulting of scrolls and then one of the wardens whispered at length in the Master's ear. Finally, after a lot of shrugging and frowning, the Master pronounced in a heavy, sullen tone: 'It seems that we must disregard the evidence of this villein. It appears that he may have been tortured and his evidence is therefore not valid. But I believe that we will hear more on this matter in due course. Sir Aymeric, proceed!'

Robin shrugged. He turned on his heel and walked over to Tuck and myself and sat down again, crossed his legs and began looking at his fingernails. He still seemed absurdly unruffled by the proceedings.

I marvelled at his composure and was trying my best to emulate it when I heard the Master saying: 'Call the next witness.'

Over the half-hour that followed, a succession of poor men and women were brought out into the centre of the church by Sir Aymeric de St Maur. Each vowed to tell only the truth, then each was asked two simple questions in English: 'Have you ever seen Robert of Locksley by word or deed engage in heretical activities that run counter to the teachings of Holy Mother Church? And have you ever seen Robert of Locksley participate in a ritual that might be considered demon-worship?'

Each time the witness came to the centre of the church and mumbled his or her way through a story – some of which were sheer moon-addled fantasy, tales of the Earl of Locksley spitting and stamping and pissing on crucifixes in secret ceremonies at the dead of night, or copulating wildly with a black goat while flying through the air; some were no more than innocuous tales of Robin taking the Lord's name in vain after stubbing his toe on a rock. All, as far as I could tell, were false. It soon became evident that all the witnesses had been well paid. One man even thanked Sir Aymeric in front of the court for the silver he'd been given.

Throughout all this – the lies and fantasies and lunatic accusations – Robin remained composed. Occasionally he would lean forward in his seat to hear a particular man or woman's testimony, but he did so in the manner of a benevolent old priest listening to the outlandish confession of one of his parishioners. Occasionally he yawned and stretched as if overcome with ennui.

And Robin was not the only one in that church who appeared to be mildly bored by this pantomime. I caught some of the knights in the round chamber yawning, too, and muttering to their neighbours. They did not seem to be overly impressed with the evidence that the Templars had manufactured against my master. In fact the more outlandish and ridiculous the stories, the less credibility they had to their audience. Sir Aymeric de St Maur, I realized with joy, had been too zealous in pursuit of his cause. We were winning; we had the tacit support of the secular knights, at least, and many Templars would believe his record of service in the Holy Land should count for much. The Bishop of London was smiling warmly at us from across the church.

Then the Master spoke: 'We have heard much evidence today concerning whether or not Robert of Locksley is a heretic and a demon-worshipper. We must disregard the testimony of the villein John, as this inquisition suspects that he may have been tortured. But I believe we have heard enough. We will hear only one more witness on this matter today and then we will make our judgement.' He paused and looked briefly at a sheet of parchment in his hand. 'Sir Aymeric, call your final witness,' the Master said.

Aymeric de St Maur walked to the centre of the church. In a loud and ringing voice he said: 'I call upon Alan of Westbury to come forward.'

And my heart froze.

I have no memory of walking the ten paces to the centre of the church, to the place beside Sir Aymeric. But I can recall clearly the intensity of the Master's bloodshot glare and his next words: 'Do you swear, by Almighty God, by the Virgin and all the saints, that you will tell the truth this day, in the knowledge that if you utter falsehoods the Lord God himself will strike you dead for your blasphemy and your soul will burn in Hell?'

My mouth was dry, my tongue suddenly seemed to be twice its normal size. I mumbled something and, at the Master's irritated urging to speak up, I found myself making a solemn oath that I would tell the truth, the whole truth and nothing but the truth. My back was towards Robin, and I was glad of it. I could not look him in the eye.

Sir Aymeric stood not two paces from me, to my front left: he waited till he had my attention and then asked me the fateful question. 'Did you witness your master Robin Hood, now styled the Earl of Locksley, taking part in a demonic ceremony at Eastertide four years ago in which a living man-at-arms known as Piers, a prisoner of war, was sacrificed to a false god? Answer merely yes or no. And remember that you are on oath to tell the truth in this holy church, before the all-seeing eyes of God Almighty.'

I could not speak. My mouth seemed to be glued shut; my jaw muscles were locked.

The Master snapped: 'Answer the question, man!'

And I found myself muttering: 'Yes.'

'Speak up,' said the Master. 'Speak up Alan of Westbury so that all may hear you.'

Sir Aymeric de St Maur stared intently at me; he was smirking like a fox who's found a way into a chicken coop.

'Yes,' I said again. 'Yes, I did witness my master taking part in a bloody ritual, a ceremony in which a living man was sacrificed to a demon, at Easter, in Sherwood, four years ago.'

Chaos erupted in the church; a great chorus of shouting voices, bellowing men. I wanted to turn and look over at Robin but I found I could not move my shoulders and neck.

I heard Prince John loudly croaking: 'Guilty! Guilty, by God.

Condemned out of the mouth of his own vassal. I say he is guilty. Burn the scoundrel! Burn him now!'

Then the Master was shouting for silence, while I merely stood there paralysed by what I had just done.

Quiet was finally achieved, and I dimly heard the Master saying: 'I think we have heard enough . . . what say you, wardens?'

I stood there before the Master of the Temple, my hands hanging loose by my side, while he conferred with his two wardens and, still staring at the floor, my mind fogged by grief, I heard him say: 'This inquisition finds Robert Odo, Earl of Locksley, guilty on all charges. He shall be taken from this place and imprisoned in the Temple crypt and in three days' time, at dawn, he shall suffer the purifying fire that will cleanse him of his foul iniquities. May God have mercy on his soul.'

I finally managed to turn my head and look over at Robin. My master was standing now, with four Templar sergeants hovering close around him while another was binding his arms in front of his body. His silver eyes bored into mine with such a look of ferocity that I was almost blown backwards as if by a powerful gust of wind. He stared at me for a long, long moment, and then he uttered one word – a terrible word, said loudly and clearly so that everyone in the church might hear it; a word full of contempt and hatred. Then the sergeants dragged him away towards the crypt. The word was ringing in my ears. And I can hear that word still, more than forty years later. The word was . . .

'Judas!'

Part Two

Chapter Eight

We are as busy as the bees now at Westbury: it is mid-June, sunny, and our broad blue Nottinghamshire skies are scarcely troubled by a single cloud – it is the time for my sheep flocks to be sheared, and the blacksmith's forge has been busy fashioning new sets of wicked-looking shears and sharpening old ones. In the hot weather the animals become uneasy, burdened as they are with their winter coats, and the shearing is a mercy to them. It is a blessing to me, too, as the price of wool has risen greatly in recent years, and I look set to make a pretty penny from the thick grey fleeces. Also, in less than a week, if the weather holds fair, I shall be sending the teams out to mow the hay meadows, to dry, then gather and stack the long grass to make winter feed for my beasts.

Osric is fully occupied in this season; he will oversee the sheep shearing, and the sorting of the fleeces, and inspect the meadows after the hay has been cut. Indeed, we all have our allotted tasks to perform, myself included. But, although there is so much to do,

I have set myself an extra task: I have decided to watch Osric from the shadows, quietly and constantly, using all the old, stealthy skills that Hanno taught me long ago. I aim to catch him at some misdeed and expose him as a villain to my daughter-in-law Marie. Then, only then, will I be free of him. I cannot sleep at night for worrying – indeed I have not slept so much as a wink for many nights now. I am still certain he is trying to murder me, but I have no proof, and proof will be needed to show Marie that she has married a monster.

It is surely a mercy that I have survived this long. Now it is time to act. So I will watch Osric, and watch well. I know that his malice is not a figment of my imagination. The other evening, about a week ago, I saw him adding a pinch of white powder to my bowl of soup as it stood on the sideboard – a slow poison, no doubt, of the type I had heard of on my travels in the East. Marie brings me supper in my chamber these days, as I work long after nightfall on these pages by beeswax candlelight – an extravagance, I know, but I feel a terrible urgency upon me. I have a premonition of my own death, and I wish to finish my tale before some evil befalls me.

I was fortunate to catch Osric in the act of poisoning my soup. I had been summoned by a groom to look at a sick horse in the stables and was returning through the hall to my chamber when I saw the mole-like fellow adding his infernal white powder to the bowl. I challenged him, of course, immediately, loudly, and the rascal had the nerve to claim that it was merely salt that he was adding to my evening meal to add savour to the broth. It was a lie, of course, I could see it in his blushing face – since when does a busy bailiff concern himself with flavouring of his master's food? I poured the bowl away without tasting it, and gave orders to the servants that

Osric must not be allowed near any dish that is destined for my table.

And yet, a part of me wishes that I had not challenged him so openly and accused him so angrily of wishing to poison me. I showed my hand to him, and it has put him on his guard. I have been watching him for a fortnight now, following him on horseback at a distance when he goes out to the fields or into the village of Westbury, watching him by day, all day, from a stool placed in a spot of shade outside the front of the hall. Sometimes I try to surprise him by appearing suddenly when he is out of plain sight, in an outbuilding, perhaps. And he often appears guiltily startled when I pop out from behind a door like a rabbit from its hole. But I have not caught him in any obvious crime yet. Indeed, most of the time he acts as innocently as a lamb, going about his business as if he did not have a care in the world. That is surely a mark of the man's devilish cunning.

Each night, I pray to Almighty God that He may hold off Osric's malice for a little longer, and that He grant me time to finish this manuscript, to complete my tale of Robert of Locksley, of Little John, of Marie-Anne, Goody, Tuck, Hanno, good King Richard and myself – for there is, I fear, only a little allotted time left for me on this Earth, and much, much more to tell.

The rain emptied from a bruise-black sky, dropping in waterfall sheets that hammered the face of the river and bounced off the dark wooden boards of our sailing barge in a continuous series of tiny explosions. We were damp and miserable, Hanno, myself and four young English Cistercian monks, crowded under a sodden canvas awning in the prow of the long boat, hooded or cowled and glumly watching the dank wooded hills of

Germany slide past on the far slopes of the riverbanks hour after dismal hour.

The abbots of Boxley and Robertsbridge, as befitted their superior rank, were ensconced in the square wooden cabin in the stern of the boat. It was drier in there, protected from the rain and river spray, but it smelled very strongly of rotting fish. As I was the leader of this company, I could perhaps have insisted on joining the abbots in their fishy box, but I found their Latin conversations schoolmasterly and tedious, and to be honest, I preferred to be at the front of the craft with Hanno. At least there I could see whatever was coming round the next bend. I had not forgotten the disastrous attack by river pirates in London; here, many hundreds of miles from home, halfway up the River Main in northern Bavaria, I felt that anything could happen.

The sailing barge – a flat-bottomed craft, eighty foot long, twenty foot wide, with one mast and a huge square rusty-red sail – was owned by a man named Adam. A stout, fair-haired Londoner with the clear blue eyes of a Norseman, Adam had been trading on these rivers for ten years or more – he also happened to be Perkin's uncle. My red-haired waterman friend had recovered from the pirate attack on the Thames and, far from blaming me for the knocks he had taken during the kidnapping of little Hugh, he seemed to feel a sense of guilt that my party had been attacked while we were in his charge, on board his skiff. Complimenting him on his fighting skill, I had made him a gift of an old short sword; now, in these dangerous, foreigner-filled lands, he had taken to wearing it all the time.

Perkin was out of sight to me at the moment, in the stern

behind the abbots' cabin, manning the rudder and steering the barge on a tack that would take us to a bend in the river. There, with the minimum of fuss, Adam and he would put the rudder across, then the boom would swing and the red sail would flap and crack briefly, and we would find ourselves on a course that would sweep us diagonally across to the other side of the river. Thus, in an endless series of elongated zigzags, we had made our way up the great rivers of Germany. When the wind was dead against us, Perkin and Adam, occasionally aided by the young monks, would pole the craft along in the shallower water by the banks. And when necessary Hanno and myself would join the monks at the six long pinewood sweeps that we carried on board, using our muscles to row us slowly upstream, deeper into the heart of the Holy Roman Empire, deeper into the lair of our King's enemies.

Perkin had arranged for me to hire Adam for the journey, although the silver I paid him was not mine but from the private treasure chest of Queen Eleanor of Aquitaine. The Queen had also given me a goodly quantity of coin to pay the tolls on the rivers, and to cover sundry expenses on the long journey. She had been understandably cool with me when I met her at Westminster Palace not two hours after the end of Robin's inquisition. The Queen was very fond of Robin, and news of my betrayal had evidently reached her. But she did not mention the inquisition at all, and I was in no state to speak rationally of it, so we confined our discussion to the hazards of the journey and the difficulties I might face in finding her son. The meeting had been brief; when we were done, she handed me a fat purse and advised me to collect my two abbots and their entourage of monks and leave as swiftly as possible for Germany. That suited me, for I had no desire to linger in England: the word 'Judas!' was still ringing in my ears and I was haunted by the image of the two rotting bird-quarried heads atop the gatehouse in Kirkton, which I felt had cursed our departure only a few weeks ago. I tried not to think about Robin, or of his fiery fate at the hands of the Templars. Thus, in the grey light before dawn, the very next day after the inquisition, my company and I glided slowly down the Thames in Adam's big sailing barge, *The Crow*, heading out to the sea to begin our quest to find King Richard.

Adam was a sturdy man, honest and not given to much emotion or boasting, but he knew the rivers of Europe, he said, as well as any living Englishman. We were in good hands, Perkin assured me; his uncle was a master sailor, a waterman of the first rank, and the ship was as robust as the man. *The Crow* was not, however, a handsome craft, and neither was it a comfortable berth. Our travelling conditions had worsened two days ago in Frankfurt when the hull was filled to deck-level and higher with logs of cut hardwood timber, leaving even less room for a passel of damp, irritable passengers. It was the third cargo we had carried so far: Adam had insisted that if he was to take us and his beloved vessel up the German rivers, he must be allowed to trade as well; his was, after all, a working boat. I was not unhappy about this, for trade gave us an ostensible reason to be travelling so far from home; and I did not want to broadcast our true intent. There were many powerful folk in the lands we were to travel through who might wish our mission to fail.

Adam looked set to make a healthy sum on this journey: he had loaded hundreds of sacks of tightly packed, untreated wool at a wharf below the Tower of London and carried them, in a rough and very unpleasant two-day crossing of the North Sea, to the Low Countries. At Utrecht, while the two abbots and I paid a courtesy visit to Bishop Baldwin van Holland at his grand palace in the city, Adam remained at the docks and arranged for the barge to be unloaded and loaded once more to the gunnels, this time with fat bales of good Flemish finished cloth.

The call that Boxley, Robertsbridge and I paid on Bishop Baldwin was the first of many visits to grand princes of the Church in the Germanic realms, and while I did not have any particular liking for these two venerable abbots in my charge, I could see the wisdom of dispatching such respected churchmen to seek out King Richard's whereabouts. As the sailing barge worked its slow way up the River Rhine, we stopped at Cologne, Koblenz and Mainz, and many smaller towns, each time finding shelter with the local abbot, or bishop or archbishop, and each time, as well as receiving the lavish hospitality due to high-ranking English clergymen, we gained a little news of the local region – and sometimes of King Richard.

The four monks who had been brought along as servants and secretaries to the abbots, as well as providing much-needed muscle power, fully proved their worth in the gathering of intelligence about our sovereign. For while the more important prelates sometimes proved reluctant to discuss rumours concerning the whereabouts of our captive King, the monks were untroubled by such discretion as they mingled in the refectory, the wash-house and the dormitory, swapping gossip with the other low-ranking clergy. In this manner they were able to pick up invaluable scraps of information.

It was as we made our way upriver from Cologne, a strong northerly wind directly at our back propelling the clumsy barge with an unusual and welcome celerity, that one of the monks, a keen young man named Damian, had reported excitedly that he had learned the King's whereabouts. Two clerks in the cathedral's cloister had told him that Richard was being held at Duke Leopold's castle of Dürnstein in Austria. While it was encouraging to have news of Richard, any news at all, my spirits nevertheless sank a little at this. Hanno said that Dürnstein was a very long way south, on the mighty Danube River near Vienna. To get there would mean leaving Adam and Perkin and *The Crow* in northern Bavaria, crossing a vast wooded and mountainous wilderness on horseback until we reached the Danube, then hiring a ship to carry us downriver to the castle. It was a daunting thought; even the rough discomfort of the English sailing barge seemed preferable to launching ourselves into the vast unknown.

I had another reason to feel uneasy: while I had been exploring the streets of Cologne, loitering by the busy wharves to watch the traders unload their exotic merchandise by the wide shimmering expanse of the Rhine, I had the strange notion that I was being followed. When I stopped briefly to pray at the old cathedral, at the shrine for the relics of the Three Kings who first adored the baby Jesus, I was certain that I could feel unfriendly eyes watching me from among the throng of pilgrims. At one point, walking alone down a darkened alleyway near the marketplace, I felt the presence of enemies at my back so strongly that I whirled around and drew my sword: but, of course, there was no one there and I felt a fool. I scanned the faces in the streets of Cologne for someone familiar, and often found features that resembled folk that I knew in England, or had met on my travels out East. But always, when I looked again more closely I realized that these were not people I had ever known before. Once I saw a pair of men, half-hidden in a crowd – one very tall, one shorter but immensely strong – and something stirred in my memory. When I looked again, they were gone.

My own enquiries among the local knights for news of King Richard had met with no success. I did, however, gather some cheering tidings from home. A German knight whom I encountered in the palace of the Archbishop of Cologne, and who spoke the most barbarous French, told me that all England was buzzing like a beehive over the news that a famous nobleman, a notorious heretic and worshipper of the Devil, had escaped from the custody of the Knights of the Temple in London. This knight, a pious dullard with a scarred pork-pink slab of a face and a sombre black surcoat, told me that six days ago one Lord Robert Otto had used his demonic powers to slip his iron fetters at the stroke of midnight, fleeing in the company of a ferocious blond giant who wielded an enormous axe. He had then disappeared into thin air, some said flying on a dragon's back, evading his just punishment for heresy at the hands of the Templars.

My mood was lifted by this news, even if it came to me in such a garbled form. But my pleasure at Robin's escape was soon dampened. The fugitive nobleman, this Lord Otto, I was told, had since been excommunicated by the Holy Church and, at the prompting of Prince John, the shire courts had declared the escaped lord an outlaw in Nottinghamshire and Yorkshire. The Prince's vassal – one Rolf Meurtach, according

151

to the German knight – had immediately marched north with an army of more than a thousand men loyal to the Prince. Finding Lord Otto's castle abandoned, Rolf had burnt it to the ground. The Lord Otto was now on the run, in fear of his life, hiding in the haunted forest of Sherwood – a place of witches and demons and wild men – where the fearless Lord Rolf would no doubt run him to earth and bring him to a place of execution forthwith.

I smiled at that, and the German knight looked at me strangely. Even if Robin had been hounded out of Kirkton by Ralph Murdac, he would be far from destitute in Sherwood. There were plenty of men there who would hide him, feed him, and fight to the death for him, if necessary. Sherwood was, as it had been for many years, the home of his heart, his spiritual sanctuary, his woodland fortress. He would be quite safe there.

So Robin was an outlaw once again, I mused to myself, with no constraints of law, or even common morality upon him. That could be very bad news for his enemies; it could be doubly dangerous to anyone who he felt had betrayed him.

But my master was far away in Sherwood and I needed to apply myself to the task at hand. So I thanked the knight, bade him farewell and concentrated on the most pressing question: Where was our King? Where in the vast wooded expanse of Europe was King Richard?

We had expected Richard to be moved from prison to prison quite regularly by his captor, Leopold of Austria. For one thing the Duke had to support an enormous household and it is the custom for great men to move about their domains spreading the load of supporting their followers evenly about their lands; and where the Duke went, Richard would go. But it also made sense for Richard to be moved from time to time. He was worth a great deal of ransom money to anyone who held him, and so long as the King's friends – or for that matter, his enemies – did not know where he was, they could not easily mount an attempt to snatch him. Not that we had rescue in mind – we would have needed a mighty army for that, not six clerics and two men-at-arms – we merely wanted to find him and begin the negotiations that would bring him safely home.

If we could establish contact with Richard, then we could be sure that Queen Eleanor, and England itself, were part of the negotiations for his ransom. The danger was that his captors – Duke Leopold, or his master Henry VI, the Holy Roman Emperor – would sell Richard to King Philip of France. With Richard languishing in a French prison, perhaps being beaten and starved, Philip could demand that our King hand over a substantial part of his French dominions, perhaps the whole of Normandy, Anjou, Maine, maybe even Aquitaine itself. He would be at the mercy of his mortal enemy. And that was not the worst of it. King Philip might well come to an arrangement with Prince John. I could easily imagine Prince John agreeing to hand over Normandy and some of the other French territories in exchange for Richard's discreet death and Philip's support when the upstart John claimed the throne of England.

If we could only make contact with Richard, then these dangers would recede, although not disappear entirely. We could make a compact with the Germans, and possibly save Richard's life, by outbidding Philip and John for his living body.

There was one factor in our favour: Henry VI proudly called himself the Holy Roman Emperor, heir to the Caesars. He liked to think of himself as the greatest nobleman in Christendom, the premier knight, a wise and beneficent ruler of millions of Christian souls. And yet, by capturing and holding a returning pilgrim from the Holy Land, he was breaking one of the fundamental laws that he had sworn to uphold. Although there was far too much cold hard cash at stake for him to simply let Richard go, he could be embarrassed into doing the right, honourable and Christian thing and releasing the King back to his own people, in return for a substantial reward – rather than delivering this hero of the holy war into the hands of his enemies. But everything depended on Richard's whereabouts being generally known. If all the world knew where the famous King Richard was being held, and if senior English diplomats were in contact with him and engaged in public negotiations with the Germans to secure his freedom, it would be that much more difficult for Henry to make a discrete, lucrative, and from our point of view disastrous, deal with Philip of France or Prince John.

Sixty miles upriver from Cologne, at the strongly fortified town of Koblenz, the enthusiastic Damian returned from a trip to the bath-house with more news of the King. A monk there had told him that in mid-February Richard had been moved to the citadel of Augsburg, in south-western Bavaria. As it was, by this time, early March, we felt we were closing in on our royal quarry. It was also heartening to know that, as we sailed southwards, Richard was being moved north by his captors, towards us.

I could finally see the sense in Queen Eleanor's plan to send us questing up the Rhine. That wide, slow river was the main artery of Europe, and it was not just the mighty torrents of water that flowed down from its source high in the Swiss mountains to the North Sea: it also carried goods, people and, most importantly to us, information.

Hanno was the next to uncover details of Richard's whereabouts. One night while I was performing some of my music for the Archbishop of Mainz, bowing my vielle exquisitely at a lavish feast given in honour of the two English abbots, Hanno had set about pursuing his love of ale in a back-street tavern in the stews of that city. One of his drinking companions turned out to have a cousin in the service of Duke Leopold, and he told Hanno that the King would shortly be moved to Ochsenfurt. At first the abbots were sceptical; Ochsenfurt was, after all, just a small, relatively unimportant town, a rustic backwater. Besides, what would rough, drunken soldiers know of the whereabouts of a king? But I believed him, and pressed my authority as leader of the expedition, insisting that Hanno would not lie. And so, having overridden the protests of the clerics, we turned the sailing barge east off the Rhine at Mainz and began to make our way slowly up the brown River Main towards Frankfurt.

At Frankfurt – a bustling place filled with hundreds of merchants from all over the Holy Roman Empire intent on making themselves rich, their shops and storehouses and myriad taverns, cook houses, brothels and churches that served their needs, huddled around the skirts of an imposing cathedral – Abbot Boxley (or possibly Robertsbridge) was able to confirm what Hanno had asserted so confidently several days before. King Richard, the Bishop of Frankfurt's slack-witted cellarer had let slip, was indeed at Ochsenfurt, only two days upriver. The cellarer had been asked to send several barrels of the finest wine to the town, which was currently accommodating a very special guest. How Robertsbridge (or Boxley) had succeeded in worming this information out of the cellarer, I never discovered, but our spirits soared at the discovery we were on the right path, and closing in fast on King Richard.

After several hours spent haggling with the Frankfurt merchants, Adam finally swapped his cargo of Flemish cloth for a load of cut timber, a rare hardwood that was prized for its density, and we set off fully laden the next morning, heading eastwards in the driving rain to bring succour to our captive King.

Two days later, the wet conditions had left us all tired, dripping and irritable. With the exception of Hanno, who was delighted to be back in his homeland, a wide grin splitting his round shaven head and showing off the wreckage of his teeth. It was late afternoon by the time we came round a bend in the river and moored at a wide wooden wharf on the southern bank that belonged to the Premonstratensian monastery – or more properly canonry – of Tuckelhausen. Ochsenfurt was less than a mile away upstream, but we hoped that, in making Tuckelhausen our avowed destination, we might go some way towards averting suspicions as to our true purpose.

Our story, which I had discussed at length with Boxley and Robertsbridge, was that they were paying a visit to Tuckelhausen because they wished to see its famous scriptorium and peruse a rare copy of the Holy Gospel that was housed there. In truth, the Gospel in question was not of any outstanding merit, but few people would question the movements of two such august abbots who had travelled so far to see it. They would tell their hosts how they had taken passage with Adam and Perkin, a couple of fellow countrymen who were transporting a cargo of building timber upriver to Sweinfurt, where the local margrave was strengthening the fortifications of his town. We agreed that I should be presented at Tuckelhausen not as an exalted member of the company but an ordinary man-at-arms, brought along as protection for the churchmen. This was not so far from the truth, and suited me well: I had plans that would be better served if I were not shown any of the few courtesies due to my rank as lord of a small manor.

After announcing the abbots' names and the purpose of our visit to the surly, white-robed canon who had charge of the wharf, he begrudgingly lent us a decrepit mule to carry our baggage, weapons and possessions. And while Adam and Perkin pretended to be attending to repairs on the sailing barge, Boxley, Robertsbridge, the four monks, Hanno and myself began the two-mile trudge in the fading light up a narrow track cut through the forest to the monastery of Tuckelhausen. The mule was particularly stubborn: it had no wish to leave its dry, comfortable stable by the river and venture out in a downpour when it was clearly time for its nightly feed. Only by hauling on its bridle and beating its hindquarters savagely with a hazel switch did we get the beast moving at all.

As we set out on the muddy track, to my left I caught a glimpse of Ochsenfurt itself, a mile away through the still skeletal limbs of the trees. It was a fortress, a compact town with high walls on four sides, built in the shape of a square with each walled side no more than half a mile long, and with four powerful round towers standing guard at each corner. Somewhere inside that stronghold, I mused, most likely in one of the four big towers, my King was being held captive. My sovereign lord, a man I respected as much as any I had met, a warrior I had followed loyally and fought beside in Outremer and with whom I had enjoyed merry-making and fine music, a man who had honoured me with his company and dare I say, friendship, was imprisoned there against his will. His enemies had seized him, a returning pilgrim from the Holy Land, against the laws of God and Man, and were seeking to make themselves rich from the sale of his person, as if he were a slave.

For the first time since I had heard the news of Richard's capture, I felt a hot surge of genuine anger in my gut. If it were ever within my power, I vowed, I would punish those responsible. And the flame of my quiet fury warmed me as we splashed along the rutted track, hauling the reluctant mule by main force, towards the drab walls of Tuckelhausen.

Abbot Joachim was rather bewildered to find himself host to a bedraggled party of foreigners when we were ushered into his cosy, brazier-warmed chamber. But he greeted his fellow abbots with a kiss of peace and ordered his servants to bring us wine and to prepare food and beds for us. We had presented ourselves at the gates of Tuckelhausen just as night was falling and the church bells were ringing out for Vespers. The monastery doors were shut, but Hanno, who spoke the local Bavarian dialect, had explained to the porters that we were a distinguished party of noble English clergymen and that we must be given entrance even at this late hour.

'But why, my noble lords, did you not write to advertise that you were paying our humble monastery a visit?' Abbot Joachim kept on asking. 'We could have prepared suitably for your visit. I fear we are in a state of some disarray here, readying ourselves for the feast of St George in a month's time. He is a very popular saint in these parts – this house is dedicated to him, as I'm sure you know – and we have many pilgrims under our roof at this moment. Indeed, the dormitory is quite full, and everything is in the greatest turmoil.'

Joachim was a worried little man, small and plump and sad-looking, with only wisps of white hair around the wrinkled bald patch of his tonsure. And while he spoke to us in Latin, his accent was so strange that it was difficult to understand what he was trying to say. On more than one occasion, we had to ask Hanno to get the Abbot to repeat himself in German so that my bodyguard could translate for us.

'If only you had given us some notice,' Joachim went on. 'Just a few days' notice . . .'

'Only the Lord God Almighty can say what happened to the messenger who carried the letter that we sent you,' intoned Robertsbridge gravely, and I realized that, for a good Christian, he was rather an accomplished liar. 'Have you much trouble with bandits in these parts?' he added.

'Oh yes, oh most decidedly, yes,' said Joachim. He seemed relieved to have found a plausible solution to the problem of our unexpected arrival. In fact, the notion that our messenger might have been slaughtered by footpads while attempting to deliver the news of our coming seemed to cheer Abbot Joachim no end. He poured the abbots some more wine, now positively beaming.

'Oh yes,' he said, 'scores of bandits, scoundrels by the dozen. I don't know why Duke Leopold does not scour them from the land, the way they trouble God-fearing folk, devout pilgrims such as yourselves. We are famous hereabouts for our wine, our sausages, our women – and our bandits. Ha ha!'

Robertsbridge and Boxley, who were standing side by side, both smiled encouragingly at him and each took a small sip of wine at the same time.

'Forgive me for asking' – the German abbot peered closely at his two fellow prelates – 'are you brothers, by any chance? Perhaps twins?'

'We are all brothers in the sight of our Lord Jesus Christ,' said Boxley with a pious smile. 'But, no, we are not from the same earthly family.'

'Ah, yes, I see, brothers in Christ – of course we are, of course we are.'

It seemed that we had confused the good man again.

While Boxley and Robertsbridge were given a fine chamber to share for the night, Hanno and I were told rather brusquely that we should make our beds in the stable. And that suited my plans very well.

The monastery was laid out in the shape of a hollow square around a big grassy court, with the big church at its eastern end. The stable stood at the western end of the square against the outer wall of the monastery, a long, warm building with a red-tiled roof and bays for a dozen animals. It was filled with the familiar homely smells of horse sweat and hay and oiled leather and, had I intended to sleep there, it would have made a very comfortable place to rest my head.

Instead, after we had eaten in the refectory with the canons and the other pilgrims and attended the service of Compline in the big abbey church, Hanno and I crossed the grassy court and, bidding a courteous goodnight to several white-robed canons that we passed, we retired to the stable. We pulled shut the wooden door and, checking that we were alone apart from half a dozen horses and the awkward old mule, began to examine the inside of the building by the light of a single candle stub. Hanno soon found the patch of damp straw on the ground at the far end of the stable that we were looking for, and staring up into the dim rafters above his head he noted that one or two tiles were missing from the roof, which had allowed rain water to leak in and wet the straw. He muttered 'Perfect!' and began to look for a way to climb the rear wall. Soon Hanno was balanced precariously on a manger, which was affixed to the stable wall at about shoulder height, while he worked to widen the hole in the roof, shoving the loose tiles aside and cursing at the loud scraping noise that they made in the quiet night.

I, meanwhile, was making my own arrangements for the mission ahead. I dressed myself in dark clothes – two tunics for the night was chilly – warm hose, stout boots and a dark cloak and hood, and smeared a mixture of candle soot and goose fat over my face and hands. It reminded me of my preparations for the attack on Kirkton: could that have been only six months ago? It seemed like a lifetime. Though I hoped that I would not have to murder anyone tonight, I made sure that the misericorde was snug in my boot – and murmured a quick prayer to St Michael, too.

Hanno had wanted to come with me on my nocturnal jaunt, but I had said no. He might have been useful, for he was a master of silent movement at night, but I felt that what I wanted to accomplish would be better done by me alone. I did not want to worry about him, or for him to worry about me, if we became separated in the darkness. And, more importantly, I needed someone to remain behind to make some excuse for my absence if one of the monks should come into the stable or if Abbot Joachim should for some strange reason summon us. In truth, I also wanted to be alone for a while. After being cooped up on board the sailing barge for a couple of weeks, the prospect of being alone in the cool purity of the night, dependent on no one, responsible for no one but myself, held a great if unusual appeal for me.

And, I confess, I was also feeling that familiar pleasurable buzzing sensation of impending action: a tightness in my stomach and a heightened glow behind my eyes. I clasped Hanno's hand warmly before he boosted me up, then, putting one foot on the manger, I cautiously popped my head through the gap in the roof that my Bavarian friend had opened. The rising peaked roof made it impossible to see anything inside the monastery, but I listened intently until I was satisfied that the whole community was asleep. Finally I levered myself up and out until I was lying face down on the sloping tiles beside the hole and, peering into the dark interior, I whispered 'Hanno!' into the space below. The shaven-headed huntsman was only just visible as a darker mass in the gloom, but I could make out enough of him by the moonlight to grasp the bulky bundle that he handed up to me. It was a large sack, with two long loops of padded cloth spaced shoulder width apart that enabled it to be slung from the back. Hanno told me that in southern Bavaria the mountain men used to wear these things when they had to carry heavy loads up and down the steep hillsides of the Alps there. Reaching into this 'back-sack', as they are known by the

Bavarians, I pulled out a coil of rope in which Hanno had carefully tied fat knots every foot and, loosening one end, tied it securely to one of the beams inside the stable roof. The rest of the coil I tossed over the outer wall of the canonry. To the sound of a barely whispered 'Go with God!' from my friend below, I began, very carefully and quietly, to climb down the rope, the back-sack looped over my shoulders, my muscles creaking under the strain of my weight, walking carefully down the ten-foot wall to the ground below.

All was quiet as I found myself standing in a muddy patch of tilled earth, some sort of vegetable garden from the look of it. Leaving the knotted rope hanging against the outer wall, I set out to the south, following the wall until I came to the corner of the monastery, and then sprinting fifty yards or so into the cover of a copse that ran east–west to the south of Tuckelhausen. As my panting breath subsided, I took stock of my situation: the rain had stopped but the sky was still filled with scudding clouds and a three-quarter moon, which provided ample light to navigate by. Too much light, if the truth be told; I had hoped for a little more cloud cover, as I did not want to be too easy to spot as I went about my business.

It was perhaps an hour or so before midnight, I judged, as I adjusted the straps on my back-sack to allow it to sit more comfortably. Checking once again that the misericorde was still in my boot, I pulled the hood on my cloak far forward and began to march eastward, towards Ochsenfurt; towards the heavily fortified town in which my King was being held prisoner.

Chapter Nine

It took me no more than an hour to cross the three miles of farmland from Tuckelhausen to the high walls of Ochsenfurt. I stayed under the cover of woods and spinneys wherever possible, or walked along the lines of hedgerows or fences to minimize the silhouette that a walking man might make on a bright, moon-filled night. At about midnight, I found myself crouched at the foot of a tree in a scrubby stand of alders, not far from the River Main, chewing on a stick of dried meat that Hanno had thoughtfully placed in the back-sack for me, and looking over at the defences of the north-western corner of Ochsenfurt, which were no more than thirty yards away.

The town was protected by a deep ditch, about three-quarters filled with rainwater, which lay in front of a thick stone wall, some twenty foot in height. At this corner of the western and northern walls, as at every other corner of this square town, was a high, round tower with arrow slits at different heights on three sides. I imagined the arrow slits coming off a spiral stone staircase running around the inside of the tower and leading to a secure room at the top. I was fairly certain that King Richard must be imprisoned in one of these towers. There was one chance in four that I was now looking at the very prison that held my King.

Richard could, of course, have been held in the town itself, perhaps in a nobleman's dwelling. But I had shinned up several tall trees as I was approaching Ochsenfurt and – apart from a large solid-looking church in the centre of the town – I could not make out another stone-built structure that would be suitable for holding a valuable captive for several days or weeks. The towers might be on the edge of town but the walls were patrolled by men-at-arms, and the only way out would have been a locked door at the base of the tower on the inside of the walls.

No, I was almost certain that Richard would be in one of the four towers. But which one?

Ten yards to my left, a well-travelled road ran east–west beside the broad, glinting flow of the Main and it entered Ochsenfurt by a strong-looking barbican beside the tower. The big wooden town gate, studded with iron for extra strength, was barred tight. It would have been closed at curfew, and would not be opened until dawn. On the battlements above the barbican, I could see the warm yellow glow of candlelight escaping from two or three windows, and the occasional moving shadow as a watchman walked past the light. I calculated that there must be about five or possibly six men up there. And these men-at-arms, charged with keeping the safety of Ochsenfurt, were awake and alert. In order to break into this town and talk face-to-face with King Richard, I would have to swim across a flooded ditch, scale a sheer twenty-foot wall, sneak past these six men-at-arms, or kill them all silently, and then wander around the maze of narrow streets after curfew, and locate my sovereign in one of four strongly defended towers – and do all this in the pitch darkness and without making a sound. To be captured would mean execution as a thief or spy.

I chewed on my strip of jerked beef and pondered the problem. It was impossible, I concluded. There was no way I could get into Ochsenfurt undetected. But that did not mean I would not be able to communicate with my King.

The big double door to the barbican was locked tightly shut, as I had already noted. Nobody could go in through it. On the other hand, it was very unlikely that anyone would come out. What sort of watchman is willing to leave his comfortable spot by a brazier, his allotted post, and venture out into the darkness? Who knows what strange, unearthly creatures, demons or witches, may lurk beyond the safety of the firelight? I thought of the superstitious villagers of Locksley and their fears of the Hag of Hallamshire, and smiled to myself. Then I dug into my back-sack and pulled out my polished apple-wood vielle and my horsehair bow. It was one of my most prized possessions, a gift from my old musical mentor Bernard de Sezanne. The vielle was about two foot long, and made up of about half neck, where I fingered the strings, and half woman-shaped rounded body, which generated its exquisite sound. It was light enough to carry in the back-sack with ease, yet fairly strong.

I repacked the back-sack, and readied myself to flee at a moment's notice, then I began to tune the instrument as quietly as I could. Mutterings of conversation came drifting down from the candlelight above the barbican, not thirty yards away, as they heard me plucking at the five strings and adjusting the pegs on the head at the end of the vielle's long neck. I could not hear the words distinctly, and I would not have understood them even if I had, but I knew that the guards were aware of my presence.

And then I began to play.

My master Robin had almost always been short of money during the Great Pilgrimage. Since he had commandeered the lucrative frankincense trade, that had all changed dramatically, of course, but for most of the time he had lacked sufficient quantities of silver to meet his obligations as the leader of nearly four hundred fighting men. And the fault had been King Richard's. My sovereign had promised Robert of Locksley a certain amount of silver in exchange for Robin's promise to come to war and bring his feared Welsh bowmen with him. Unfortunately, as is often the way with rich men, and especially kings, Richard had been slow to pay what he owed to my master, and Robin had suffered a lack of ready funds as a result.

As a favour to Robin, I had used an opportunity to play music with Richard to remind my King of his debt to Robin, and we had enjoyed a sort of musical duel: I had sung a verse suggesting that Richard should pay up promptly and Richard had replied by telling me not to stir up trouble. It had all been done in a spirit of fun and laughter, but the outcome was that Robin was paid a proportion of the silver he was owed, and Richard and I had formed a bond as fellow verse-makers.

That dark night, seated on the cold earth outside the barbican of the main gate of Ochsenfurt, I played the music that accompanied the song that Richard and I had written together. It was a simple, distinctive melody, repeated twice and then elaborated on in the third and fourth lines, before returning to the main melody again. I bowed the opening notes, and sang:

My joy summons me
To sing in this sweet season . . .

I bowed the next few chords and continued:

And my generous heart replies
That it is right to feel this way.

And then I stopped and listened. There were raised voices coming from the barbican, and a few incomprehensible shouts of enquiry, but I tried to erase them from my hearing. I was straining to hear if my sovereign lord, Richard the Lionheart, King of England, Duke of Normandy and Aquitaine, Count of Anjou and Poitiers, would join me in my carolling from inside his prison cell. If the guards in the barbican could hear me, I was sure that anyone kept imprisoned in the adjoining tower would be able to hear me, too.

I waited for a few minutes. In silhouette against the battlements of the gatehouse I could see a man-at-arms standing with a flaring torch in his hand, peering out into the darkness. But I held my peace. I doubted that they would sally forth to find me, and even if they did, I would be able to slip away before they could catch me. The man on the battlements turned his head and said something to someone behind him. And then fixed the torch in a nearby becket and went back into his warm guardhouse. Once more, I thought, just one more time, and then I'll go.

And I drew my bow across the strings of the vielle, and once again I sang the first verse of 'My Joy'. There were more shouts from the guardhouse and two men appeared, this time on the battlements, clutching bright torches. Since I had not received the response that I was looking for, I backed away into the darkness, leaving the men-at-arms atop the barbican to shout their querulous challenges into the empty night.

I walked southwards, away from the river, keeping a little further away from the town wall and the water-filled ditch, but still holding them in sight. It was not just the barbican that had conscientious sentries: each of the four town walls was patrolled by alert soldiers, too. But there were not so many men concentrated near the south-western corner of Ochsenfurt when I arrived there a few moments later and found a spot under a bush from which to observe the second tower. The shouts of the guards at the barbican had drawn a single man, running from the western section of the town wall; I had seen him trotting in the opposite direction to me as I approached the second tower.

Oddly, I also believed that I could hear a strange noise behind me; a heavy crunching tread, like a huge beast moving ponderously through the undergrowth. When I stopped to listen, the noise also stopped. A quiver of ancestral fear ran through me, the notion that something was out there, behind me in the blackness, something that meant to do me harm. I shrugged off my nerves, telling myself to get a grip on my courage. It was most likely a boar or a stag, raiding the rich farmland for something good to eat; or perhaps a sleepy cow blundering around in the darkness.

The second tower, on the south-western corner of the town, looked deserted. Not a chink of light to be seen; nothing stirring at all. I waited perhaps a quarter of an hour, huddling in my bush, and then, straightening up, I bowed the first chord and sang the first verse of 'My Joy'. Nothing. No response from the tower, no angry cries of alarm from the guards. I tried the second verse:

> *My heart commands me*
> *To love my sweet mistress,*
> *And my joy in doing so*
> *Is a generous reward in itself.*

Again: nothing. That second verse had been written by King Richard himself – it was a witty reply to my own first verse, using many of the same words to give a different meaning to the verses. Richard had been justifiably proud of his composition. I doubt very much he would have forgotten it. But: nothing. So I packed up the bow and the vielle into the back-sack, and began to move off eastwards towards the third tower.

The approach to my third performance spot was easier than the last two as there was a small wood to the south of Ochsenfurt which made it possible to come undetected to a place close to the walls. The third tower looked as unpromising as the second; there were no guards in evidence and not a chink of light showing. I wondered whether I had made a mistake, that Richard was not imprisoned in one of these tall round fortifications; maybe he was not in Ochsenfurt at all. Perhaps he had been moved once again to another location altogether. Was I just wasting my night, when I could be tucked up in the warm hay of the stable listening to Hanno's snores?

I unpacked the vielle, feeling a little discouraged, and with very little ceremony I launched once more into the first verse of 'My Joy'. Again, there was no response, not a sound from either a guard or royal prisoner. Dispirited, I began a listless rendition of the second, the royal verse. And then it happened.

A light showed at a tiny window at the top of the tower; a little spark of good cheer. I stopped playing, dumbfounded. It couldn't be, it couldn't be . . .

And then I heard a voice: not strong, nor particularly tuneful, the voice of someone only just awakened – but familiar, very familiar, and it made the skin all over my body pimple like a plucked goose's flesh. The voice sang:

> A lord has one obligation
> Greater than love itself
> Which is to reward most generously
> The knight who serves him well.

It was Richard. I had found my King. And he had remembered, and sung back to me, the verse I had written so long ago, to remind him of his debts to Robin.

I had tears stinging my eyes as I struck the strings of the vielle for the final verse: and I sang it in unison with my lord, my captain, my King, his voice growing in strength with every note.

A knight who sings so sweetly
Of obligation to his noble lord
Should consider the great virtue
Of courtly manners, not discord.

When we had finished, there was a long silence. My throat was too choked to speak. And finally, I saw a pale face at the window high up on the tower, and a royal voice called out: 'Blondel, Blondel, is that truly you? Or are you some night phantom sent to taunt me in my misery?'

'It is me, sire. It is Alan Dale. It is truly me, and we – myself and my lord abbots Boxley and Robertsbridge – have come to accomplish your freedom. Take heart, sire, your friends are close at hand.'

At that moment, something flashed in the corner of my eye. Purely out of instinct, I moved back half a step as a shining steel sword blade slashed past my face, missing my nose by a quarter-inch. If the blow had landed, it would have hacked straight through my skull, killing me for sure. But, God be praised, I was young then, and very fast. I dropped the bow and turned to face my attacker with only a frail wooden vielle in my hands. He was a tall, very thin man, taller than me by half a foot, and he was not slow either. And suddenly I knew him. He was the man I had seen beside the fire with Prince John, at the siege of Kirkton six months ago. I had no time to reach down for my misericorde, but my beloved musical instrument was enough to deflect the next strike; a lightning lunge at my heart. By God, he was quick! Holding the instrument by the neck, with the sound box towards my enemy, I caught and deflected his sword as it flickered towards me – and what a

sword: a long, slim blade, chased with gold, a crosspiece decorated with ropes of silver, and a large blue gem, a sapphire, I
assumed, set in a ring in the centre of the silver pommel. I saw
all this in an instant, and at the same time, my vielle swept up
and to the right and pushed the magnificent blade safely past
my body. I riposted instinctively; hours and hours of training
in the strike. And if the vielle had been a sword, my counterblow
would have killed him. As it was, the blunt end of the vielle's
round body smashed into his face with enough force to crush
his nose and send him staggering back. I fumbled at my boot
top for the dagger; I needed steel for this work, not frail wood.
He looked angry and surprised as we circled each other.
I watched his sword arm, waiting for his next move and trying
not to think of how much I wanted to own that lovely blade,
but my hind brain was shrieking another warning: one that
I could not at that moment decipher.

I had the misericorde in my left hand and the vielle in my
right when he attacked again; a scything diagonal back-hand
cut with the long sword aimed at my head and coming fast
from my right-hand side. I swept up the vielle and the sword
crunched into it, leaving me unharmed but with a tangle of
splinters and kindling, held together with five cat-gut strings
in my hand. I dodged the next blow, and hopped over a slash
at my ankles, trying to get in close to use the misericorde – all
the while, my brain yelling its inchoate warning – and as he
was turning after his low sweep, I jumped forward, jabbed at
him with the misericorde – a feint – and swung the wrecked
vielle at his head. He avoided the blade with a neat half-turn
but the rump of the smashed instrument pivoted around the
back of his head, wrapping the cat-gut strings around his throat.

Then I pulled. He dropped that wonderful sword and turned away, both his thin white hands flying to his neck to loosen the strangling cat-gut. I dropped the misericorde in turn, and leapt on his back, using my weight to drive him to the ground, my hands scrabbling for the cat-gut, wrenching it tight, the vielle strings cutting deeply into his long throat. I hauled for my life, with one hand on the neck of the instrument and one on the wreckage of the bridge. He gurgled wetly, his eyes bulged, his tongue protruded like some evil purple sausage as his body kicked and writhed under mine. I knew he was dying; all I had to do was hold on and pull the vielle strings tighter and tighter . . .

And then something exploded in the side of my chest, I heard the crack of bone as my body flew off the supine swordsman and flipped over. As I lay on my back, the cat-gut still in my grasp, still around the thin man's neck, I saw a giant form, round as a glacial boulder, barely human, looming above me. I knew that I had been kicked in the ribs as I had never been kicked before; it felt like a hoof-blow from a fear-maddened stallion. I also knew what my brain had been screaming at me as I fought the swordsman: Where is his friend? Where is his giant, muscle-bound companion from the fireside? I knew now.

The ogre – for there was no way on God's green earth that this monstrous fellow could have been wholly human – raised a gigantic foot, ready to stamp on my two wrists which were still half-hauling on the cat-gut and strangling the life out of the tall man. Hurriedly releasing the vielle strings, I pulled in my arms just as his foot came stamping down on the place where they had been moments before – and I swear I felt the earth shudder with the impact of his boot. I rolled away from the pair of them: the thin one, now kneeling and coughing and groping for his sword, and then rising, impossibly quickly, shining blade in hand; and the ogre, striding towards me with an insane gleam in his piggy little eyes. He appeared to be unarmed but, seeing his massive ham-like hands clenching and unclenching in front of him as he advanced on me, I knew that if I allowed myself to be caught by them, I was a dead man. My misericorde was gone, lost in the struggle, and I am ashamed to say that I did not hesitate for an instant. I turned and ran, as swiftly as I could with my damaged ribs. I ran like a craven hare into the trees behind me.

With a sword in my hand I fear no man; but unarmed against a first-class swordsman and a monstrous creature from some feverish nightmare . . . Anyway, enough of my poor excuses, I fled. I ran for my life. The ogre lumbered after me for twenty yards or so, panting and growling behind me like a bear, but my pain and fear drove me onwards and I soon lost him in the thick cover of the wood. As I ran, I could hear the shouts in German from a couple of men-at-arms on the walls. And above their harsh cries, I could make out the calls of my King in good, clean French, demanding to know what had happened beneath his prison tower. But he received no response from his loyal subject below. I needed all my wind just to run.

My ribs were giving me a deal of trouble. So much so that I found I could not climb the knotted rope that was still hanging down the side of the wall when I reached Tuckelhausen half an hour later. I called softly for Hanno, but received no response. Doubtless my friend was sleeping soundly in the soft

175

hay. I was reduced to tossing stones through the hole in the roof, hoping that the noise of their rattling on the tiles or landing inside the stable would wake my friend. Fortunately it worked and I soon saw his round, shaven head poking out of the hole in the tiled roof.

Hanno managed to haul me up without too much difficulty, and not half an hour later I found myself gulping from a flask of wine, and wiping the greasy soot from my face as I told my friend the news and he strapped up my battered side tightly with long strips of linen.

He was overjoyed to hear that we had successfully located King Richard, but alarmed by the attack on me by the two mismatched assassins.

'Who are they, Alan, and why do they want to kill you?' he asked with a puzzled frown. 'If they are in the service of Duke Leopold or the Emperor Henry, they must surely arrest you and you are then hanged in the square as a spy. What does this mean?'

'They are Prince John's men,' I told him, and explained that I had seen them before, outside Kirkton, bringing a message from Prince John to Sir Ralph Murdac.

'Ach so, but why do they want to kill you?' asked my friend. He was a master of stealthy movement, was Hanno, in daylight and darkness; he could hunt and track animals and men better than any other fellow I ever knew. But he was not swift of thought when it came to the dark motives of princes.

'Prince John does not wish Richard's whereabouts to be known to the world,' I said, trying to explain it as simply as possible for Hanno's benefit. 'The Prince must have spies in Westminster. When they told him that we were setting off on this mission to find Richard, he gave this unlovely pair of killers the task of making sure we did not find him. If we were to quietly disappear on this journey – both of us and perhaps the monks and abbots, too – who would know about it? It might be weeks, even months, before another diplomatic party was dispatched to try to find our King. And that delay would give Prince John more than ample time to make an arrangement with Leopold.'

'Do they attack us again?' asked Hanno.

'I don't think so,' I said, although I was very far from sure. 'But we must be on our guard, and the sooner we get the abbots to Ochsenfurt, into the presence of the King and registered as an official English embassy, the better.'

So, the next morning, an hour or so before noon, I stood once more before the gate of the barbican, at the north-western corner of the town of Ochsenfurt, while Hanno bawled up at the guards a translation of our names and rank and the purpose of our visit. It felt very different from the last time I had been before this portal only hours previously. The abbots and I were dressed in our finest clothes; clean white woollen robes for the clergymen and tall staffs topped with golden crosses, and a scarlet tunic embroidered with silver thread for me, topped by a fine new grey woollen hat. I did my best to look lordly as Hanno bellowed that we had come to pay our respects to Duke Leopold of Austria and to pay a visit to his illustrious prisoner King Richard the Lionheart of England.

The wooden iron-studded gate swung slowly open and we were ushered into Ochsenfurt by a squad of ten mail-clad men-at-arms, each armed with spear and sword and proudly bearing the symbol of a red ox, the town's badge, on the chests of their snow-white surcoats. We were escorted through the narrow streets into the centre of town to the antechamber of a great hall, where we were offered refreshments – politely declined – before being shown into the great hall itself and the presence of Duke Leopold, loyal vassal of the Emperor Henry, ruler of much of the southern German lands, former pilgrim – and the mortal enemy of our good King Richard.

Leopold was a tall, dark, hawk-faced man, with eyes that seemed to glitter like black gems. He listened attentively to our speech, delivered in elegant Latin by Abbot Boxley, the Duke nodding and smiling occasionally, and then we all waited while a fat priest in a fur-trimmed robe translated it into German for him.

He spoke for a while in his native tongue, seemingly welcoming us to his lands, and then beside me I heard Hanno make a sharp intake of breath. The fat priest then translated.

'My noble lords,' said the cleric in strongly accented Latin, 'the Duke bids you welcome to his hall and to this his fiefdom. If it pleases you, you may stay as long as you wish in the Duke's dominions, under his protection, and rest your bones after your long journey. His Grace is pleased to have the company of such a distinguished group of pilgrims, and he feels that you will do honour to his household by your presence,' the priest went on, 'but . . .' Here the fat man paused and gulped. 'But his Grace fears that you are labouring under a misapprehension. His Grace has no knowledge of the King of England, and is certain that the noble Richard the Lionheart is not at this time within the confines of the town of Ochsenfurt.'

We were stunned into silence by this outright lie.

Robertsbridge began to speak, shooting little angry glances at me between phrases: 'Your Grace, we have it on good authority' – he turned his head and glared at me – 'we have had some indications, rather, that King Richard may be a prisoner here within these walls, awaiting ransom by his loyal friends.'

The priest translated, and the Duke replied through him. 'You are mistaken. The illustrious King of England is not here. I am afraid you may have been the victims of a practical joke; perhaps an amusing schoolboy's prank. I can assure you, on my honour, that your King is not here.'

Chapter Ten

The abbots were angry, furious even, and Robertsbridge even accused me of making the whole story up, or of dreaming it in a drunken stupor. Icily I informed them that my cracked ribs were quite real, they were paining me considerably that morning, and I would stand by everything I had told them about my adventures last night. Then I demanded, through Hanno, that the Ochsenfurt men-at-arms take us to the third tower on the south-eastern corner of the town. Immediately.

Incredibly, they obeyed my orders. As we climbed the narrow spiral staircase, the whole troop of us, the four monks and the two abbots puffing and panting in my wake, I knew with a sense of gloomy certainty that the room at the top would be empty. And so it was.

It was a high, circular room with few furnishings: a narrow cot, a table and stool. Nothing else. The stout door, I had noticed on the way in, was bolted on the outside rather than from within the room. The wooden floor was slightly damp, and there was not a trace of dust anywhere. Strangely, perhaps, I was cheered by this: the room had been cleaned only this morning, and the floor had been thoroughly washed. And although I knew I had not been dreaming my encounter with Richard the night before, it was pleasing to have such proof, if you can call a damp floor proof. Someone, without a doubt our good King Richard, had been incarcerated in this high room until a few hours ago, and since then someone else had made efforts to erase all trace of his presence here.

When I explained this to the abbots, they seemed unconvinced. But they did not go so far as to call me a liar to my face. We all trooped down the stairs, and were escorted by the Ochsenfurt men-at-arms to our quarters, a large two-storey timbered townhouse opposite the church of St Michael, in the centre of town, which had been set aside for the use of high-ranking travellers.

We gathered gloomily at the long wooden table in the parlour and while the young monks bustled about bringing us bread and cheese and wine from the well-stocked pantry, I brooded on what we were to do next.

Suddenly I looked up from my cup of wine, and asked: 'Where is Hanno?'

Nobody seemed to know. I could not remember having seen him since we had left the great hall and the audience with Duke Leopold. He had translated my demand for the Ochsenfurt men-at-arms to take us to the tower, but no one knew what had become of him after that. I was not overly concerned, however, despite the threat of the two assassins. I knew that my wily hunter friend could take care of himself. He had probably just wanted a little liberty to explore Ochsenfurt, drink some of the local ale, and talk his own language for a few hours.

We did not need Hanno for our discussions. Indeed, there seemed little to discuss; we found ourselves completely at a loss as to how to proceed. Robertsbridge was all for returning to the Duke and threatening him with excommunication if he did not reveal Richard's whereabouts. Boxley, I believe, just wanted to go home. For myself, the prospect of returning to Queen Eleanor with the news that I had sung merrily with her son but had not been allowed to speak to him and had been turned away with an obvious lie was unthinkable. I argued that, since his two hired killers were in the vicinity of Ochsenfurt, it was fair to assume that Prince John was in touch with Duke Leopold over the matter of Richard's ransom. This was bad news, as was the Duke's refusal to acknowledge that Richard was in his custody. We could only assume that Leopold planned to hand over our King, either to Prince John or to King Philip of France. Helpless to prevent this from happening, our best hope was to remain in Ochsenfurt until the Duke tried to move Richard, at which point it might prove easier to establish contact with him.

The abbots and I were still sitting despondently in the parlour, sipping wine and racking our brains while the day quietly slipped away, when the door crashed open and Hanno came staggering into the room. He was very drunk.

'I fin' 'im,' slurred my Bavarian bodyguard, a thick waft of strong ale billowing out with his breath.

'You are inebriated, man,' snapped Robertsbridge. 'Go to bed and trouble us no more. We have important matters to attend to here.'

'I find King Richard,' Hanno said, making an effort to speak our language more clearly. 'I find your lost lord. Come, I take you to him.'

We hurried out into the street where Hanno introduced us to Peter, a burly man-at-arms in the Ochsenfurt surcoat, who beamed at us with a face as red as the ox device on his chest. He was even drunker than Hanno. He was also, we soon discovered, King Richard's gaoler.

As we walked towards the southern side of the town, I noticed that there seemed to be some event, a grand arrival of some sort, with trumpets sounding and bells ringing, monks chanting, taking place at the barbican gate, but we were too excited and preoccupied to investigate further. As we walked, Hanno related to us what he had been up to the past six hours, apart from imbibing vast quantities of the local ale. While we went off with the men-at-arms to inspect the third tower, he had slipped away, leaving the town and circling its outer walls until he came to the spot beneath the tower where I had played my vielle the night before. Had we but looked out of the small window in Richard's cell we would have seen him below us. At this point Hanno interrupted his narrative to hand me my misericorde, and I gratefully sheathed it in my boot. He had found my dagger, along with the marks of the fight, on the ground. He had even found the remains of the vielle and the bow, both sadly beyond repair. Then he had tracked the foot-steps of two men, one with long narrow feet, the other with huge round ones, into the wood and had discovered the site of their bivouac. Approaching with caution, Hanno had found the place deserted, but the warm ashes of the cooking fire told him that it had only recently been occupied. According to

Hanno's almost supernatural fieldcraft, the two men had left their camp about dawn and made their way north towards the River Main, possibly planning to escape by boat. As Hanno related his tale, he seemed to grow more sober with every passing moment.

Rather than attempting to track them further, my cunning friend had returned to Ochsenfurt and made for the nearest soldiers' tavern. There he had set about ingratiating himself with a man-at-arms, buying him several pots of ale. Hanno's new friend had then taken him to another tavern, and another, in search of the beaming brick-faced idiot who now stood before us: Richard's gaoler. Hanno, as well as plying the fellow with drink, had promised him a purse of silver if he would allow us to speak with his special prisoner for quarter of an hour. Apparently the buffoon had not been told who his prisoner was, only that he was to guard him well.

As we hurried through the streets, Hanno told us that Richard had been hooded and bound, then moved from the tower at dawn and unceremoniously locked in an earth-walled root cellar under a grand house near the southern wall of Ochsenfurt. The house was empty and the only guards, four of them, were under the command of this Peter, evidently a habitual drunk, who was now shambling along beside us, alternately grinning and tugging his greasy forelock at the abbots.

It took but a few moments to reach the house, and while the oafish gaoler fumbled with a key, I congratulated Hanno on his resourcefulness, handing him the purse from my belt with which to reward Peter. 'Ach, it is nothing,' said Hanno modestly. He seemed to have thrown off the effects of the ale almost entirely. 'This is a very small town, everybody knows everybody's business here. I grow up in a small town just like this one. You can never keep a secret in these little places . . .'

'You did it perfectly,' I said, knowing that it would please him. He grinned and nodded happily.

The gaoler threw open the door and bowed low, ushering us into the dank, earthy space. While Hanno remained outside to keep watch, the two abbots and I ducked our heads and made our way cautiously into the dim cellar. I had my hand on my sword, unsure what to expect, and when something moved with a clink in the far corner, I half-drew my weapon.

There was barely enough light to see, but as my eyes grew accustomed to the darkness I could make out the form of a man, a tall man, lying in the corner. He was chained by the ankle to an iron stake driven deep into the floor; his face was hidden by a bag made from a dark cloth of some kind and his arms were tightly bound by the elbows behind him. Suddenly I was extremely angry. This man was a king, and a hero of a righteous war against the enemies of Christ, not some common felon awaiting a shameful execution. I cut through his bonds with my sword and pulled the bag off his head. I could do nothing about his iron fetter.

'Sire,' I said gently as King Richard rubbed his arms to bring back the circulation. 'Sire, we are here. All will be well now that we are here to help you.'

King Richard blinked and stared at me in the dim light of the cellar. 'Blondel,' he said, almost whispering my nickname. 'Blondel – I knew I was not dreaming. It *was* you singing last night, not some foul trick of my ears or a night demon. I knew it.'

'Sire . . .' Abbot Boxley took a step towards the King. 'We

come here with the full authority of your mother the Queen to negotiate for your release. England stands ready to buy your freedom. And we shall not leave your side until your liberty is accomplished.'

King Richard sat up. He seemed to be recovering swiftly from his ordeal. He rubbed his eyes and looked at the abbot standing before him in his pristine white robes.

'Ah, it is my lord Abbot Robertsbridge, if I am not mistaken. Good to see you, man. Very good to see you.'

Boxley recoiled just a shade at the King's words. 'Sire,' he said, 'I have the honour to be the Abbot of Boxley. My lord Robertsbridge is over there by the door.'

'Of course he is, of course,' said the King. 'And you are both very welcome in my sight. It's, ah, John, isn't it?'

The Abbot of Robertsbridge replied from the doorway: 'We both bear that Christian name, sire. But, if I may make so bold, we have little time for such pleasantries and much to discuss concerning your ransom – and certain events in your kingdom that have occurred in your absence. Your brother, Prince John . . .'

Leaving the abbots and my King crouched on the dirty earth floor of the root cellar in earnest discussion, I drifted outside to the fading light of the day. Hanno was talking in Bavarian and laughing with Peter the gaoler by the main door of the house, and I wandered over to them as casually as I could. The red-faced man smiled at me and nodded ingratiatingly, and as I approached he seemed about to say something. What he was intending to say, I will never know.

My left arm flashed out and I grabbed him roughly by the throat, squeezing his windpipe with a powerful grip and slamming him back into the wall of the house. My misericorde was in my right hand, and I placed its needle tip under his left eye. Hanno growled at him from over my shoulder.

'Listen to me, you rancid turd,' I said, speaking slowly and harshly in English, my eyes boring into his frightened face. 'That prisoner is a king – the King of England, no less – and you will treat him with the respect he deserves while he is in your care. I want food and wine and clean linen brought to him, and water for washing. And I want it done now.'

I was truly angry. My right hand, the one that held the dagger poised to plunge into his eye, was shaking slightly in my rage. And, as Hanno translated, I glared at Peter, giving him the full force of my righteous ire.

'Know this,' I grated, 'if you mistreat him, if you do not show him the courtesy that is his due, I will take your eyes. And your nose and your lips.' I tapped him on the mouth with the tip of the misericorde.

Hanno repeated my message in Bavarian. Then I continued: 'Though it might cost me my life, I will blind you, torture you, and kill you very, very slowly. Then I will come to your house, and kill all your family, and burn it to the ground. And if a cowardly rat such as yourself has any friends, I will kill them all and burn their houses too. Do I make myself clear?'

Even before Hanno had translated my words I could see that Peter understood me. He gibbered something at me, and then Hanno leant forward, his face a stone mask, and shoved the little purse of silver in the man's mouth, silencing his sobbing words.

Disgusted, I released him and turned away, heading back to the dank cellar to see how my spiritual lords were faring. Behind me the gaoler was shouting for his comrades, and issuing a stream of orders, telling them, I assumed, to bring food and wine immediately.

Unbidden, Robin suddenly came into my mind, his handsome face smiling cruelly at me as he enquired, *So, Alan, are you now using fear to bend weaker men to your will? You become more like me every day.* I shook my head to rid myself of the sound of Robin's mocking laughter, and saw that the abbots Boxley and Robertsbridge were emerging from the cellar, looking grave yet satisfied. The gaoler was by now bobbing around me, chattering in Bavarian and offering God knows what services, but I did not deign to look at him. A second man-at-arms had appeared and was in the act of shutting the cellar door when, from within, Richard cried out: 'Hold! Wait a moment!' And I put a hand on the man's arm to halt him.

King Richard stared out at me from his dank and miserable cellar, with the door half-closed, looking directly at me through the gap. He said nothing for a few moments – and then he spoke these words:

> *A lord has one obligation*
> *Greater than love itself*
> *Which is to reward most generously*
> *The knight who serves him well.*

My heart was full of wild emotions – anger and love and shame – as the cellar door banged shut on my sovereign lord. And as I turned to join Hanno and the abbots, now impatient to confront Duke Leopold, I thought, *I am your loyal soldier, Lionhearted Richard, I am your vassal to command; I swear it now, silently, before no mortal man but before God Almighty himself. I swear it. Till death, I shall always be the King's man.*

We marched straight to the great hall in a tight phalanx of outrage, determined that our encounter with the King should not be denied. The abbots to the fore, we demanded that Leopold's men-at-arms admit us immediately to the Duke's presence. Somewhat surprisingly, they offered no resistance but opened the heavy doors. We walked straight into the middle of a lavish celebration.

The hall fell silent as we entered, the feasting stopped, a juggler who had been performing dropped one of his silver balls, letting his jaw hang open. In a ringing voice, my lord Robertsbridge began to inform Duke Leopold in crisp Latin that he had just ended a conference with King Richard in which he had found our lord in chains and lying in his own filth. He was halfway through his demand that our King should be treated with the respect that was his due as a Christian monarch when his voice faltered and came to a halt. I could see why. Robertsbridge had been addressing Duke Leopold, but whereas earlier that morning the Duke had been seated in the position of highest honour that place had now been taken by another man. And though I had never before laid eyes on him, I knew immediately that I was looking at Henry the Sixth of that name, the King of Germany, lord of much of Italy, overlord of Duke Leopold of Austria, God's anointed representative on Earth, the Holy Roman Emperor himself.

The greatest prince in Christendom was a slight man in his late twenties, medium height, with a bush of curly brown hair beneath a golden crown, and a wispy beard a little lighter in

189

colour perched above a narrow line of a mouth. He looked amused rather than angry at Robertsbridge's passionate tirade, and when the abbot stuttered to a halt, he raised a pale hand and addressed our party in clear and fluent Latin.

'My lord abbot, calm yourself, do please compose your spirit,' the Emperor commanded in a warm tone, but with an edge of cold steel to it. 'There has been some regrettable misunderstanding, it seems. Certainly King Richard is here in Ochsenfurt, we know that *now*, and I have just given orders that he should be housed in apartments fitting to his exalted station.'

Robertsbridge put back his shoulders. He poked out a bony accusatory finger at Duke Leopold: 'That gentleman denied it this very morning. He told me to my face, he swore on his honour that King Richard was not in Ochsenfurt. He lied to—'

'It seems that my noble cousin Leopold was mistaken,' the Emperor interrupted smoothly. 'Some months ago a penniless vagabond pretending to be a Templar knight was arrested in a house of ill-repute within the Duke's domains and since then we have been trying to ascertain his true identity. As you have been able to confirm this, we are now satisfied that our masquerading vagabond truly is King Richard of England himself.'

'Since *now* you recognize who he is – a genuine pilgrim returning from the Holy Land, a noble knight sworn to Christ's service – then perhaps you will kindly release him to us this instant,' said Robertsbridge coldly.

'Alas, alas, there have been many grave charges laid against your King – tales of his consorting secretly with that devil Saladin, betraying the Great Pilgrimage, and even ordering the murder of our cousin Conrad of Montferrat in Acre last year.

190

I am afraid your noble King Richard must answer to these charges before we can consider allowing him to go free.'

The charges were all patently false, ridiculous even. The Emperor was merely seeking a legal pretext that would allow him to keep our sovereign in custody.

'I must beg you to reconsider,' said Robertsbridge. 'The imprisonment of King Richard is in direct contravention of His Holiness the Pope's decree on the sanctity of those returning from the Great Pilgrimage.'

Henry attempted to look genuinely troubled by the difficulty of balancing the trumped-up accusations laid against Richard and the Pope's decree: he wrinkled his brow and scratched his head. He frowned, cupped his chin and pretended to be thinking deeply. Then he brightened. Had he been a mummer rather than lord of half of Europe, he would have certainly starved to death.

'I would dearly like to release the noble King Richard into your custody, I dearly would, but alas, I fear I cannot. These grave charges against him must be answered. Until such time as we can arrange an investigation into his alleged misdeeds, the King of England shall remain with me – not as a prisoner but as an honoured guest, housed in suitable comfort and security.' Beaming like a village idiot, the Emperor continued: 'And I very much look forward to spending time with him in the coming weeks. I gather that he and I share a love of poetry and music. Well then, we shall make music together while he is my guest.' At this point I felt his sharp eyes search me out. 'We shall make our music by day, of course,' he said, speaking it seemed directly to me, 'in a civilized hall. Rather than outside the walls like common thieves in the dark of night.'

However, Robertsbridge had not become a very high and mighty churchman by accident; he had bones of iron. 'Then, my lord, as his trusted friends and counsellors, we shall stay with our King and see to his comfort and safety until this matter has been properly resolved – unless you have some objection . . . ?'

'Indeed not, my lord abbot. You and your men are most welcome at my court. Most welcome. Now let us eat!'

There was nothing else to do but join the feast.

We spent a sleepless night. After the feast was over, back at our guest house, the abbots sat up till dawn writing many letters to the great men – and women – of England and Normandy, while Hanno and I packed our possessions, cleaned our swords and armour and prepared to carry these precious missives on the long journey home.

We were to leave the abbots and their monks with King Richard and retrace our steps to *The Crow*, which would carry us down the Main and the Rhine, all the way back to the North Sea and across it to England. The letters we would carry were of vital importance; in effect we were being entrusted with King Richard's lifeline, for these letters were his only link to his supporters in England. Undoubtedly Prince John's assassins would stop at nothing in their efforts to prevent the letters from reaching their destination. Still, I was confident that, with Hanno at my side and a yard of steel in my hand, we would be more than a match for them. There would be no shameful running away this time, I told myself.

*　　*　　*

192

Bidding a fond farewell to the abbots by the barbican gate at the north-western corner of Ochsenfurt, Hanno and I shouldered our back-sacks and were soon trudging down the road beside the Main towards the Tuckelhausen wharf where we had left *The Crow* two days earlier. I have to admit that I was exhausted after two sleepless nights and the dramatic events that had occurred since we moored at the rickety monastery wharf. But I was buoyed by our success. What a tale I would have to tell Perkin! We had completed our mission; we had found the King and made his life a little safer and his person a little more comfortable – for the moment. Soon all Europe would know of his whereabouts; he had been brought out into the light, and the risk of murky, dishonourable, hole-and-corner dealings between his enemies was diminished. Despite my tiredness I was happy; warmed by the glow of our victory and looking forward to telling Perkin all about my adventures, singing with the King and fighting the two assassins – no doubt he would be suitably impressed – and then I would curl up in the stern cabin under a blanket and sleep the sleep of the just while Adam and he crewed the big black sailing barge downstream towards home.

It was Hanno's sharp eye that noticed it first: a wisp of grey smoke against a grey cloudy sky, just a tendril. When he drew my attention to it, I muttered something about a local peasant's campfire, my mind split between happy thoughts of returning home and the need, given my exhausted state, to concentrate on putting one foot ahead of the other. But as we approached, the wisp of smoke thickened, fattened and grew darker until we both knew we were looking at a disaster. Hanno and I broke into a run at the same time, sprinting up the road towards the wharf as fast as we could under the weight of the heavy back-sacks. The column of smoke turned black and evil, twisting up into the sky like a fat snake, dark as sin and speckled with bright flecks of orange sparks that danced upward in the roiling stream.

We rounded a bend and blundered straight into the scene of a catastrophe: *The Crow* was blazing from stern to bow, its cargo of hardwood timber the perfect fodder for a holocaust. The heat from the flames was ferocious, and we could not approach closer than a dozen yards to the burning craft. But I could make out the body of a man through the smoke and flames, pierced many times, lying in a pool of sizzling blood at the prow of the barge, his blond hair frizzling, curling and blackening in the heat, and I could smell the pork-like stench of his roasting flesh. It was Adam. His face was turned towards me and his blue seafarer's eyes stared into nothingness. I crossed myself and began to mutter the *Ave Maria* over and over to myself under my breath – for Adam's dead body was not the worst sight that polluted our gaze on that cursed morning: on the wooden jetty, before the roaring boat, was a far worse sight.

Through the eddies of choking smoke, I could see the arms, legs and torso of a young man, and a yard or so away was his head: a snub-nosed, red-haired head. It had not been severed by a blade; from the neck protruded strands of tissue, ligament, veins, and a sharp dagger spike of white broken bone, while the skin of the neck was stretched and floppy. Perkin's head had been ripped off by immensely powerful hands, much as one might decapitate a chicken. I felt the gorge rise in my throat, but fought back the urge to vomit. Rage consumed me: I was in no doubt as to who had done this.

Hanno, who had been questing around the beaten ground

beyond the gusting veil of smoke, soon confirmed my opinion. 'It is them,' he said simply. And he indicated two sets of footprints: one set long and thin, the other huge and round, like the paw print of an enormous beast.

I pictured the two assassins as I had first set eyes on them by the light of Ralph Murdac's fire, and found I was almost crying with fury at what they had done to my friends. My sword was in my hand and I felt an almost overpowering urge to kill, to hack and maim – to bring my blade against these two monsters in the name of justice.

'They are not long gone,' said Hanno. He was looking at me with searching, furious eyes. 'We must catch them. Come, Alan, I can track them. They are not so far ahead of us. Come, let us go after them now.'

And I wanted nothing more than to do just that. God above knows how much it would have pleased me to strip off my back-sack, toss it down, and run these foul, misshapen creatures to earth so that I could hack them into gobbets. What I did next was one of the hardest things I have ever had to do in my life.

'No, Hanno,' I said. And I found I was breathing hard, almost panting. 'No,' I said again through gritted teeth. 'We must see that these letters are delivered. If we were to catch them – as I earnestly pray to God and all the saints that I may do some day – one of us might be injured and that would lessen our chances of successfully carrying these precious messages back to England.'

Hanno looked at me, dumbfounded. Then he slowly nodded his round shaven head. 'It is your duty, no?'

'Yes,' I sighed. 'It is my duty. But I swear now, before you, my friend, that I shall have vengeance on these creatures before I see Heaven. I swear it on the name of the Virgin, and I call upon St Michael, the warrior's saint, to witness my vow. You have heard me, they have heard me, and now we must get away from here as swiftly as we are able. We need a boat. Any kind of boat will do.'

For the second time in a matter of days, I was running from an encounter with these two murderous bastards. In the name of duty to my King, I was sacrificing my personal honour. But I felt slightly better for my vow of vengeance; not entirely comfortable, but calmer. There would be a reckoning one day: I was certain of it. And on that day I would carve them both into bloody lumps.

But in the meantime what we needed, what I prayed for, was a boat . . .

And it seemed that God had been listening to my prayers, for within the hour – while I knelt by Perkin, straightening his dead limbs and placing his poor head as close to his neck as possible, my eyes burning from the smoke and barely able to breathe – Hanno reported that not ten yards from the smoke- and blood-stained jetty he had found a craft hidden in the reeds: a battered skiff just big enough to hold two heavily laden men.

'It must belong to the white monk who tends this wharf,' said Hanno. My friend's words prompted another question: Where was the surly Premonstratensian canon?

We found him soon after, seated behind the hut that he used for shelter, an extra mouth gaping below his chin: his throat had been cut from ear to ear. I gazed at the man's body, the front of his white habit sodden and scarlet with his blood, and a terrible weariness came over me. I had seen so much death, too much. Would there ever be an end to Man's evil? Why did God allow his servants to be slaughtered like this by men who were clearly spawned by the Devil? I could find no answers. All I could do was repeat my vow to St Michael that I would take red vengeance for these foul acts before too long.

Leaving the dead where they lay, trusting that the monks of Tuckelhausen would bury them and say a Mass for their souls, Hanno and I clambered into the skiff. Setting our leather back-sacks in the middle of the vessel, and taking up two paddles that we found in the bilges, we set off downstream, rowing slowly and steadily, and letting the slow current do most of the work.

I passed the remainder of that day in a stupor, head wearily nodding on my breast as my muscles automatically worked the paddle, though my cracked ribs sent pain stabbing down my left side with each stroke. But with God's help, and Hanno's unflagging work, we reached Würzburg that same evening. And while I was staggering with pain and exhaustion, Hanno arranged for us to occupy palliasses in the almshouse of the cathedral. I was asleep as soon as my head hit the thin, damp straw mattress.

For two days I slept, waking only occasionally to answer the calls of nature and to eat a little soup that Hanno brought to my palliasse. I was exhausted, worn thin in soul and body by the harrowing fall of events. And my ribs were hurting worse than ever. But while I was idle, Hanno was not. On the morning of the third day, he introduced me to a badly scarred, grinning rascal named Dolph who, for the princely sum of five shillings, was willing to take us in his trading galley all the way to Utrecht. It was an extortionate price for such a voyage, but I had the money – Queen Eleanor was paying, after all – and while the man looked to me like a pirate, Hanno, it seemed, trusted the fellow. I never did discover whether Dolph was truly a river pirate, but I did find that he was a man of his word. While I slept for most of the journey, nursing my aching ribs, Dolph took us quietly and efficiently down the rivers Main and Rhine, and seven days later, with a cheery nod and a hand clasp, he deposited Hanno and myself together with our precious back-sacks at the docks in Utrecht.

Three days later, I was standing in my salt-stained clothes in a private chamber of Westminster Palace, face to face with my King's venerable mother, Queen Eleanor of Aquitaine.

Chapter Eleven

The Queen looked as lovely as ever, dressed in a burgundy gown with pearls at her throat, and her auburn hair caught up in a golden net. But looking closer, I could see that her fine features were a little worn with care, and for the first time I could begin to see her true age in the lines on her still beautiful face. Her reception of me was far warmer than at our last meeting, and she rose from her high-backed chair to greet me, ordering a servant to bring wine and asking after my health in a most considerate manner.

I handed over the letters which were addressed to her – I had dispatched Hanno to deliver the rest – and stood patiently while she read them, sipping from a silver-chased wooden cup of wine and admiring the gold-embroidered tapestries on the walls of the chamber. The Queen was not alone, of course. Walter de Coutances, the Archbishop of Rouen and the Queen's most loyal counsellor, was in attendance, too. He seemed barely able to restrain his impatience while she read through the letters, almost snatching them from her fingers the moment she had finished reading them and devouring the contents the way a starving man wolfs down a plate of food.

'You have done very well, Alan,' said the Queen with a smile. 'And I am most grateful to you. We all are. Your service shall not be forgotten when this business is over.'

I was muttering something about not seeking any reward, that the honour of serving my King was ample reward in itself, when the archbishop rudely interrupted me.

'It seems that Boxley and Robertsbridge have the situation in hand. They say they will stick like glue to the King until we can arrange the ransom,' he said to the Queen, ignoring me completely. 'But it is going to be expensive, very expensive . . .'

'The Church in England must be made to play its part in raising the money,' said the Queen, fixing the archbishop with a meaningful look. 'I am thinking we must appropriate the gold and silver plate from every parish church in the land. And Boxley suggests that we take some of the Cistercians' wool crop, too – that will be worth a pretty penny.'

'Yes, that might be possible,' said Coutances. 'And the nobility must pay its share, too, but I fear that will not be enough.' He shook his head sadly. 'Some of the burden will have to fall on the common people. I'd urge a general tax of one quarter the value of all moveable property. We will need to collect the silver – there will be a vast quantity of it – at a central point. Here in the crypt in the Abbey, perhaps, or in London at St Paul's . . .'

Suddenly reminded of my presence, the Archbishop frowned at me. 'Perhaps, my lady, we might discuss this in private . . .' And he inclined his head in my direction.

200

'Alan, will you excuse us, please?' she said to me with a lovely smile.

Making my bow, I withdrew, leaving the old man and the Queen to their deliberations.

I had no desire to linger in Westminster. I had a horror of running into Marie-Anne, who I had heard had not followed Robin into the woodland exile of an outlaw, but had remained under the protection of Queen Eleanor in the safety and comfort of her court. After my betrayal of her beloved husband at the inquisition in Temple Church, I knew I could not face the accusatory look in her eyes should we meet.

I was happy, though, to be reunited with my grey gelding Ghost, who had put on an alarming amount of weight in the palace stables while I had been in Germany, and who had completely recovered from his bruised hoof. He was happy to see me, neighing and nodding with pleasure, when I brought him a special feed of warm mash that evening, and I took my time over brushing his coat, vowing that I would take him out for a long gallop the next day.

While I was fussing over my animal friend – I believe I was braiding his tail like a besotted stable hand – I heard a familiar voice calling me by name and wishing me God's peace, and turned to find myself facing a slim, fit-looking man of medium height, with cropped, iron-grey hair and muddy green eyes.

It was Sir Nicholas de Scras, an old friend and well-liked comrade from the Holy Land, who had tended me when I was sick with fever in Acre. But while his face was wonderfully familiar, there was one thing about Sir Nicholas that was different: his surcoat. When I had known him in Outremer, Sir Nicholas had been a Hospitaller, a member of a religious knightly order similar to the Templars, but concerned with healing the sick as well as fighting the infidel. Their surcoat was an austere black with a small white cross on the breast. The man who stood before me in the stable was sporting a dark-blue garment with three golden scallop shells on the front around a representation of a dolphin.

'Sir Nicholas,' I almost shouted, clasping his hand warmly. 'I am so pleased to see you! But what brings you to England? Have the Hospitallers abandoned the Holy Land to the heathen Saracens?'

'They have not, and God willing they never shall,' my old friend said, smiling back at me. 'No, it is I who have abandoned the Hospitallers.'

'How so?' I asked, amazed.

'It is a sad tale,' he said, his eyes crinkling with sudden unhappiness, 'and one that would be better told over a cup of wine. Will you join me? I know of a tavern that will suit our needs admirably. It is not far.'

And so I found myself once again at the table in the Blue Boar tavern where I had caroused with Bernard six weeks previously, sharing a flagon of the same green Rhenish wine with my old friend Sir Nicholas.

After some gossip about the Queen's court at Westminster, I urged Sir Nicholas to tell me how he had come to leave the Hospitallers. And so he began: 'I would not have left, had it not been for the death of my elder brother Anthony. He died in the autumn – fell from his horse; he cracked his pate, breathed his last three days later. It was a silly, pointless death, and not worthy of a fine man. But he is with God now, and so beyond the cares of this world.

202

'His poor wife, Mary, is left with two small sons. The eldest, William, will inherit our lands in Sussex, but he is a child, barely able to walk let alone administer an estate or defend his property during the coming years of blood and violence. And so, when news reached me of Anthony's death, I was left with a stark choice: return home to England to protect my brother's family or remain faithful to my Order.'

Sir Nicholas took a gulp of wine. It was clear that he was still not entirely reconciled with the choice he'd made.

'For seven days and nights, I prayed. I spent a week on my knees in the Church of the Holy Sepulchre in Jerusalem. Under the truce with Saladin last year, after King Richard departed Outremer, we Christians were permitted to visit the holy sites unmolested. So for a long week I asked God for guidance. Should I go home to defend my family's lands or remain with the Hospitallers? And through Heavenly Grace I was granted a sign.

'The silence of that holy place was suddenly broken by two boys, a Christian and a Muslim, who ran into the church shrieking and laughing at some game of their devising. In that moment, I knew that God was sending me a message. Those two happy children were not much older than my nephews, and, though they were of different faiths, born of enemies, during the truce when they were allowed to mingle, the boys had managed to find a fresh, innocent joy in each other's company. I knew then that God meant for me to make my own peace with the Saracens, leave the Holy Land and return to protect my brother's boys.'

He wiped away the suspicion of a tear, and I admit I felt like shedding a few myself, moved as I was by his tale.

'I went to see the Grand Master the next day to tell him of my decision, and of his mercy and doubtless because the truce meant that he had a lesser need for experienced fighting men, he agreed to release me from my vows. So, here I am, back in England for good. Tomorrow I must travel onwards to Sussex to take up my sword on behalf of my family. But I must tell you, Alan, it was not easy to turn my back on the Order. Even though I believe that God directed my actions, I cannot help but feel that, in some way, I have behaved shamefully.'

He fell silent, and for a few moments I said nothing. I could only wonder at the strength it must have taken for him to break his sacred vows, to give up his calling for the sake of two small boys who were not even his own. Once again Robin leapt into my mind; I recalled his sacrifice on behalf of another small boy who was not his son. There was something of Robin in Sir Nicholas, I mused: a ruthless fighting man, doubtless a fearsome killer of men, but with a streak of compassion, too, and a fierce sense of family duty.

'You said that bloody violence was coming to England,' I said, mainly to break the silence. 'What did you mean by that?'

Sir Nicholas had composed himself by now. 'Oh, this business between Richard and John. They are both sons of King Henry and both want the throne. And while Richard has it now, he is imprisoned in the wilds of Germany. Who knows when he will return? Meanwhile, John is gathering his power, calling barons and knights to his banner, recruiting fighting men . . . Even if Richard were to return soon, he would have an almighty battle on his hands. John has taken Tickhill Castle and Mount St Michael and Marlborough and Nottingham castles. It will not be an easy matter to dislodge him from these fortresses when – or even if – Richard returns. And for all we know, the King could already be dead.'

I longed to blurt out all I knew, to set his mind at ease on that score, but my mission to Ochsenfurt was supposed to remain secret for the moment and I could not allow myself to betray the Queen's confidence. Out of the corner of my eye, I saw a big man in the corner of the room. It was the boorish fellow Tom with whom I had fought the last time I had been drinking in this place. I stared over at him, a challenge in my eyes. But when he saw me looking at him, he hurriedly finished his tankard of ale and shambled out of the tavern without a backward glance. I put him out of my mind and concentrated on what Sir Nicholas de Scras was saying.

'. . . I miss Outremer,' he said, a low hum of emotion in his voice. 'I miss the certainty of the cause; of knowing that we were engaged in God's work, serving Him in everything we did. I had a place in the world, a purpose. Now, I don't know. Nothing is clear any more. I had friends there, good friends, but I know almost nobody at court now. And in Sussex . . . well, I left my brother's hearth a long time ago. It's a good twenty years since I was there. England is a foreign land to me now.'

I looked at Nicholas. The wine seemed to have made him a little maudlin.

'Do you remember Sir Richard at Lea?' he asked, his muddy green eyes clouding with sorrow.

I nodded, and took a frugal sip of my drink.

'I miss him. He might have been misguided enough to join the Templars, but he was a true Christian, a true friend. It was not a death worthy of a noble Christian knight, to be cut down like that, guarding some merchant's caravan. I'd like to get my hands on the men who killed him, would that I knew who they were. Bandits, just . . . fucking scum.'

I was surprised by his use of such earthy profanity. I could not imagine the Sir Nicholas I had known in Outremer, the holy warrior, the man dedicated to God, using such a term. And I did remember Sir Richard at Lea. He had been a good friend to me, too.

I also remembered Sir Richard's death, for I had been there, only yards away, when he died. I remembered the casually efficient way that Little John had cut the Templar knight's throat at Robin's command after Sir Richard had been captured. It was a source of pain to remember it. Shame, too. I had railed madly at Robin for ordering the death of such a good man. In fact, I had fallen out with my master badly over it and had even considered leaving his service as a result. The 'fucking scum' Nicholas was talking about were Robin's men; we had robbed the caravan purely so that Robin could make an unsubtle point to the wealthy frankincense merchants of Gaza, to convince them that they should deal exclusively with him.

Apparently, Sir Nicholas had no idea as to the identity of Richard at Lea's killers, and I was thankful for that. I prayed that he would never discover the truth.

'So, what will you do now?' I asked Sir Nicholas. He fixed me with his clouded green eyes, and said: 'Tomorrow I travel to Sussex, to Mary and the children. But I shall not remain there long.' He paused and looked down at the scarred tabletop. 'I have taken service with Prince John,' he mumbled.

'What?' I said, incredulous. 'What did you just say?'

He looked up and his gaze firmed. 'I have sworn allegiance to Prince John, the man who will undoubtedly be the next King of England!' He said it defiantly. 'I am no longer a Hospitaller, a warrior for Christ; I have a duty to defend my family, and

Prince John is the coming man. Richard may be king now, but he is king only in name. John will be on the throne before long. I have taken a side, the right side, the side that I believe will be victorious in the end. And by doing so, by supporting John, I believe I have guaranteed the safety of my brother's family.'

I hid my astonishment by taking a sip of the green German wine. This was treasonous talk. Sir Nicholas had always appeared to me to be a man of simple faith, a man who healed the sick and fought valiantly, selflessly, against the enemies of Christendom. I had never seen this pragmatic, political side of him. This English Sir Nicholas, in his blue-and-gold surcoat, talking of 'fucking scum' and admitting to high treason was a different creature entirely.

'It is on this subject that I wanted to talk to you tonight,' Sir Nicholas continued. 'Prince John will be generous to any fighting man who wishes to join his cause. And I was minded of this the moment I spotted you in the stables. You are an honest man, Alan. And you are an accomplished fighter: I saw you charge the Saracen right wing at the battle of Arsuf, and I was impressed. That was a bloody day! A good day! You should join with John now – it will make your fortune in the years to come.'

'But John is such a . . .' I began.

'Prince John is the man who will be king,' interrupted Sir Nicholas, staring hard into my eyes as if willing me to under-stand his actions, perhaps even to forgive them, and to make everything in his life right by following in his footsteps. 'Think about it,' he said. 'Just consider your position for a moment. I have heard it said that you betrayed your master at the inquis-ition in Temple Church. That it was your testimony that clinched his guilt. Is this true?'

I blushed with shame. 'It is true,' I muttered. This time it was I who could not meet his eyes.

'I do not blame you,' he said. 'I heard that you swore a mighty oath in the church before God and the Virgin to tell the truth and the whole truth. How could you do otherwise? No, I do not blame you – you have behaved as a good Christian must. And so, as I say, *I* do not blame you – but the outlawed Earl of Locksley surely will.

'And, from what I know of the Earl's reputation,' he went on, 'I am certain that he will try to take his vengeance upon you. He is not a man to allow one of his servants to betray him without striking back. He will seek to make a bloody example of you. Am I not right?'

'You have described him perfectly,' I said.

'And so, what will you do now? Go back to Westbury and oversee your tenants and collect your rents and wait for his vengeance to fall upon you? Or will you find new and more powerful friends? As I see it, you have no choice. You must go to Prince John at Nottingham and swear allegiance to him as soon as possible.'

I said nothing. His logic was flawless. Sir Nicholas waved to the tavern-keeper to bring another flagon of green wine. I realized then that the last one was empty, and he had drunk most of it.

'Come, Alan – Prince John is no monster. He is not such an evil man, merely a trifle high-handed, and for that you must blame his ancestry and his exalted birth. He is the son of a king, and will be a king himself. Believe me, he knows how to reward loyal service. You have never wronged him person-ally, have you?'

I shook my head. I had not. I had been humiliated by him once, but I had never struck back, solely because I had never had the opportunity. I doubted that he would even remember my name.

'Go to him, kneel before him,' urged Sir Nicholas. 'Humble yourself before the next King of England and you will be safe from the Earl's wrath. More than that, you will prosper and gain wealth and honour in this life.'

I could say nothing against his arguments.

'I will send word ahead that you are coming with my blessing. Now, tell me you will accept service with Prince John and I will smooth the path for you. You will receive a royal welcome. Come, man – say you will serve him. Tell me that you will!'

I looked up into his muddy eyes, now blazing with a verdant fervour that I had never seen in him before.

'I will,' I said.

As we left the tavern, I realized that I had taken too much wine, but I had not had nearly as much as Sir Nicholas. It was long past curfew and the streets were silent and deserted. After my reluctant acquiescence to his suggestion that I join Prince John, Nicholas had insisted that we drink a good deal more, and the talk had passed on to more congenial subjects. It was well past midnight when we staggered from the tavern and into the street outside, and while the sleepy tavern-keeper locked and barred the door behind us, complaining about customers who kept him from his warm bed, Nicholas muttered something about relieving himself and wandered around the corner, where he began to piss like a war horse.

I stared up at the starry sky and the bright full moon that hung like a fresh cheese above the rooftops. I hummed a little music to myself while I waited for Sir Nicholas to finish his business; my head was light but I was enjoying the feel of the cool air on my face. A beautiful night . . .

And I became aware that I was not alone. I could see perhaps a dozen figures, moving purposefully out of the gloom from the far side of the street, twenty yards away, grey shapes against the blackness, and the cold wink of steel blades in the moonlight.

As fortune would have it, though I had no more protection for my body than a tunic and short cloak, I was wearing my sword. In one smooth movement I drew my weapon and prepared to sell my life as dearly as possible. *At these odds*, I just had time to think, *I am a dead man.*

A snake of ice slithered in my belly and I realized that I was afraid. The dark mob were now advancing swiftly. They came at me without a sound, spreading out into a semi-circle to envelop me, surround me and cut me down, but I was already moving to the left, keeping my back to the wall of the tavern and forcing the oncoming men to crowd each other and change the shape of their attack. I counted eleven of them and then gave up, but I could see that they were far too many to fight one man with any efficiency – but who needed efficiency? Even if I managed to down three or four of them, they had no lack of men to take their places.

In the middle of the crowd, clearly visible in the light from the full moon, I could make out the looming form of Tom, the man I had fought on my last visit to this God-cursed drinking den. He had evidently neither forgotten nor forgiven our bout. No words were spoken, and none needed to be said. It was clear

Tom wanted revenge for the thrashing I'd handed him – and this time he'd brought a sword and all his friends to the party.

I took a pace forward and took up the high guard position, my long blade held in my right hand vertically, the hilt in front of my face, the point lancing towards the star-speckled sky; I had the misericorde held low and to the side in my left hand. Then I waited for their attack.

It was Tom who began this deadly dance, with a mighty over-hand hack at my head; this served as the signal for all his confederates to pile in. I blocked Tom's cut with a semi-circular sweep of my sword, knocking his blade down and away, and I would have followed on with a hard thrust from the misericorde, but a man to my left swung an axe at my legs and I had to jump to save my ankles – and from then on it was sheer bloody mayhem. Blades were slicing, cutting, spearing at me from three sides, and I was moving as fast as I could, blocking, dodging, parrying, striking out wildly just to stay alive. I took a knife cut to my unprotected ribs, on the cracked left side, but managed to drop one man with a dagger-punch to the belly, and, as he wheeled away screaming, I took the hand of another man, hacking it clean off at the wrist with my sword. But I was deeply in trouble – and I knew it.

A blade probed out of nowhere and burned along my jaw before I could block it, and I wondered how much longer I could keep the mob at bay. My face was bloody and my side torn, and I could see the rest of my life as being measured in less time than it takes a leaf to fall. At that moment, as I ducked a swinging sword, I caught a glimpse of a snarling face above a dark surcoat and a whirling silver blade: Sir Nicholas was charging into the fray from my right.

My friend made no sound but for the wet smack of his sword

chopping a way into the throng of men around me. His first strike lopped a man's head off, and then he was carving his way towards me leaving screaming mutilated men in his wake. Slice, lunge, sweep, parry, lunge. It was an awesome sight, and a part of me just wanted to stand and admire the former Hospitaller's formidable battle skills as he hacked with pitiless efficiency through the mob. He dispatched one assailant with a dancer's grace, thrusting his sword through the man's belly, immediately pulling out the blade and cutting the legs from beneath another. Somehow I came out of my reverie in time to block a savage sword swipe from big Tom. But this time I managed to slam the point of the misericorde into his upper thigh, following up with a lateral sword chop to his waist that dropped him to the ground – and then they were all running. Well, those who were able to run. Half a dozen bodies littered the mud- and blood-churned street, including the groaning form of Tom, who was trying to rise on his injured leg.

Sir Nicholas rested the point of his sword on the ground and leaned on it for a moment. His breathing was deep and unhurried. I stepped to where Tom knelt and kicked him over on to his back. Booting his weapon out of reach, I put my knee and my full weight on his chest, and the point of the misericorde under his chin. 'Who sent you?' I demanded, hot blood running down my jaw and dripping on to his dirty upturned face. 'Who ordered you to kill me?'

'God damn you!' he said, glaring at me with huge, pain-filled eyes, and spat at me. As I leaned back to wipe the gob of spittle from my cheek, a sword tip out of nowhere speared down past my chest, and sliced into his neck, cutting the artery there and spraying me with gore. Tom clutched at his red, wet neck with both hands, and in the few moments it took me to pull back out of reach of the spatter and sheathe my miseri-corde, he fell still – silenced for ever.

I turned and looked up the length of the blade at Sir Nicholas, a question in my eyes.

'That was for his insolence,' said my knightly friend. 'He spat upon you, he defiled you – and I could never allow a churl such as this to show disrespect to a man who fought so well for Christendom.'

I said nothing for a moment, for my emotions were mixed. I was disappointed that we would not now be able to get any information from Tom, and yet I owed my life to this slight, deadly man standing above me. Had he not come to my rescue, I would be as dead as the big man now lying before me in a lake of his own precious life fluid. So I rose painfully to my feet, mopped the running blood from my face with my sleeve, and thanked Sir Nicholas from the bottom of my heart for coming to my aid.

'It was nothing, my friend,' he said. 'If I had not drunk so much wine, I would have been faster. Are you hurt?'

My wounds, thankfully, were not serious. The cut in my left side, slicing straight through the big purple-yellow bruise from where the ogre had kicked me, was shallow and only three inches long. Hanno would stitch it for me in the morning. Sir Nicholas, having studied my jawbone, told me I needn't worry about the copious bleeding. Then he slapped me on the back and said that I would have a fine scar to remember the fight by. In truth, I have always been watched over by God and the saints in battle – either that or you could say that I had the Devil's own luck.

And so Sir Nicholas and I, leaving seven dead bodies lying in the street for the local watchmen to find and bury, or the wandering street pigs to eat – I cared not – walked back to Westminster Hall to seek out our pallets.

At noon the next day Hanno and I set off towards Nottingham and Prince John. We had travelled only as far as Charing when we saw a horse-borne party trotting towards us. As they drew closer, I saw with a sinking feeling that it was Marie-Anne, accompanied by another woman, a priest, and a dozen men-at-arms in Queen Eleanor's red-and-gold livery. The street was narrow at this point, so Hanno and I directed our horses over to the side to allow the party to pass. I said no words of greeting; indeed, I looked down at Ghost's grey neck hoping that I would not catch the eye of Robin's countess and only peeped at them out of the side of my eye.

I need not have worried. Marie-Anne, looking almost regal in her haughtiness, walked her horse past mine, head high, eyes looking straight ahead, without even giving me the merest glance. The woman riding beside her was Godifa, and I could not help but notice that she was looking spectacularly beautiful. Her hair beneath a simple pure white headdress shone like gold, her neck was long and slender and she held her chin high, which brought out the line of her jaw and elegant cheek-bones. She did not vouchsafe me the slightest look either. But the priest – it was Tuck, of course – hauled back on the reins as he came close, halting his mount and hailing me cheerfully. The men-at-arms riding behind him were forced to steer their mounts around the stationary priest in order to keep up with their female charges.

'Alan,' Tuck yelled, although we were only a few yards apart. 'Well met. You are back from the German lands, I see. And I hear your mission was successful. Well done! You have served the King well. But what has happened to your face?'

I lifted a hand to the freshly sewn cut on my jaw and was about to answer my old friend when I was interrupted by the Countess of Locksley. She did not speak to me, but rather called back over the rump of her horse to her confessor.

'Father Tuck,' she said, in a high imperious voice, 'do not dawdle and pass the time of day with street scum and traitors. You will attend to me. Come up here, ride next to me this instant.'

Tuck shrugged, half-smiled an apology, his round face screwed up with unhappiness, but he did as he was ordered and spurred his horse to catch up with his mistress.

Hanno and I turned in our saddles to watch the party ride south towards Westminster. I was about to make some light remark to him when the right-hand lead horse peeled away from the cavalcade and a small figure began to gallop back towards us, her skirts flying in the wind. When she drew level with us, Goody hauled on her reins and brought her mount to a standstill, its legs pawing the air in front of Hanno and me. I noted that she had become an accomplished horsewoman since I had last seen her. When had I last spent any time with her? I thought to myself. Did I even really know her? Two red patches of rage coloured the soft, creamy skin of her cheeks as she brought her animal under control. And I could imagine, quite easily, that sparks were actually flying from her shining violet-blue eyes.

'I cannot believe that you have the nerve to show your face in this country,' she began, her voice low and crackling with anger, 'after what you have done to Robin, after all he has

215

done for you . . .' She swallowed a breath. 'You deceiving, back-stabbing, hateful man!'

'Goody,' I pleaded, 'if you will let me explain—'

'You can keep your explanations. I don't want to hear your lies – I don't ever want to see you again. And to think that once I felt . . .'

She was magnificent – utterly beautiful, ravishing. Flushed, sparkling, her anger was a rare and rich jewel. If I had not been the object of her wrath, I believe I might have savoured that moment for many a year. As it was, I could only feel my cheeks flushing bright red to match hers; and a trickle of fresh blood seeping from the cut on my face.

'Goody,' I tried once again. 'You don't understand; you cannot understand . . . when they asked me those questions in the church . . .'

'Don't you dare to speak to me! Don't you ever speak to me again. I hate you, I hate you!'

And, to my astonishment, she burst into tears, wheeled her horse and, spurring savagely, galloped back to join the Countess's cavalcade, which was by now more than a hundred yards away.

Hanno had found something fascinating on the nail of his index finger and he was giving it his full attention. For myself, I was in no mood to discuss being snubbed and scolded by a pair of highly strung women, so we mutely turned our horses' heads north towards the great Roman road and put as much distance as we could between us and the scene of my humiliation.

Chapter Twelve

Two days later, on a golden spring afternoon, with the sunlight glancing through the narrow windows, illuminating the swirls of smoke in the air and making mad and merry patterns on the rush-strewn floor, I stood before Prince John himself in the great hall that occupied the middle bailey of Nottingham Castle. The Prince was in a fine humour, feasting at one end of a long table laden with roast chickens and other dishes, laughing and jesting with a short companion seated to his right. Although the huge space of the great hall contained several dozen folk – knights, men-at-arms, priests, servants of all kinds – they were the only diners. I had been admitted to the hall by the Prince's chamberlain, and loudly announced, but I was left to stand there, with Hanno at my side, waiting at the end of the long wooden board to be noticed by the most powerful man in the country; the man who Sir Nicholas avowed would surely be the next King of England. Yet it was not Prince

John who drew my eye as I waited patiently; it was his small, dark companion who commanded my attention. He seemed to be enjoying the Prince's particular favour that afternoon, talking intimately with his royal master, making half-heard jests and sharing the big silver platter of succulent roast fowl. It was the erstwhile Sheriff of Nottinghamshire himself: Sir Ralph Murdac.

I was glad to note that his crippled left shoulder was still wedged high, but otherwise Murdac seemed in good health, a little heavier than when I had last seen him and clearly prospering in the Prince's service. His familiar expensive black silk tunic was topped by a rich fur-lined mantle, though the weather was warm enough for this to be mere ostentation. His stubby fingers, smeared with chicken grease, now sported half a dozen chunky golden rings topped with fat, square-cut glinting jewels.

Riding through the town of Nottingham on our way to the castle had brought back evil memories of my younger days there as a starving cutpurse, and that bad feeling remained with me now that I was in the very heart of England's strongest fortress. I felt unnerved, unmanned: this castle had fearful memories for me. When I was a boy it had loomed over the town of Nottingham, a source of raw Norman power. From its gates mail-clad men on horseback had emerged to terrorize the population, collecting taxes, violating young maidens and summarily hanging anyone who opposed their will. In this very hall just three years ago, these two men had humiliated me, forcing me to sing for them when I was cold and wet and tired, and then tossing me pennies as if I was some starveling mountebank.

Feeling the stirrings of rage in my belly, I suppressed them almost immediately. For the weeks and months ahead I needed to be what Tuck would have called a 'cold-hot' man; that is, a man who keeps his rage hidden deep inside and only shows an icy indifference to the world. Robin was such a man, I remember Tuck telling me shortly after I joined the band of Sherwood outlaws in what seemed like another age. But like the shivering thief I had once been, I was hungry now, and even as I eyed Murdac's golden rings with a larcenous envy that I had not felt in years, my stomach growled, a long, low sound like a war hound giving warning that it was about to attack. The noise was loud enough to startle Ralph Murdac and his royal master from their crisp, golden chickens. And they simultaneously looked up at me.

'I beg your pardon, sire,' I said, spreading a servile grin across my lips.

The Prince must have known that Hanno and I were standing there, for we had been but ten paces from him for some while, but it had amused His Royal Highness to ignore us. My wayward stomach, it seemed, had forced him to acknowledge our presence.

'Ah, there you are,' said the Prince, suddenly all smiles and affability. 'It is young Alan of Westbury, if I am not mistaken; the famous *trouvère* and noted swordsman. And my servants tell me that you are the man we have to thank for locating my noble brother King Richard in his stinking German prison – you know, I had feared that he might be dead . . .'

As he said this, something flashed across his face, just for an instant, a look of – was it fear? Anger? Then it was gone and he was all bland smiles again.

'Well, don't stand on ceremony, my boy, come and join us.

219

Could you manage a little chicken?' The Prince clapped his hands and a servant appeared suddenly, as if by some mountebank's conjuring trick. 'A cup of wine and a stool for my young friend, and be quick about it,' he ordered in his harsh cracked voice.

So I sat down at the board with Prince John and Sir Ralph Murdac. It was a situation that I could never have conceived of five years ago. I could scarcely believe it now. I saw that Hanno was being led away by one of the servants – presumably he was to be fed in the kitchens or somewhere more suited to his lower rank. I helped myself to a small piece of chicken breast, and a hunk of fine-milled white bread.

'You know Sir Ralph Murdac, of course,' said Prince John, nodding at my mortal enemy, the man I most wanted to kill in the world, who sat on the other side of the table from me chewing a drumstick and regarding me down his nose with those icy blue eyes.

'Sir Ralph,' I said, managing a condescending smile, and nodding my head in a casual manner as if I regularly sat down to break bread with murdering little shit-weasels.

And then I spoilt it all. I caught a waft of Murdac's perfume, some foul lavender-based concoction and, as I always did when its odour raped my nostrils, I gave a mighty sneeze, a huge nasal trumpet blast, and then another. A chunk of half-chewed chicken shot out of my mouth and spattered the crisp white linen tablecloth.

'I see your base-born manners have not improved,' sneered Murdac. 'But then, blood will out, as they say . . .'

'Good God,' croaked the Prince, interrupting his friend. 'Are you sick, young Alan? You haven't caught some Oriental plague,

I trust, from your long sojourn in the Holy Land? Or some German ague? He-he-he!' He seemed to find this very funny and chortled to himself for several moments, the red ringlets of his shoulder-length hair dancing with his merriment. *Do not punch him in the face, Alan; do not do it*, I thought. *Be the cold-hot man. Be calm, or all is lost.*

'I am quite well, sire. It is perhaps a slight chill, that is all. I thank you for your royal concern.'

'Well, I won't keep you long, not if you've got a chill – or the dreaded plague. He-he-he! I understand that you wish to serve me – is this the truth?'

I merely nodded; I did not trust myself to speak.

'Well, you are in luck. Sir Nicholas de Scras, one of my finest knights, has personally recommended you. And that is good enough for me. We know whom you served before, and indeed *why* you are seeking a new lord, but I think the least said about that affair on St Polycarpus's Day the better. Don't you?'

'I don't trust him,' Murdac said bluntly. 'I think he is a spy sent by Locksley and he means to betray you.'

I stared hard at Sir Ralph, boring into his chilly blue eyes with my own angry brown ones. But I kept my mouth shut. The cold-hot man, that was me.

'Nonsense, Ralphie,' said Prince John. 'We were both there in the Temple Church when he betrayed his heretical master. We saw it with our own eyes; heard it with our own ears. And now that Locksley is loose, he will surely be coming for this fellow; very fond of vengeance is our Robert Odo. The boy's clearly desperate; masterless, damn near penniless – he's got nowhere else to turn.'

The Prince had dropped his shallow pretence of being a friendly, jolly companion; he was talking about me as if I were not even in the great hall, let alone seated two feet away from him.

'We'll watch him, of course. He has a well-earned reputation as a slippery fellow. Low-born fellow, too, I hear. But if he plays us false – well . . . we will deal with that if and when. I need fighting men, Ralphie. Besides, Nick de Scras vouches for him, and that's good enough for me.'

Prince John looked at me directly now, and his voice changed and became harsh once more. 'Let me speak plainly, Dale. I will give you the manors of Burford, Stroud and Edington. They lie in the West Country, not far apart from one another, and make up one knight's fee. I expect you to do me faithful service in return. If you betray me, if you even disobey me, you will lose the manors – and your head. Am I clear? Now, do you accept my offer and will you swear to serve me loyally?'

'I accept,' I said.

'Good,' said the Prince. 'I will have the charters drawn up and we will do the homage ceremony tomorrow at noon in the chapel. Now get out.'

I was on my feet before I knew it. 'I thank you, sire, from the bottom of my heart for this opportunity to serve you,' I said, bowing low. 'I am most grateful for your royal kindness.'

But the Prince had returned to his plate of greasy chicken and so I bowed once more, ignoring Sir Ralph completely, and reflecting, as I made my way out of the great hall, that I would have to get better at this royal boot-licking. After all, I might be required to do it on a daily basis.

The next day after a solemn Mass in the great chapel, during which I prayed even more fervently for my soul than usual, I knelt before Prince John, placed my hands between his, and swore a solemn oath before God. We then exchanged the kiss of peace and I ceremonially received three bulky parchment scrolls, hung with big green and black discs of sealing wax, which confirmed me as the lord of the plump West Country manors of Burford, Stroud and Edington. It would seem that I was going up in the world.

After the ceremony, my new master called his knights together to witness what he called an 'amusement'. A local freeman known as Wulfstan of Lenton had been accused of moving a marker stone, so as to encroach on some ploughland on one of Prince John's estates. In reality, I had been told by a castle servant, a Nottingham man whom I knew slightly from earlier days, Prince John's steward had moved the stone and Wulfstan had merely restored it to its original position. Normally, since good King Henry had reorganized the law, the case would have been tried by the defendant's peers, twelve good men and true from the surrounding area, but Wulfstan clearly did not believe that he would receive a fair trial in a court packed with Prince John's tenants and cronies. Thus, claiming that he was the great-grandson of Saxon thanes, and therefore had the right to bear arms, he demanded the old-fashioned wager of battle – to the death: a trial by combat.

He was a rather slack-witted man, as fair-haired as Goody and with a bushy beard obscuring his face, but he was as proud as Lucifer. And I cheered him, silently, deep in my heart, for preferring to fight than allow his ancestral lands to be encroached on by his powerful royal neighbour.

A square area about sixty foot on each side had been marked out with ropes in the outer bailey of the castle, inside the long wooden stockade that surrounded the entire fortification, but outside the stone walls of the castle itself. The stone core of Nottingham Castle was shaped like a swaddled baby, with a circular upper bailey at the south end – the baby's head – and a slightly bigger oval middle bailey – the baby's swaddled body – connected to it and lying directly to the north. Both upper and middle baileys were built on a massive sandstone outcrop, the highest landmark for miles around, and they were walled with granite and dotted with high square towers every fifty paces or so for extra strength. Between the upper and middle baileys, indeed connecting them at the baby's neck, loomed the great tower, a high square stone fortress that was the ultimate stronghold of the constables of Nottingham, the final place of refuge in a siege, if all went badly for the defenders. On the eastern and northern sides of the castle was a wide area known as the outer bailey, filled with tradesmen's shacks, animal pens, stables, workshops, cookhouses, a few guest halls, some storehouses and, next to a deep well, a large newly built brewhouse where the ale for the whole castle was made. The outer bailey was protected by a twenty-foot-high earth-and-timber stockade – the castle's first line of defence.

The area roped off for the list lay to the north and east of the stone-built part of the castle, and it was thronged by castle denizens and by people from the thriving market town outside the walls to the east – my old hunting ground in my days as a hungry cutpurse.

The crowd was packed three deep around all four sides of the list and already there was a hum of excitement at the coming contest. Each combatant was to be armed with a sword and shield, and I suspected that Wulfstan might have believed that he was actually going to fight Prince John himself. If that was true, he was in for a shock, for John had naturally delegated a champion to do his fighting for him. I confess, when I saw who the champion was, I had to suppress a start of unease myself. And the sight of his huge companion had me reaching instinctively for my sword hilt.

The man who would do battle with Wulfstan was the tall, thin swordsman who had attacked me outside the walls of Ochsenfurt. His ogrish companion stood guarding Wulfstan with one massive hand holding him casually by the back of the neck as if he were measuring it.

I nudged a knight next to me and, indicating the two grotesque assassins, asked, 'Who are those men?'

'Have you not yet had the pleasure of their acquaintance?' He smiled at me in a not altogether friendly way. 'The tall one is called Rix,' he continued. 'The quickest man with a sword you will ever see. His gigantic friend is Milo – and, as you can judge for yourself, he is barely a man at all.'

'They serve the Prince?' I asked, although I already knew the answer.

'They kill folk for him,' was the knight's terse reply. And he would say no more on the matter.

At a signal from Prince John, Milo released Wulfstan and gave him a little push so that he staggered into the centre of the roped-off square of packed earth. The freeman stood straight, rolled his shoulders, shook his arms to loosen the muscles and used a piece of leather thong to tie back his long thick blond hair. He was a man of about thirty, I guessed, of middle height, deep in the chest and strong from long days of labour in the fields. Wulfstan went over to the far corner of the list where a standard yard-long sword with a leather-wrapped wooden handle and a stout six-inch crosspiece had been propped next to a kite-shaped shield. These were weapons that were carried by any ordinary man-at-arms in England; indeed, their like could be seen slung on the backs and about the waists of about two dozen of the men who were crowded round the square field of battle at that very moment. I myself was carrying arms that were not dissimilar.

Then Rix entered the list, hopping over the rope on his long legs like a stork. He was dressed in a homespun tunic the colour of straw, belted at the waist, with his long sword hanging in a scabbard on his left side. He was bareheaded and his brown hair was cut short across the brow and shaved on the scalp at the back, high, from the neck up beyond his ears, in an old-fashioned style that would have suited a Norman of his great-grandfather's day, one of William the Bastard's men. His face, like his body, was long and lean, and he seemed entirely calm, like a man going about his daily business, rather than one about to engage in mortal combat to determine the Judgement of God.

Rix pulled the slung shield off his back and slid his left arm through the grips, and then he drew his sword. Once again I was struck by how beautiful the blade was: slightly slimmer than a normal weapon, and tapering gracefully to a razor point, the blade engraved with tiny golden letters along the fuller that ran down its centre. From where I stood, it was impossible to decipher their meaning. The magnificent blue sapphire, set into a thick ring of silver at the pommel, flashed as it caught the light on that bright spring day. It was a sword fit for a king, an Emperor even, and I wondered where he had obtained it. No doubt from some nobleman that he had slaughtered. I wanted it. I lusted after that sword; I desired it so much it was an ache in my heart.

But there was no time then for these covetous thoughts. At the crook of a finger from Prince John, who was seated in a high-backed chair in the middle of the northern side of the square and surrounded by his closest knights, Rix and Wulfstan came and stood before him, the blond Saxon eyeing his opponent with just a hint of trepidation. He was right to fear him, I thought. Standing in the eastern side of the square, I could see both men in profile, and I saw that Rix was a full head taller than his adversary, although with Rix's slimness I would have guessed that Wulfstan weighed a shade more. Both men made a solemn declaration that they had not eaten that day and that they had no hidden witch's enchantments or magical gewgaws about their bodies that would give them an unfair advantage in battle. Wulfstan then declared loudly that he was fighting to preserve his land, the land that had belonged to his father and his father's father before that, and he called on God Almighty, Jesus Christ, and all the saints to aid him in this matter and prove for once and all time that his cause was right.

Then they began.

Wulfstan wasted no time. He charged at Rix with a wild yell and began to batter at the taller man with a welter of hard blows, wildly swinging with his strong right arm, and battering his opponent with powerful cuts at his head and shoulders. Rix fended off the attack with ease, blocking with his sword and letting the blows slide off his shield, slowly retreating before the fury of his foe. Wulfstan, I could see, was not unused to the sword: someone had instilled the rudiments in him and he would have made a decent if not particularly skilful man-at-arms. I had trained worse men than him for Robin, and he had a passion, too, a rage in him that gave force to his sword cuts – he was fighting for his honour, for his family lands, and he knew in his heart that his cause was just.

But he was no match for Rix.

In the middle of a storm of blows from Wulfstan, the tall man's long blade lanced out over the top of Wulfstan's shield and plunged deep into the top of his opponent's left shoulder. It was like the strike of an adder: fast, precise, deadly. Blood spurted red from the wound and Wulfstan fell back with a cry of rage and pain. His shield sagged, his torn shoulder muscles unable to support its weight. Then Rix struck again, once more on his opponent's left side, the shield side, his sword flickering out almost delicately to carve a bloody furrow in Wulfstan's cheekbone.

The blond farmer charged once more, red droplets flying from his face into the clear air; a howling surge of fury and desperation and blurring, hacking sword, but Rix merely blocked, dodged, ducked a blow, stepped forward and back-swung gracefully, chopping into the meat of his opponent's bare right forearm. Wulfstan screamed and staggered back. He could barely hold up his shield with his left, and his sword arm now had a chunk of purple flesh flapping from it. He could no longer either attack his foe or properly defend himself and it was only a matter of time before blood loss pulled him down. He was a dead man – and he knew it. Every man watching knew it too.

A more merciful opponent would have finished him then, but Rix seemed to have no compassion in his lanky black soul. The next few minutes were excruciating, as Rix circled Wulfstan inflicting minor cut after minor cut. He slashed at his calves and drew a spray of blood, sliced into his side, into his right thigh, and carved a furrow on the right side of his face to match the one on the left side, this time taking the eye along with it. He was slowly cutting his opponent apart. Very slowly chopping the life from him.

The crowd had been cheering the display, whooping and applauding the first blood, but gradually the noise died away to a few scattered shouts as Rix played with Wulfstan as a cat plays with a wounded mouse. The Saxon could no longer protect himself, staggering about the square, weak with loss of blood, sword and shield held in drooping blood-slicked hands, and all the while Rix danced in and struck, each time leaving the man weaker and more gory, but disdaining to make the killing blow.

My stomach was sickened by this display. I have seen much of battle and death but this slow draining of a man's courage and life force, mocking his pain and making sport with his pride, was too much for me. I looked over at Prince John, hoping that he would stop this cruel exhibition, but he sat there grinning, pointing and clearly sharing a joke with Sir Ralph Murdac, who was standing at his side.

The Saxon was by now on his knees in the centre of the list; he had dropped both sword and shield and he knelt there passively, head hanging low, beard dripping blood, as Rix took two steps in and sliced off an ear. Wulfstan made a low bellowing noise of pain and frustration but he barely moved except to rock to one side when the ear was lopped. He merely waited like a bullock for the release of death.

I had had enough.

I stepped over the ropes, and drew my sword.

'Hey! You there, Rix, or whatever your name is. He is finished. Let him be,' I said, striding into the centre of the square with my sword in hand.

It was an idiotic thing to do, and went against all the plans and stratagems that I had so carefully made. And, given his prowess with a sword, it was quite possibly suicidal, too. But I could not stand there and watch him torture a brave warrior any longer. So much for my being a cold-hot man.

Rix turned to face me, his beautiful blood-washed sword in hand. His smile broadened. 'You have a proper weapon this time, boy, I see,' he said in good French. 'Not some child's musical toy.'

Although he had insulted my much loved and very much missed vielle, I was pleased to note that he still bore the circular red mark from its strings around his neck. I lifted my blade and saluted him. 'This time I do – and it is this weapon that will cut short your miserable life, you soulless, night-skulking man-butcher.'

'No,' shouted a harsh voice. 'No, I will not have it! I will not have my men brawling with each other over a trivial matter such as this.' Prince John had seen fit to take part in the dispute. 'You sir, Dale – you will not interfere with my justice. This very morning you swore an oath to be my faithful vassal – have you proved to be an oath-breaker so soon? I command you to withdraw from the list. Now. And you, Rix: that is enough. You have done well, but you are dismissed. Let Milo deal with him.'

230

Rix shot me a malevolent glare. 'We will try this matter another time,' he said before wiping the gorgeous sword carelessly on his yellow tunic hem, sheathing it, turning his back on me, walking away and stepping long-legged over the rope to disappear into the crowd.

'You're damned right we will, you murdering bastard,' I muttered, sheathing my own weapon. I walked back to the ropes, but I could not help myself from turning as I reached them. As I watched, the giant form of Milo padded over to the kneeling, blood-drenched Wulfstan, and with one seemingly effortless wrench of his meaty hands quickly snapped the man's neck and sent him instantly to the next, and I most earnestly pray, better world.

Perhaps as a punishment for my unruly behaviour, Prince John decided that I should become a tax collector. With a shameless disregard for truth, decency and knightly honour that stole the very breath from my lungs, the Prince announced that he would take it upon himself to begin collecting the taxes to pay for King Richard's ransom. He gathered a score of knights in the main courtyard of the middle bailey and harangued us for an hour about the fate of his poor brother, kept in chains in Germany, and exhorted us to hear no excuses, listen to no lies, to search every croft and cot diligently, and spare no one in gathering funds for the enormous ransom that doubtless would soon be demanded for his dear brother's release. The ransom silver, Prince John informed us with a perfectly straight face, would be kept safely here in Nottingham Castle, under his watchful eye, until the time was right to release our beloved sovereign. This drew one or two sniggers from the assembled knights, but their merriment was quickly quelled by Sir Ralph Murdac's cold blue eye searching for culprits in the throng. He stood beside his master like a faithful hound, in his shadow, shoulder wedged up high, and surveyed the crowd of fighting men in the courtyard for signs of disloyalty. Naturally his eye alighted on me. I gave him a big, toothy grin. And a lascivious wink.

No one in that packed bailey believed for a heartbeat that Prince John had any intention of handing over the silver once it was collected. And that was fine; we were all his loyal men, and we would all share in his future good fortune, if, Heaven forbid, something fatal were to befall good King Richard.

And so I became a tax collector, which was, I can heartily assure you, one of the most distasteful labours that I have ever undertaken.

A few days later, we cantered out of Nottingham: myself, a big sergeant and six mounted men-at-arms and a rat-like priest called Stephen. I had dispatched Hanno on some errand the day before and did not expect him back for several days. Father Stephen carried the parchment rolls in his saddlebags; the long lists therein recorded the wealth of every single hovel, cottage, farmstead and church in the manor of Mansfield, the area we had been assigned to gather revenue from that day. Other parties of knights and men-at-arms had been dispatched to various manors, towns, districts and villages for the same purpose, and there had been much discussion and some complaints when the assignments had been handed out by Sir Ralph Murdac. Some men had demanded larger areas, others had whined that the manors in their allotted sector were too poor to be worth much. It was clear that many of the knights who had flocked to Prince John's banner were privately reckoning how much they could squeeze from the places they were taxing, and just how much they could get away with keeping for themselves. To swear allegiance to Prince John, I realized with a sinking heart, was to receive a licence to plunder.

England had made itself especially beautiful on that April morning as I rode north through Sherwood at the head of the column of eight men. The sun smiled down on us in a kindly manner, the sky was a deep untarnished azure, bright new green leaves rustled in the slight breeze, bluebells carpeted the shady ground beneath the tall trees, jays swooped among the branches and wood pigeons carolled sweetly to us as we passed. I glimpsed a hump-backed boar through the thick forest undergrowth, rooting for last year's acorns; and a slender fallow deer, just standing and staring at us with its enormous eyes, and I was instantly transported to happier days, hunting with Robin and his outlawed men in these parts; days full of ale and laughter and comradeship and the excitement of the chase.

As we rode through villages, scattering piglets, chickens and geese before the hooves of our horses, I could see the peasants planting onions and leeks in the little plots of land outside their cottages, and peas and beans in the big communal fields outside the village. These were the men and women who worked, who supported the whole kingdom on their sturdy backs. My family had once been like them, and though I had risen to become a fighting man, I always reserved a loyalty for them, and a respect for their endurance and quiet courage. I knew these good people, I had grown up around them, as one of them. These were the folk whose sweat and toil would create the silver that one day, I prayed, would bring King Richard safely home.

We stopped at noon at an alehouse, and while my men ate bread and cheese and sucked down the local ale at a rough table in the sunshine outside the house, I spoke to them about our mission, and told them what I expected from them when we reached the manor of Mansfield.

'We are not going there to loot,' I said sternly to a gathering of big, violent men in iron-ringed coats with sharp swords strapped to their waists. 'We are not going there to steal. We are going there to collect the rightful taxes that are due, and not a penny more.'

There was some grumbling and muttering at this. I waited patiently for silence and then continued:

'Most especially we are not going to rape, or abuse, or kill anyone. Do I make myself clear?'

'Begging your pardon, sir, but what is to be our share of the take?' asked the sergeant, a fat man, grey at the temples and scarred from battle.

'We do not share in what you call "the take". Do you not receive a daily wage of two pennies from Prince John, a recompense for service to your lord? That is your share of the take. That is the money you are being paid to perform this labour. I want you all to understand this. Every coin that we raise will go to Nottingham. Father Stephen has the amounts that we are to collect listed on his rolls; we will collect them, with firmness and fairness, and deliver every penny to the account-keepers in the castle.'

There was an outbreak of tumult, angry men hammering pewter mugs on the tabletop and shouting at me. I had not made any new friends with my little speech. The priest, our lettered clerk, looked at me with his darting, rodent eyes; then he looked away quickly. I would find no support there.

'So what do you get out of this, eh?' said the sergeant. He was red in the face and waving his finger underneath my nose. 'Kindly tell me – and the lads here – what *your* share will be. More than the few extra pennies we might have scraped up, I'll be bound.'

I grabbed his finger in my left hand and his wrist in my right, and twisted, bending the digit back against the joint. He gave a high-pitched animal scream of pain that shocked the noisy table into silence. I leaned into him so that our faces were only inches apart.

'When you address me, Sergeant, you call me "sir". Do you understand?'

'Yes,' he said, and I could see that his fat face was greasy with pain-sweat.

'Yes what?' I demanded, and gave his finger joint a sharp twist. He howled again but managed to squeal: 'Yes, sir! Yes, sir!'

'Not a penny of this tax money will stick to my fingers – nor to yours. Is that understood?'

'Yes, sir.'

'Fine,' I said, and released him. 'Now, all of you, get mounted. This respite is over; we're riding out.'

The mood in our little cavalcade after that was as sour as a bucket of week-old milk that someone has pissed in. I rode at the head of the column, with the sergeant riding immediately behind me, nursing his twisted finger and shooting me looks of molten hatred. I suspected that I was the least popular captain in England that afternoon – but I did not care. I did not believe they would try to murder me, and risk incurring the wrath of Prince John. And if they did not like me, well, I could live with that. The most worrying thing was that I could hear the echoes of Robin's voice in my ear saying, *Interesting – once again you turn to violence, Alan; inflicting pain to impose your will. I'll make a real man of you yet!*

I began to sing loudly to myself as I rode, chiefly to drive the sound of Robin's laughter from my head.

Chapter Thirteen

Our first stop that afternoon was at a church serving a tiny hamlet about three miles south of Mansfield. The old priest protested when I sent in the men-at-arms to strip the altar of a pair of golden candlesticks and a wide silver plate, but he desisted when Father Stephen informed him that we were collecting for the ransom of the King. Whether he believed us or not, he was not foolish enough to question eight armed men.

One of the soldiers suggested that we might take a burning torch to the soles of the old priest's feet to see if he had any more silver hidden away but, with a sigh, I said no and explained again the rules of our mission that day. No robbery, no abuse, no rape, no murder. The message finally seemed to sink in then, and we were in and out of the church in less than half an hour, having taken everything of value that we could see.

Our next stop was the manor of Mansfield. It was a royal

manor, set in a bowl of countryside on the western edge of Sherwood Forest, much irrigated by rivers, and held by a mutton-headed steward called Geoffrey who had lost a foot fighting for Richard in France during the interminable wars between the Duke of Aquitaine and the late King Henry.

Geoffrey was happy to pay up the three shillings and eight pence that Father Stephen demanded of him and, as the day was drawing on, he offered us accommodation for the night to spare us the fifteen-mile ride back to Nottingham. We spent the rest of the afternoon collecting money from the village, which went without incident – except that one old woman claimed she had no coin and we were forced to accept a scrawny and ancient cockerel instead. Then we returned to the manor house and presented the bird to Geoffrey's cook, as recompense for our bed and board.

Geoffrey provided the men with a small barrel of ale, several loaves of bread and a big pot of frumenty, a cracked-wheat porridge flavoured with cabbage, leeks and chervil, and allowed them to take their ease in the stables. And while the men relaxed with a pair of dice and the remains of the ale, Father Stephen and I repaired to the hall to eat a tough chicken stew and drink wine with the steward.

The meal was served by a pretty girl of about fourteen years, I would have guessed, blonde and blue-eyed, like an angel. She reminded me a little of my lovely Goody in her looks, though she did not have Goody's alarming fire and passion. But she brought the food swiftly and served it neatly, and busied herself unobtrusively tidying up the table when we had eaten. I saw Father Stephen watching her movements with his dark little eyes and wondered how seriously he took his vows of chastity.

After the meal, I asked the steward for news of the area and he told me two things that were of much interest to me. Firstly, the notorious outlaw Robin Hood had been very active in the area in recent weeks, robbing churches and churchmen as they passed through Sherwood Forest. Robin had even attacked a large manor over towards Chesterfield that belonged to Sir Ralph Murdac, robbed it, driven off the livestock and burnt it to the ground. I reflected that my lord had not been idle while I was in Germany, and he had clearly not forgotten his code of vengeance: Murdac had burnt his castle at Kirkton, so Robin was paying him back in kind.

But, according to Geoffrey, the locals had worse to fear than the depredations of ruthless outlaws. Stories abounded of a black witch, a hideous crone with strange demonic powers, who had been seen by a number of people as far afield as Derby and Sheffield. It was said that she could turn a man to stone with one look from her terrible eyes; that she could curse a pregnant woman's unborn child; and that the Devil visited her every night and they fornicated in a foul and unnatural manner beneath the stars, the witch crying aloud in her ecstasy in a Satanic tongue. Father Stephen crossed himself hurriedly, and the steward followed his example as he ended his tale. Clearly the Hag of Hallamshire had not been idle either while I was away. I recalled Elise's words to me in the winter, when she passed on the warning from the wise woman Brigid, and felt an unfamiliar prickle of unease at the base of my spine. I crossed myself, too.

Just then, a long, loud wailing cry shattered the night, and I jumped to my feet. It was the cry of a woman in torment and it was coming from the courtyard just outside the hall. I clutched at my sword hilt, and while Father Stephen fell to his knees, hands clasped in prayer and gibbering in terror, the steward grabbed a lantern and he and I made our way out of the hall, across the courtyard and over to the stable.

Inside the stable, my eyes were met by a most disgusting sight. By the dim light of the lantern, I could see a pair of round hairy buttocks pumping away like a pair of blacksmith's bellows on top of the little blonde girl who had served our dinner. The culprit was one of the men-at-arms under my command, and he was clearly raping the poor girl on a large mound of hay. Once again she gave that long wailing cry, clutching at his back and bucking her hips – no doubt trying to heave him off her frail young body.

I took a step forward and grabbed the man by the scruff of his tunic, and hauled him off the girl – kicking him sharply in the face to subdue him while I drew my sword and put the point to his neck.

'You will hang for this,' I grated. 'I warned you twice and now you will see that I was not jesting. No man under my command will be excused rape or any other crime.'

The man was huge-eyed with shock and surprise; I could see in the thatch of hair at his crotch his manhood shrivelling fast. He mouthed something at me but no words came out. Behind me I could hear the rest of the men-at-arms stirring. I turned my head and saw the fat sergeant coming forward from the depths of the stable, rubbing the sleep from his eyes.

'Fetch a rope,' I told him. 'We are going to hang this son of a bitch right now.'

Behind me I heard the blonde girl cry out: 'No, please, sir . . .'

'But sir,' said the sergeant, coming round to stand by his comrade, who had still not uttered a word in his own defence. 'He didn't rape her. She was willing, right willing, only she's a noisy lass, sir, as all will agree. I'm sorry if you have been disturbed.'

My sword point was still at the half-naked man's neck, but I turned my head to look at the serving girl. The steward Geoffrey had found a blanket to cover her nakedness, and her eyes were wide and stained with tears. 'Did this man rape you?' I asked her, trying to sound as kindly as I could in the circumstances.

She shook her head. 'No, sir, it wasn't like that. Alfie and I was just . . . just fooling around, you might say.'

I put up my sword, and stepped away from the half-naked man-at-arms on the stable floor, feeling like the biggest fool in Christendom. 'Ah, well, I see . . .' My cheeks were growing hot, and I could think of no dignified way of ending this encounter. 'Well,' I said again, 'in that case, ah, carry on . . .'

And blushing like a fourteen-year-old milkmaid, I left the stable and its chortling inhabitants and fled back to the safety of the hall.

Riding back to Nottingham the next day the mood among my men had changed from hatred to ridicule: it was not a pleasant journey for me, hearing fake amorous cries coming from the men-at-arms and stifled giggles for fifteen long, slow miles. Maybe I should have hanged the man after all. It would have saved me a deal of embarrassment. But we returned to the castle with saddlebags filled with silver and gold, after stopping at two more churches on the way back home. And when I delivered the loot to the clerk in charge of storing

241

Prince John's hoard in the bowels of the great tower, I received a compliment from the man for the amount of silver we had turned in. Prince John himself even gave me a friendly nod that evening in the hall when I was eating my supper. Clearly he was happy that I had brought home the bacon – for one of his other tax-gathering parties had not: apparently while passing through Sherwood Forest they had been robbed of every penny of their tax silver by a gang of hooded bowmen, led by a giant blond man wielding a double-headed axe.

It was my old comrade Sir Nicholas de Scras who told me the tale the next day. He was visiting Nottingham with messages for Prince John, and I confess I was very pleased to see a friendly face in that castle full of thugs and bullies.

'The timing was impeccable,' said Sir Nicholas as we shared a jug of ale and a bowl of earthy-tasting fish stew before a brazier in one of the guest halls in the middle bailey.

'Locksley's band of robbers waited until Prince John's men had finished completing their collection – and the tax men had done well, their saddlebags must have contained nearly five pounds in silver – before they struck. John's men were passing through a narrow defile near Hucknall when up jumped a score of archers who loosed a storm of arrows into the column of men. It was sheer bloody slaughter, by all accounts. Men and horses stuck like pin-cushions. Only two men escaped alive,' Sir Nicholas told me, 'and one of those is very near death. Prince John is furious. He actually began frothing a little at the mouth when he heard the news – just like his father used to do – and his chaplain and his household knights had to lead him away. This is no exaggeration, I swear; I saw it with my own eyes.'

He was still smiling quietly at his royal master's intemperate rage when Sir Ralph Murdac came striding over to our table. 'So this is where you've been skulking,' the little man said to me, with a curl of his red lip.

'Sir Ralph, how pleasant to see you again,' said Sir Nicholas, rising gracefully to his feet to greet him. 'Won't you join us? How is the good lady Eve, your delightful new wife? In the pink of health, I trust.'

Ralph Murdac ignored him, he was staring at me with fury in his eyes. 'You know where he is, don't you?'

'I beg your pardon: where who is?'

'Don't play with me, you dirty fucking peasant. You know where he is, don't you? The God-damned Earl of Locksley – you were part of his foul gang of thieves not so long ago, as I recall, and even if you have been cast out as a traitor from their maggoty band of cut-throats I am certain you must know where to find them.'

'I have no idea where the Earl is at this moment. I have neither seen nor spoken to him since the inquisition at Temple Church. He is a desperate man on the run, an outlaw, and I cannot tell you where he might be. I can, however, tell you this: if you ever call me a "dirty fucking peasant" again, I will cut off that shrivelled lump of cheesy gristle that hangs between your legs and feed it to you. Do you hear me, Murdac?'

I had leapt to my feet and half-drawn my sword, and Murdac's hand was reaching for the dagger at his waist, when Sir Nicholas took up position directly between us. 'Hold hard there, my friends,' he said soothingly. 'Be at peace. There is no need for hasty words. Of course, Alan doesn't know where Locksley is, Sir Ralph. Nobody does but his fellow outlaws.

And there is no need for language of that sort – either of you. Let us sit down and have a quiet drink and all can be resolved.'

Sir Ralph said nothing; he merely turned on his heel and walked away: left shoulder high, his stride long and infused with frustrated fury.

'He really is an ill-mannered lout,' said Sir Nicholas when the former Sheriff of Nottinghamshire was out of earshot. 'Very loyal to the Prince, I've been told. But not one of nature's charmers.'

I shrugged and said nothing. I was thinking about the day when I would be free to kill Sir Ralph Murdac. As far as I was concerned, it could not come soon enough.

'So you don't know where he is, by the by?' asked Sir Nicholas in a kindly voice. 'It would make things so much easier all round.'

'I'm afraid not,' I replied. And it was true. 'When I was with him, Robin had more than a dozen hide-outs, scattered all over the countryside in Nottinghamshire, Derbyshire and Yorkshire. Doubtless he's acquired a few more since then. He has many friends in Sherwood. He could be almost anywhere; even in Nottingham town itself. I have no idea.'

'And if you did know where Robin was,' Sir Nicholas said slowly, but still in his kindest, most reasonable tone, 'you would tell us, wouldn't you? I mean, sometimes – well, we all feel the pull of old loyalties. But the past is the past, and it's best to be honest in these matters. Some people feel that you might have mixed emotions about serving our Prince John . . .'

'I don't know where Robin is.' I looked directly into Sir Nicholas de Scras's muddy green eyes. And I said slowly and clearly: 'I swear by Our Lady Mary, the Mother of Jesus Christ, that I do not know where Robert of Locksley is hiding. Do you not believe me?'

'Of course, I believe you. But it's best to be sure. Now, have I told you about Ralphie Murdac's new wife? Eve, her name is – daughter of Sir John de Grey – and she is absolutely enormous. Huge! As big as a house. She must weigh at least twice what he does. But then she does come with some hefty property: the manor of Standlake in Oxfordshire is hers, she had it from her father. And now, I suppose, Murdac holds it in her name. But you should see her, Alan. Enormous, I tell you!'

'My God,' I said, smiling at my friend, 'can you imagine little Ralphie Murdac climbing aboard this Mistress Eve! It must be like a field mouse coupling with a milk cow!'

And we laughed heartily, not quite meeting each other's eyes.

For the rest of that spring and into the summer of that tiresome year, I gathered taxes from the good people of Nottinghamshire, from the rich and the poor, from church and alehouse, from blacksmith and merchant, ostensibly to amass funds for King Richard's ransom – although few in Nottingham Castle mentioned our captive King during those warm months. Prince John did a great deal of travelling during this time, visiting his other castles in England at Tickhill, Lancaster and Marlborough and, some whispered, making secret trips to France, Normandy and the Low Countries to recruit knights to his banner and hire mercenaries. Sir Ralph Murdac was appointed Constable of Nottingham Castle by his royal master, and a knight named William de Wenneval was made his deputy. I stayed out of

Ralph Murdac's path as much as possible – I was afraid that I would lose my temper and attack him on the spot. When not out scouring the countryside for silver, I spent any free time I had with Hanno.

We practised our sword-work together every morning, explored the castle during the daytime, and kept ourselves to ourselves in the evening, occasionally visiting The Trip to Jerusalem, a warren-like tavern carved out of the soft sandstone rock beneath the castle, near the upper bailey on the southern side. It was a cosy place with a cheery clientele, and Hanno had made friends there. At one time, before Nottingham Castle had been rebuilt and expanded by King Henry, The Trip had supplied ale to the whole garrison. But its position outside the walls meant that in the event of a siege the castle would be denied its crucial ale-making services. Consequently, a new brewhouse had been set up inside the outer bailey, where it could be better protected, and The Trip now relied upon trade from off-duty men-at-arms and knights who wished to escape the castle for a few hours and enjoy a period of peace and quiet outside the walls. The ale was excellent, but on the evenings that we went there we mostly remained aloof, politely refusing to join in the revelry of Prince John's men. On one occasion I was asked by a knight if I would perform some of my music for him and his friends, but I refused, saying that until I could replace my vielle with an instrument of similar quality, I could not do justice to my compositions. He was offended by this refusal, as were his friends, and coupled with my stand-offish behaviour and my refusal to line my own pockets at the peasants' expense, it must be said that I was not a popular member of the Nottingham garrison.

From time to time, word filtered in about King Richard. After I had seen him at Ochsenfurt, he had been brought to Speyer, accompanied by the abbots Boxley and Robertsbridge, where the Emperor had staged a trial in front of the most senior churchmen and nobles of the German realms. Apparently, our King had acquitted himself well, refuting with ease the charges of betraying the Great Pilgrimage and of murdering Conrad of Montferrat, the King of Jerusalem. His eloquence and charm, his status as a pious knight captured while returning from the Holy Land and the fact that the charges were quite obviously false, meant that he elicited much sympathy from the German nobles – in fact, he made a number of good friends.

After the trial, it appeared he had come to some sort of arrangement with Emperor Henry. He was now being held in the Castle of Trifels, high in the mountains to the west of Speyer, and it was reported that negotiations for his ransom and return to England were proceeding smoothly. The trial having failed, Henry had come up with a new pretext for holding Richard: apparently the Emperor was demanding a fee for his services in 'reconciling' the Kings of England and France – and a figure of 100,000 marks had been mentioned. Richard, of course, would remain his 'honoured guest' until the money had been paid. But all could see that this fee was truly nothing more than ransom by another name.

Meanwhile, Philip Augustus, the as-yet-unreconciled King of France, had invaded Richard's duchy of Normandy and was busily capturing castles and lands at an alarming rate.

But that was happening far away, and we had enough to do in Nottinghamshire without worrying about distant battlefields. We had our share of the extortionate 100,000 marks – about

67,000 pounds, perhaps twice the sum the whole country yielded for King Richard in one year – to collect from the long-suffering folk of northern England.

The attacks by Robin's men on the tax collectors had continued all summer long, and many believed he was using some kind of witchcraft to see the future, for his outlaws always seemed to know where and when the richest convoys of silver would pass. His bowmen would swoop out of hiding, sometimes masked, sometimes merely disguised in deep hoods, and shoot down the mounted men-at-arms guarding the packhorse train, or drive them off. Then the outlaws would make off with the silver, still contained in the chests on Prince John's pack animals, escaping back into the wilderness of Sherwood before any pursuit could be organized.

Sir Ralph Murdac, infuriated by the Earl of Locksley's success, had taken to sending more and more armed men out with the bigger convoys of tax collectors, sometimes as many as thirty or forty or even fifty men-at-arms to protect each train. Robin, however, declined to take on the heavily armed convoys, selecting the weaker ones and continuing to wreak havoc and deny much silver to the Constable of Nottingham's treasure vaults.

Convinced that the local people must be helping Robin in some way, perhaps informing him when tax convoys would be passing or acting as spies for his outlaw band, Murdac ordered that villages that had already been taxed should be taxed again, and again, as a punishment. The villagers responded by melting away from their holdings and taking to the forest. Deep in the safety of Sherwood, Robin fed them and sheltered them; some he armed and trained for battle. Thus he swelled the numbers of loyal men-at-arms under his command.

Though it pained me to be forced to carry out Sir Ralph's orders to tax a countryside that had already paid up more than its fair share, I had no choice but to obey. I would try to ensure that we made as much noise as possible, shouting battle cries and blowing trumpets as we approached a village or manor, allowing its occupants to slip away before we arrived. And I forbade my men to chase after peasants fleeing into the forest, saying that it was unsafe to do so: who knew what or who might be waiting in ambush beyond the lush green curtain of trees? It gave me a reputation as an unadventurous commander, timid and very careful of his own safety – which irked me a good deal. But it could not be helped.

Other leaders of tax-gathering bands were not so gentle or fastidious. I heard terrible reports of villagers summarily hanged, men and women tortured with fire and boiling water until they gave up their meagre pennies, stock animals killed or confiscated, churches sacked and burnt, girls – or even young boys – raped for the amusement of the Prince's men-at-arms. It was as if John's troops were an occupying force; an enemy ravaging the land rather than Englishmen lawfully raising revenue in the King's name. But the worse the depredations carried out by Prince John, the more men flocked to Robin's outlaw banner and the more powerful the Earl of Locksley became.

And Nottingham was not the only stronghold from which Prince John's men were sallying forth to wring silver from an unwilling countryside. The powerful stone castle of Tickhill, on the Yorkshire border, which was held by the famous knight Sir Robert de la Mare, had been amassing coin for Prince John over the past six months, and one chilly September morning fifteen knights and men-at-arms, including myself, rode out from Nottingham to Tickhill, thirty miles to the north, with instructions from Sir Ralph to escort a wagon train filled with silver coin back to Nottingham.

The previous day, Murdac had summoned me to his large private chamber on the western side of the great tower and informed me: 'You are too idle and too cowardly, Dale, that is what the men say about you.' I bit the side of my tongue until I could taste blood but said nothing.

The lavish room had been empty when I entered it, but Ralph Murdac had emerged a few moments later from behind a curtain that shielded the privy. The seat of ease was at the end of a short passage, and was built into the outside western wall of the chamber. It was a rare luxury to have a garderobe, as these conveniences were sometimes called, in a private chamber, but it meant that a man could relieve himself in comfort – his waste dropping down through a wide chute and ending up in a midden pile outside the walls of the castle – without having to wander the dark stone corridors to use the common privies frequented by the ordinary men-at-arms.

'It's about time you started earning your keep here,' he snapped, seating himself at a table piled with parchments. 'You won't be in command. Frankly, from what I hear, I don't believe you're up to it – it's your base blood, of course. I don't know what His Highness Prince John was thinking. You'll take orders from Sir Roger Fotheringhay on the mission and you leave at dawn. That is all. Shut the door behind you on the way out.'

And with that he gave me a brief contemptuous look, picked up a goose-feather quill, pulled a piece of parchment towards him and began scratching at it. I said nothing; I merely shrugged, turned and walked out of the room.

I left the door open – but it was a poor revenge for having to swallow being called a lazy coward.

The journey to Tickhill Castle, a full day's ride, was uneventful: it was a strongly built fortress with a high stone wall surrounding the bailey, and a tall keep built in the centre on top of a twenty-foot mound. The fifteen of us under Sir Roger's command were allocated a section of the hall to sleep in, but we had not much space per man, for the castle seemed to be crammed with fighting men: including our party, I counted nearly a hundred men-at-arms of various ranks at the evening meal, and in the bailey the stables were filled to bursting with horses of all shapes and sizes. *Something is up*, I thought to myself. *Where did all these men come from – and where are they going?*

It has to be said that the organization of Tickhill under Sir Robert de la Mare was impressive. His servants worked all night to prepare the three wagons for the journey and to load them with the silver-filled strong-chests. Locked, chained tight, personally sealed by de la Mare, then covered with mounds of rough sacking to disguise their presence, six immensely heavy chests were loaded into each wagon and, just before dawn, three teams of eight oxen were yoked into position to pull the weight of Prince John's ill-gotten silver all the way to Nottingham. Our fifteen men-at-arms, yawning and scratching after a short night's sleep, formed up on either side of the ox-wagons. The castle gates swung slowly open, the drivers cracked whips, called to their animals and prodded the oxen's rumps with sharp goads, the men-at-arms clicked their tongues to their horses and the whole convoy began its ponderous passage on the road south.

We travelled at the speed of the slowest ox and so, when we stopped at midday for a bite of bread and a drink of ale, we had come no further south than the village of Carlton in the district of Lindrick. At an alehouse near the old Saxon church of St John the Evangelist, Sir Roger arranged food and drink from the local hostelry. He seemed nervous and agitated, and he kept giving me strange, flickering glances, as if he were somehow frightened of me. Perhaps he was uncomfortable that I had been demoted for this expedition, that I had to take his orders when I had previously been a captain of my own team of tax gatherers. But I paid it little mind. It was a cold, sharp day, grey skies and a whiff of rain on the breeze, and we ate a joyless meal in Carlton in near-silence. I just wanted to get back on the road to Nottingham with the least possible delay, and I was in no mood to swap pleasantries with my fellow men-at-arms. Half an hour later, my wish was granted and we set off again.

We were no more than half a mile out of Carlton, passing through a place where we were hemmed in by dense woodland to the west with open farmland to the east, when the arrows began to fly. The first I knew of the attack was a sudden hiss and thump, followed by a scream of pain from the man-at-arms in front of me, who folded over in his saddle clutching an arrow shaft which protruded like a thin, straight branch from his belly.

Sir Roger shouted something and I turned Ghost right, facing towards the woodland in the west: I could see indistinct shapes moving in the forest gloom and arrows flickering out from the trees like horizontal hail. Scores of shafts flashed by me, on either side, and in an instant the mounted men and their horses were screaming and dying left and right. Hooded men, dark and menacing, wielding long war bows, advanced towards me through the trees like murderous wraiths, shooting as they came on. Ghost whickered and shied between my thighs and I tried to calm him as the deadly shafts sped past his flanks and sank into the flesh of his fellow beasts. One horse, spitted through the neck, screamed and reared. I saw a man-at-arms cursing an arrow in his left arm, trying to remove it, just as two more shafts smashed into his chest. I watched, immobile but for my jittering horse, while Sir Roger to my left took an arrow to the face, his helmeted head snapped backwards by the shaft before he slid dead as a boulder out of the side of the saddle. Death passed by me, surrounding me, close enough to touch, close enough to smell and close enough to feel the wind of its passing and hear its awful hiss and thump, hiss and thump. One knight, his horse stuck deep with three arrows, and he sporting a fourth jutting from his waist, managed to draw his sword and tried to charge the shadowy bowmen advancing through the woodland. He put back his spurs, shouted a feeble war cry; then his horse surged forward and he was met with a dozen more shafts that slashed out of the trees simultaneously, some taking his horse in the throat, while four or five thudded into his mailed chest. He and his mount were dead before they had travelled five yards.

And yet in all this carnage, amidst all this death and blood, Ghost and I remained untouched. I dropped the reins on the saddle horn and raised both hands, palms forward, fingers spread in the universal sign for surrender, crooning softly to Ghost to give him courage, and trying to hold him still between my knees.

Looking round quickly, I saw that all of our men-at-arms were down, and most of their poor horses were wounded or dead. The hooded wraiths with their long killing bows were no more than twenty paces from me, walking steadily forward with the soft, purposeful tread of executioners. Then I heard a familiar voice, one I had not heard for six months or more, shouting: 'Cease shooting, men; hold those arrows. Cease shooting, you rascals!' And out from behind a tree not twenty yards from me stepped a tall handsome figure in dark green, wrapped in a raggedy grey cloak, an arrow bag at his waist, a bow in his right hand.

'Hello there, Alan,' said Robin. 'And how have you been keeping?'

Chapter Fourteen

The Earl of Locksley's men, marshalled by Little John with his enormous old-fashioned double-edged axe, swiftly dispatched any of the men-at-arms who still lived. I stepped down from Ghost's back and embraced Robin. My throat was choked with emotion: I had not realized till that moment how much I had missed him in the long deceitful months at Nottingham. And there were many other familiar faces grinning at me from under their hoods: Much, the son of a well-to-do miller, who loved the violent outlaw life more than the safe respectability of grinding wheat for a living; Owain, the master bowman, a valiant Welsh warrior and old friend who had made the journey to Outremer and back with me; young Thomas ap Lloyd, wielding a bow that had been cut down to match his youth and size; Little John came over and gave me a bear hug that nearly crushed my ribs; then he slapped me on the back and told me he was proud of me.

And then there was Robin.

My lord, the Earl of Locksley, looked closely at me, his bright silver-grey eyes staring deep into mine. 'How goes it in Nottingham, Alan?' he asked. 'They don't suspect that you are still my man, do they?'

'I don't think so. Well, they cannot be certain – but, Robin, how much longer do I have to play this role? They will find out soon: they must know that somebody is giving you information about the convoys' movements.'

Robin stroked his lightly stubbled chin. 'I think you must play this game just a little while longer, Alan, if you can stand it. The silver we take from Prince John goes directly to Queen Eleanor in London. And every penny we take weakens him and brings King Richard's release a little closer.'

'Every penny goes to the Queen?' I said, tilting my head in a query.

'Yes,' said Robin, pretending to look outraged. 'Well, I do have some expenses, obviously. But the vast majority of the money – well, most of the money – goes south to London. Don't you trust me?'

I just looked at him and raised an eyebrow. Suddenly, we were both laughing madly.

Breathless with mirth, Robin managed to splutter out: 'I'm not doing this to enrich myself, Alan, on my oath. I don't need it. The Outremer trade still flows like a great glittering river. This is all for Richard. It also happens to amuse me to play the rogue again – but, upon my sacred honour, Alan, this deadly game is to buy King Richard's freedom.'

I wiped the tears of laughter from my eyes, and said: 'I think I can carry on the subterfuge a little longer, if you wish me to, and for the King's sake, but not past Christmas, I beg you. I'm not sure I could stand it any longer than that without running mad and cutting Murdac's throat in his sleep.'

'That's not a bad idea,' said Robin. 'Although you'd never survive to tell me the tale. No, regretfully, you'll have to play the part for a little longer. Another three months should do it; till Christmas, as you say. But at the first sign that they suspect you – you and Hanno get yourselves out of the castle. Promise me that, Alan? The first sign of suspicion, you get out of there. I need you alive and well, my friend, not dangling from a gibbet in Nottingham market.'

While I had been talking with my true lord and master, Robin's men had been busying themselves around the wagon train, gathering up weapons and mail coats, giving a merciful release to wounded horses, soothing the nerves of the surviving ox drivers by swearing that they would not be harmed if they co-operated with the raggedy hooded men in green and russet who now swarmed over the wagon train looking for plunder. A couple of the outlaws had been fruitlessly trying to break into one of the silver chests, but its strength had defeated them for the moment.

Little John had had the foresight to post sentries north and south on the road, and it was a rider, galloping furiously towards us down the road from the north, who interrupted my conversation with Robin.

'Sir, sir,' the man shouted as he drew near the wagons and flung himself from his horse, 'there are horse soldiers coming, proper cavalry, about sixty of them, heavily armed, lances, swords, shields, and coming up very fast!'

The laughter was wiped from Robin's face in an instant.

'Sixty, you say?' he asked the sentry.

'At least, sir, not more than a mile or two away.'

A strange look crossed Robin's face, one of cold doubt. He looked at me hard – it was not a pleasant expression.

'What?' I said. 'Don't you trust *me*?'

I was hurt by that look, but then I knew that Robin had a very suspicious mind. I pushed my hurt aside, and continued: 'Forget about that for now. With only these men' – I gestured at the twenty or so raggedy outlaws, now joking and laughing among the wagons, so different from the murderous menacing wraiths of a quarter of an hour before – 'with only these men, you either have to run and leave these silver wagons to the enemy, or fight for it. And if you fight, you will lose. Then we will all die.'

'Fight or run?' Robin thought for a moment. 'I will do both.' He raised his chin, and using his battle voice, a timbre designed to be heard clearly over the carnage of warfare, he shouted: 'Archers – form up on the treeline. Now. Move! John, over here, a moment of your time, if you please,' And in a quieter tone to me he said: 'And you, Alan, need to get out of sight. I don't want any of these horsemen seeing you with me.'

I understood him, it was the sensible thing to do, and although I was most reluctant to be dodging yet another fight, I led Ghost into the woodland and tethered him to a small bush fifty yards from the road. Then I crept back towards the highway and began to climb the tallest, leafiest tree I could find, ten yards back from the public thoroughfare.

Peering out between the leaves some little time later, I saw a thin, single line of perhaps three-score horsemen, pennants flying, spear points glittering, red-and-blue surcoats flapping in the breeze, coming over the brow of the field on the far side of the road about three hundred yards away at a gentle trot. The attacking line looked spindly, elongated, lacking in depth and power – and yet it was the perfect formation to attack archers.

Robin's meagre numbers – I counted fewer than twenty-five men – were in a loose line on the western side of the road, where the trees began. The archers had planted three or four arrows, bodkin-point down in the ground in front of them, but most still had full arrow bags at their waists. They were waiting for orders. At one end of the line stood Little John, bowless, but with his double-headed axe in hand, feet planted as strongly as the oak tree that stood behind him and a gentle smile on his broad brown face. At the other end of the line was Robin, bow at the ready. He wasted no time.

'Nock,' Robin shouted in his brazen war voice. And a score of men put arrows to their strings. The cavalry had seen our men by now and were increasing their speed to the trot – they were perhaps two hundred and fifty yards away and approaching fast.

'Draw,' shouted Robin. With a sound like a great creaking barn door, twenty-odd bows were drawn back until the goose-feather fletchings tickled the archers' right ears. The cavalry were at the full canter now, sweeping down in an irresistible wave of big horses and big heavily armed men; their lances were couched and they were set to crash into the archers, skewering their unprotected bodies, and trample Robin's few men into bloody rags.

'And loose!' said Robin. A score of shafts hissed out in a

grey blur towards the galloping enemy. Even at two hundred yards, half a dozen saddles were emptied in a trice. But still the enemy came on, the line thinner and with many a gap, but unstoppable nonetheless.

Once more Robin gave the orders – nock, draw and loose – but faster now, and once more the arrows slashed out towards the charging horsemen, spitting men and animals indiscriminately. But the cavalry were only a hundred yards away now and the dreadful pounding of the destriers' big hooves filled my ears.

'Shoot at will,' bellowed Robin. 'Loose, loose, loose!' The archers were desperately plucking arrows from the ground and, almost without seeming to aim, shooting as fast as they could at the looming mounted warriors. The cavalry line was no more, it was just a collection of knots of charging horsemen filled with battle fury from the killings they had endured, thundering towards the frail line of archers, their bright spear-points seeking our flesh – and they were so nearly upon us!

'Into the trees! Into the trees!' I could hear Robin's bold voice above the war cries of the knights, and the screams of wounded men and horses, above the drumming of hooves on hard earth only fifty yards away. His order came just in time. The archers turned as one man, and pelted backwards into the thick woodland. I saw them running beneath me, bows still in hand, to take up new positions on the far side of a small clearing. As the archers ran across the clearing I saw the taller men ducking in a strange way, all of them bobbing their heads slightly at exactly the same spot in the clearing.

And then I smiled; for I saw what these men were ducking to avoid. It was a stout chain of steel links, rubbed with dirt to hide the gleam of metal, and it was stretched between two giant oaks twenty yards apart on either side of the clearing, secured fast to the tree trunks. The archers were forming up on the far side of the open space: not hiding, but in plain view, and they nocked arrows once again and waited for the pursuing cavalry – inviting them to attack.

They had only moments to wait.

Some three dozen horsemen came barrelling into the woodland at almost the same time. Seeing the archers in a loose huddle at the far side of the clearing they dug their spurs into their horses' flanks and, shouting with excitement, charged straight at the footmen. The chain, which had been set at about six foot above the ground, caught two of the leading horses by the throat, and they went down in a tangle of kicking legs. The chain missed a third animal which was charging with its head held low, but swept its rider out of the saddle, almost cutting the man in half. Hard on their heels came the rest of the horsemen, their mounts crashing into the fallen horses with the terrible sound of tumbling half-ton bodies and the awful crisp snapping of equine legs. It was sheer bloody chaos: a seething tangle of horses and shields and lances and struggling men. One horse went mad with fear and began kicking and biting anything within reach. Most of the cavalry, however, stopped their mounts in time, and reined up panting and swearing, seeking a way around the mound of thrashing bloody horseflesh and the stunned and broken men-at-arms.

While this horse-borne carnage was erupting, the archers had not been idle. They nocked, drew and loosed without ceasing, pouring out a torrent of deadly arrows; not the measured volleys of before, but individual shots, well aimed and at

261

very close range. I saw a shaft, loosed thirty yards away, pass right through a man's chest and still stick six inches deep in the flank of the horse behind him. Another shaft, shot from twenty yards, punched straight through a man-at-arm's shield, through his chain mail, piercing deep into his chest. Soon the clearing was filled with heaps of dying men and kicking, screaming horses. One knight managed to make his way around the bloody mound of twitching chaos – and Little John met him with a sweep of his double-headed axe, slicing the knight's horse's head clean off with one blow. The knight died moments later as four arrows thudded into his belly.

And the enemy had had enough. The surviving horsemen, those who had come last to the fight in the woodland, the men who had hung back, turned their mounts and fled, streaming away back out of the trees towards the open farm land. Of the sixty men that had come on so proudly against Robin's archers, I saw fewer than a dozen knights make their escape.

It was a stunning victory. Robin's tiny force of raggedy peasants and outlaws, armed with little more than a few sticks and lengths of hempen string, had defeated – almost annihilated – a force three times their size of armoured, well-trained men on horseback.

And Robin had lost only a single man. We found his body by the treeline. He was a squat, well-muscled archer but he must have been slow to run on Robin's command, for he bore the classic death wound of a fleeing infantry man pursued by a mounted knight: a bloody hole in his back where the knight's lance had pierced him as he ran for his life.

The archers showed no pity to the wounded men they found,

ignoring appeals for mercy and all talk of ransom, and cutting their throats without regard for rank or status. Then they immediately began to search the bodies for coins.

One of the ox-drivers had been killed, too. Some escaping knight, overcome by frustration at his defeat or just plain bloodlust, had hacked into the back of the man's head as he was passing the wagons, and now the poor driver lay dead at the feet of his draught animals, his brains softly leaking from his cracked skull into the green grass.

'Greetings, young Alan,' said Little John. 'Did you enjoy my little trick?' He gestured with a vast hand at the mound of dead and dying horses in the centre of the clearing, now being picked over by outlaw archers looking for valuable weapons, armour, silver bridles, expensive horse knick-knacks and, as always, food and drink.

'It was astounding,' I said. And I meant it. 'But where on earth did you get the steel chain?'

'I made it,' said Little John, with undeniable pride in his voice. 'God's great pimpled buttocks, did you think it fell from the sky or was given to us by the fairies?'

'But—' I said, and stopped.

'Forgive me, Alan. I was forgetting,' said Little John. 'You've been away from us for a while. I learnt the blacksmith's trade in London. Just by happenstance, you might say. I needed to be near the Temple Church – Robin's idea, of course – and there was a blacksmith's right opposite the place. So, for a goodly fee, and no questions asked, I became a rather elderly apprentice for a few days. I learnt a thing or two, as well.'

My mind went back to a figure I had glimpsed on the day

of Robin's trial. A tall blond man with an eye patch who seemed to have absolutely no interest in a large force of mounted soldiers appearing right on his doorstep.

'So it was you who arranged Robin's escape?'

Little John laughed. 'My master at the smithy was asked to provide the Templar's gaoler with the locks and chains to shackle Robin. And I arranged with the blacksmith to have the honour of undertaking the task.'

I snorted at this. The thought of Little John as a biddable blacksmith's apprentice was almost too comical to believe.

'I locked up Robin in the presence of the gaoler, but – would you believe it? – I botched the job: loose pin in the locking mechanism. Well, I was so ashamed of my shoddy work that I thought it would be better to take Robin and myself away from there as soon as possible. Once Robin was loose, we only had to kill a couple of Templar sergeants, climb a wall, and ride like Hell for Sherwood. The whole thing went as smoothly as shit passing through a goose.'

The big man was laughing now, and I joined him. I was very pleased to see Little John again: I had missed his rough good humour, appalling impiety, and his unique attitude to life, viewing the world as such an easy place in which to live. As we laughed, Robin came over to me.

'It's time you were going, Alan. So, I'm afraid, you need to decide – where do you want it?'

'What?' I said, stupidly.

'Your story when you get back to Nottingham is that you were wounded in the fight – knocked out, perhaps – and when you came to, you were the only man left alive. Does that sound plausible?'

'Oh, ah, I suppose so . . .'

Robin looked over at Little John, and gave a tiny nod.

And I ducked.

A fist like a granite boulder whistled over my head, its massive flight ruffling my blond hair, and I turned to look at Little John in alarm.

'Stand still, Alan. It's got to look authentic,' said John, frowning. 'Unless you'd rather have a flesh wound?'

'We could always do that,' said Robin, drawing his sword. My lord was enjoying this – the steel-eyed bastard.

'All right, all right.' I braced my feet, clamped my mouth shut and closed my eyes.

Are you ready?' said John.

'Yes – just get on with it,' I said through gritted teeth.

The blow, when it came, was like a whack in the face from a well-swung mallet. I was knocked up and backwards, and landed with a winding thump on the horse-churned grass of the clearing. A moment's deep blackness, then bright-red sparks shooting through my skull. When I opened my eyes, Robin was standing over me, his face full of concern.

I sat up groggily, and spat out a fragment of tooth. I could feel blood running down either side of my mouth from my smashed nose. I saw that my hands were trembling as I gently felt my squashed hooter. By the wiggle at the bridge, I knew it was broken.

Little John came over to me, leading Ghost.

'Can you sit a horse?' asked Robin, helping me to my unsteady feet.

'Course he can,' said Little John, handing me the reins. 'Christ's crusted bum-crack, the boy's no weakling. And I only gave him a gentle tap. He'll be fine.'

My head spinning, my face dripping gore, I climbed wearily up on to Ghost's back.

'I'll pay you back for that one day,' I mumbled to John, before nodding painfully at Robin and guiding Ghost out of the clearing and back on to the road to Nottingham.

It took me half a day to ride back to the castle: my head was splitting, my mouth and nose throbbing with pain. I amused myself on the ride back by thinking of ways I could revenge myself on Little John – nothing dreadful, I mused, but it'd be good to get my own back on the big lug.

It was dusk when I rode through the wooden gates of the outer bailey and up the rough road to the stone walls of the castle. I did not bother to wash before reporting to Sir Ralph that catastrophe had occurred to his Tickhill silver convoy. I figured that a bloody visage might speak volumes in my defence. And so, with the skin on my face cracked with dried blood, and my nose and mouth swollen and still smarting badly, I entered the great hall in the middle bailey to make my dolorous report in person to the Constable of Nottingham Castle.

Murdac was not alone: while I had been away Prince John had returned to his strongest English fortress, and as I walked over to his throne, I felt an air of something not quite right stir the hairs on the back of my neck.

I bowed to the Prince, and nodded at Sir Ralph Murdac, who as usual was standing hunch-shouldered close beside his master. On the other side of the royal chair was a third man: Sir Aymeric de St Maur, the Templar knight. *Interesting,* I thought to myself – *the Templars are siding openly with Prince John.* And then I pushed the thought aside and began my

266

report on the robbery of the silver wagon train by the notorious outlaw Robin Hood and my fictional role in its heroic but unsuccessful defence.

The three men listened to me in silence and I was just finishing my tale, describing how I came back to consciousness to discover the wagons were gone and I was surrounded by the mounds of dead, when Prince John interrupted me: 'You really are quite a good liar, for a steaming pile of low-born pig shit.' He sounded as if he genuinely meant it.

'A liar, sire? I hope not . . .' I said, trying to look confused, but with my belly dissolving.

'Be silent,' said the Prince. 'I have heard enough of your dissembling. Guards, bind him.'

Half a dozen men fell upon me and removed my sword, misericorde, and my mail coat. My hands were roughly tied behind my back. I did not resist: the only way out of this was to keep my head.

'Sire, might I be permitted to know the meaning of this? Is it some playful jest? A game, perhaps?' I asked with as much humility as I could muster.

'You know very well what is happening,' Sir Ralph Murdac answered for the Prince and smiled nastily at me. 'We have known for some weeks now that you, through your German servant, have been supplying information to the outlaw Robert of Locksley. Did you think we were completely stupid? You have forsaken your oath of loyalty to your Prince; you are forsworn, and a traitor. You have betrayed us and will suffer the penalty that is your due.'

If Sir Ralph was visibly enjoying himself, Prince John seemed merely bored. 'You have fulfilled your function here,' he croaked. 'Once we were sure that you were still labouring on Locksley's behalf, we hoped to use you to trap the man. If you knew that a great shipment of silver, weakly guarded, was coming here from Tickhill, you would be bound to inform your master. And he would be bound to try to steal it. We arranged for a force of knights to trap him in the very act of the robbery – but it seems they failed to defeat Locksley's rabble. I am at a loss to explain why – we sent sixty brave knights to intercept him. Perhaps your master really does consort with the Devil – if such an unlikely creature really exists.'

At this, Sir Aymeric de St Maur gave Prince John a sharp look. But the Templar said nothing.

Prince John continued in his harsh voice: 'Your usefulness is over, Dale. Too many of my men have died at Locksley's hand, and I will lose no more. It is time for you to pay for your crimes – and his. So I have arranged a match tomorrow afternoon, a public wrestling match: you will fight my champion to the death – as a little "amusement" for the loyal men of Nottingham. Tomorrow you will face Milo in the list; no weapons, no rules – man to man. And you will die.'

Part Three

Chapter Fifteen

All is not well here at Westbury. The peril from Osric has grown and looms much nearer – he now has a confederate! I saw my bailiff meet his accomplice in secret in the back of one of the disused stables at the edge of the courtyard, the night before last. As I peered through a chink in the wooden slats of the wall, I saw Osric by the light of his lantern, greeting and conversing with a soberly dressed man in a neat black skullcap – but one look at his evil face, brown, creased and warty, and I knew that he meant no good. He is dark of eye, dark of dress, dark of heart – bent and stooped and old, almost as old as I am. The two conspirators talked for a long while, but in tones too low for my worn-out ears to hear. The dark man seemed to be angry about something. Osric soothed him and it seemed that their disagreement was soon resolved, for the stranger passed Osric a small clay pot, sealed with wax, and received a couple of silver coins in return – whatever was in the pot must command a high price. By his dress and demeanour, I guessed that this dark man was an apothecary and that the clay pot contained some sort of poison.

Black rage at Osric's perfidy boiled then in my gut and yet I did not challenge my bailiff openly, as I did the last time. He would no doubt have found some seemingly plausible reason for his secret meeting after nightfall with a purveyor of poisons, although what that might be, I cannot imagine. Instead, I went to Marie and told her what I had seen of her husband's conspiracies. It was an even graver mistake.

'You are a stupid old fool!' Marie said, when I awoke her that same night with my tale of Osric's sinister business with the apothecary in the stables. She had already taken to her bed, but I wanted her to see with her own eyes their plotting. 'To even think, to even entertain the notion that Osric means you harm – it is ridiculous, absurd even. He respects you, and wishes you nothing but health and prosperity. Has he not shown it with his work here at Westbury? He has made this little manor a great success. Go to bed, you silly old dotard, be grateful for Osric's hard work, and put these idiotic thoughts from you.'

She is clearly in league with him: I see that now. I was a fool to reveal my suspicions to her. Osric and her, newly married, greedy, ambitious, impatient: of course, they both wish me dead. With me gone, they can do with the manor as they will. Perhaps Osric will install one of his tall sons as the lord. I fear for little Alan, my heir: who will protect him? Not I. I am an old man now, how can I stand against the combined cunning of Osric and Marie? I feel my doom approaching.

And there is worse to relate. This very night, not an hour ago, as I worked on this parchment with scant thought of the danger that surrounds me, I drained the last drops from a wooden mug of ale and discovered a white powdery residue in the bottom of the mug. The poisoners have struck! The contents of the clay pot have found their way into my belly and there is toiling, moiling through my guts to achieve my destruction. I feel Death's bony hand upon my shoulder. I made myself vomit, of course, as soon as I saw the white residue. I spewed in my chamber pot until I could bring up no more. But I can feel the poison working in my body: I am growing sleepy, so very careworn and tired. But I must not sleep, I must go on and finish this tale before the cursed white powder drags me down into the grave.

I have barricaded the door against them, and routed out an old sword from my chest, which now leans unsheathed against the lectern that I stand at and write upon. If they try to break into my chamber tonight I will defend myself, and perhaps kill one or both of them. But I do not wish their deaths as they wish mine; I merely pray they will leave me in peace for one last night. If I am to finish this tale before I am called to God, I must endeavour to write on as quickly as I am able . . .

There is a great comfort to be found in prayer, particularly when you are certain that you will shortly be face to face with your Creator. And I prayed that night in Nottingham Castle as I have never prayed before. I did not fear death, but I did not want to perish. I did not want my earthly life to be ended by Milo, that monstrous half-human being, for the amusement of Prince John, Ralph Murdac and all the other castle knights that I had come to despise. And if the measure of a man is how he faces up to his Fate, I fear I did not measure well. I prayed, I prayed again and then I prayed some more.

The guards had taken me to the lowest part of the great

tower, in the cold stone heart of Nottingham Castle, cut my bonds, and thrown me into a storeroom half-filled with sacks of grain. It was completely dark in there, and silent too, but for the occasional scurry of a rat – but to be honest it was not uncomfortable. When I had finished praying, I laid my body down on two large full sacks of barley and thought about how I had ended up here.

I remembered Robin's face when he told me what he wanted me to do, in Westminster, the day before the inquisition at Temple Church. His silver eyes were blazing with intensity and he said: 'I know this will be very hard for you, Alan, and dangerous, too, and I would not ask it if it were not of the utmost importance – but we must have a man inside Prince John's camp.'

I asked him why we could not merely bribe some servant. And he shook his head sadly. 'We need a fighting man. I need to know how many men will be with each tax-gathering party, and their strength, their weapons and morale. It needs an experienced soldier. And, don't forget, you will have Hanno with you for company. He will run all the messages to me, and for safety's sake you and I will have no contact after this ridiculous inquisition until your time with Prince John is over.'

'But, Robin,' I protested weakly, 'the world will think me a man of no loyalty, a cur who turned traitor on his lord . . .'

'It is necessary, I'm afraid, Alan. Everyone must think that. If they do not believe that you have genuinely betrayed me at this inquisition, Prince John will never take you into his service. You and I will know the truth – that you serve me still. And be honest with me: you did not like my playing the bloodthirsty part of Cernunnos; as I remember it, you were quite angry with

274

me at the time. All I am asking you to do is to tell the truth to the inquisition when they ask it of you. You can do that, can't you?'

'But what about you, Robin? What about your life?' I said. 'If the Templars find you guilty at the inquisition tomorrow your life will not be worth a rotten turnip.'

'I have made arrangements. Do not concern yourself about that. Now, will you do me – and our good King Richard – this great service?'

I sighed: 'Yes, sir.' I could summon little enthusiasm for his plan: betrayal, ignominy, the very real chance of a felon's death on the gallows. Still I said yes. I could never refuse Robin, no matter how unpleasant or difficult or dishonourable the task he proposed to me.

'You know that I will not forget this? That I will be for ever in your debt?' He gripped me by both shoulders.

'Yes, sir.'

'Good man!' he said, and he slapped me on the back and left me to my preparations for an immediate departure to Germany after the Templar trial.

And so for six long months I had been acting my part as Prince John's man and feeding information to Robin through the good offices of Hanno – where was he? I wondered. I had dispatched my wily German friend the day before yesterday to pass on the news of the great silver wagon train to my master and I had not seen him since. Had Prince John's men taken him? Was his corpse at this moment twisting in the wind on the town gibbet?

I had not intended to accompany the wagon train of silver. All those months ago Robin and I had agreed that, to try to avoid doubt falling on me, he would not rob tax-gathering parties of which I was a member. I had only joined the force of knights guarding it at the last moment, on the specific orders of Ralph Murdac: clearly their suspicions of me had finally come to a head. I felt my throbbing nose and ran my tongue over the chipped tooth. There had been no need, it occurred to me then, for that brutal knock from Little John. I could have stayed with Robin and saved my own life. Right now I could be riding Ghost through the cool clean spaces of Sherwood, free and clear, beside Robin and Little John and all my friends – rather than lying here, with the Devil beating his drums inside my head, waiting to be ripped apart by that grotesque monster Milo.

I realized that I was pitying myself and stopped abruptly. I was not dead, not yet. I got up from my barley sacks and began to make an examination of the storeroom. It was small, perhaps four paces by five and seven foot high. The door was a solid one made of thick elm boards, bolted securely from the outside. I pressed my ear to the door and heard – nothing. I wasted a few moments banging on the door and shouting for a gaoler but got no response: it must be the early part of the night, I reckoned, about eight of the clock. Either the guards were asleep or eating, or no one had bothered to post them. There was nowhere I could go, deep as I was in the bowels of the great tower, no chance of escape, so perhaps there was no need to detail guards to watch a locked door all night.

The walls of my cell were cool, dry smooth sandstone, with no breaks or cracks or fissures that I could discern, and there were no tools or weapons in the room of any kind. By touch I found an empty bucket, and a jug of cool water. I drank deeply and relieved myself in the bucket. And that was it, apart from some sacks of barley and a couple filled with oats. I did not know the underground ways of the great tower well, having only been down here on two or three occasions – Hanno knew it far better than I, as there were innumerable cellars and kitchens and pantries down here under the big square keep and built into the thick walls surrounding the upper bailey, and he often spent time down here in the warren of corridors and disused rooms, engaging in illicit trysts with some of the castle's serving girls. But I had a rough plan of the castle in my head and I reckoned that I was not far away from the closely guarded underground treasury where Prince John was keeping the silver from his summer's tax gathering.

I prayed a little more, this time for strength in my coming ordeal, and then settled back to think about Milo. I pondered the question of how a smaller, lighter man could defeat a much larger, heavier one, but my thoughts on the little I knew about wrestling kept being interrupted by disturbing images of Goody.

In my mind's eye I could see her sweet face, her soft golden hair and her thistle-blue eyes sparkling with happiness – or sudden, incandescent rage. I realized that more than anything in the world I wanted to see her again, one more time before I died. I would like to hold her tightly in my arms and tell her that everything was going to be all right. I wanted to apologize for deceiving her as to my true role among Prince John's men. And, so badly, I wanted to touch her soft cheek, and kiss her on the lips . . .

I had to use a deal of force on myself to stop these thoughts sliding into greater sinfulness. She was as a sister to me; she looked to me for the protection of an older brother. Who was

I to start thinking about kissing her? Besides, she despised me: 'You hateful man,' she had said. 'I never want to speak to you again.' These harsh words were burnt into my heart. Yet, if she only knew . . .

Stop, Alan, Just stop. Milo: Milo is the problem at hand; you must concentrate on defeating the ogre if you want to live . . .

And at some point in this strange half-dreaming, half-anxious state, I fell truly asleep.

I awoke just after dawn and drank some more water. And then I sat and waited, munching a handful of loose oats, sitting on the barley sacks, and I waited and waited. After what must have been several hours I started hammering on the elm door, and demanding proper food and more water. I heard footsteps and a harsh voice in English told me to hold my noise. And then the footsteps went away and I sat for hours in the darkness thinking about my fate and singing long, jolly *cansos* loudly to myself to keep my spirits up. I must have dozed again, for the next time I was awoken it was by the door of the cell crashing open and the dim light of the corridor outside spilling violently into the room. Four men-at-arms burst in and grabbed me by the arms and hustled me out into the passageway. I had no time to resist, and before I knew it I was being marched up the stone steps to the ground floor of the great tower, out of its iron gate, past the eastern side of the great hall and across the middle bailey with the afternoon sun slanting down. I was escorted roughly out of the barbican and north towards the new brewhouse, with the four men-at-arms close around me until we approached the wood-and-earth palisade at the east of the outer bailey that marked the limits of the castle.

The whole outer bailey was buzzing with men-at-arms and

servants and clergy; almost every one of Prince John's dependants, it seemed, wanted to watch the afternoon's 'amusement'. And there in the centre of the roped-off area of the list, sixty foot by sixty foot, stood Milo.

He was even bigger and uglier than I remembered. Dressed only in a loincloth and a pair of heavy leather boots, I could see that his entire body was covered in sweat-matted black hair. Thick slabs of muscle stood out on his chest, his belly was huge and round but did not look remotely soft, his arms were as big as my thighs and his short legs were like the cross-beams of a great hall. He smiled at me cruelly from across the list, his little piggy eyes buried deep in a doughy baby's face. I scowled back at him: but the ice snake slithered in my belly once more and I knew he could break my spine as easily as a man snapping a stick of kindling. I realized, too, that I had been misled about his height, for without lanky Rix to make him seem short – and the tall swordsman was nowhere to be seen on that afternoon – I saw that he was almost as tall as me, and I am six foot high in my hose.

I tore my gaze away from his mountainous muscle-bound shape and studied Prince John, seated in his customary high-backed chair on the north side of the list. Sir Ralph was beside him, standing on his left, looking over at me with a placid, contented stare. A knight in a dark blue surcoat on the other side of Prince John was whispering urgently in his ear: he was a slight man of medium height, with cropped grey and black hair. And I saw, with a little leap of hope in my heart, that it was Sir Nicholas de Scras.

At that moment, Prince John nodded and said something quietly to Sir Nicholas, and the former Hospitaller came striding across the open space of the list towards me. His face bore a warm, slightly sad smile of greeting and he started to speak when he was still more than ten paces from me.

'Alan, Alan, we can stop all this unpleasantness. We can stop it right now. But I will need your help.'

I spread my hands in a query. 'What can I do for you, Nicholas?' I said.

'You can stop this barbaric display with just a few words, just a few well chosen words.'

I frowned: 'You want me to beg? You want me to plead for my life – to them?' I gestured at Prince John and Sir Ralph Murdac, who were eyeing me from beyond the ropes. I put my shoulders back, and jutted my jaw. 'I will not!'

'No, no, Alan, nothing like that. I would not insult your honour in such a way. But you must tell them where the heretic outlaw Robert of Locksley is hiding.'

I looked straight at him: his kindly green eyes were beseeching; I could sense him willing me to tell him.

'I do not know where he is,' I said.

'Alan, I understand that you serve him, that you have always served him; that you tricked me when you said you wished to serve Prince John, and came here as a – as a ruse. I forgive you for all that. But this is your life we are talking about. You must tell me where Robin is, or how we might find him. You must! If you don't, in a few moments that brute yonder will tear you apart.'

Very slowly and clearly I said to him: 'I do not know where the Earl of Locksley is and, even if I did know, I would not reveal to you or to anyone else in this castle his whereabouts.'

'Alan, I beg you . . .'

I remained silent. There was nothing more to say.

Sir Nicholas shook his head sadly and looked at the ground. 'Then may Holy Mary, the Mother of God, watch over you now at this the hour of your death,' he said, and made to walk away.

Suddenly he turned back, and stepped in close. He slanted his head towards Milo, who was stretching his giant muscles for the bout, hands clasped above his head, twisting and turning his huge body in the afternoon sun. In little more than a whisper, Sir Nicholas said: 'His left knee is weak. He twisted it a few days ago while exercising. His left knee, understand? God be with you.' And with that he went to rejoin his royal master on the far side of the ropes.

Two men-at-arms stepped forward and roughly pushed me towards the centre of the list, towards Milo.

Prince John stood. In a loud, carrying voice he said: 'Alan Dale, you are guilty of high treason against my person, of disloyalty, of oath-breaking, of serving a demon-worshiping outlaw – and now you will face your just punishment. You will die today for your crimes – and here is your executioner.'

He ended his little speech with a shout on the word 'executioner'. And at this Milo lifted both his massive arms above his head and the crowd gave a roar of approval. It sounded like the howling of a pack of hungry wolves. And I have heard that sound before.

'Begin!' said Prince John, and abruptly sat down.

Milo walked over towards me slowly, his piggy-baby face smiling, his arms opened wide, massive paws open, fingers outstretched as if in a friendly greeting, as if inviting a cosy hug. He spoke then, his voice deep and grating, like the roots of a mountain being pulled out: 'I'm going to crush you, little man. I'm going to pull your head off as I did your little friend in Germany!'

I made no reply, but moved backwards, slowly, edging around to my left. I thought of honest, blue-eyed Adam and my red-headed friend Perkin, and the heat of rage at their senseless deaths flowed through my veins like hot wine. I was going to kill this man-beast, I told myself. I might die in the attempt, but as I had vowed to St Michael all those months ago on the banks of the River Main, I would have my vengeance this day.

The sun was low in the sky to the west and I wanted, if possible, to have it shining into my grotesque opponent's eyes, so I continued to circle to my left. I also watched the way that he walked as he followed me round, a bear's shuffle – and I saw that Sir Nicholas was right. He was favouring his left leg and had just a trace of a limp. The ogre grinned at me. 'Come here, little man, and I promise it will be very quick. Come to Milo.'

And suddenly, as I neared the southern rope, still circling westwards, he broke into a lumbering run, closed with me and made a grab for my body. I dropped to a crouch, my left hand on the ground, and lashed out with my right boot, catching him a hard blow on the side of his left knee. He gave a howl of rage, and stumbled a half-step forward, arms swinging to envelop me. I dodged under his massive right arm and danced away behind his back. And I felt the first flickering of hope. He was slow, he was very slow – and that kick to the knee had hurt him.

I moved backwards towards the western end of the list. I could hear booing from the crowd at my cowardly retreat, but I knew that if I wanted to live long enough to take my vengeance I had to stay away from his crushing embrace. Milo growled something unintelligible and charged at me. I feinted to the left and as he moved that way to grab me, I dived to the right under his arms once again, landing on the hard-packed earth of the list but immediately flipping my body over, swinging my leg and landing another hard kick on his left knee. He howled and went down on the injured joint, his broad, fur-matted back towards me.

Then I made a mistake.

I jumped to my feet, leapt on his back and locked my left forearm around his neck from behind, squeezing it tight with my right forearm in a choke-hold. By God, his neck was thick – it must have been a good foot wide. But though I squeezed with all my considerable strength, hoping to cut off his wind and prevent the blood getting to his massive head, it was like trying to strangle an oak tree. Milo rose to both feet, with me clinging tightly to his sweat-greased hairy back, lifting me off the ground as if I were a child and he were giving me a pig-a-back ride.

I could dimly hear the roar of the crowd, sounding like the beating of the angry sea against a cliff. Milo shook his body in a series of enormous heaves, to the left and right, trying to dislodge me. My stranglehold seemed to be having no effect on him whatsoever. As he shook his great squat body, mine flew from side to side with each heave, but I clung on for dear life, trying to keep my purchase on his neck and exert as much pressure as possible. I could feel the rumbling of his ogre's rage

283

through the bones in my left forearm. Then he changed tactics. His huge right fist swept up and backwards over his own shoulder, smashing into the right side of my head. It was an awkward blow, and only delivered with half-force, but it slammed me to the left and I could feel my grip slipping; then he punched me with his left hand, catching me full on the left ear and sending me crashing to the ground, my head spinning. He turned and stamped at my chest and just in time I rolled, and rolled again on the hard earth as he came raging after me, stamping and roaring. If a blow from one of those huge feet had landed on me it would have crushed my chest like a rock dropped on an egg. But I kept rolling and rolling just ahead of his stamping boot. In desperation I swung my own boot at him laterally, and by God's grace I caught the left knee again, from behind, kicked it right from under him, and he dropped to the floor with a bull-bellow of rage.

As I scrambled to my feet I saw that he truly was hurt. But I found I was breathless and still dizzy from the punches I had taken to the head, my legs felt like water, and I had a strong urge to vomit. Milo struggled to rise, and could barely put any weight on the injured limb once upright. Yet for all his inhuman looks, he was no coward. He roared: 'Now you die, you little worm.' And he came charging at me once more, his feral anger giving him the strength to run on that injured knee.

And I knew what I had to do. It was a move that little Thomas ap Lloyd had shown me many months ago in Kirkton, a wrestling trick that he had devised himself, he claimed, to use a bigger, stronger man's weight and momentum against him. He had used it on me, and easily thrown me – and it was not only my pride that had been bruised that day. I offered up a very quick prayer to Michael, the warrior saint, and, as Milo charged at me once more, hobbling forward with a surprising turn of speed, I committed myself to little Thomas's strange wrestling manoeuvre.

As Milo's enormous hands reached out to grab my body, I fell straight back before him, tucking my knees up into my stomach and rolling backwards on my spine, curled up like a new-born baby. When Milo stumbled over my prostrate body, his meaty hands groping the air, I grabbed his wrists, jerked him forward and shot my feet suddenly upwards into his stomach – and, using all the main strength in both my young legs, I heaved him up and over my body.

He flew.

He flew over my extended legs, sailing into the blue sky, his huge body turning a full circle in the air and smashing down a full three yards away, landing with an earth-jarring crash – on his left leg.

I jumped up and ran at him, my mind barely registering the broken left limb sticking out under his prone body at an unnatural right-angle. His screaming drowned out the roar of the crowd as I raced in and smashed my right boot as hard as I could, squarely into the side of his face as he lay on the ground, roaring with agony. His head jolted with the impact of my foot, but still he seemed hardly to notice it and continued groping madly at his twisted knee, and squealing like a half-butchered pig. I shouted: 'For Perkin!' – and stamped with the full weight of my boot-heel on his broad cheekbone, and was rewarded with a loud and welcome crack. He was trying to move, to sit up, so I gave him another belting kick to the right eye, pulping it and knocking his giant head backwards with its impact, and another hard-swung scything boot to the temple, and yet another that must have dislocated his jaw, and another, smashing into his cheekbone. His head was now bloody and raw, and hanging loose on his bull neck, but I did not let up – thinking of the deaths of my friends, I carried on kicking and stamping, landing blow after blow with my booted feet into that huge bloody baby-giant poll. I was filled with a black and terrible rage that afternoon, fuelled by fear of this monster sprawled before me and a deep well of hatred for all those around me, and for longer than I like to recall I kicked and hacked, stamped and ground at his gory, pulpy head, until my stout leather boots were slick with his blood and skin and tissue, and he moved no more.

I finally stopped, panting, shaking with emotion, and looked around the crowd of men-at-arms at the ropes. They were absolutely silent and none would meet my mad, glaring eye. I looked over at Prince John; his mouth was hanging wide open, showing little yellow teeth and a bright pink tongue. Sir Ralph Murdac beside him looked white and shocked.

Prince John recovered first. He croaked, 'Seize him!' and suddenly I was surrounded by a dozen men-at-arms with drawn swords. I readied my soul for death. 'Take him . . . away,' the Prince managed to say.

And as I was being dragged back towards the keep by rough hands, I heard Prince John shout after me, his voice shaking with emotion: 'You are not free of this matter, you filthy cur. You will not escape your crimes. You will hang for this, you will hang for this, you diabolical, blood-crazed . . . animal; before God, I swear you will hang at dawn tomorrow.'

*   *   *

286

Back in the storeroom, I wept. I do not know why, but often after a fight I feel a terrible sadness, a soul-sickness, come over me. It is one that I can usually control, but in that dark, desperate place, still trembling with rage after beating Milo, I allowed myself the weakness and comfort of a woman's tears. It did not last for long and I must admit that, afterwards, I felt a good deal better.

Over the next few hours, I took stock of my situation: to the good, I had defeated a monster who had sought to tear me apart; my enemies had arranged a humiliating death for me and by great good fortune – and here I blessed little Thomas ap Lloyd and his oddly effective wrestling tricks – I had avoided my fate and taken a suitable revenge for Perkin and Adam. I still lived. More than a little bruised around the face and neck, I grant you – I had taken savage punches from both Little John and the monster Milo in less than two days – but for the most part hale and well.

To the bad: I was to be hanged like a common criminal in the morning.

I bathed my sore face in what was left of the water, and drank some of it too, tasting the metallic tang of my own blood in the jug. I prayed once more for salvation – either in this life or in the next. And then I lay down once again on the barley sacks and tried to sleep.

I had barely closed my eyes when the door of the storeroom opened and two men entered. One of them fixed a burning torch to a becket in the wall and when my eyes had adjusted to the harsh light, I saw that it was Sir Nicholas de Scras. I had half-expected a visit from my friend, but his companion came as a complete surprise: it was Sir Aymeric de St Maur, the Templar knight.

Sir Nicholas handed me a jug of ale, a loaf of rye bread and a small bowl of cold mutton stew. And I found that I was starving. The two knights watched me as I ate hungrily and slaked my thirst, saying nothing, only staring at me by the flickering light of the torch. When I had wiped the last of the gravy from the bowl with the remaining crust of bread, I broke the silence: 'Thank you,' I said. 'And to what do I owe this unexpected courtesy?'

'You know what we want, Dale,' said Sir Aymeric. 'Or rather, *who* we want. You are Locksley's man and you must know how we can find him. And we can force you to tell us if we have to.' He smiled cruelly. 'I find that a hot iron applied judiciously can loosen the most stubborn tongue.'

I could not suppress a quick shudder. I had once been tortured by Sir Ralph Murdac with hot irons and that foul memory is one I do not care to contemplate. And I remembered the poor wretch dragged to the centre of the Temple Church at the inquisition, and tried not to imagine what Aymeric de St Maur had done to him to secure his testimony against Robin.

I shook my head: 'I am getting tired of telling you people this. But I will repeat it for you once more and then I will speak on this subject no more. I – Do – Not – Know – Where – Robin – Is. I serve him, yes, and gladly. But we arranged matters so that I would never be able to betray him – even on pain of torture or death.'

Sir Aymeric de St Maur glared at me. For a few moments no one spoke. Then he said: 'We have sent men to bring in your servant – the foreigner. And when we have him, we will see if a little heat will loosen *his* tongue. Or perhaps, watching his agony, you may feel more inclined to talk.'

I closed my lips, clenched my teeth and determined that I would say no more.

'There is no need for this sort of unpleasantness,' said Nicholas de Scras calmly. 'Sir Aymeric, would you be so good as to leave us. I'd like to talk to Alan alone. Of your goodness, will you grant me this small mercy?'

Aymeric stared at Sir Nicholas for a few moments; he seemed taken aback. Then, turning to leave, he said grumpily, 'Very well, but mark you this: if he will not talk to you, he will talk to me before morning.' And with that parting threat hanging in the air like a foul odour he left the storeroom, banging the elm-wood door shut behind him.

Sir Nicholas and I stared at each other for several moments. And then the knight said, 'It is still not too late for you, Alan.' His voice was pleading, kindly – like a father trying to persuade a recalcitrant child. 'We can end all this, and set you free to go wherever you will, if only you will help us. Please, Alan, for your sake, and mine: help me to help you.'

I said nothing, locking my jaw and looking him in the eye; and my silence seemed to draw speech from him.

'I do not have many friends,' said this one-time Hospitaller, 'and I have even fewer now that I have left the Order. But I thought once that you and I might become close. And when they hang you tomorrow, I will feel a great sadness that another man who offered me the promise of brotherhood has perished. Of course, it is entirely your own fault: if you would only speak to me about your friend Robin, if you would only trust me, I could save you, even now. But you have chosen to die. And I can understand that. I honour your loyalty to your lord, but you have shown your mettle a hundred times; you have proved

289

your courage and your worth as a faithful vassal, and now it is time to think of yourself. To save yourself. Alan, I beg you: save yourself!'

He paused for a while to give me the chance to speak. But I said nothing, merely stared at him, my tongue locked.

'I had a friend in Outremer, a good friend,' Sir Nicholas continued. 'He was your friend, too, I believe. His name was Sir Richard at Lea – and you know how he died. You know . . . you know who it was who killed him.'

He paused again and looked at me, and this time I could not meet his eye.

'You know that your master Robert of Locksley callously ordered the death of a good man; he killed my friend and yours, just so that he could enrich himself like some filthy merchant with the trade in frankincense.'

I was surprised. I could not understand how Sir Nicholas knew all this; the knight seemed to be able to see directly into my mind. Then he relieved my puzzlement.

'In Acre, in the hospital there, I tended you when you were sick,' Sir Nicholas said. 'Do you not remember?' And I nodded and remembered his kindness to me. I felt an overwhelming desire to speak to him, to thank him, and only with some difficulty did I manage to hold my tongue.

'I tended you, I sponged the night sweat from your body, and soothed you when you raved. I listened to your ranting, night after night: and I remembered it. Do you know what you said in your delirium? Do you know who you accused of the murder of Sir Richard at Lea? I think you do. You named Robert, Earl of Locksley, as his killer. And you called him a monster, a demon-worshipping fiend. All that I know of Locksley's crimes, I know because you told me during those long, fever-racked nights in Acre.'

Sir Nicholas's face had grown more gaunt and his voice had become a little harsher, a little less kindly and fatherly.

'You have already betrayed Robin Hood, your friend, your master. Did you not know that? It was I who told the Templars where to look for the evidence of his heretical beliefs; his God-cursed sacrifices to woodland demons. And I received all that information, every scrap of it, from you, from your sickbed ravings.

'You have already betrayed your master! You are already a traitor – and a real traitor this time. But now you can save your skin, and live a long and happy life. All you have to do is talk to me. You called him a monster. And he *is* a monster. He killed my friend, my true friend Richard – all for the sake of some filthy incense money! Help me, Alan. Help me to bring that monster to justice and let our noble friend Sir Richard at Lea rest peacefully at last in his grave.'

I stared at the floor: my jaw muscles flexing, my teeth squeaking with the effort of keeping quiet.

The silence stretched out for an eternity. And, finally, Sir Nicholas gave up. He got to his feet and banged on the store-room door to bring a guard.

'Why will you not help me, Alan? Why?'

He stood in the open doorway; I never expected to see him again in this world and so, at last, I spoke.

'I swore an oath to Robin, long ago when I was just a boy. Though I was not yet a man, I swore it: I swore that I would be loyal to him unto death. And I intend to keep that oath. It is something a man like you, a breaker of holy vows, a man who turns his back on his comrades, could not possibly understand!'

Sir Nicholas flinched at my words, as I had intended him to; and two smears of red appeared on his cheeks. He made the sign of the Cross on his breast, in the place where a white cross had once been sewn on his black Hospitallers' surcoat – the sacred mantle that he had discarded.

'God will judge all of us in His own good time,' he said and, pulling the torch from the becket on the wall, he made to leave.

'Wait, Nicholas,' I said. 'I have a question for you. As I am to die tomorrow morning, as a kindness, answer me this: why did you kill the big man Tom outside the Blue Boar tavern in Westminster? He was wounded and he might have talked, but you quickly silenced him. Why?'

Sir Nicholas cocked his head on one side and looked at me, the torchlight flickering across his face and casting his eyes in deep shadow. 'After what you have just said to me, I am not sure that I wish to oblige you.' He looked at me a while, then shrugged. 'Well, I suppose it can do no harm . . .' And he smiled sadly at me, more like his old self again. 'I knew that Prince John had sent men to murder you – but I did not know who they were. I thought that those men outside the tavern might have come from the Prince. And if they had, and the big one had admitted his mission under questioning, I knew that you would never have willingly come to Prince John's banner. That was my reasoning. I wanted you to come to John so that I could get to Robert of Locksley. I thought that if we were on the same side, you might let slip something that would allow me to reach him. It seems I was wrong.'

Our eyes locked for a couple of heartbeats. I said nothing more. Then he half-saluted me with his right hand, and stepped quickly out of the room and the door closed quietly behind him.

When Sir Nicholas had left me, I tried once more to sleep. I could not: there were too many images rushing around inside my head for peaceful slumber. Visions of Robin, and Little John, and Sir Richard at Lea's terrible death in the blood-clotted sands of Outremer, and images of Goody and Marie-Anne; of Milo's bloody head lolling by my boots; of Ralph Murdac's shocked expression. And then there was the hanging. I was going to die in a few short hours. I had seen my own father hanged when I was a boy, torn from his bed and strung up by Sir Ralph Murdac's men, and the memory disturbed me still. I could see his hideously distorted face and bulging eyes as the rope choked the life from him, and I pictured once again the piss dripping from his kicking heels. Was my fate to be the same as my father's? Had I been born to hang?

At a little after midnight, after several sleepless hours, the door of the storeroom opened once again – this time very softly – and Robert Odo, the outlawed Earl of Locksley, stepped in.

Chapter Sixteen

I did not know immediately, of course, that it was Robin. The door just swung open – in the intense blackness of the roots of a castle at midnight I heard it more than saw it. And then he spoke: 'That you, Alan?' And even in his hoarse whisper, I knew my lord had come and all would now be well. I can remember vividly the emotion I felt at the time; like a great warm wave that flooded my soul with joy. I knew Robin would lead me out of that dark place and into the light, to safety.

I had the urge to throw my arms around him – but I controlled myself, as a man should. I did not want Robin to think that I had been frightened for my life. So I merely whispered: 'What took you so long? I've been bored almost witless waiting for you to turn up.'

Feeble stuff, I know, but I sensed Robin smile in the darkness. 'I'm a very busy man,' he whispered back, with the hint of laughter in his tone. 'So much silver to steal, so many ruffians to rescue.' Then he continued, still in a low, barely audible voice: 'Are you fit, Alan? Are you injured? Do you think you can climb a rope?'

I admitted that I was largely intact.

'Then come on – unless you'd rather stay here and wallow a while longer in your comfortable little cell.'

We slipped out of the door and, in the dark corridor outside, I sensed a shape and heard another familiar voice: Hanno. There was a rustle of cloth and Hanno handed something heavy to Robin and my lord quickly returned to the store-room. He was gone a few moments, and I grabbed Hanno's arm and asked him in a whisper what Robin was doing.

'A wolf's head,' said my friend. And I imagined his awful grin in the darkness.

'What?' I whispered back.

'He leaves a big wolf's head in there, Alan. It is freshly cut this morning from an animal trapped in Sherwood.'

'For God's sake, why?' My voice was rising in volume. This seemed to be behaviour that verged on madness. Why were we standing there in that dark corridor talking about decapitated vermin? I was suddenly alarmed: had the strains of outlawry turned Robin insane?

It was Robin himself who replied, coming silently out of the storeroom door, but bolting it shut with a loud click. 'Terror, Alan – just giving them the fear,' he whispered. 'You know how I like to do it – minimum effort to create maximum terror.'

Then we were off: with Hanno leading, we crept down the dark corridor, Robin bringing up the rear. We turned right, and swiftly left – Hanno seemed to know exactly where we were going, but I did not. The punches I had taken to the head must have made me slow-witted, for it only dawned on me then, as we padded silently through the passages under the great tower and the upper bailey in the dead hour after midnight, what Robin had been doing back in the storeroom. He was trying to convince the castle's men-at-arms that I had been spirited away from my condemned cell by wild magic. And by leaving a severed wolf's head, he was saying that it was he – Robin Hood, the outlaw earl with the wolf's head device on his banner – who had accomplished this demonic trick.

If people generally believed Robin to be guilty of heresy, consorting with devils and spirits, and so on, he had only himself to blame. Hard on the heels of that thought came another: he welcomed people believing that he had extraordinary, demonic powers. I recalled a spectacularly ugly, one-eyed friend called Thomas from my early days as an outlaw who had told me that Robin dabbled in all this devilish stuff to add to his mystique with the country folk. But it was obvious that he enjoyed it too. It was forbidden, wrong, ungodly – and Robin revelled in that type of thing.

Something else occurred to me belatedly. I touched Robin's sleeve and whispered: 'How did you get in here? And where are we going now?'

He chuckled almost silently and said: 'You'll soon see!' And I had to be content with that.

At the end of the next corridor we all paused, and flattened our bodies against the cool sandstone wall. Around the corner came the sound of footsteps: a lone soldier's boots. One man and a glow of light.

I felt the warmth of Hanno's face next to my ear, and he breathed three words: 'Watch and learn!'

The unfortunate man-at-arms came round the corner and Hanno leapt on him as quick as a hunting weasel, his left hand clamping over the man's nose and mouth, his right arm punching a long dagger into his unguarded belly just below the rib-cage, and then twisting it upwards into his chest. The man was smashed back against the far wall, dropping the horn lantern he was carrying with a clatter; he had been taken completely by surprise, and was only able to utter a few muffled grunts of pain and shock before Hanno's long, questing blade found his heart, ripped it open and, with a gout of hot blood, the man-at-arms slumped to the ground, a twitching, unstrung marionette, who was very soon still.

'Do you see?' Hanno was at my ear again. 'That is perfect. The dagger goes in, here, and then up, here' – he was poking at my abdomen with a rough finger, but I was in no mood for more lessons in silent murder; I was looking at the dead man by the light of his dropped lantern, studying the comical look of surprise on his face – and his belt. For tucked into it, on the left-hand side, was a triangular-bladed stabbing weapon with a plain wooden handle and a stout crosspiece in steel. It was my misericorde. By happy chance, this was one of the men-at-arms who had seized me in the great hall two days ago. He must have thought the misericorde a legitimate prize of war. Well, it was mine again now. I took it from the dead man's belt and slid it into my left boot. I took his sword and sword belt, too. And suddenly all my fears melted away. Whatever happened tonight, I would not allow myself to be recaptured. I had a weapon in my boot and one at my waist, and I was prepared to kill the whole world if necessary.

Robin knelt beside the lantern, opened the little horn door

and pinched out the candle inside – and once more we were plunged into absolute darkness.

Hanno led us silently and swiftly onwards, down a dank set of stairs, through a door and into a short corridor, where we paused again. I could see another glow of light seeping from around the corner. Motioning us to stillness and silence, Hanno dropped quietly to the floor and peered at boot-level around the corner from where the light was coming. He stood again and moved in close to Robin and me: 'Two of them,' he breathed. And putting a palm on my chest, and shoving me gently against the wall he whispered: 'You stay here, Alan. Don't move.'

My master nodded at me, and then pulled up his hood to cover his face. And with that my two friends, the one with a bare round shaven head, and the other shrouded in his hood, both armed and very dangerous, stepped around the corner and left me alone in the gloom.

I heard Hanno say loudly in his best English accent: 'Hello, you fellows, be so good as to tell me: is this the way to the cheese store?' Then there was a thump and a muffled scream and a clatter of falling metal and a horrible wet gurgling sound. And suddenly I knew exactly where in Nottingham Castle we were. We were just outside Prince John's treasury. Just yards away from the greatest haul of silver coin in central England.

When I peered round the corner I could see Robin and Hanno, each manoeuvring a slumped guard's body and arranging it so the arse was on the ground, legs extended, back to the stone wall of the corridor. They were evidently trying to make it appear as if the men were asleep at their post by the door. The ruse would not have fooled anyone for very long: the spreading pool of blood beneath each corpse told the truth.

Taking a heavy bunch of keys from one of the dead men, Robin inserted one into the big iron lock and turned it. As I approached down the corridor, he flung the door open and held up the horn lantern, relit from the guards' candle stub, to cast its glow inside the room.

It was like a dragon's treasure cave: a glittering hoard. There were small barrels overflowing with silver pennies, iron-bound chests containing precious gems, small round sacks of coin piled in heaps, silver and gold plates and candlesticks, cups, knives, mazers, serving dishes, bright pieces of women's jewellery, and all the moveable wealth of middle England scattered about the place on shelves, in wooden boxes and casks and even in mounds on the floor. As the candlelight was reflected, sparkling and bouncing off this incredible accumulation of booty, I sensed that even Robin was stunned to see so much wealth in one place.

But he did his best not to show it. Instead he busied himself pulling open his cloak and unwinding a series of confections of rope and cloth bags from around his waist. He hurled a couple at me and I caught them in the air. Unfolding them, I found that they were pairs of rough canvas bags attached to stout networks of rope. Hanno showed me how to wear them: he filled the two canvas bags with silver pennies then draped the heavy bags over his neck so that the chinking burdens hung from a kind of harness under his arms, gently nudging his ribs. Then he grabbed another pair of bags and began again.

'Only coin, I think,' said Robin. 'Leave all the bulky stuff. And carry no more than you can comfortably run with, boys. Quickly now!'

And we fell to with a will, using our hands to shovel the bright discs of silver in glittering cascades into the bags and then hanging them around our necks and shoulders, festooning our bodies with a fortune. I could not resist a quiet laugh: if I were to die at this particular moment, I thought to myself, I would die a very rich man.

Robin passed me a wide leather belt upon which were hung six big leather pouches at equal distances. I strapped it around my waist and filled each pouch with golden coins: fat, greasy, glittering Bezants, the like of which I had not seen since my time in Outremer. I looked at the other two men: their eyes were bright with greed and the simple delight of seeing precious metal shining in the candlelight. And our joy was infectious.

Finally, Robin called a halt to our plundering: 'No more,' he said. 'No more, or we will not be able to move.'

I was fingering a beautifully carved golden cross, studded with precious gems. 'Alan, put that down and let's be away from here,' he ordered.

For a moment, I considered defying him, I wanted that cross; it was so beautiful, so fine – surely I had earned it for all the recent strains put on my loyalty to him? – such is the dark pull of treasure on a man's soul that I gave Robin an evil glare, and considered shoving it in my boot top – and then I came to my senses and replaced the gorgeous cross on a nearby shelf. And reluctantly we left the treasury, Robin locking it carefully behind us.

We stepped over the two corpses, chinking slightly as we moved, each carrying in the region of sixty pounds of precious metal hung in dozens of bags slung from cords and ropes about our bodies. As we staggered our way down the corridor, once more in pitch darkness, I laid my hand on Hanno's shoulder ahead of me, with Robin moving heavily behind me. We were carrying as much coin as we could, yet we had hardly made a dent on the contents of the treasury – at most we had taken one tenth of all the silver and gold there. I marvelled at how much wealth Prince John had accumulated in the past few months – despite Robin's constant depredations on his wagon trains. John must easily be the wealthiest man in England by a long mile. As I thought about this, I missed my step and blundered into the back of Hanno, and the bags of coin at my chest banged into the ones slung at his back with a grinding squeak. 'Be quiet!' hissed Robin savagely. Mutely I accepted his rebuke.

More than anything I dreaded running into a party of men-at-arms: under normal circumstances, with Robin and Hanno at my side, we would have been a match for any group of armed men – even a dozen of them. But encumbered as I was, with that dead weight of metal around my neck, shoulders, chest and waist, I would be as slow-moving in a fight as the ogre Milo; I was not sure I could defeat even one half-competent man-at-arms. And so I prayed that we would not be discovered as we proceeded as silently as we could down each corridor and passage, following Hanno's unerring sense of direction in the dark.

Finally we stopped by a big door in the sandstone wall, Hanno lifted the rusty latch and we stumbled into a dusty room and quietly shut the door behind us. I heard Robin scraping away with a flint and steel until he had a glow, and then a small flame with which to light the candle inside the lantern. By that guttering light, I saw that the walls of the room were stacked with barrels of varying sizes, all thickly covered with cobwebs. Wine barrels, ale casks, huge tuns – dozens of them. I tapped one or two of them experimentally and found them to be empty. The cobwebs should have given me a clue: clearly this room had not been used in years. To be honest, I was sorely disappointed: I could have done with a drink – the excitement of the night and the effort of carrying all that weight of metal had made me thirsty.

Hanno beckoned me over to the far wall, where an old curtain was hanging from a rail. He pulled back the curtain to reveal another door, very wide and low – no more than five foot high – and like a conjuror at a county fair, he pulled a big iron key from his pouch, brandishing it in the dim light of Robin's lantern. I was mystified, but followed Hanno when he unlocked the door, stooping to get through the low entrance and into a very small chamber beyond. Once Robin had joined us, Hanno solemnly locked the low door behind us, tucked away the key, and gestured with a flourish at a structure in the centre of that small space. It appeared to be some sort of well housing: a wide circular stone wall about knee height and six foot in diameter, above which stood a small crane arm, with a heavy-looking block-and-tackle pulley. A thick rope dangled from the crane arm, falling away into the darkness of the well.

I frowned: I knew that the castle had a deep well in the outer bailey near the new brewhouse, and huge cisterns for storing rainwater in the roof of the great tower in case of a siege, but I'd had no idea there was a well here, at what I judged to be the south-eastern side of the upper bailey. Surely we were too high up here for men to have found water by digging through the sandstone. I peered down into the shaft of the well but could see no more than ten feet down. And I could discern no flickering shine of reflection off a surface of water. Perhaps a dry well, then?

Robin came over to me, grinning happily: 'What do you think, Alan – brilliant, isn't it? Underneath that uncouth, ale-guzzling exterior, your man Hanno is a *bona fide* genius.'

I was very slow that day, I confess. And my puzzlement must have been obvious. Robin laughed: 'Come on, Alan – you can work it out. What is that room out there?' He indicated the low door we had just passed through.

'It's an old buttery,' I said. 'But it looks as if it has not been used for some time now.' I was still none the wiser.

'And what do butteries contain?'

'Butts,' I said stupidly. 'Butts of ale and wine, and so on and so forth.'

'And where do butts of ale come from?'

Suddenly I had it. 'From a brewhouse. From the new brewhouse in the outer bailey,' I said excitedly, my brain finally working at full speed. 'But before that was built three years ago, they used to come from the old brewhouse outside the castle walls, which was next to The Trip to Jerusalem tavern. So this is not a well . . .'

Hanno came over to join us by the wide shaft. 'That is the way that the ale is delivered to the castle in the old days. They make it in the brewhouse and put it into barrels and then they bring the barrels up this shaft so the men can be drinking it in the castle. But nobody uses it now. It is forgotten, I believe. Perfect, eh, Alan? A perfect way out.'

'Shall we?' said Robin with a smile, gesturing at the rope that hung down into the darkness.

Climbing down that rope with sixty pounds of metal strapped to my body nearly ripped my arms from their sockets. But it was only a short descent – no more than twenty feet. Soon all three of us were standing, hearts pounding with exertion, in a low chamber, five paces by five paces, quarried out of the sandstone deep beneath the south-eastern wall of the upper bailey, beside a tunnel with hacked-out shallow steps leading away downwards and eastwards into the darkness.

Robin, lantern in hand, led the way. The candlelight danced and flickered on the close yellow walls, making eerie patterns and shapes with the rough, pebble-dotted sandstone rock so that, to my tired and punch-drunk brain, it seemed the tunnel was peopled with demons, fairies and bizarre creatures. It was hard to believe that it had only been that morning when I had stomped Milo into bloody mush. I felt I had entered some other, magical world. The tunnel turned this way and that and I saw that there were other passages leading off the main thoroughfare to unknown destinations deep in the rock on which the castle was built. A man could get lost here, I thought, in this underground maze. And perhaps, once lost, he would enter a fairy realm and never be seen by mortal eyes again.

But at last our spooky twisting passage down the tunnel came to an end and I found myself with Robin and Hanno in a long, low cellar, once again filled with empty casks, but this time clearly in use. And not long afterwards, having passed through several wider caverns cut from the soft sandstone, we emerged out of the darkness, through a heavy leather curtain and into the back room of The Trip to Jerusalem.

As we stepped, blinking, into the tavern, I saw a cosy, homely sight laid out before me. Little John was seated at a table by the fire with two small children. Unaware of our presence, he threw a pair of dice, and the children – a boy and a girl, both little dark-haired mites with big deer-like eyes – cried out joyfully at John's bad luck with the gambling bones. I saw that John's double-bladed axe was leaning casually against the table by his side. Over by the counter, I saw something of quite a different tenor. The children's parents were standing by the racks of flagons and mugs and ale-pots, staring at John, immobilized with fear. I knew them slightly: they were the young couple who ran The Trip – and I have never seen two people look more terrified in my life. The woman was clutching at her husband's arm, and every time Little John made a sudden move, to scoop up the dice, say, and throw again, she flinched as if Sir Aymeric's hot irons were being applied to her parts.

Over by the door that led to the rest of the tavern stood two tall, grim-faced hooded men, armed with sword and bow – men I knew, and who nodded a greeting to me. And my heart sank a little. While I was most grateful to Robin for rescuing me, for saving me from torture and certain death, I still balked slightly at his ruthless methods. He had clearly threatened this good couple's children to ensure their co-operation. And while it was a very effective way of guaranteeing our safety that night, as we emerged weighed down with booty from our adventure in Nottingham Castle, I could not but feel a chill in my bones at the soul-suffering that Robin had inflicted on these decent people.

Having said that, no one had been hurt, and we passed the rest of the night with great conviviality in The Trip to Jerusalem, feasting on honey cakes and ham and preserved berries washed down with ale provided by the frightened brewer and his wife, while Little John set riddles for the children to guess, and allowed them to ride on his back as if he were a horse. They were enchanting creatures, about five or six years old, I would say. And I privately swore that they should come to no harm, even if it meant facing Little John and Robin over drawn blades.

A few hours before dawn I asked Robin how he had known that I needed to be rescued. And I thanked him profusely, if a little drunkenly – for I must admit the ale had taken a hold of my tired head – for saving me.

'It was the wagons,' said my master, looking fondly at me over a foaming mug of good Trip to Jerusalem ale. 'The wagons we captured outside of Carlton. There was no silver in them. Nothing valuable in them at all. Those great chests in the three great wagons, so firmly locked and sealed by Sir Robert de la Mare, were full of no more than sand and gravel.'

'So we knew you were neck-deep in the shit, young Alan,' interrupted Little John. 'It was obvious: Murdac had hoped to trap us with the lure of silver, but he wasn't prepared to risk the actual precious metal. We knew then that the game was up – that the minute you put your nose back inside Nottingham, you were headed for the noose.'

'They sent two men to arrest Hanno here,' Robin said, 'but he's not a man to be led meekly to the gallows.'

'I kill them both – pffft, pffft!' Hanno moved a flat blade-like hand back and forward across his own neck, and made a strange whistling noise between his broken teeth. 'Then I take Ghost from the stables and fly north to Sherwood, very fast. I am lucky to be able to track down Robin that very same day.'

'Still, I think we have more than compensated ourselves for the lost wagonloads of silver,' said Robin with a smile, and he nodded towards the pile of bulging sacks of coin in the corner of the room. By my reckoning we had removed nearly two hundred pounds of coin from Prince John's treasury – and I couldn't help but return his smile.

'To John Plantagenet's princely generosity,' I said, lifting my mug of ale. Robin laughed, and my friends all repeated the toast and we drank.

At dawn, with two packhorses tottering under the weight of precious metal, we rode through Nottingham town, hooded, anonymous and looking as innocent as six heavily armed and badly hungover horsemen can. I was happy to be astride Ghost once more, and even more pleased to be in the company I was – free at last of the subterfuge of the past six months. The tavern-keeper and his wife and their two sweet children waved after us as we rode away, the children looking happy, tired and just a little madcap, having spent the whole night awake with playful grown-ups, the parents relieved but still a little shocked and fearful. We made it out of the northern gates of Nottingham town as the church bells were ringing out for Prime and set our horses' heads north on the road to Sherwood.

Chapter Seventeen

I was tired, deep in the bone tired, and when, a day later, we reached Robin's Caves, an old outlaw hideout in the heart of Sherwood, the first thing I did was sleep for several days. But while I was restoring my muscles and sinews, and allowing my bruised face to heal, with lazy days spent pottering around Robin's sprawling camp and long nights on a comfortable over-stuffed straw pallet inside the main cave, Robin was busy.

He invited friends, and fellow outcasts from Sherwood, and men loyal to King Richard from all over the north of England to join us in a feast under the stars in the Greenwood – and to hold a council of war. The country was on the verge of outright civil war, Robin told me; small groups of supporters of John had clashed with those of Richard in pitched battle on several occasions in the past few months, and Richard's men had had the worst of it. Now they came to us, in their hundreds – poor men, knights, even a minor baron or two – to sit at a huge circular table in a clearing near Robin's Caves, around a huge roaring fire, and gorge on roast venison, and wild boar, and mutton, on stews and puddings, and pies and autumn fruit, and cheese; all at the outlaw Earl's expense. Vast quantities of ale and wine were drunk, too, but by and large the company remained orderly. The feasting lasted for several days, and there were games and competitions, wrestling and foot races, for those sober enough to participate.

Father Tuck turned up – coming all the way from London; deserting his mistress the Countess Marie-Anne for a few days but bringing her love and affection to her husband. He had messages too for Robin's ear from Queen Eleanor of Aquitaine and her senior counsellors Walter de Coutances and Hugh de Puiset. Even William of Edwinstowe, Robin's older brother, came for one day. He and his men-at-arms kept themselves to themselves and ate and drank sparingly. William and Robin had a long, intense conversation at the back of the main cave, which I was not privy to, but it seemed to have a satisfactory conclusion, for they embraced stiffly after the talking was done, and soon afterwards, William and his men rode away towards the south, heading for London, according to the gossip around the campfires.

One day while we were sitting alone, indulging in yet another massive bout of gluttony, I plucked up my courage and directly asked Tuck for news of Goody.

'Oh, she is very well. And I think she must be happy, too. She has a gentleman admirer who calls on her every day bringing flowers and sweetmeats, costly silks and perfumes.'

'What did you say!' Suddenly I felt sick and pushed away my plate, still piled high with rich food.

'I said young Goody now has a gentleman admirer,' Tuck repeated calmly, and then he drew my platter towards him and, with dainty fingers, he picked up and took an enormous bite from a crisp slice of a suckling pig.

'And who is this lecherous bastard? Some scabby, rat-faced, turnip-muncher, I make no doubt!' I realized that my voice had grown rough and loud and my cheeks were glowing hot.

Tuck leaned his head back and regarded me over his big red nose as he chewed. When he had finished his mouthful of pork, he said: 'He is Lord Chichester's eldest boy, Roger. A handsome lad, and quite refined – the ladies all say so.' And he grinned at me.

'All the ladies say so! I'll wager they do. And you let this philandering, over-bred, chinless stripling get close to my Goody! How could you, Tuck? He'll be smarming all over her, trying to weasel his way into her bedchamber with pretty words – sweetmeats, silks and perfumes, indeed! I hold you responsible, Tuck. God's bones, I'd like to meet this horny little rich boy. If he has so much as laid a hand on her, I'll cut his balls off, I'll . . .'

'Calm yourself, Alan! Do calm down. Why don't you ride down to London yourself and you can meet this boy Roger. You will find that he is a very chaste and God-fearing fellow, mild-mannered . . .'

'Chaste and mild-mannered, my arse,' I muttered. 'Nobody called Roger has ever been less than a full-blooded whore-mongering lecher . . .' And then I stopped. I knew I was making a rare idiot of myself, but perhaps Tuck was right. Perhaps it was my duty, as Goody's friend and honorary older brother, to pay a visit to this Roger person and make damn sure that he understood a few basic rules of gentlemanly behaviour: like no touching Goody, no fondling, no kissing – in fact, no speaking to her alone, or gazing at her longingly from afar, or sending her little scented love notes . . .

It was clearly my week for making a fool of myself. I brought up the prospect of a southern journey with Robin the next evening after a late supper. Most of the guests had departed by then and there were only about thirty of Robin's senior men gathered around a table in the main cave finishing a modest meal of soup and bread and cheese. To my surprise, Robin thought it a good idea.

'You can escort a packhorse train of silver to London for me,' he said. 'You've been sitting about for too long now. It's been – what? – three, four weeks since we pulled you out of Nottingham. I reckon it's about time you did something useful. Take at least twenty men with you, and be very, very careful. I've just heard that you have been formally declared outlaw by the shire court – it's Prince John's doing, of course – and there's a price on your head: a pound of finest silver. Congratulations!'

I beamed at him. I felt a strange kind of pride to be an outlaw; I had been too insignificant to be properly outlawed when I was last living wild in Sherwood. Now I was a dangerous, wanted man with a price in silver on his head. And I rather liked it.

Robin continued: 'Take heed, Alan, and be extra vigilant. Any man may take your life now and claim the reward, and if word gets out that you are carrying large quantities of specie, half the footpads in England will be lying in wait for you. And if you lose that money, I will be extremely displeased.' And he gave me a cold, hard stare.

Then his expression softened. 'When you get to London you can give my love to Marie-Anne, and little Hugh – and to Goody, of course.' And he smiled at me, with a glint of something knowing in his odd grey eyes.

Despite his warning, I was feeling very pleased with myself. A pound of precious silver for my life – it was a goodly sum. I thanked Robin, and was about to leave the cave when a thought struck me and I turned back to my outlawed lord. 'What is the price on your head now, Robin? Tell me honestly, I beg you.'

For a moment my master seemed almost embarrassed. Then he looked straight at me: 'I'm told it is up to a thousand pounds by now.'

I felt instantly deflated. 'A thousand pounds! A *thousand* pounds!' I said the words too loudly, almost shouting – in that company, nobody raised his voice to Robin – and a tense silence descended over the supper table. But for some reason I couldn't stop myself: 'And what about John Nailor?' I demanded of Robin, once again too loudly, and nodded over to the giant form of my blond friend who was watching us, grinning evilly from the far end of the table.

Robin coughed: 'Ah, um, I think it is five hundred pounds of silver at present!' He smiled mockingly at me. 'And I believe even Much the miller's son is worth ten pounds – and that's dead or alive, of course.'

'This is outrageous!' I was suddenly very angry. 'Why am I only worth one paltry pound of silver? That is nothing – nothing but a damned insult! I've a good mind to complain . . .'

'To Prince John?' said Robin, with a straight face, and the whole table – thirty big, tough, dirty outlaws – erupted in a deafening wave of laughter. I flushed a deep red, turned on my heel and stalked out of the cave with as much dignity as I could gather around me, while a cascade of boozy laughter and crude half-heard jests swept me out into the chilly night.

I rode south on a blustery October day with twenty heavily armed, mounted men at my back; half Welsh archers and half men-at-arms, guarding five packhorses each with two stout wooden chests strapped to its back. Beside me rode Hanno – and Thomas ap Lloyd. The dark Welsh boy had told me that he wished to become my squire, and train to be a fully fledged warrior one day, and while at twelve summers he was a little old to begin training, I felt he had promise, and that I owed him something for showing me the wrestling trick that I had used to defeat Milo. So he came, too, trotting along on a pony that was as brown, quiet and well mannered as he.

When he asked if he might serve me, I had asked him one crucial question in return.

'What do you know of your father's death,' I said, looking directly into his calm oak-brown eyes.

He looked right back at me, his gaze perfectly level, and said quietly and soberly: 'I know that he was offered money by Sir Ralph Murdac to kill the Earl of Locksley. I know that my life and the life of my mother were threatened by Murdac to encourage my father to comply. And I know that, instead of attacking our lord, he attacked you in the dark in the Earl's bed-chamber, by mistake, and that you fought and killed him.'

'Do you blame me for his death?'

'No, sir, I do not,' he said, and I was certain, as certain as I am of Damnation or Salvation, that he was telling me the truth. 'My father was forced to do what he did by Murdac, and you killed him in self-defence,' he continued. 'He died by your hand, but his death is not to be laid at your door. You were protecting yourself, and your lord, which is right and proper. I blame Sir Ralph Murdac for my father's death – and if I ever have the opportunity, I shall have my vengeance upon him.' He said these words quietly, calmly and with an incredible conviction for one so young. I believed him utterly.

'Then we shall get along very well,' I said, and took him into my service.

We had ridden no more than ten miles south of Robin's Caves, and our horses were only just getting into their stride for the long journey, when one of the scouts who had been ranging ahead of the column rode back to me and reported that there was a strange woman, apparently alone, chanting nonsense by an old stone preaching cross a mile or so down the road. I had told the scouts that they were to report anything out of the ordinary to me directly they saw it – for I went in mortal terror of a well-laid ambush or some ruse by Prince John's men that would rob me of the silver hoard the packhorses carried.

As we approached, I saw a small figure, hooded and swathed in heavy black wool, with her arms stretched out sideways in imitation of Our Lord's Passion, standing beside the cross which stood on a mound of earth next to the highway. It seemed that she was speaking to that holy symbol. And with a shock that was like a plunge in an icy mountain tarn, I realized that she was speaking in the Arabic tongue.

Suddenly the woman turned her body towards us and swept off her hood. I held up my hand to halt the column but I believe the whole cavalcade would have been stopped by her appearance alone. She had a truly hideous face, mutilated so much that it was almost beyond recognition as belonging to a human being: the nose was missing, leaving two large holes in the centre of her face, surrounded by ridged scars, like a truncated pig's snout; I saw that her ears, too, had been hacked off crudely, and her lips were gone as well, so that her narrow yellow teeth showed in a dreadful skull's grimace. Her hair – grey and long and matted into rats' tails – was whipped about her gaunt white face by the wind, and two dark eyes glowed in their sockets like the black-burning fires of Hell. She looked like a witch from a child's nightmare. From behind me I could hear the frightened muttering of the mounted men. And yet, for all her cruel looks, I knew she was no hag; in truth, I knew that she was not yet twenty summers old.

You see, I recognized her. This wreck of a young woman, this demonic personification of ugliness, with a face that would curdle fresh milk, had once been my lover. I had once smothered that terrible visage with my kisses and received them, too, from her now absent lips. For this was Nur, the once-exquisite Arab slave girl that I had met on the long journey to Outremer. There was a time when I had been entranced by her beauty – by her midnight hair that spilled like dark oil down her back; by her huge brown eyes and snow-white skin; by the soft, generous curves of her body and the way she gave it up so joyfully for my pleasure. But then my enemy, Malbête, had taken her and his men had abused her brutally before hacking away her luminous, radiant looks with their blades; desecrating her perfection to punish me. She had shown her mutilated face to me, one dark night when I lay in a sickbed in Acre, and I had screamed in horror at her disfigurement – and she had fled.

That had been two years ago, and I'd not seen her since. Yet here she was before me, in Nottinghamshire, as real as the rough stone cross on the grassy mound behind her.

'Nur,' I said. And then was lost for words; pity and shame welling up inside me in equal parts.

'Alan, my love, we meet again,' she said, holding out her arms as if to embrace me.

I flinched at her use of the words 'my love'. And I tried to ignore the invitation in her open arms. With her beauty gone, I had been forced to face the truth: that I was a shallow man, interested only in the outward form of a woman. I discovered that I was a man who could not love, truly, deeply, with the heart and not just the eyes, as women claim to do. I had behaved most ignobly – for, although she had run from me, I had not searched for her. It was my fault that she had come to look this way, yet I could not even make amends by giving her the love that she surely deserved for all her suffering.

'Nur – what are *you* doing here?' I said, trying to sound as if I had just encountered an old acquaintance in a tavern – and hating myself even as I spoke. 'Why did you leave your home-land? We all thought you must have gone back to your village, to your family. But here you are!'

'I followed you, my love' – I flinched once again at those words – 'I followed you halfway across the world, through storm and drought, through pestilence, fire and battle; I followed you hungry and shoeless . . .'

As she spoke, my mind traced her journey. I could only dimly imagine the hardship and dangers she must have faced, a woman alone, travelling so many thousands of miles of wild and lawless road.

316

'But why?' I said. 'Why follow me? What do you want from me?'

'Did you not promise, when you held me in your arms aboard that Frankish ship, to love me for ever? Did you not vow it? I have come to you. I followed you to prove that, despite my misfortune, despite my ugliness, I am worthy of your love. My darling, my true love – I have come back to you. We can be united once again.'

My stomach felt as if it were filled with clay. I *had* promised to love her for ever; I had said so many things in the heat of passion, then – but now I could not even bear to look at her, let alone touch her; the idea of kissing her made my belly squeeze tight up into my chest.

How could I tell her that I would never love her again, that I could never love her again?

'But why were you waiting here, on this spot?' I asked, still in the same jolly tavern-acquaintance tones.

'I have been waiting for you. And while I waited, I have been talking to your Christ God,' she said, indicating the stone cross behind her with a dirty, bony finger. 'I have been telling Him about my troubles and asking Him to heal my wounds.' Here Nur waved a dirty hand across her poor tortured face. 'And he spoke to me!'

I could feel all the men behind me crossing themselves. Out of the corner of my eye, I saw young Thomas straining forward in his saddle to get a closer look at her deformed face. But Nur had not finished.

'He spoke to me – your Christ God! And He promised to heal me, and He has promised me that we shall be together. You and I, Alan, my love, together at last.'

317

I could not help noticing that her command of English was much improved since I began teaching her our tongue on the voyage to Outremer two years ago. But I also felt an almost uncontrollable urge to run from her, to gallop far, far away so that I would never have to see her poor mutilated face again or feel the shame that it aroused in my breast.

'I think we must be married soon, my love; your Christ God has decreed it,' Nur continued. And behind me I heard a man-at-arms snigger and I stiffened in my saddle. I had to tell her once and for always that I did not love her.

'I am afraid that cannot be, Nur, my dear,' I said, trying now to sound like a kindly uncle. 'We may have shared our lives in Outremer, but here I am a different man. I can never be with you. I am not the marrying kind, alas. And I cannot linger here chatting either, for I must ride south this day on important business. Here, take this,' I said, and, feeling like Judas's paymaster, I plucked a small leather purse containing a dozen silver pennies from my belt and held it out to her. 'Take this purse and follow the road north from here, and you will be stopped by two armed men. Say that you come from me and that you are to be given food and shelter. Robin of Locksley is there; you remember him. Go to Robin and he will shelter you until I return.' I threw the purse to her and her bony hand, snaked out and snatched it out of the air.

'I must come with you, my love, wherever you go. We are one, you and I – we must never be parted again,' said Nur in a weird sing-song voice. It was as if she had heard nothing of what I had just said. The purse had disappeared somewhere inside the folds of her black robe.

'It was very pleasant to see you again, Nur, after so long. But much as I would like to hear the tale of your travels, I cannot take you with me. You must go north to Robin; he will care for you until I return. Try to understand . . .'

'No, it is you who must understand, my love.' Nur's voice had changed; it was higher in pitch, louder and dangerously approaching a shriek. 'You belong to me! Your Christ God has told me this, today! He spoke to me here, in this place. You belong to me now. You have always belonged to me; and you are mine now and for ever!'

'Stand aside, Nur!' I said, trying to sound soldier-like and forceful, not like a man pleading for sense from a madwoman. 'Stand aside, for I must ride on and I cannot take you with me. We will speak some more when I return. Go north to Robin. And may God be with you!' And at that I spurred my horse onward, and the convoy of twenty mail-clad men-at-arms clattered after me.

Out of the corner of my eye, I saw Nur step backwards to avoid being trampled by the moving column of horses. She retreated up the mound on which the cross was set and began to curse and scream in Arabic at the men riding past her. I understood only a little of her speech; I had been taught a smattering of it by my friend Reuben, who came from those parts, but I believe she was wishing that their bladders be afflicted with red-hot maggots, their eyes filled with tears of fiery acid, and damning their souls to be dismembered and roasted for eternity in the seven hells of Jahannam – or some such vicious gibberish.

I turned around in the saddle to remonstrate with her for these curses and saw, just as the last horse was riding past her position on the cross mound, a small black figure launching itself at the rearmost archer in an attempt to climb on to the back of the man's saddle. The archer, a big, brawny fellow, stiff-armed her away in mid-air and she landed sprawled in the mud behind the horse's tail. I gave the order to trot and, with a deep feeling of shame burning in my heart, I led the column swiftly away from the stone cross and from the shrieking, bawling, raggedy, mud-smeared figure in black – huge nostril-holes gaping, teeth permanently bared, grey rat-tail hair snapping in the breeze – as it howled blood-chilling threats of eternal damnation in our wake.

The rest of the journey south was mercifully uneventful. In the late afternoon of the third day after my disturbing encounter with Nur, the cavalcade trotted along Watling Street, through the city wall at Newgate and into the noisy crowded streets of London. Ahead of us the tall spire of St Paul's Cathedral seemed to beckon us to journey's end, and in no time at all we were dismounting in the cobbled courtyard in Paternoster Square outside the huge old church and calling for stabling, grooms and porters to help us carry the heavy chests of silver down into the crypt, where the rest of the ransom hoard was being stored under the seals of Walter de Coutances and Queen Eleanor of Aquitaine. A clerk noted the amount of silver we had brought him, a little over five hundred pounds, on a vellum scroll with an air of total ennui – and I realized how little he or any London folk cared about our contribution.

I understood the clerk's indifference when I caught a glimpse of the inside of the crypt over his left shoulder as he stooped to make a note of our delivery: the vast space beneath St Paul's was filled to the roof with chests and barrels and heavy sacks of silver coin. We had been amazed by the wealth of Prince John's treasury in Nottingham – but this was of another order entirely. It seemed as if all the wealth of the kingdom had been gathered here, every peasant's half-penny, every merchant's shilling had been collected; every miser's purse shaken out, every baron's money chest emptied, every church altar stripped. And not just money from England – King Richard's overseas possessions had played their part too: Normandy, Anjou and Maine had sent silver by the cartload; his wife Queen Berengaria had organized the collection of taxes in Aquitaine far to the south. I realized later that I had been staring, over the back of that bored clerk's rough woollen robe, at piled-up treasure with a value of about 100,000 marks – more than sixteen million silver pennies – a staggering thirty-three tons of bright metal. It was truly a king's ransom!

Queen Eleanor herself received me that same evening in her chamber off the great hall of Westminster. As always, she was gracious and ordered wine and sweetmeats to be served and thanked me in her warm husky voice for bringing Robin's silver safely down from Sherwood.

She made a point of being kind to me, asked after my health, and mentioned once again my exploits in Germany with flattery, charm and gratitude. For all that she was the most powerful woman in Europe, the wife of kings, the mother of kings, I found myself talking to her almost as if she were my own mother.

'And how is my disreputable Lord of Locksley? Still causing trouble in Sherwood, I'll be bound.' The Queen laughed to show that she meant him no ill, and her smoky purr, as always, sent a delicious tingle down my spine.

'I'll wager he's having the time of his life,' said a figure lounging in a dim corner of the chamber that I had not noticed before. His face was in shadow, but I could see that he cradled a lute in his arms, and gracefully he struck a chord and sang a few lines of poetry – my poetry, to be precise.

> *Oh, the merry old life of an outlaw bold,*
> *Offers more reward than silver or gold.*
> *There's women and feasting, and wine to be poured*
> *And battles aplenty – you'll never grow bored . . .*

Perhaps poetry is not the right word. Doggerel, you might call it. It was one of many simple songs, set to simple tunes, that I had composed for the outlaws of Sherwood in my younger days. These ditties celebrated the life and deeds of Robin Hood, although not always with a firm allegiance to the truth, and they had spread across the country in the past few years being sung in alehouses and taverns, in hovels and manor houses from the Pennines to Penzance. Robin pretended to be indifferent to them, but I knew that he secretly loved being so celebrated by the common people of England.

'That will do, Bernard,' rasped Queen Eleanor, with just a suggestion of a chuckle in her voice. 'If you wish to indulge your taste for low entertainments, I suggest you take the young Lord of Westbury off to one of your vile dens of iniquity – some cheap tavern where both of your . . . ahem . . .' the Queen cleared her throat delicately, '*musical* talents will be properly appreciated.'

Bernard de Sezanne set down his lute and came out of the shadows, a smile wreathing his ruddy, handsome face.

'As ever, Your Highness, your slightest wish is my command. Come, Alan, I know just the place for us: the food is almost edible, the drink is very good – and the girls are simply unbelievable!'

I bowed low to the Queen, trying not to grin too widely, and left the royal presence with my old friend – to seek out wine, women and low entertainments.

I awoke the next morning with an aching head, and a gritty feeling in my mouth, but with my spirits unaccountably high. I felt a sense of freedom that I had not enjoyed for many a month. Bernard had been on excellent form the night before, taking me down the river in a barge and over to the other side to a disreputable house owned by the Bishop of Southwark where we had guzzled wine and Bernard had besported himself with three young girls who began the evening dressed as novice nuns – I did not believe that they were really novices, destined one day to become Brides of Christ, but you could never be too sure with the bawdy Bishop of Southwark's girls.

I have never quite felt comfortable in my bones paying for the love of women – although I will not condemn those who do – and so I confined myself to watching Bernard as he cavorted with his three lovelies, passing the odd cup of wine to him when he felt in need of refreshment, and passing ribald comments when I felt they were called for.

Once Bernard had quenched his lust – and I must say that, for a man in his late thirties who loved to complain so much about being aged and infirm, he had a prodigious amount of stamina – we paid off the girls and fell to talking of recent affairs of the kingdom.

'You know, they nearly have it,' Bernard said to me, wiping his sweaty face with a towel. 'A hundred thousand marks – I never thought they'd do it. But by hook or by crook – by crook mostly – the Queen, may she live another thousand years, has gathered the first tranche of the money together for Richard's ransom. The Emperor's ambassadors are coming next week to collect it.'

'The first tranche?' I said, surprised. 'I thought a hundred thousand was the full price for his release.'

'No, no, my boy,' chuckled Bernard. 'Never underestimate the greed of princes. Emperor Henry has decided to squeeze Richard until he squeaks – he's upped the price. Now he wants a hundred and *fifty* thousand marks in cash, or the equivalent in well-born hostages.'

'But that is impossible – the country has been bled dry. There is no more money in England – anywhere. I know, I did a good deal of the bleeding!'

'They'll do a deal, Alan. They always do. But the important thing is that the German ambassadors are coming and, once they've got their money, they'll have to set a date for Richard's release. And once that has happened, the tide will turn in our favour.'

'What do you mean?'

'For the past year, all the knights and barons of England and Normandy have been trying to divine who will win this great struggle between Richard and John. Obviously, they all want to be on the winning side. When Richard was in prison, and John triumphantly capturing castles left and right all over England, everyone looked at John as the eventual winner. The longer Richard was locked up, the more our King's support melted away – apart from a few staunch fellows such as me, you and your outlaw friend Robert of Locksley, of course.'

Bernard paused, took a swig of wine, and went on: 'Once a date has been set for Richard's release, all the fighting men in England will have to reconsider their positions. When Richard comes home he's unlikely to look kindly on those who supported his brother's bid for the throne. He's more likely to waste their lands, slaughter their soldiers and dispossess their children. So everything is in flux right now. People are already beginning to switch back to Richard's side. Things are looking up for us.'

I pondered Bernard's words the next morning as I sluiced my aching head at the pump in the courtyard outside Westminster Hall, while Thomas stood behind me with a towel and a clean shirt. Bernard was right, I concluded. Things were indeed looking up. But I had another reason to be cheerful that day. I was going to be paying a visit to my master's wife Marie-Anne and her baby son Hugh – and I'd also get a chance to see my lovely Goody. And there was something in particular, something very special indeed, that I was planning to ask her.

Chapter Eighteen

The Countess of Locksley had taken a large two-storey, timber-framed house on the south side of the Strondway, the main road leading into London from Westminster. It was the inn or town house of Lord Wakefield, who was presently in Normandy, and Marie-Anne had filled it with her women and her dogs, and a dozen or so of Queen Eleanor's jolly Gascon men-at-arms.

I rode up there on Ghost on that crisp morning, with the frost still on the grass either side of the wide road even though it was near nine of the clock, and I reflected that my life was far from unsatisfactory that cold autumn day. As Bernard had said last night, all being well, King Richard would soon be released from his German prison. Better yet, my musical friend had told me that Goody was stricken with remorse over the way she had spoken to me at our last meeting. According to Bernard, she now looked upon me as some sort of hero who had hoodwinked Prince John and allowed Robin to collect a fortune in silver on King Richard's behalf. A hero, no less. I liked the sound of that.

Although I was prepared for a change of heart from Goody, I did not expect the enthusiasm I received when I arrived in the big courtyard of Wakefield Inn, dismounted and handed Ghost's reins to a waiting groom. I was dimly aware of a human-shaped streak of white and gold coming towards me at speed and then Goody was in my arms, her body wrapped tightly around me, her lips kissing my face over and over while she wept and apologized and kissed me again.

Finally she drew breath and pulled back from her embrace: 'Oh, Alan, can you ever forgive me – the things I said to you . . . I didn't understand . . . I thought that you had . . . but of course, you never would. Not you . . .'

Her face was quite delicious: cold and beautiful, like a bowl of wild strawberries and fresh cream – blotched pink around her sparkling violet-blue eyes where she had been crying, the deep flushed red of her soft lips, a glimpse of pearly teeth, and all set off by her silky white skin. I could have eaten her alive. Instead, I kissed her full on the lips.

And she kissed me back.

My mouth melted into hers; our tongues probed, duelled, entwined; her taste was slippery sweet; warm and soft and utterly wonderful. My arms were locked around her thin back, and hers around my neck; and I could feel every curve of her lithe young body pressed hard against mine, and soon that familiar hot rush of blood to my loins . . .

'Godifa, what on earth do you think you are doing?' said a sharp voice from twenty yards away. And Goody broke our long kiss, and turned her golden head to look behind her.

Advancing across the courtyard, through a sea of dogs, with an irritated frown wrinkling her normally perfect brow was Marie-Anne, Countess of Locksley, Robin's wife, Goody's guardian, and my hostess. I was aware that half a dozen servants were standing in the courtyard gawping at Goody and myself and the expression of our love like a passel of slack-jawed half-wits. I gave them all my fiercest battle scowl.

'Marie-Anne – look, it is Alan!' said my lovely girl.

'I can see that. And that is no reason to eat him alive out here in the courtyard. Stop making a spectacle of yourself and bring him inside.'

'But it's Alan!' Goody said again, and I could hear the incredulous joy in her voice.

'I know, my dear, I know. Now, let's take him inside,' said Marie-Anne, and she took me by the elbow. So, with two of the most beautiful women in England on my arm, I was escorted into the big warm hall of Wakefield Inn.

That deep kiss was the last one I received from Goody until we were formally betrothed. Marie-Anne insisted on this, and Goody and I meekly agreed to remain chaste until we were duly affianced. Then it was agreed that Hanno, Thomas and I would move into Lord Wakefield's big house along with Robin's twenty men-at-arms – for there was plenty of space and stabling for everyone. Goody and I spent that autumn in a happy blur of mutual, unfulfilled but passionate love.

To be near Goody was to be in Heaven: I could not take my eyes off her, she seemed to me to be the embodiment of perfection: the way she moved, the shape of her hands and arms, the curl of bright hair that escaped from under her plain white cap – everything about her was utterly entrancing, intoxicating to me. We took long rides together in the countryside around Westminster – always accompanied by Marie-Anne and a couple of maidservants and Thomas, and protected by Hanno and a handful of Robin's men-at-arms, for I had learnt my lesson after the incident with the river pirates, and I never ventured far in those days without half a dozen good men at my back. There was also the matter of the price on my head; it might be a paltry pound of silver, but many desperate men might wish to claim it. Word had reached us that bands of Prince John's soldiers were roaming the countryside, robbing and murdering at will. And though these men were operating near John's strongholds in the north and west of England, I did not wish to take any unnecessary chances with my beloved's life – or, now that I had found true happiness, with my own.

But despite the fact that we were not entirely alone on our horse-borne pleasure jaunts, I felt as if we were. Goody was the only person I was aware of in that throng, the others mere shadows against her brightness, and I watched her swiftly changing, almost flickering moods as a mother watches her newborn baby. When Goody was happy, my heart soared with hers; when she frowned, I was gripped with anxiety; when she exploded into one of her sudden sun-bright fiery rages, I trembled just a little.

I have never felt a love like it before or since. It was not a lustful love, of the kind that I had felt with Nur and a handful of other women; I did not want to possess her body, to be naked and sweaty, to be rutting like some farmyard animal with her. I just wanted to be with her all the time, for all time. I wanted to be next to her, looking at her, gazing into her eyes.

I wanted to bask in her beauty, receiving it like summer sunshine on my upturned face. I loved her wholly, without reservation, and I believe she loved me equally. We told each other that we did, often, and made excited plans for a formal betrothal and marriage when King Richard was safely home from Germany.

The news from that quarter had been good. The ambassadors of the Holy Roman Emperor had accepted the hundred thousand marks in silver – I had been part of the armed guard that delivered it to their ship, which had been moored at Wapping, a grubby little village downstream from the Tower of London. And word had reached us a few weeks later that Emperor Henry had finally determined a date for Richard's release: the seventeenth day of January, St Anthony's Day.

In December, just before Christmas – with suitable regal pomp, a whole gaggle of senior nobles and churchmen and a powerful force of Gascon guards – Queen Eleanor of Aquitaine took ship and departed for Germany with a small part of the extra fifty thousand marks that the Emperor had demanded and a number of well-born youths, the sons of English and Norman nobles, as hostages for the rest of the money. It looked very much as if Richard would soon be safely home and Goody and I would be betrothed.

We kept Christmas Day quietly with a service in the chapel at Wakefield Inn, the solemn celebration of Christ's birth conducted by Father Tuck. My friend had grown a little leaner over the past year and his tonsured hair was now entirely grey. In fact, I had been slightly surprised by his appearance when I came south from Nottingham: he looked like an old man. But then, he was well advanced in years. He had been a middle-aged monk when Robin was a boy – and Robin by now was nearing thirty. However, Tuck was still an active man, and he still knew a thing or two about the world. When he heard my confession on that cold Christmas morning, he asked me, after I had finished recounting my humdrum sins, a mildly blasphemous word here, a lustful thought there, whether there was anything else that was on my conscience, and I told him about the meeting at the stone cross with Nur, and my feelings of shame at how I had treated her. I wanted her to be happy, I truly did, but I had no idea how I could make this a reality without sacrificing my own happiness – and Goody's.

'Those in love wish all the world well,' said Tuck, smiling at me with his kind nut-brown eyes set deep in his apple-wrinkled face. 'But in this case I do not think you can help her. Nur's suffering has plunged her into madness, and nothing – at least, no human enterprise – can bring her out the other side. You must pray for her, and hope that God will show her the light of his mercy.'

We feasted all that Christmas Day on the Yule boar – a huge animal that Robin had sent down from Sherwood, with his love, and that we had been roasting over a slow fire since dawn – and a largely restrained and mostly sober merriment continued for the Twelve Holy Days. On the eighth day of Christmas, January the first, we exchanged our gifts. Goody gave me a fine sword-belt buckle, chased in gold; I gave her a simple silver bracelet – and, as a sort of jesting love token, a ginger kitten. When Goody and I had first met in the house of her father, an irascible old rogue who lived deep in Sherwood, I had rescued a kitten for her from a tree, and Goody told me that it was then that she had first begun to love me. I was stunned when she told me that – I had seen her then as an unhappy little girl, feisty and fearless, not as the love of my life. But God moves in mysterious ways, as Tuck was forever telling me, and I had no doubts now that Goody and I were destined to be together for the rest of our days.

As my Christmastide gift, Marie-Anne, my wonderful and wealthy hostess, gave me a new vielle to replace the one that I had broken in the fight with Rix. It was a beautiful instrument, with five strings pegged at the end of a long neck, elegant curves and a deep sound box. It was fashioned from polished rosewood, a deep, warm reddish-brown colour, and came with a matching horsehair bow. And after a lavish supper that day I was easily persuaded to perform with my gorgeous new instrument for the party at Wakefield Inn.

Being in love gave every *canso*, *tenso* or *sirvates* that I performed a special resonance: the words of love between a knight and his lady, honestly written when I was alone, but somehow callow and empty, suddenly came alive and acquired a new meaning under Goody's influence on me. And at the end of one song of tragic love, one that I had written blithely three years ago, I found that my eyes were wet with tears.

'For Christ's mercy, play something a little more cheerful,' said Tuck, dabbing his eyes with a linen kerchief. 'You'll send us all to bed in floods of tears at this rate.'

Goody was openly sobbing. 'It was so beautiful, Alan,' said my love. 'You are so beautiful . . .' Her words were thankfully muffled by a napkin with which she was mopping her streaming face, but I realized that I had to change the mood and so we ended the evening with a rollicking, bawdy composition about a one-legged old woman with seven young lovers – one lover

332

for each day of the week – each of them also missing one vital limb. And we did all go to our beds in tears after all, tears of laughter.

In the second week of January, a cold, snow-bound season, I visited Westbury. Ghost was unhappy to be abroad in that frigid time, but Baldwin, my steward, seemed pleased to see me in his dry, unemotional way when we finally arrived after three days of plodding through snow on iron-hard roads. I spent several days with him in the warm, smoky old hall going over the accounts of the manor; we had made a small profit the previous year, and a good harvest meant that the granaries were full and there would be more than enough for everyone at Westbury to eat over the cold months. I returned to London a week later feeling well pleased with Baldwin's running of the estate, and content that he should continue to act for me there in all things.

Sometimes I believe the Devil has a special watch put upon human souls who are happy – and when he finds sinless joy he focuses all his malice upon it and directs his minions to work night and day to turn it sour. For the moment I returned to Wakefield Inn from my trip up to Westbury, things began to go horribly wrong.

As I approached the Inn, walking my tired Ghost along Strondway in the half-light of dusk, I thought I saw a small, huddled figure in a voluminous dark gown scuttling away from the gatehouse. I dismissed the wretch as a beggar, but I had cause to think again when I found myself outside the big wooden iron-studded gate. Somebody had defaced the entrance to the courtyard with a strange and evil symbol: an image no more than one foot square that seemed to resemble two figures, possibly a man and a woman, grotesquely deformed and grappling with each other in mortal combat. It had been scratched deeply into the wood at about head height, and coloured with a substance that I suspected was blood. I told the porter, who was asleep in his cosy lodge by the door, and who had heard nothing, to erase the evil symbol immediately with a pumice stone and stiff scrubbing brush. Then I tried to put it from my mind.

As I walked across the courtyard and into the hall, stamping the snow off my boots as I went, I came across a sight that chilled my already frozen body to the marrow. Goody was sitting on a bench by the hearth fire snuggled up to a handsome young man.

And they were holding hands.

He was a slim lad, about my height; exquisitely dressed in samite and furs, and with fine, pale blond hair. His face, I suppose, was one that women would call handsome: at least he had soft, regular features and no moles or growths or missing parts to disfigure it. I would have called it insipid, even weak, for my part. But there he sat, this golden youth, clutching at Goody's hands with his long fingers.

Both Goody and her damned swain rose as I strode over to them, my hand on my sword hilt. I saw that the boy was unarmed, and a part of me cursed his soul, for the chance to pick a fight and cut him down where he stood would have been a fine thing, I thought angrily, a fine thing indeed.

'Who are you? And what the Devil do you think you are doing here?' I snarled at this baby-faced, samite-clad, hand-holding mountebank.

'Alan,' said Goody sharply. 'Behave yourself! This is Roger

334

of Chichester, a very good friend of mine. He is merely paying me the courtesy of a friendly visit to wish me joy of the season.'

I growled at him under my breath, and gave him my nastiest, most dangerous glare. But I managed to keep my mouth shut.

'A pleasure to have made your acquaintance . . . sir,' said this presumptuous little popinjay. 'I regret that I do not have the honour of your name.'

'This is Alan of Westbury,' said Goody, her face flushed, her lovely violet eyes kindled with sparks of anger, 'and he is behaving today like an overbearing, ill-mannered lout.'

'Ah, well, then, ah, I will leave you in peace, ah, and I bid you God speed, ah, until we meet again . . .' stammered this over-dressed love-puppy.

'I doubt very much we will meet again,' I said shortly. 'God be with you!' And I turned away from him rudely and began to fiddle with the clasp on my damp riding cloak. I heard rather than saw Goody usher this silly lad over to the hall door, and send him gracefully on his way, and then she came back over to me by the fire.

'What is the matter with you? Why were you so unpleasant to dear Roger?' asked Goody when she returned. 'There was no need for that sort of rudeness. You have quite upset him.'

'I don't care – and I don't care for him. Who is he, anyway?'

'I have just introduced you: he is Roger, Lord Chichester's eldest son and heir. What's more, he is, as I have said, a good friend of mine.' She was beginning to sound very angry; there was a rasp in her voice that I had heard before. Foolishly I ignored it.

'He was holding your hand: in future, I don't want him alone with you in this house.' I realized that I too had raised my voice.

335

'This is not your house; nor yet is it your hand. And I will spend my time with whomever I wish.' Goody was nearly snarling now, her blue eyes flaring brightly at me like a wildcat's.

'I forbid you to see him!'

'What did you say?' She was very nearly spitting the words, and her voice was quite as loud as mine.

Rashly, I repeated myself: 'I forbid you to speak to this "dear Roger" person again.'

Goody's face was white as a lily except for two points of vivid red on each cheekbone. She said coldly, and slowly, her voice now chillingly calm: 'I will speak to whomever I like, whenever I like; and you will find, sir, that I will *not* speak to those who do not respect my rights and wishes.'

And with that she spun on her heel and marched off towards the end of the hall and the stairs up to her private quarters.

I found myself with a raised forefinger, pointing at her departing back, and uttering the words: 'Well, I shall speak to whomever I wish too, ha-ha, and see how you like . . .' But by then she was gone.

For the next few weeks, Goody refused to talk to me at all. It was as if the fire of her love for me had been totally extinguished, as if a barrel of snow had been poured on to a hearth, suddenly blotting the blaze and replacing it with an icy white mound.

I was rather taken aback by her sudden change of attitude: the day after the argument I had tried to apologize to her when our paths crossed in the upstairs corridor. It had been a silly argument, I said, faults on both sides, and I was sure we could each forgive the other for our hasty words. She cut me dead.

And, after that, she refused to even remain in the same room with me. Whenever I entered the hall, she found an excuse to leave; if I entered a chamber she was in she would stalk out leaving an invisible chill in the air.

At first I was bewildered by her rejection of me, and then, after a whole week of icy silence, I was secretly rather impressed by her strength of will. She was punishing me, I knew, and she was relentless. But after two weeks, I began to grow annoyed. I spoke to Marie-Anne about the matter, and she urged me to apologize again to Goody.

'You have no rights over her, Alan; not yet. She is not betrothed to you, nor married. And she has always been a very independent girl. Why do you not go to her and beg her forgiveness.'

'But it is not my fault, this stupid rift. She was flirting with this Roger fellow. What was I supposed to do? Encourage them? Show them to a comfortable bedchamber? Bring them some warmed blankets?'

'You have nothing to fear from Roger. He is not . . . he is not a threat to you and Goody. If you love her, why not apologize again? It cannot possibly hurt anyone.'

But I could not bear to humble myself before her only to incur her icy scorn. And so we went on as before, ignoring each other day after day, trapped in a frigid howling silence. I lost myself in exercise and self-indulgence: beginning Thomas's training to be a knight with sword lessons, and long hours on the back of a horse; and occasionally going drinking with Bernard to his favourite places of 'low entertainment'. His advice, predictably, was to get myself a plump whore and forget about Goody entirely. But I could not – and staying in

Wakefield Inn and catching fleeting glimpses of my love, seeing her white indifferent face, was sheer bloody torture. Almost as bad as the hot irons, I thought. Indeed, I would gladly have undergone a night of torment in some stinking dungeon if it meant that my bond with Goody could be healed. I couldn't sleep; I couldn't eat. My head was filled with thoughts of sorrow, pain and death from sun-up to bedtime.

And then things took a turn for the worse. I was in an eating house on Bankside, a place that served food all day and all night for the men from the ships who came to eat there when they had finished unloading cargoes at odd hours, when Bernard joined me.

He was not in good form. For once he was sober, and his happy, boozy face was grey and tired. But he tried his hardest to make light of the grave news he bore.

'There has been a little setback with the King,' he told me. 'Did I not warn you that the greed of princes was limitless? It seems that King Philip of France and Prince John have joined forces and made a counter-offer for King Richard's person.'

'What?' I felt as if I had been smacked in the face with an open hand. 'What kind of counter-offer?'

'You know that Prince John is in Paris now, and looks set to stay there at Philip's court?'

I nodded – it was common knowledge: now that King Richard's release was supposedly imminent, Prince John had fled to the protection of his French allies, skulking away and leaving his loyal followers in England to hold his captured castles for him.

'Well, I overheard Walter de Coutances telling the Queen that Philip and John had sent a letter to Germany offering the

Emperor a further eighty thousand marks to keep Richard in prison until Michaelmas. And I understand that the Emperor is extremely tempted to accept it.'

It was a massive blow for our cause, perhaps a mortal one: but a part of me could see that it was a clever move, too, on John's part. The Emperor would keep the hundred thousand he had already been paid by Queen Eleanor, but delay releasing Richard until the end of September, eight months hence, which was the close of the campaigning season. In the cold, wet months between September and March, by common custom, very little fighting took place between warring knights. It gave Philip and John, in effect, a whole year's grace to capture more of Richard's castles both here and in Normandy and to shore up their support against him. And when it came to Michaelmas . . . Well, who knew what would happen between now and then? Richard might die in captivity, or be assassinated by Prince John's agents. Or another year in prison might be bought for yet more perfidious silver.

I had thought that my soul was at an all-time low already, with the freezing of my love affair with Goody. But at this news I realized that there was yet further for my spirits to fall.

After my old music teacher's announcement, we ate a joyless meal at the Bankside food-shop, sunk in gloom and having little to say to each other over our stale pasties and sour wine. Bernard left without even getting drunk.

The next morning, I was awoken from my slumbers by the sound of high-pitched screaming. It was a servant, one of the kitchen maids whose task it was to set the fires before daybreak. She was standing at the opened gate of Wakefield Inn and pointing to a rickety structure, a makeshift gamekeeper's gibbet that had been erected before the portal at some point during the night. It was a simple affair, and at first I thought it was some sort of joke: a crosspiece made from a long crooked hazel bough, about the width and length of a spear shaft, supported at either end by two tripods of hazel wands. And from the crosspiece were hanging a dozen miserable animal shapes.

As I walked closer to the gibbet I could see that the two shapes in the centre were larger than the rest: they were a puppy, a newborn floppy-eared rascal that belonged to one of Marie-Anne's dogs – and Goody's ginger kitten, her Christmastide gift from me. Both had been eviscerated, their entrails dangling around their pathetic little furry legs, and strung up by the neck with twine to the crossbar. On either side of the puppy and the kitten hung half a dozen rats, starlings, a robin, and even a baby field mouse. It was a gruesome collection of corpses, eerily like the sheriffs' gibbets strung with the bodies of hanged thieves that could be seen in most towns in England, only much smaller, and in a weird way more poignant. But it was not the collection of dead animals that shocked me most. On the front gate, in blood, had been scrawled a message. It was in Arabic, and although I could not read that language with any proficiency, I could make out these words. It said: *True Love Never Dies.*

Nur!

She must have followed me south from Sherwood and observed me with Goody. And now she was telling me that she knew that I had found love again. I shuddered on that cold January morning at the sight of her crude daubings in – whose? – blood. And I remembered the hideous figures scratched in the wood of the gate, which I had seen on my return from Westbury only a few weeks before. Could Nur truly be a witch? Did she have powers? Was she the Hag of Hallamshire? And was she now using her magic against Goody and me?

I took a grip of myself. And then gave orders for the servants to take the gibbet away and burn it before Goody or Marie-Anne could see it.

For days afterwards, as I went about my business in London – visiting Bernard in the taverns at Westminster, at horse and lance training with Thomas on the broad high heath near the little village of Hampstead – I kept seeing a small black figure out of the corner of my eye. But, always, when I turned to look properly, it was gone. Whatever else Nur had learnt in her long travels from the Holy Land to England – witchcraft, sorcery, the casting of foul curses – she had also mastered the art of concealment in rough country almost as well as my friend Hanno.

But I did not actively seek out Nur, track her down or lay an ambush, for I still suffered from feelings of shame about the way that I had treated her. I did wish to speak to her, if only to urge her not to threaten either Goody or myself with her devilish tricks. It had been clear that the puppy and the kitten had been meant to represent Goody and myself, and the other dead animals our servants and friends. It felt like a curse on my soul, a black witch's slow-burning malediction – and I wanted her to lift it. And in some way I wanted to make amends for her suffering; but also I had to make her accept that I'd never love her again.

If I am honest, I must admit that I did not relish another

encounter with her. Any threats to her, I knew in my heart, would be empty. I could not lift my sword to her after what she had endured at the hands of Malbête and his men. More than anything else, I just wished her gone.

There are those who say that God and the Devil are engaged in a constant struggle for the souls of men; and most agree that God is mightier than the Evil One. And so it came to pass that God triumphed and the evil time at Wakefield Inn came to an end.

It ended, as in my experience so many bad things have, with the arrival of Robin – and he brought with him wonderful news.

My master clattered through the inn's gate at the head of forty cavalrymen, straight in the saddle, proud and accoutred for war. And after embracing Marie-Anne and greeting Tuck, Goody, Hanno and me, he made a point, I noticed, of sweeping up little toddling Hugh in his arms and tickling the boy until he screamed with joy. Then he called everybody into the hall and, warming his hands in front of the hearth fire, he said casually: 'Richard is free.'

His words were greeted with a stunned silence. We had all grown so used to our King being a prisoner in Germany – he had been there for more than a year by then – that his words took us all by surprise. So Robin repeated himself:

'King Richard, our noble sovereign, is free. He has been released by the Emperor and, even as I speak, he is travelling with his mother towards England.'

'But what about Prince John's counter-offer – the eighty thousand marks to keep him till Michaelmas?' I said, a little bewildered.

'Oh, I'm sure the Emperor was tempted. But Richard has made a good number of friends among the German princes, and they would not have stood for that sort of underhand behaviour from their overlord. Holding a nobleman for ransom is quite acceptable, but to accept the ransom money and then renege on the deal would have provoked outrage. Emperor Henry would have faced rebellions left, right and centre from his vassals – he might even have been overthrown and lost his title. He's already been excommunicated by the Pope, and that makes everyone, even the most ungodly German baron, uneasy. Besides, he would have made a bitter enemy of Queen Eleanor – and she is not a woman whose wrath can be taken lightly. So he did the sensible thing: he took hostages for the rest of the money that the Queen had promised him and released Richard into her care a couple of weeks ago. He has a few matters to attend to in Europe, but our King should reach England in ten days or so, weather permitting – and then we'll see the royal cat set among the disloyal pigeons.'

Robin grinned at me, a merry devil-may-care sparkle in his silver eyes. 'I've had messages from Richard's people and we have orders to meet him at Sandwich – and then we march north, gathering fighting men on the way – we go to retake Nottingham. It appears, Alan, that we may soon be able to settle our accounts with Ralph Murdac.'

I felt dizzy with joy. All that I had been striving for over the past year, all that I had endured – the long journey to Germany, the deaths of Perkin and Adam, the strain of deception while I was playing the loyal man in Prince John's camp, the wrestling match with Milo and the terrible night as I waited to be hanged like a felon – now it all seemed worthwhile. Good King Richard was coming home, and all would be set to rights. I found myself grinning like an idiot at everyone in our company and, by accident, my gaze fell on Goody.

She looked directly back at me, something she had not done in weeks. And quickly, privately, she smiled at me. In a heartbeat, our quarrel was over: in that moment it seemed absurd, ridiculous – a foolish trifle, an evil enchantment that had been conjured up solely to divide two young lovers, a thing of no substance at all, mere thistledown on the wind in the wild joy of King Richard's return.

We moved towards each other, almost as if drawn by some invisible force, and then she was in my arms, held tight, squeezed, her white face pressed into my neck, and I could feel the burn of her tears.

Chapter Nineteen

King Richard stepped off the gangplank on to the wharf at the port of Sandwich on a bright, sunny March morning, and the cheers that rang out from the hundreds of men-at-arms gathered to meet him were loud enough to deafen the Heavens. He was thinner than when I'd last seen him, very pale, and looked a little older too – but he was still that strong, confident man who had led us to victory in Sicily, Cyprus and Outremer. His chief men – the earls and bishops and great barons – all those few who had remained loyal to him during the dark times – were gathered in the forefront of the crowd at the quay-side, with their own loyal men behind them. And hundreds of small boats filled the brown water of the harbour with spectators, local Sandwich men and women, all wanting to catch a glimpse of the King's triumphant arrival.

As our sovereign stepped off the narrow wooden walkway that ran down from the high deck of the ship, he staggered a little and then righted himself and smiled, and it felt as if the world was warmed. We cheered him, three times three, until our voices were hoarse. And Richard smiled and nodded at individuals in the crowd, lifting a thin hand to acknowledge a face here and there. He greeted each of the assembled magnates by name, walking slowly along the front of the shouting, jostling crowd, and giving each of them a word or two of thanks. Our King stopped by Robin, clasped him by the hand and pulled him forward. He muttered something in Robin's ear and they both laughed, and then his eye lighted on me, standing as I was, directly behind my lord.

'Blondel, well met,' said the King. 'How goes it with England's most talented *trouvère?*'

'I don't know about that fellow, sire,' I said, suddenly shy of conversing with the King, 'but I can tell you that *I* am quite fit and well and ready to serve you.'

Richard laughed. 'Good man. But we shall need your sharp sword more than your sharp wit in the next few weeks, Alan. And it may be some time, I fear, before we hear your elegant verses again,' he added, looking grave.

'I am yours to command, sire,' I said, bowing.

The King nodded. 'And I have not forgotten the debt I owe you for Ochsenfurt,' he said.

I could find no reply but merely smiled mutely at him, and then he was off, past me and greeting the Earl Ferrers, who was standing nearby. I felt as if, for a moment, I had been standing by the blaze of an open hearth, and the warmth of the King's greeting was sufficient to linger with me for hours afterwards.

As I was making my way through the throng back to the

manor house where Robin and I were to sleep that night, I felt a hand on my arm and turned to see two bald elderly men, similarly dressed in white robes, much stained by travel. They were smiling at me, like old friends, which in a way they were. The foremost man extended a veined hand with a large jewelled ring on it for me to kiss. I bobbed down and made my obeisance, and grinned up at the abbot: 'My lord Boxley,' I said. 'How very good to see you again. May I congratulate you on bringing our noble King safely home.'

A brief look of irritation flitted across his lined face, but he quickly recovered and smiled wryly at me: 'I see that my good friend Alan is pleased to make merry with me,' he said. 'For he knows full well after all our adventures together in Germany that *this* is the Abbot of Boxley,' he indicated his companion, who was nodding and beaming at me, 'and I have the honour of Robertsbridge.'

'Of course, of course, please forgive my foolish levity. I am most happy to see you both and long to hear of all your endeavours over the past few months – it cannot have been easy but you have certainly triumphed . . .'

After one night at Sandwich Manor, and an interminable meal with the two abbots, during which they gave me a blow-by-blow account of the negotiations to free Richard, we all took horse and followed the royal object of their efforts to Canterbury the next morning. As we rode, more and more knights and barons and their men-at-arms flocked to join in the procession – some men coming from as far afield as Cornwall to join the King, until we were a veritable army on the move.

On reaching the cathedral at Canterbury, Richard prayed at the shrine of Thomas à Becket and then commanded the

Archbishop, Hubert Walter, a loyal, jolly but warlike prelate, to perform a Mass of thanksgiving for his safe release in the open air so that all the army could take part. After the service, the King called his chief vassals to him in the cathedral's chapter house, and I was fortunate enough to be invited by Robin to attend him at the meeting.

As Robin mingled with the other earls and barons, greeting old friends and making new ones, I sat in one of the carved stone thrones around the walls and, with my back to the cool stone, I daydreamed about Goody.

After our passionate embrace, a tearful scene had followed: I had apologized to Goody for my jealousy and rude behaviour to Roger and she had begged my forgiveness for her coldness towards me, and we had laughed and joked and made everything right between us. We agreed to ask Marie-Anne, Goody's legal guardian, to arrange a betrothal between us as soon as was humanly possible – and vowed never, ever to quarrel again.

Goody had said: 'You have no need to feel jealous of Roger – he does not love girls. In fact, he came to me that day to tell me his heart had been broken by another boy.'

I felt as if a weight had been lifted from my own heart – suddenly everything seemed to make sense: his finely tended good looks, his meticulous, elegant dress, his bewilderment at my boorish aggression. Truly, Goody and Roger were no more than friends. And I thanked God.

I confessed to Goody the whole story about Nur. Even telling her about the curse I believed that she had cast on our love in revenge for my abandoning her, and how her malicious enchantment had been the real cause of our quarrel.

Goody went very quiet when I had finished telling my tale,

and then she gently took my hand in hers and very quietly but firmly she said: 'I don't believe in enchantments, and I'm not frightened of unhappy women who go about pretending to be witches. You are not to blame for Nur's misfortune; it was your enemy Malbête, not you, who cut away her beauty. And you cannot be blamed for the death of your love for her. Perhaps you did not truly love her before her misfortune; perhaps you did. It matters not. You do not love her *now*; and nothing she can do will persuade you to change your heart. You must give her a living, a cottage and some land to till in Westbury, some compensation in silver, perhaps, but that must be the end of the matter.' She looked deep into my eyes with her lovely thistle-blue ones and said: 'You are mine, now, not hers – and she has no right to meddle in our lives. If she does, I will make her regret it . . .'

I was startled out of my pleasant reverie in the chapter house by the sight of Robin talking to his brother, William of Edwinstowe, and a tall, familiar-looking knight. The knight wore a pure white mantle emblazoned with a blood-red cross on the breast; he was evidently Templar – of the very Order that had hounded Robin into outlawry only a year ago.

He was, in fact, Sir Aymeric de St Maur himself.

I sat upright with a jerk, my hand going instinctively to my sword hilt: the last time I had seen this man was in Nottingham Castle when he had been threatening me with hot irons to make me betray the very man with whom he was now congenially conversing not ten paces from my seat. The Templars had kidnapped little Hugh, tried my master for heresy, attempted to have him burnt at the stake and, on his escape, had had him excommunicated. And yet here was Aymeric, gossiping with

Robin like a pair of goodwives at market. I had assumed that the Templars were backing Prince John's cause – but now it seemed I was wrong. William of Edwinstowe, standing between his brother and the Templar knight, put a hand on each of their arms, smiled, said something quietly and walked away into the throng. And Robin and Aymeric were nodding, smiling at each other and now, miraculously, giving each other the kiss of peace before they parted – as if they were old and trusted comrades. I stood up as Robin came over to me. He laughed out loud when he saw my amazed face.

'That surprised you, Alan, didn't it?' he said with a wide, easy grin.

'I don't understand,' I said. My jaw was sagging.

'It's all about the money, Alan,' said Robin. 'It usually is. Sometimes with a little revenge thrown in, sometimes some honest religion, sometimes it's a question of bruised pride. But mostly it's about cold hard silver.'

'What are you talking about?' I said, bewildered.

'As of today, when I've had a moment to dispatch a few letters to my people in the East, we are no longer in the frankincense trade.'

I goggled at him. 'But why?'

'To keep the peace, mainly; and to get these damned Templars off my back,' said my master. 'That's really all those holy hypocrites wanted from me. That whole inquisition flummery about heresy and demon-worship was just a way of forcing my hand. And I have been persuaded to submit to their wishes.'

'Explain!' I was beginning to be irritated by Robin's flippant answers.

He sighed. 'The Templars are taking over the frankincense

trade in Outremer. In exchange, my excommunication is rescinded; the interdict on the Locksley lands is lifted; and the Templars have withdrawn their support for Prince John and come over to our side. My brother William has arranged everything: he acted as a go-between, he spoke first to the Master of the Temple two months ago, and brokered the whole deal from start to finish. With a little help from Queen Eleanor's people.'

'But what about all the money? You will lose thousands in revenues every year!' I was also thinking of the good men who had died for that God-cursed frankincense trade, and of one good Templar knight, a noble man and a staunch friend, in particular.

'I believe I may be, ah, compensated for my losses,' said Robin, nodding towards a tall regal figure with red-gold hair who was at this moment striding energetically into the chapter house at the head of a crowd of knights and priests. 'The King insisted on my making peace with these holy hot-heads – and promised royal rewards if I did so,' said my master with a wry grin. 'And there is some more good news: you and I, Little John – everybody – we are all to receive full pardons for our alleged crimes and misdemeanours. We are wild outlaws no longer, Alan; we are now honest king's men.' His extraordinary silver eyes twinkled at me, as if in jest, but I detected a note of wistfulness in his tone.

As ever, King Richard was decisive: in a loud voice he gathered everyone into the centre of the chapter house and in very few words he welcomed all to the Council and called on Hubert Walter, the Archbishop of Canterbury, to summarize the state of the campaign against John's forces.

The Archbishop, a short, wide but very muscular man, beamed at the company. 'It goes well, Your Highness,' he began. 'It goes very well indeed. As you may already know, my men have already recaptured Marlborough Castle in Wiltshire, and without too much trouble, I may say. Hugh de Puiset sends to say that he is outside the walls of Tickhill Castle on the Yorkshire border – and he writes that Sir Robert de la Mare is almost ready to surrender the fortress, assuming we can give certain guarantees of safe conduct, no reprisals, full pardons, and so forth.'

'Give them,' said King Richard curtly. 'I want the castles, not the misguided men inside them.'

Hubert Walter continued, with a nod at his sovereign: 'Lancaster Castle has fallen to de Puiset's brother Theobald – and as for Mont St Michel in Cornwall . . .' Here the Archbishop consulted a scrap of parchment. '. . . It seems the constable, Henry de Pumerai, died of fright when he heard Your Highness had returned to England.'

The room erupted in a roar of laughter, a mass of burly men doubled over in hilarity, slapping each other on the back and knuckling their own eyes, and even the King joined in, tears of mirth streaming down his pale cheeks.

At last, the Archbishop called the chapter house to order: 'There is one last nut to crack, Highness, and then all England is yours: Nottingham Castle.'

'Tell me about Nottingham,' the King growled.

'Well . . .' the muscular prelate began. The King silenced him with a wave of his hand. 'Not you, Hubert. You've done your bit. Locksley, that's your neck of the woods. What news of my royal castle of Nottingham?'

All eyes in the chapter house were now on my master. He sucked in a big breath and began to speak. 'Sire, as my lord Archbishop has already said, Nottingham is a tough nut. It is the last hold-out of Prince John's men, and knights and men-at-arms loyal to your brother have been mustering there for the past few weeks since your release. There must be as many as a thousand fighting men there now – including a contingent of two hundred first-class Flemish mercenaries: crossbow men, and very good, I'm told.'

Robin paused for a moment to collect his thoughts: 'Nottingham has ample provisions for at least a year. It has several layers of defences, so that even if we take the outer walls, they can retreat into inner fortifications, and even if we take those, they could defy us from the great tower for many months. Some men say that Nottingham is absolutely impregnable; that it cannot be taken by force. Ever.'

'But can *we* take it?' The King was frowning at Robin.

My master looked straight back at him, but for three heart-beats he did not reply. Finally he said: 'Yes, sire, yes, it can be taken. It will cost many lives, but, yes. Assuming that Prince John does not return to England with a great army and march to its relief. We can take it. But the price in blood, the price in the lives of your men, will be very high.'

The King looked thoughtful. 'Who is there at Nottingham now?' he asked.

Robin replied, with no emotion at all in his voice: 'The castle is presently being held by Sir Ralph Murdac, your royal brother John's constable, who was sheriff of Nottinghamshire, Derbyshire and the Royal Forests under your father.'

'Murdac, that slimy little shit-bag? Is he still on the

chessboard?' said the King, with more than a little surprise in his voice. 'I thought he had been banished, or exiled, or outlawed or something. The man's no better than a thief. A damned coward, too.'

'He is no fool and he should not be underestimated,' said Robin. 'And he has a strong garrison at his command. It will be no easy matter to winkle him out.'

'Why do you defend him? He is no friend of yours,' said the King. 'If I remember rightly, you have crossed swords with him on several occasions. And wasn't there some saucy rumour . . .' the King stopped, embarrassed.

'He is no friend of mine – that is certain,' Robin said coolly. 'I would happily see him hanged as a traitor from the nearest gallows. But it would be a grave mistake to underestimate him. As we speak, my men are now outside the castle walls, with the Earl of Chester's forces, keeping him under surveillance. There are not enough loyal men to hand – a few hundred at most – to keep Murdac penned in if he really wanted to sally forth. But my guess is that he believes he is safe behind those walls, and he is sitting tight and holding out until Prince John sends a relief force from France.'

'We need not fear my royal brother overmuch,' said Richard. 'He is not a man to take a country, or relieve a castle even, if there is anyone with even the slightest will to oppose him.' Dutiful laughter echoed round the chapter house – it was a jest Richard had used before. Even Robin smiled tightly.

'Well, gentlemen,' said the King. 'It is quite clear what we must do: we must go north, to Nottingham, and dispossess this Murdac creature of my castle – and perhaps I shall hang him from the nearest gallows, too, just to please you, Locksley!'

Robin smiled again, and made the King a deep, graceful bow.

King Richard was clearly a happy man – after a year of humiliating and frustrating inactivity, he was back in the saddle with loyal companions at his side, and a bloody campaign to fight to restore his kingdom. More than anything in this world, our King loved a good fight, and his enthusiasm and confidence lifted our hearts. We rode out from Canterbury the next day, some four hundred souls: barons, knights, men-at-arms, bishops, priests, royal servants, huntsmen, whores and hangers-on. The men were boasting of the great deeds they would do in battle and jesting crudely with each other. The whole column was in tearing high spirits, eager for a fight, and from time to time snatches of song would break out and spread down the lines of men, growing, blossoming like a forest fire until we were all bawling our hearts out in time with the stamp of marching boots. We were still badly outnumbered by Prince John's forces, but we knew, you see, we knew in our very bones that we would be victorious when we reached Nottingham. After all, we had King Richard to lead us, and with the finest warrior in Christendom as our lord, who could possibly prevail against us?

The whole country seemed to realize this, too. As we made our way north from Canterbury, to Rochester, then London for a brief stop of one day, and on again to Bury St Edmunds, we were joined by a constant stream of men-at-arms: country knights rallying to the royal standard, tough young lads looking for a bit of adventure, and canny barons, smelling Richard's victory on the wind and wanting to renew their allegiance to him before his ultimate success.

At Huntingdon, we were met by William the Marshal and a hundred well-equipped men-at-arms from Pembroke. The Marshal's brother had only recently died but William had chosen to forgo attending his funeral to meet us, just to demonstrate his loyalty to the King. It was a touching scene: this thick-set, grizzled veteran of scores of bloody contests embracing our thin, pale King. Both men were in chain-mail under their surcoats, but while William was clad from big toe to fingertip in heavy links, I saw that Richard was wearing only a much lighter, shorter, sleeveless mail coat, of the kind some men had worn in Outremer. It was easier to bear if you were weak, wounded or suffering from the sun's oriental heat – but it was not as strong as the heavy chain-mail in deflecting a blow. And I wondered privately whether Richard, after his inactive year in captivity, was truly fit for a bruising battlefield.

By the time we made our camp outside Nottingham, pitching our tents in the deer park to the west of the castle, we were a thousand men strong – and our numbers were boosted by another four hundred when we linked up with Ranulph, Earl of Chester, who had been watching the castle from the high ground to its north, and David, Earl of Huntingdon. The latter had been sent by his father – the Scottish King, William the Lion – who was a great friend of Richard's and determined to support him in the struggle against Prince John. David, who also happened to hold the English honour of Huntingdon, brought with him a powerful force of knights. And we were glad to have them.

At a meeting in his royal pavilion in the deer park, in a

space packed with loud, eager, armoured men, Richard gave a rapid series of orders to his barons. The whole of Nottingham Castle was to be encircled by our troops immediately, this night. Now.

'He wants it sewn up as tight as a mouse's arse,' said Little John to me after we had met in an alehouse in the eastern part of Nottingham town. Little John had been in command of Robin's contingent of a hundred or so archers who had been left in the north, with the Earl of Chester's men, to keep an eye on Ralph Murdac. 'Nothing is to go in or out,' said my giant blond friend, as we sat at a rough bench sharing a gallon of weak ale, a big bowl of watery turnip soup and half a loaf of stale rye bread.

I had been shocked when I rode into Nottingham that afternoon. A swathe of the town some hundred and fifty paces across, just to the east of the castle, had been completely destroyed. Streets that I had known well, indeed, that I had walked down just a few months ago, were gone, along with the shops and taverns, peasant hovels and workshops that had once lined them. All that remained now were smouldering ruins and piles of grey ash.

John told me how a force of two hundred knights and men-at-arms had ridden out of Nottingham Castle under cover of darkness two nights before and, using ropes and the muscle power of their big destriers, they had pulled down all the buildings, tearing them quite literally apart. Then, without a thought for the ordinary men, women and children who might be trapped inside their dwellings or trying to salvage their meagre possessions or save their beasts, Murdac's men had set fire to the wreckage of straw-thatched roofs and broken timber beams,

357

tumbled beds and furniture. It was only by God's grace and the hard work of Little John and his archers, who fought the fire all night, that the whole of Nottingham town had not burnt down. As it was, John's blond eyebrows had been singed off, which gave him a slightly surprised look. And three of his archers had been badly roasted and would be unable to fight.

And the point of all this cruel and wanton destruction? To create an open space which would allow the crossbowmen on the eastern wall and in the big gatehouse of the outer bailey to see what they were shooting at, and to deny cover to an attacking enemy.

Cruel, it might have been, but it was also the wise, the clever thing to have done. As Robin had said, Sir Ralph Murdac was no fool.

Nottingham Castle's fortifications followed the contours of the massive sandstone outcrop on which it was built. The castle proper – that is, the upper bailey, the great tower and the middle bailey – sat on the highest part of the outcrop, protected on its western and southern flanks by unscalable hundred-foot-high cliffs topped with thick twenty-foot-high stone walls. There was no way in from that direction.

Below this, and to the east and north of it, was the outer bailey: the largest, most open part of the castle, housing stables and workshops, as well as the new brewhouse, a cookhouse and a bakery. This outer area did not have the luxury of stone walls but, in truth, it did not need them, for it was ringed by a ditch and an earthen rampart, six foot high, on which was entrenched a heavy wooden palisade another twelve foot in height. And now it looked down on the town across a huge smouldering scar of empty space.

Standing in the ditch on the outside of the outer bailey walls, a man would have to jump – or fly – more than twenty foot up in the air to clear the defences. And while he was attempting that impossibility, he would be continually assailed by the crossbow bolts, spears, rocks and arrows of the defending men-at-arms. Even if the attacker managed to get over the twenty-foot-high defences, he could only be supported on the other side by any of his fellows who had managed the same incredible feat – and there would be few enough of them alive after charging through a blizzard of crossbow bolts across the hundred and fifty yards of scorched and emptied land on the castle's eastern side.

King Richard had ridden once around the whole circuit of Nottingham Castle when he arrived that afternoon, the twenty-fourth day of March, by Tuck's reckoning, eleven hundred and ninety-four years after the birth of Our Lord Jesus Christ. The King was accompanied by a dozen knights and the royal standard, with its two golden lions on a red background, was proudly displayed for the benefit of the hundreds of enemy heads that peered at him over the battlements. Afterwards, at a meeting of his senior commanders in his pavilion in the deer park, Richard declared succinctly: 'It's the gatehouse. That is truly the only way in. We take that and we can flood the outer bailey with our men. With God's help, and given a bit of battle chaos, we can follow them, get right in amongst them when they retreat, and take the barbican of the middle bailey next. If we take that, the castle is as good as ours. So, first we take the gatehouse.'

I admired his confidence: but I could not share it. His breezy talk of taking gatehouses and barbicans and baileys, as if they were a child's castles in the sand of a beach, made me nervous. From my time as a member of the castle garrison, I knew that the stoutly built wooden gatehouse that pierced the wall of the outer bailey on its eastern side housed about a hundred heavily armed men under the command of a couple of captains and a senior knight. Worse still, the King had promptly assigned the difficult and bloody task of capturing it to the Earl of Locksley, and Robin, naturally, had given the task to Little John – and to me.

So, over watery turnip soup and weak ale, Little John and I discussed our plans for the next morning, when, at dawn, with only a hundred men each, we were going to storm the gatehouse of the outer bailey and attempt to deliver the royal castle of Nottingham up to its rightful owner.

Chapter Twenty

It was cold; a thick frost had turned the black scar of land between the gatehouse and the first houses of the town into a dull smear of grey. I peered out of the side door of a large wool warehouse on the edge of the grey strip of frosty-burnt ground in front of the eastern wall of the outer bailey. It was perhaps half an hour before dawn, and the first inkling of paleness was visible in the sky behind me. I could see my breath steaming in white plumes in the cold air. At my back were Hanno and Thomas – who was unhappy because I would not allow him to join in the assault on the left flank, the southern side of the massive wooden gatehouse. I knew that it would be a hard, gory slog of an assault – we all did – and, perhaps sentimentally, I wanted to spare Thomas, who was still no more than twelve years old, the bloodbath that was about to take place.

Though his disappointment had rendered him silent, Thomas

did not sulk. He assisted me with a smooth efficiency as I dressed for battle, helping me to wriggle into an old patched mail coat, which I wore over a padded aketon; fitting my helmet on neatly – a plain steel cap with a nasal guard – and strapping it under my chin. My long leather gauntlets, with sewn-in steel finger and forearm guards, had been waxed and oiled until they were supple, and so had my sword belt, with Goody's silver Christmastide buckle at the front securing it around my waist, cinched tight to take some of the weight of the mail coat. Thomas had cleaned and sharpened my old sword and oiled the misericorde that now sat in its sheath in my boot. I had never been so pampered before going into battle, and I found the sensation a pleasant one. When Thomas handed me my shield, which he had freshly whitened with a thick layer of lime wash and repainted with Robin's device of the black-and-grey snarling wolf, I was ready to fight – ready save for the cold, empty feeling in my belly when I dwelt too much on the task we were about to attempt.

I looked behind me into the gloomy interior of the warehouse. The side walls and the far end of the building, twenty paces away, were stacked high with bales of wool, but it was the men I was looking at. Ninety-four of Robin's hand-picked men-at-arms, each wearing a long dark surcoat of green cloth over whatever oddments of armour that he had, stood watching me, waiting for the signal to proceed. A few of them were checking their blades, or the leather straps of their shields, and some were on their knees, uttering a last prayer before we went in to battle. I looked at my company – former outlaws, thieves, runaways and ne'er-do-wells, even some, I noticed, who had once served in Murdac's ranks – and I tried to appear unconcerned about the coming slaughter. They were all good men, brave men, I thought to myself, whatever they had done in the past. All was now forgiven. I did not feel worthy to command them. There wasn't a man in that warehouse who was not afraid; but I knew that every man there would rather die than show it.

We had managed to commandeer five wooden thatching ladders, each more than twenty-five feet long, from the towns-folk. And the two men assigned to carry each one were closest behind me. The ladders were unwieldy things to transport, and the men carrying them were the best in the company, men I knew personally from Sherwood or Outremer. They were men I trusted with my life. In truth, all our lives were in their hands.

Hanno leaned towards me, and said in a low voice: 'Do not worry, Alan. It is good. We can do this.' And I nodded at him, managed a smile, and said, 'I know, Hanno, I know. I'm sure it will be a wonderful success.'

I was lying: I was nervous and very far from sure that we could achieve what we had been asked to do that morning. I looked out of the door once again at the gatehouse, its boxy shape looming black in the half-light before dawn, half as high again as the gate that it guarded. We were going to attempt to run towards it, enduring the spears and arrows and crossbow bolts of hundreds of enemy soldiers, prop the thatching ladders up against the palisade, climb up into the teeth of a determined opposition, get over the wall, and fight our way down to the ground – and somehow survive long enough to open the gate and allow our mounted troops to gallop into the outer bailey and capture it.

It seemed ludicrous; a method of self-immolation, not a

serious battle plan. But, if that proved to be the case, at least we would not be dying alone. Little John and another hundred or so of Robin's men would be attacking the north side of the gatehouse at the same time as us.

I looked north, up the slope of the hill along the grey frosted line of the burnt area, at the singed line of houses and shops that now marked the new edge of Nottingham town, and heard a horn sound a single long blast in the chilly air. As I watched, I saw a huge warrior, bareheaded and with bright yellow hair in two long, thick braids on either side of his head, stepping out from a big house sixty paces away. He carried a huge double-bladed axe and an old-fashioned round shield. He lifted the axe and shouted something loud and rough and joyful, and more men spilled out of the house, carrying their slender wooden ladders.

I turned into the warehouse, meeting dozens of pairs of expectant eyes, and said in a loud clear voice, 'Right, this is it. We form up outside, now.' And then I stepped out into the grey dawn, turned to face the gatehouse and commended my soul to God and St Michael.

Within the gatehouse, the enemy had not all been sleeping; their sentries were alert. There were shouts and angry cries, and whistle and trumpet blasts as the garrison of the wooden fortification was roused as fast as possible from their bed rolls. A hundred and fifty yards away, heads began to appear on the palisade, little round black shapes, clustering thick as elder-berries on the crenellated wooden walls. A single crossbow twanged from the gatehouse, a sergeant shouted something angrily, and a bolt whizzed past a good twenty yards to the right of my waiting men, who were by now formed up in a loose mob behind me, the ladder-bearers to the fore.

And then there was more movement to my right as Robin stepped out from between two houses, slightly up the slope from our position, and a great mass of men followed him – archers, more than a hundred of them, all in uniform dark green, but few with more than a scrap or two of armour. They shuffled into a loose line, two ranks deep, between my position and Little John's men, with Robin at the southern end. My lord raised a hand in cheery greeting to me, put a horn to his lips and blew two short notes.

And the archers began to shoot.

With a tremendous creaking of wood, a hundred men pulled back the hempen strings on their powerful yew bows, leaned far back and loosed. Up, up, almost vertically, they climbed into the grey dawn sky, seeming to pause in the air for a moment at the top of their parabola, before plunging down, down, the shafts falling on to the gatehouse and into the bailey beyond it, and slamming deep into the logs of the building and into the men sheltering behind the wooden walls, driving down into their cowering bodies like a solid, killing rain.

Even from more than a hundred paces away, I could hear the cries of pain from the defenders as the lethal yards of ash wood, tipped with four-inch-long, needle-sharp bodkin points, cascaded down upon them, punching through the padded jerkins of the crossbowmen, and plunging deep into the mail-clad shoulders and chests of the enemy men-at-arms with awful force.

Robin's archers waited a few moments to check their range, and then they hauled back their bows once more and loosed another storm of wood and steel up high in the sky to fall like the wrath of God upon the enemy. And then a third wave of death swept up, seemingly swallowed up by a pale and hungry sky, before being spat down venomously on the defenders below.

It was time to go.

I turned to look at the men behind me. I knew that I should find something to say to those frightened, familiar faces – Robin would have had said exactly the right thing, at that time, to put courage into their hearts. But I had nothing to offer. I pulled out my sword, raised it in the air and said: 'Right, let's go. Keep your shields high. For God and King Richard – forward!' And I set off at a jog across the burnt strip of land towards the imposing bulk of the gatehouse, the soft ash puffing beneath my running feet.

For a moment, I feared that nobody would follow me; that I would be charging across that wasted strip of land on my own to certain death. But I was too proud to look behind me – and, eternal praise be to Almighty God, the Father, the Son, and the Holy Ghost, I soon heard the rattle and chink and thump of running men behind me. My heart soared. I was about to take my sword to a hated enemy, and I was charging into battle at the head of as brave a band of fighting men as had ever trod this earth.

We had crossed fifty yards of open ground before the first crossbow bolts began to fly: black streaks of death hissing from the battlements like a demonic swarm of hornets. I felt rather than saw a quarrel smash into the top right corner of my shield. I heard a cry behind me and turned my head. At least four of my men were down, just from the first crossbow volley. The ladder-man directly behind me had dropped his burden and was kneeling on the grey-black ground, coughing blood, a quarrel protruding from his neck. The bolts were whistling past me left and right, I stopped and took a step back towards him, and he looked at me with beseeching eyes. Men were falling all around me, quarrels were whipping past in long black blurs – the earth seemed to be moving beneath my feet; I had the strange sensation that I was in the midst of a wild gale on a storm-tossed sea. I sheathed my sword and held out my right hand to the ladder-man, but at the last minute hardened my heart and grabbed the first rung of his ladder instead. Keeping my shield arm up, I shouted: 'Come on, come on; let's get this over with quickly.' And those of us who could still run stumbled forward again, the bolts hissing and cracking around us.

I heard Robin's horn ring out three times, and was dimly aware that the deadly rain of our arrows had ceased. But I had no time to ponder what damage might have been done to the enemy by my lord's arrow-storm: his barrage did not seem to have slowed their deadly crossbow work one jot. Men continued to fall all around me, skewered, punctured, plucked from this life by the wicked black bolts. I feared that there would be not one single man alive by the time we made it to the wall. By God's mercy, I was mistaken.

In what seemed no more than a few moments, two score of us survivors were panting, sweating, cursing below the high wooden walls of the palisade and the four remaining ladders were sweeping up through the grey air in a great arc to thump on to the battlements. 'Up, up!' I shouted, but I might have saved my breath. The men – God bless them – were swarming up the frail ladders like monkeys up a ship's rigging, and I began to climb too, awkwardly with one hand on the rungs and my shield held above me, behind a heavy-set man with bright red hair and a vicious-looking spiked axe in his right hand. The ladder bounced alarmingly under our combined weight, and I heard a cry above me and was nearly swept from the ladder as the red-head crashed into my shield, a long spear waggling from his chest, before crunching to the ground below me. I looked up and stared into the eyes of a terrified man, no more than two or three yards away, glaring down at me between two crenellations on the battlements. He leant forward to loose his crossbow at me and, by the grace of God, even at that close remove, he missed – and I swear I flew up the final rungs of the ladder and launched myself over the top. The man's bow was now unloaded, but as my feet landed on the walkway behind the palisade, he swung it at me in a short, hard arc. If it had landed, it would have crushed my skull, but I caught it on my shield, batted it away and, using my kite-shaped protection like an axe, I hacked the edge into his jaw. He fell away, inside the walls, down into the outer bailey, screaming wordlessly, blood flying. I took a brief moment to draw my sword – a heartbeat, but I had no more time than that. A man hurled himself at me from my left and I smashed him away with my blade.

The walkway and the ground beneath it were littered with dead, victims of the arrow storm, but more men in strange red livery were running along the walkway at me from both sides, converging from all around the palisade on the gatehouse. A crossbow twanged and more by luck than judgement I managed to get my shield up in time; the bolt ricocheted off its curved surface and away. And then I was fighting by pure instinct. I went right towards the gatehouse to engage a swordsman who was cutting at me. He came on too fast, and I dodged his wild swing at my head, lunged and stabbed him deep in the stomach. The man behind him was more cautious: he feinted at my legs

368

and then chopped at my neck and I had to block with the shield before dispatching him with a short, hard thrust under the chin. Suddenly, the blood was singing in my veins; all my earlier nervousness burnt away by the heat of battle. I was inside the walls of the castle, fighting for my lord and my King, and slaying their enemies with a righteous fury. And I was no longer alone. As I cut the legs from beneath a big crossbowman with a low, vicious sweep of my sword, I glimpsed more of my men behind me on the walkway of the palisade. There was Hanno, snarling and hacking at a mob of men-at-arms who had appeared from the south. And another two of our men came boiling over the wall. Three men, now four and five. They were tumbling over the top of the ladder and taking their swords with a deadly swiftness to the enemy. And my ladder was not the only one that had successfully surmounted the palisade – I could see two others further along the wall, and the men, my brave men, Robin's wonderful fearless men, pouring over the top like the bursting of a dam.

I charged towards the gatehouse, skewering a man who was emerging from its cover straight through the cheek, mangling his face and ripping the blade free, running heedlessly past him as he dropped screaming to his knees, and now I was entering into the gloom of the narrow building. A tall knight, his face red with fury, ran at me out of the upper storey of the gatehouse, mace and sword whirling. I gave ground, two steps, three, until I was once again outside the structure, half stumbling over bodies as his berserk onslaught drove me backwards. There were flecks of white spittle at his lips, which were drawn back in a grimace of mindless rage. He lunged at me with his sword, and I stepped back and away to my right towards the palisade, dodging the blow. He swung at my head with the mace, screaming something at me, and lunged again with his blade. I parried the mace with my sword, and blocked the sword with my shield; for a moment we were locked together, faces only inches apart. Then I bullocked my head forward, smashing the steel rim of my helmet into his teeth, snapping several off at the root, and he stepped back, bloody-mouthed, in surprise – and into thin air.

The battle-crazed knight fell fifteen foot on to the hard-packed earth of the outer bailey. I could hear the crack of his neck from the walkway, and he twitched only once before he lay still.

With the knight's death, the defence of the gatehouse and our section of the palisade came to an end. The surviving crossbowmen were running. Hurrying, stumbling, jumping down the wooden steps that led to the ground, and streaming away from the gatehouse, back towards the castle. And we ran after them – jubilant, hearts pounding, muscles glowing. Our men were hoarsely cheering themselves and their achievement – but we had no time for celebrations. 'The gate!' I shouted. 'Get to the gate. We must open the gate.'

And I led more than a score of men, fizzing with victory, to the huge wooden door of Nottingham Castle, where another fight was already reaching its climax. Little John, like some giant Saxon war god of old, his yellow braids swinging in time with the sweeps of his double-headed axe, was cutting his way methodically through a gaggle of terrified enemy men-at-arms, but I could see that his assault on the north side of the barbican had been even bloodier than ours. There were very few men in Robin's dark green livery fighting beside him – perhaps a mere two dozen of the hundred that had set out such a short time ago.

We men of the southern attack charged into the fray, yelling our war cries and brandishing weapons – and the enemy melted away before us, deserting the gate in panic and retreating a hundred yards or so to where a dozen knights on foot were rallying the fleeing troops and preparing for a counter-attack. We had only a very little time, for there were so few of us – fewer than fifty men still on their feet, the mingled remnants of both attacking parties – and if we did not get the gate open swiftly, the enemy would mass in their hundreds and easily overwhelm us.

Two of Little John's men were fiddling with the cross-bar that held the swinging sections of the great door together. There was some kind of locking mechanism, a bar-and-lever combination, and the men, it seemed, could not fathom how it might work.

The enemy knights had stopped roughly forty fleeing cross-bowmen, and I could see them reassembling, calmer now, under orders again, loading their weapons, using the hook on their belts and a foot in the stirrup at the end of the bow to haul the drawstring back.

Worse, a large crowd of men-at-arms – perhaps a hundred or more in Murdac's black surcoats with the red chevrons – was pouring out from the barbican in the middle bailey. Reinforcements. Things were about to get very, very bad.

'Hurry!' I snapped to the men pushing and pulling at the cross-bar on the gatehouse door. 'They are coming. We have only a few moments before they attack.'

'Get out of my way,' boomed a deep confident voice that I knew so well. And I saw Little John shove the men aside and swing his blood-soaked axe double-handed at the oaken beam that barred the door.

Thunk!

But even Little John's mighty blow only chipped out a slim bright brown-yellow splinter of wood an inch thick from the cross-bar. The wood was old oak and tough, and the bar a foot wide. We didn't have time for John's rough carpentry.

'Form a line here,' I shouted. And with one eye on the mass of black-and-red enemy a hundred yards away, I pushed and pulled Robin's men into two ranks, the front rank kneeling, the second rank standing, shields to the fore.

Thunk!

Out of the corner of my eye I could see that Little John was beginning to lay into the crossbar with a slow but steady rhythm. Then Hanno was by his side, following John's blow immediately with one of his own from a smaller, lighter, single-bladed war axe.

Thunk! Think!

The two axe blows made strikingly different sounds.

'Stay tight, and keep your shields up,' I shouted to our raggedy wall of forty or so men. But the men needed no urging, for the crossbowmen had reloaded and soon, as everyone could plainly see, their wicked bolts would begin to fly again.

Thunk! Think!

I looked behind me to the east and saw that the sun was fully up by now. It was going to be a lovely spring day.

'Here they come!' I shouted. The crossbowmen had divided into two groups of about twenty men each and were advancing on either side of the main body of a hundred or so of Murdac's men-at-arms. At seventy yards they began to loose their quar-rels. Not as a volley but individually: two or three men shooting, then stopping to reload while the others advanced. These were

372

clearly first-class troops, well disciplined and brave. They kept up a nearly constant rain of missiles on our thin, weak shield wall, forcing our men to cower behind their flimsy protection to avoid being spitted like hares.

Thunk! Think!

A man standing beside me on the edge of our double line screamed suddenly and fell backwards, a black bolt thrusting from his eye.

'Keep those shields up!' I shouted, and crouched down myself in the front rank beside the men, trying to keep my body as much as possible behind my kite-shaped shield.

The two groups of crossbowmen were now so close that they could hardly miss. And between them the men-at-arms were advancing in a purposeful manner, swords drawn, some armed with short spears or cut-down lances. I knew that at about twenty yards away they would launch into a run and smash through my thin line of exhausted, battered men. We had, by my reckoning, only a few moments before we were overrun by the enemy. The crossbow bolts were rattling against the shield wall, occasionally finding a gap and giving rise to a yelp or scream.

Thunk! Think!

'God's bulging bollocks!' shouted a great voice, clearly in pain. And I turned to look back at Little John, who was peering over his own shoulder at a black quarrel sticking out from his huge right buttock; his green hose were glistening black, soaked with blood. But he merely shrugged the pain away, leaving the evil-looking bolt in place, and turned back to his task.

Thunk! Think!

I heard Hanno yell something but could not make it out. The enemy men-at-arms were only forty paces away now.

Thwick! A different sound. I risked another quick look behind me and saw that John had finally chopped his way through the bar. Limping more than a little, he was helping Hanno to swing the heavy wooden portal open. I looked out of the gap between the slowly opening doors of the gatehouse and saw a sight beyond it that made my heart leap with joy.

Horsemen.

A great mass of armoured horsemen, led by a tall knight in brightly polished, gold-chased helm riding a magnificent destrier beneath a red-and-gold standard. And beside him was another familiar figure, faceless in his flat-topped tubular helmet but wearing a deep green surcoat with a black-and-grey wolf's mask depicted on the chest. The horsemen came on at the trot. They were only thirty yards away. The lead horseman lowered his lance, and all his companions – at least three-score knights – followed his example in a wave of white wood and glittering steel. A trumpet sounded and the cavalry came up to the canter. It was Richard, my King, coming to the rescue. And my liege lord, the Earl of Locksley, was riding at his side.

Another trumpet rang out. The horsemen charged.

'Down!' I shouted. 'Everybody down. Lie down. Lie still, lie absolutely still if you want to live.' And as one the men in the shield wall dropped to the muddy ground. I could feel the wet earth vibrate under my cheek, and hear the rumble of massive hooves, and I dared not look up as the household cavalry of Richard Plantagenet, by the Grace of God, King of England, Duke of Normandy and Aquitaine, Count of Anjou and Maine, a company of some of the finest and bravest knights in Christendom, poured over our prone bodies like a rushing equine waterfall, jumping cleanly over the cowering bodies of forty prostrate men in a welter of pounding hooves and flying mud, before spurring on to smash straight into the advancing line of black-and-red men-at-arms, lances couched, a battle cry roaring from every mounted warrior's throat.

When I finally lifted my head I saw a scene of utter carnage. King Richard's cavalry had crashed into Murdac's men-at-arms like a mighty tempest blowing through a field of stacked wheat, the twelve-foot razor-tipped lances skewering bodies and hurling the enemy several yards backwards. Those who had not been pierced by their spears or crushed by the giant hooves of the knights' destriers had scattered. And when the lances were gone, snapped off, impaled in heads or buried deep in infantrymen's bellies, Richard's knights pulled out long swords or a mace or an axe and the butchery continued. I saw Robin lopping the sword arm from a man-at-arms who had been foolish enough to turn and face him. But even those who ran rarely escaped. I watched a fleeing crossbowman easily over-hauled by a horse-borne knight, who hacked down in passing, slicing open the poor man's unprotected face. Three knights surrounded a knot of struggling men-at-arms, battering at their heads and upheld arms with mace and sword until all the footmen had fallen in a sodden, twitching heap. Everywhere running men-at-arms were being sliced and hacked and battered by the victorious knights; no quarter was given, and none of the enemy were thought to be worth ransoming, so scores died, and their bloody rag-doll bodies were trampled and torn time and again under the hooves of the knights' big horses as they criss-crossed the outer bailey looking for fresh prey. The lucky ones, or those enemy crossbowmen and men-at-arms who could run the fastest, made it back to the barbican in the middle

375

bailey, and were quickly pulled inside for safety as the thick iron-studded oak door slammed shut behind them. But they were few, very few.

Richard's knights, however, did not have it all their own way. After the initial onslaught was over, from the walls and towers of the upper and middle baileys, Murdac's surviving Flemish crossbowmen took their revenge. Foot-long oak bolts, tipped with sharp iron, hissed from the battlements, sinking deep into horse and rider without discrimination. Javelins were hurled downward, and huge boulders, too. One unfortunate knight, unhorsed outside the barbican of the middle bailey and battering futilely with his sword hilt at the barred door, was fried alive when a cauldron of red-hot sand was poured on him from a murder-hole above. I saw another knight, cursing and crying with pain, pinned through the meat of his thigh by a black quarrel to the wood of his saddle.

But the outer bailey was ours. When the defenders who had remained there were all dead, mortally wounded or captured, and there were no more easy targets for the roaming knights' swords, most of the mounted men, panting and praising God, retreated back beyond the open gate of the captured gatehouse and out of range of the defenders' deadly missiles. There was nothing else for them to do: the main castle was shut tight, secure from their blood-spattered blades, and their horses could not gallop through the grey stone of its massive walls.

We men in Lincoln green had picked ourselves up from the ground by this point, though we had taken no further part in the fight for the outer bailey. A few of the brighter enemy men-at-arms had thrown their weapons away and run towards us, shouting as they came that they wished to surrender. They escaped the wrath of the knights, and took refuge with us, under guard, on the far side, the town side of the gatehouse and the wooden palisade we had so valiantly captured. The outer bailey of Nottingham Castle belonged to King Richard's men – but we could not easily move about in it, except by running and dodging and hiding behind the few scattered buildings there, for fear of the crossbowmen who now lined the castle walls, seemingly determined, even though the fight for that ground was over, to pick us off one by one.

King Richard came walking unhurriedly across the open space, horse-less and hobbling slightly. For some reason – most probably ignorance of who he was – the crossbowmen seemed to be sparing him. He stopped in front of the right-hand part of the wooden double door that Little John had managed to open in the nick of time and greeted me cordially:

'Blondel, how goes it?' he called. 'You survived, I see.'

'I'm well, sire. Quite miraculously unharmed.'

The King nodded distractedly and just then a crossbow bolt slammed into the ground between us. It seemed that the bowmen on the castle's stone walls had finally woken up to the fact that the King was in their sights. Richard ignored the bolt sticking out of the earth in front of him, and a second one that landed on his other side but closer to the royal foot. He was staring up at the wooden bulk of the gatehouse. We were at the extreme range of the crossbow's power, more than a hundred and fifty yards from the battlements of the middle bailey, but Richard must have known that, with his light desert armour, any quarrel that struck him could still do considerable damage. The King's self-possession, I thought admiringly, was remarkable.

Two household knights came hurrying up to their sovereign as he stood in the doorway of the gatehouse gazing silently up at its structure. They were carrying two large shields and, standing behind the King, they lifted the kite-shaped objects to protect his back from any further insult from the castle crossbowmen.

'You did very well, Blondel,' said the King ruminatively, 'to capture this gate. I thank you for it. But, you know, we cannot hold this place . . .'

A crossbow bolt skittered off the shield being held by one of the knights standing protectively behind him, and my concentration was diverted momentarily so that I did not hear what the King said next.

'. . . it's a shame really, but it can't be helped,' he said.

'I beg your pardon, sire,' I asked, embarrassed by my inattention. 'What did you just say?'

'I said, my good Blondel, that you are to take your men and burn this gatehouse to the ground. Destroy the whole outer palisade too, while you are at it. If we cannot hold the outer bailey, then they shall not have it either. Burn this and all the defences that you can get at. And when we have done that, I shall send heralds to talk to this Murdac fellow, to see what he has to say for himself.'

It was easier said than done to burn the palisade. I gathered up the survivors of that morning's attack, borrowed a score of Robin's archers, and we set about placing dry straw and brushwood faggots doused with oil along the inside and outside edges of the palisade, ready to put it to the torch. We were harassed constantly by the crossbowmen in the middle bailey and I had to use a screen of men carrying shields on both left and right arms to keep those men laying the fire safe from the darting quarrels of the defenders.

I lost one man killed and two injured in the process, and it was grim work. We were not taking part in a mad rush for glory, with the rage of battle pounding in our ears, but doing heavy, difficult, dirty work. What is more, destroying the outer bailey's defences made the sacrifice of precious lives that morning seem a terrible waste. But when a King commands, you obey.

It was gone noon by the time we finished, and I released the men to find food and rest as the first flames began to crackle and burn along the line of palisade. I put the torch to that damned gatehouse myself, piling straw and brushwood on either side of the wooden doors, then throwing a burning length of pine into each pile and retreating beyond the burnt strip as the column of smoke rose into the blue March sky. My task accomplished, I walked back into the town to seek out Robin and receive fresh orders.

I found the Earl of Locksley in a big townhouse in the centre of Nottingham, drinking red wine and joking with Little John. Robin was sitting on a stool in the corner of the room with his left leg extended. He had a bloody bandage on his thigh, but he assured me jovially that it was a clean javelin wound and would surely heal, given time – if he was only allowed a little peace and quiet. Little John was lying flat on a big table in the centre of the hall, naked from the waist down. His right buttock was swollen and bloody and the black shaft of the quarrel was sticking up vertically, protruding about six inches from the mound of pink-white flesh. Nonetheless, John seemed to be in very good spirits. A nervous barber-surgeon was fussing around the big man's nether regions, mopping at the blood that was trickling down his hip and muttering. The man, who was clearly rather frightened, kept picking up an instrument that resembled two spoons fixed together – the bowls facing each other, and the whole contraption attached to the end of a short, thin iron shaft – then putting it down again.

Robin saw me peering at the instrument and said: 'It's a tool for removing arrow heads from deep wounds. The spoony part is inserted into the wound, closed around the arrow head, which allows the head to be withdrawn without causing any more damage. Totally unnecessary, in my view – Flemish cross-bowmen don't use barbed arrows for warfare. But Nathan here insists it is a marvellous invention and the decision must be his: after all, Nathan is the man who is to operate on John, when he can summon up sufficient courage.'

I looked at Robin quizzically. And my master said: 'John has threatened to break both of Nathan's arms if he causes him any unnecessary pain.' And he gave me a lop-sided smile.

Little John was grinning owlishly at me from his position on the table. I could see that, unlike Robin, who was merely relaxed, John was thoroughly drunk. He had also been tightly strapped to the table, with several thick leather bands securing his huge chest and both meaty legs. I walked over to him. 'Now then, John,' I said, selecting my most patronizing tone. 'There is no need to throw your weight about here and make such a childish fuss about a little thing like this.'

And with my index finger I flicked the shaft of the quarrel that was sticking out of his arse cheek – hard.

It wobbled satisfyingly, and John bellowed with rage and pain and tried to struggle free of the leather bonds that strapped him to the table. Out of the corner of my eye, I could see Nathan the barber-surgeon looking stunned and Robin, heedless of his javelin wound, convulsed with laugher on his stool in the corner.

'That,' I said to the red-faced giant now writhing on the table and trying to reach me with great backward sweeps of his massive hands, 'was for the punch in the face that you gave me at Carlton.' And I grinned broadly at him to display the tooth he had chipped.

'And this is to teach you not to bully poor barber-surgeons—' I grabbed the shaft of the quarrel and pulled it free of the wound with one swift, clean jerk of my wrist. It came free easily, accompanied by a splash of black blood.

Followed only by John's booming roar of outrage and the sound of Robin's helpless laughter, I ran from the room and tumbled out into the street, hardly able to contain my own mirth. It had been a long, difficult day, but that image of Little John's crimson face, contorted with impotent fury, was one that would warm me on many a cold night for years to come.

At dusk, the King summoned his chief counsellors to his big pavilion in the deer park. I accompanied Robin to the meeting, but only after I had ascertained that Little John was *hors de combat*, sleeping off a vast quantity of drink in a comfortable bed in the town, his bum cheek now cleaned, stitched and bandaged by the surgeon. I had resolved to stay well out of his way for a few days, at the very least, until he had calmed down; possibly a month – maybe even a year or two.

All the King's senior barons and knights were there, crammed into the stuffy tent, some bearing the marks of the day's battle.

The Scotsman, David, Earl of Huntingdon, was chatting to Earl Ferrers, who had been lightly but unluckily wounded in the face that afternoon by a quarrel fired from the castle. His men had made a valiant attack on the barbican of the middle bailey, and had very nearly taken it. But the falling of dusk, and a surprisingly determined resistance by the defenders, had forced them to retreat at the last, leaving their dead in piles in the ditch below the middle bailey's stone walls. William, Baron Edwinstowe, standing alone near the back of the pavilion, gave me a cautious nod and a half-smile; I bowed slightly in return. Ranulph, Earl of Chester, stood with Sir Aymeric de St Maur and another grey-haired Templar knight talking quietly in a corner of the tent. While we waited for the King, Robin and I passed the time in conversation with William the Marshal – he had been one of the knights who had charged to our rescue that day with Richard, and he had slain many of the enemy that morning with his own hand. I thanked him for saving my life, and the lives of my men.

'I should be thanking you,' said this grizzled old war-hound. 'Without your valiant assault on the gatehouse, we'd never have taken the outer bailey.'

'Not that it has done us much good,' said Robin with a grimace. 'Ferrers' assault on the barbican failed. We are still no closer to taking the stone heart of Nottingham. You might say that we just wasted the lives of a good many men today – mostly my men.'

I knew that Robin's wound was paining him, but he was also genuinely angry about the carnage that had occurred during the taking of the gatehouse. Of the one hundred and ninety-odd men-at-arms who had charged with Little John and me that morning, more than two-thirds were now dead or wounded. And many of the badly wounded would not live through the night. Robin's forces had been severely depleted by the attack, and we could not even say that we now had mastery of the outer bailey. No one did.

'I don't care for that sort of talk,' growled the Marshal, looking sharply at Robin. 'It was bravely done, and Alan here is to be congratulated for a difficult task accomplished.' I smiled gratefully at William. And Robin grinned a little ruefully at me. 'You are right, Marshal,' my lord said. 'That was remiss of me. You did very well today, Alan. And I thank you from my heart for your gallant efforts.'

I wasn't sure I liked the word 'efforts', but before I could raise the matter, Robin changed the subject.

'What news from the heralds, Marshal?'

The old warrior scratched his grey head. 'Nothing very surprising: the castle still formally defies us. The only ray of sunlight is that the heralds have reported that there are those inside who, it is believed, would surrender to the King in the right circumstances. But not while the Constable, Sir Ralph Murdac, is in command there. The wretched fellow is apparently devoted to Prince John, and he has told the heralds that he does not believe that the foe encamped before him really is King Richard. He is saying that our army is commanded by an imposter, some jumped-up knight pretending to be Richard!'

Robin snorted. 'That's a good one – the King is an imposter! And the idea of Ralph Murdac being devoted to anyone is quite amusing, too. That little hunchbacked rat has nowhere else to go, and he knows it, so he's dressing it up as knightly loyalty. But that's all by the by. I take it that there is no chance of a nice peaceful surrender, then?'

'None – while Murdac remains Constable,' said William. 'We must take the castle by force. It will have to be done the hard way, the old-fashioned way.'

'Maybe – but then again, maybe not,' said Robin, musingly. 'Will you excuse us, Marshal? I need to speak to young Alan on a private matter.'

And, hobbling slightly from his javelin wound, he pulled me aside and began to whisper quietly into my ear.

By rights, I should not have spoken out at the King's Council. Although I believed Richard was fond of me, I was a nobody, a mere captain of men, a youth, not yet twenty years old, of no family to speak of, and with only one small manor to my undistinguished name. But I did speak, and it changed my life. And, as it was his idea, I have Robin to thank for the results.

The meeting began with the King addressing the assembled barons and bishops, offering a brief word of thanks to the Marshal, the Earl of Locksley, Earl Ferrers and several of the other knights there for their actions that day. Then he moved on to give a résumé of what the heralds had reported: namely, that the castle still defied us, and would continue to do so under the command of its present Constable. The King did not mention that Murdac considered him to be a jumped-up imposter. Rightly so: even royalty must safeguard its dignity.

'So, gentlemen,' said the King, 'what we need to do is bring those big walls down. I will teach Sir Ralph Murdac to defy me, by God's legs I will! I have given orders to my artificers to build a couple of siege engines by morning, a powerful mangonel and a good-sized trebuchet, and over the next few weeks I plan to reduce the east wall of the middle bailey to rubble. I took Acre, and that was considered an impossible task, and I can damned well take Nottingham. But I'm afraid, gentlemen, it will take some time . . .'

'Sire,' I said. I still find it hard to believe that I had the courage to interrupt my King in mid-flow, and I would not have done so were it not for Robin's insistent elbow nudging my ribs, but I did. And this is what happened.

At first the King did not notice me. 'We need to bottle them in securely,' he was saying. 'I want no food, water or provisions, and particularly no men or information going in or out of the castle. You, my lord of Chester, will take the southern section, by the cliffs . . .'

'Sire,' I said again, and this time the King noticed me.

He looked slightly annoyed to be interrupted, and I suddenly wondered if I was making a huge mistake.

'What is it, Blondel?' the King said, coldly.

'Sire,' I said for the third time. And my tongue shrivelled in my mouth.

'Yes?' The King was definitely getting testy. 'Now that you have interrupted me, Alan, speak if you have a mind to.'

I finally managed to get my words out: 'What if we were to, ah, get rid of Murdac? What if we were to – well, ah, kill him, or remove him from command of the castle in some way? Wouldn't that change things for us?' As I said it, I knew it sounded absurd, the sort of thing a silly child might say, and I could feel my cheeks redden as some of the most powerful barons in England stared at me, astonished at my impudence.

The King looked at me for a long, long moment, and for

an instant I believed that he would order the guards to drag me away from the tent and have me hanged, drawn and quartered.

'And *how* would you accomplish this?' the King asked, frowning.

'I know of an old servants' entrance into the castle, sire. It is forgotten; I believe it remains a secret known only to a very few. It leads from a tavern below the southern wall of the outer bailey to a small unused buttery inside the upper bailey of Nottingham Castle itself.'

My voice was growing in confidence as I spoke. 'It is a narrow passage, and I do not believe that a large number of men-at-arms could use it. The noise a large party of men would make would ensure detection. And once detected, they could be easily slaughtered one by one as they emerged into the castle. But one man, treading lightly, could secretly gain access to the castle this way, I believe. He would then have a good chance – if he did not put too high a value on his own life – of finding Sir Ralph Murdac and killing him. Perhaps in his chamber at night as he slept, perhaps in some other way – but I think it could be done.'

'You may have something, Blondel,' said the King, and he smiled at me. And instantly, all the other great men in the tent were beaming, too. 'Without Murdac, as you say, we'd have a much better chance of getting these rascals to surrender my castle. Would you do this for me, Alan? It is a risky – one might say downright foolhardy – proposition . . .'

'Yes, sire,' I said simply. And what else could I say? He was my King.

Richard nodded to himself as if confirming something that

he already knew, and then he looked over at Robin. 'Do you know about this forgotten servants' hole, Locksley?'

'No, sire,' lied Robin. 'But I have full confidence in Alan of Westbury. If he says it exists, it surely does, and, if anyone can accomplish this most dangerous and difficult task, it is he.'

I looked at Robin, a little surprised at his praise and by his denial of all knowledge of the tunnel. He grinned over at me and gave me a suspicion of a wink. And I smiled back.

When I tell the old tales of Robert, the cunning Earl of Locksley, of the wily outlaw Robin Hood, all too often I stress the times when he behaved badly. I tell far too often of his cruelty, or of his greed for silver, of his indifference to the sufferings of those outside his family circle, and his contempt for Holy Mother Church. And all too often I forget to mention the one thing that was perhaps his most outstanding characteristic: his kindness. If you served him well, he would pour out his benevolence on you without ever counting the cost to himself. He was, at heart, a very kind and generous man – at least to those whom he loved.

Robin had wanted me to raise the subject of the tunnel with the King because he wanted Richard to know how resourceful I was; and for the King to reward me in due course. Robin could have claimed credit for the scheme himself; he could have said that he had shown the tunnel to me, and used it to rescue me from imprisonment inside Nottingham. But he did not. That was the sort of man he was. And so, with a careless smile and a half-wink, he secured the King's personal favour for me, and dispatched me on a great and perilous adventure – and quite possibly to my death.

Chapter Twenty-one

Hanno led the way, holding up a single horn lantern with a stub of candle in it. The yellow walls of the tunnel seemed even more grotesque than before, with weird faces seeming to leer out at me from the walls, mocking my ambitions: going into the castle on a mission of murder was far more daunting than coming out of it to freedom and safety.

It was close on midnight, and although I had not slept since the day before last, I was not tired. In fact I was burning with an excited rage that seemed to banish all my fears. I knew that, if things went wrong, I would have only a small chance of survival – but, for the opportunity to kill Sir Ralph Murdac, to take revenge for so many hurts and insults at his hands, and to do an invaluable service for my King, it seemed a risk worth taking. I was young then, and adventure and risk had a certain appeal merely for their own sake.

There were also a number of things to my advantage. I knew

the castle, and the members of the garrison there knew my face, but possibly not my true allegiance. With so many folk changing sides in the contest between King Richard and Prince John, I was fairly sure that if I was stopped by suspicious guards and questioned, I could convince them that I was back on Prince John's side. And my presence in the castle would seem to be proof of that. Both Hanno and myself were also wearing the black surcoats with the red chevrons of Murdac's men – taken from prisoners captured in the battle for the outer bailey – with our swords belted over the top. And so I felt confident that any man-at-arms seeing me – a familiar face, inside the castle, wearing Sir Ralph's livery – would likely consider me friend rather than foe.

The main problem would come when we emerged at the mouth of the ale-shaft; I did not know whether the old buttery had been discovered as my method of escape. After all, five months ago a condemned prisoner had disappeared in the middle of the night, killing three men, stealing a large quantity of silver and leaving a bloody wolf's head in his prison cell – what would the garrison have made of it? Would they have searched for a secret tunnel, or remembered how the ale had previously been delivered to the castle? Would they have put it down to witchcraft? Did they believe I had magicked my way out of there? Or would they have assumed that I made my escape by more ordinary means, bribing a guard with a bag of silver and slipping quietly over the castle walls? I had no way of knowing.

I was fairly sure that Sir Ralph Murdac would not be familiar with the lower reaches of the castle: it was an area frequented by servants, cooks, butlers and so on. Not by knights, and certainly not by the Constable himself. I was staking my life that the old buttery and the ale-shaft were as we had left them – staking Hanno's life too.

I had initially meant to go on this mission alone, but Hanno had insisted on accompanying me. 'You get lost in those tunnels – ha-ha – and in the bottom of the castle too!' Hanno was jovial as ever and seemed totally unconcerned about the danger when we talked quietly in the main room of The Trip to Jerusalem tavern – now deserted, for the brewer and his young family had wisely fled when the castle had been encircled by King Richard's troops. Hanno was supposed to be seeing me off on the mission, but instead he said: 'Best I come with you to keep you out of trouble; maybe teach you something.' And I did not protest too much. I was very glad to have him by my side.

When we approached the final steps of the tunnel, and reached the chamber directly below the shaft that led up to the buttery, we killed the horn lantern and stood absolutely still, listening for sounds of danger from above. Nothing. Not a sound.

I stretched out my hand in the darkness and made contact with the rope. The same rope that Robin, Hanno and I had climbed down five months ago. It seemed incredible but, apparently, the buttery and this secret way into the castle were still quite unknown to the defenders.

I climbed up the rope into the dark shaft. My arm muscles were soon protesting; though I carried no shield, I was weighed down by my mail coat and sword, and by the heavy back-sack that I wore. But very shortly I sensed a space around me, and groping quickly with my left hand, I found the lip of the housing. Then Hanno was there, lighting the lantern, and I was using his big key to unlock the low, wide door that led to the old buttery.

So far, so good. The buttery, as far as I could tell, was the same as it had been five months ago.

A clatter, an appalling din of wooden noise as a small ale cask fell to the floor with a crash, toppling from a pile of larger ones. Then there was a high-pitched squeal of rage and something dark moved very fast in the corner of the buttery. My heart seemed to explode and I had my naked sword in my hand before I knew what was happening.

Hanno and I stood frozen in silence. There were no further sounds. Then Hanno laughed quietly. 'It is just a rat,' he whispered. 'But he gives you a good fright, yes?'

I said nothing, but re-sheathed my sword, cursing my jumpiness. And a few moments later Hanno and I were walking confidently along the corridor outside the buttery in the bowels of the upper bailey, in the very heart of Murdac's stronghold.

At this hour the interior of the castle was largely still – there would have been sentries on the ramparts, and groups of men-at-arms bunched together in the towers on the walls, and in the guardhouses and barracks in the middle bailey, but this part of the castle was eerily quiet. Hanno and I passed only one person as we made our way towards the great tower and Ralph Murdac's chamber: a servant carrying a tray of wine cups. The surly devil ignored us, brushing past in an irritable manner. It seemed that our surcoats gave us the invisibility we craved.

We passed a guard room at the base of the great tower, and as we walked past, I could not help glancing through the door.

My eyes just had time to take in the homely scene: two or three men-at-arms in red-and-black surcoats playing dice at a table in the centre of the room by the light of a single candle, and a dozen soldiers snoring in cots around the edges of the chamber. We walked past without inviting any comment; indeed, without even being noticed. My nerves began to ease: we were going to succeed! God willing, we were going to make it all the way to Murdac's chamber – where Sir Ralph was no doubt slumbering peacefully – without a single challenge.

The chamber of the Constable of Nottingham Castle was on the western side of the great tower, on the second floor. I had not been there since that fateful day in September the year before when I had been summoned by Murdac and told that I was to accompany the silver wagon train from Tickhill back to Nottingham. Hanno and I arrived there, walking normally along the stone corridors and pretending to converse with each other in low tones, like any two men-at-arms on a midnight errand from their captain, or just stretching their legs after a long stint of sentry duty.

We stopped just short of the chamber, hearing the sound of pacing feet, and after a cautious peep around the bend, Hanno whispered in my ear that there was only one man doing duty before the door. My German friend reached down and pulled the misericorde from my boot: 'Do it quick and quiet,' he said into my ear, putting the weapon in my hand. 'No noise, no fussing.' I nodded, my heart hammering. It was time once again for cold-blooded murder. I peeked round the corner, too, and took a look at my victim. Like the sentry outside Kirkton Castle a year and a half ago, the man-at-arms outside Murdac's door was young. But this time, when I looked into my soul, I found I had no qualms about taking his life – it was necessary, I said to myself, and that was all that really mattered.

My heart quietened, I took a deep breath and moved fast, without hesitation. Two quick and silent steps, as he was turned away from me, and I grabbed his nose and mouth with my left hand and slotted the misericorde hard and neatly into the back of his brain with my right. It was as easy as sliding a well-greased bolt on a cellar door. The blade glided home, the man kicked once and collapsed into my arms, a dead weight. That was it; there was nothing more to it.

Silently, Hanno was by my side. 'Perfect,' he said. And I was very pleased.

I passed the sagging corpse into Hanno's arms, cleaned my misericorde on the dead man's surcoat, slid the weapon back into my boot, drew my sword, took a deep breath and burst through the door of Murdac's chamber, with Hanno hard on my heels, dragging the limp body of the sentry behind me.

After the gloom of the corridor, Murdac's room was shockingly bright, lit as it was by two large candle trees. It was a comfortable chamber, spacious and warm, with costly furs scattered over the polished wooden floor, and a fire burning merrily in a large fireplace built into the outside wall. In the centre of the room was a large table, and seated at the table, his glorious long sword drawn on the surface before him, was Rix.

The tall man picked up the sword, and I could not help admiring its blue pommel jewel glinting at me in the candlelight, and the elegance of the long slim lines of the blade. I was entranced by the weapon, and my eye caressed it, even as Rix pushed back his chair, stood to his full height and said in French: 'Ah, you are here at last. Sir Ralph has been half-expecting an assassin. And how fortunate that it should be you! We have some unfinished business between us, I believe.'

I nodded but said nothing to the tall man. Instead my eyes roamed the room, seeking out the target of our deadly intentions, the Constable.

A sumptuous four-poster bed stood against the far wall of the chamber with the thick curtains drawn. And, as I looked at it, a dark and tousled head poked out from between the drapes, blinking wildly, like a mouse coming out of its hole. It was Ralph Murdac, and his expression when he saw me was one of equally mingled fear and surprise.

'You!' he said incredulously. 'You, of all people! Alan Dale – the traitor, the thief, the gutter-born rat who wants to be a knight. That it should be you who has come for me, sword in hand, in the dead of night – I can scarce believe it. Kill him, Rix; kill him now! Slice the nasty jumped-up little peasant into pieces.'

Rix stepped away from the table and, at Murdac's command, he saluted me with his beautiful sword, holding the hilt to his brow for a moment, before sweeping it into the first position of the serious swordsman: *en garde!*

'Get over to Murdac,' I muttered over my shoulder to Hanno, without taking my eyes off Rix. 'Grab him; hold him fast; keep him out of the fight. I'll handle this one alone – I made a vow to St Michael to cut down this long streak of shit, and I mean to honour it.'

I felt Hanno move away from me in the direction of the big bed and I took a step towards Rix. With no preliminaries at all, I swung my blade as hard and as fast as I could at his head.

His sword leapt upwards and he parried my blow with a clang of steel. But I was already swiping low, aiming to sink my sword into his calf muscle. Miraculously, his long blade was there before mine, once again blocking my strike with ease. I lunged with all my speed at his chest; he nonchalantly flicked my blade out of the target area and it slid past his left arm into space.

Then he attacked: a feint at my body, then another, followed by a lightning strike at my throat. By God, he was fast; much faster than me. By sheer luck I managed to avoid being spitted on his sword, sweeping my own blade up just in time. I deflected his lunge into the air above my left shoulder and counter-attacked, against his right, hoping for a score on his sword-arm that would slow his terrifying speed. But, once again, he swept my blow away almost contemptuously.

I could hear muffled thumps and yelps coming from the four-poster bed, but I dared not look away from Rix, even for a moment. I thrust again at his chest, and he swatted me away. I hacked low; he merely stepped back. Then he attacked once more, striking left and right, high and low, his weapon a lethal silver blur, and it was all I could do to keep his sword point out of my flesh. It occurred to me then, in a blinding moment of clarity, that I was going to lose this fight. He was the better swordsman; there was absolutely no doubt about it. I was giving ground slowly, making nothing of the fight; merely blocking, parrying, dodging and ducking. I was outclassed, overmatched – I was going to be cut to pieces.

We fought on almost in silence, the only sound the clang and clash of our blades, and the panting of my breath. As Rix stepped away momentarily and began to circle round to my right, I caught a glimpse of the four-poster. And saw my German friend, calmly sitting on the edge of the bed, the curtains drawn back, his arm curled around Ralph Murdac's tousled little head, as one might carry a ball, his long knife at the Constable's throat. Murdac was very pale, his crisp blue eyes under Hanno's muscular arm were enlarged with fear, and a trickle of blood was leaking from his mouth. Hanno was frowning at me; he looked almost comically disappointed. But holding Murdac as he was, he could not easily release him and come to my aid against Rix. I could expect no help from that quarter.

I jerked my attention back to the fight just in time: Rix's sword came lancing towards my eye and I parried and slashed at him wildly. He blocked and riposted, and I hacked again at his head with all the savagery in my soul. He merely ducked the blow. He was perfectly balanced, and as cool as a river trout. I, meanwhile, was red-faced and panting with exertion. I aimed another tremendous hack at his shoulder, which he blocked. His counter-stroke, a lunge at my heart, nearly skewered me, but I jumped backwards in the nick of time. My left foot landed on a fine bearskin rug, the rug skidded on the polished floor, and before I knew it I had landed painfully on my arse, and my sword was skittering and bouncing away across the shiny wooden floor to my right.

Rix stood over me. He smiled coldly, saluted me once again, and lifted his sword over his head. I was scrambling on my knees before him, staring up in shock and fear as his beautiful sword rose in the air, my hand reaching desperately for the bottom of my left leg . . .

My fumbling hand found the misericorde. The triangular blade slipped loose from its boot-sheath and I brought it up and struck like an angry viper, slamming it down in a hammer blow straight through Rix's soft kidskin shoe, nailing his left foot securely to the wooden floor.

He screamed – he screamed one word, loud enough to wake the dead: 'Miloooooooo!'

But I did not listen; I was scuttling away after my sword. I collected the weapon, regained my feet and, while Rix tried to turn right towards me, his long limbs tangled because of his pinioned foot, I stepped in to him, swung back and chopped the blade down hard into the angle between his neck and his left shoulder, giving it all my strength, and cutting a foot deep into his chest cavity. For a shaved moment, I caught a glimpse of grey flabby lungs deep in his gasping purple torso before the blood welled and filled his chest.

And he was down.

I tugged my sword loose from the shattered bones and meat of his thorax, and only just in time. There was movement from the far side of the room, a curtain was torn back – it was the heavy curtain that covered the entrance to Murdac's privy – and out of that dank passageway stumped the ogre, Perkin's killer, Adam's assassin, walking on one good leg and one wooden one. The half-man whom I had believed I had stamped to death in the list in the outer bailey five months ago was resurrected. Milo was doing up his broad belt, and staring about him with bovine stupidity.

Time is a strange beast: some moments seem to last for ever, yet others go by in a flash. I felt as if I had been fighting Rix for hours, but I realized later that it can have been no longer than a hundred heartbeats or so, just the time it had taken for Milo – who was on the seat of ease in the privy – to finish his business, wipe himself, drop his tunic and do up his belt, and come to see what all the clang and clatter was about in Murdac's chamber.

Milo saw me standing over the bloody dead body of his friend, blinked, scowled, gave a feral shout – and charged. And though his left leg, above the knee, had been replaced with a strapped-on leather cup attached to the stump of his thigh, and a stout bar of wood to walk on, he moved at a pretty decent lick. I knelt quickly beside the tall swordsman's gory corpse and picked up his lovely weapon with my left hand; then I stood to meet the ogre's hobbling charge, a sword in each fist.

In the three heartbeats before he reached me, I had time to notice that he still bore the marks from our battle in the lists on his face. He had but one good eye; small and piggish, and glaring with bottomless rage, and his hairless head was a crumpled mass of scar tissue from the battering my boots had given him, all yellow and shiny and furrowed, with barely any recognizable features at all. A flashing image of Nur came into my head: and indeed they would have made a pretty pair. His head was like a ball of beeswax that has melted after being placed to warm too near the fire. He looked even more monstrous than he had before our battle. Yet I was amazed that he lived at all, for I had been sure that I had stamped his vital spark to extinction – but live he did, and now he sought revenge.

When Milo was a mere yard from me, I twisted to my right out of his path like the Saracen dancers I had seen in Outremer, twirling in a complete circle, fast, and hacking down hard on his outstretched left arm with Rix's gorgeous sword. The blade sliced clean through the thick knotted muscle and solid bone just below his elbow, cutting away his forearm with a single blow and leaving him, roaring with pain, the blood jetting from the stump. But I wasted no time in gloating at his injury; instead, continuing my twisting manoeuvre, I found myself behind him and cut down with a smooth sweep into the slab of solid muscle of his right thigh using the plain old sword in my right hand. There was not enough power in my strike to cut through that knotted limb, but he did fall to his knees squealing with pain.

I took his remaining hand then: a neat downward blow with Rix's incomparable sword slicing all the way through like a hot blade through butter, sending his pudgy, ham-like fist thumping to the floor. He was a dead man then, of course: both arms useless and unable to rise on his one wounded leg. And I stood before Milo, between his half-kneeling, blood-drenched massive body and the long heap of his friend, and looked at him for a moment or two, remembering the wrestling match in the list, and the crunching explosion of his boot in my ribs in Germany, and the sight of the torn bodies of Perkin and Adam as we found them on the bank of River Main. He stared back at me with his one mad eye. There was nothing to say, and so I held my tongue: I merely gave him a merciful end, thrusting with both swords simultaneously into his huge breast, the two long blades plunging deeply into the chest cavity, driving towards his engorged ogre's heart.

'Not so bad,' said Hanno from the bed, where he was still holding Ralph Murdac securely around the neck. 'But very far from perfect. I think the tall, skinny one is going kill you, for sure. You are sloppy, too confident and your attacks are obvious. You must practise, Alan. Practise more. You must try to do better in future.'

I stood there between the corpses of the two men I had just killed, and nodded my head in agreement. Hanno was right, I had not deserved to win the fight against Rix. It was all very well being able to dispatch a half-trained man-at-arms in a mad battlefield mêlée, but faced with a serious swordsman such as Rix I had very nearly lost my life.

'Shall I do this one for you?' said Hanno, jerking his chin down towards Ralph Murdac's terrified little face. 'Show you the proper way?'

I shook my head. 'Just tie his arms and bring him out here on the floor. I want him for myself.'

While Hanno bound Sir Ralph Murdac with his belt and a strip torn off the bed-sheet, tying the man's elbows behind his back and his wrists to his feet so that he was in a permanent kneeling position, I moved the heavy table up against the door, blocking it. Milo's roars must have roused some of the garrison, I reckoned, and it would not be long before someone came to investigate. The big table, heavy as it was, would not hold Murdac's men back for long, but it might give us an extra moment or two to escape. And we were not planning to leave by the door anyway.

I shoved the plain old sword back in my scabbard and came over to where Murdac was kneeling, with Rix's magnificent, gore-smirched blade in my hand.

Murdac could not take his eyes off the sword. When I held it low before me, he seemed fascinated with it, watching the red blood drip slowly from the tip on to his wooden floor.

'Stretch out your neck,' I said. 'It will make it cleaner, and quicker for you.' And I lifted the long blade, holding it cocked in two hands above my right shoulder like a professional executioner.

Murdac turned his face up towards me, his pale cheeks stained with tears. 'Please, Alan,' he said. 'Please, do not kill me, I am begging you.' And the tears rolled down his handsome cheeks, and dripped from his perfect little chin.

'You deserve it many times over,' I said, and I had to harden my heart, because the sight of his small quaking, sobbing body was weakening my resolve.

'Please, Alan. By all that is holy, spare me. Spare my life. I will go away, I will leave England and never return. I have money, you know . . .'

'We do not have time for this nonsense,' said Hanno. 'Strike, Alan, and let us be on our way.'

I moved my arm back another inch, and Murdac shouted: 'Wait! Wait – if you kill me Alan D'Alle – which I know is your true name – if you kill me, you will never know the secret of your father's death.'

I rocked back on my heels, as if I had been struck a blow. 'What secret?' I managed to stammer out. 'What is this secret?' I lifted the sword higher.

Just then there was a loud hammering at the door of the chamber, and the sound of rough soldiers' voices.

'Alan, we have no time. Strike!' said Hanno.

There was more hammering on the door, and a man shouted: 'Sir Ralph, Sir Ralph, is all well with you in there? Constable, are you unharmed?'

'What is the secret? Tell me now or die.'

'It concerns your father's time in Paris. I know the name of the man who ordered his death.'

'You ordered his death. I know this to be true.'

'It is true that I ordered him hanged, but I received orders from someone, a very powerful man, a man you cannot refuse. He told me to accomplish your father's death. Swear before Almighty God and on the Holy Virgin that you will spare me – and I will tell you his name.'

'Constable – Sir Ralph, are you there? Are you all right?' the man-at-arms outside the door demanded.

'Tell them that all is well in here or I will kill you now, I swear that before Almighty God.'

'All is well,' shouted Murdac immediately. 'There is no cause for alarm. Go back to bed!'

The hammering stopped. I saw that Hanno was uncoiling a long thin rope that he had taken from his back-sack – and for a second I wondered if it would be long enough, and strong enough for what I had in mind. We needed a hundred and fifty foot of very strong rope for my plan to succeed. I shrugged off my own back-sack and kicked it over to Hanno.

'Who is in there with you, Sir Ralph?' shouted the man from beyond the door.

'I am with my friends. Go away and cease troubling me with your impudence!' Murdac sounded convincing. Pleased with his performance, he was nodding and smiling at me in an eager manner.

I swung my hands down in a short hard arc – and smashed the silver pommel of the sword into Murdac's temple. He gave a soft sigh and flopped to the floor.

'We are taking him with us,' I told Hanno. And to his credit, my doughty German friend merely nodded, shrugged and moved off towards the privy, carrying the bundles of rope in his arms.

*   *   *

There are some experiences that are almost too unpleasant to recall, and so I will only briefly tell of the passage down the exit chute of Murdac's privy. After I had recovered my misericorde – it took a deal of strength to prise if from Rix's foot bones and the grip of the polished wooden floor – we dropped the unconscious Ralph Murdac down the chute first, after tying him securely to the end of Hanno's rope and lowering him none too gently through the shit-rimmed hole to a shoulder of sandstone rock thirty feet below. Then, reluctantly, we followed him down.

Our boots sunk deep in crusted ordure, we paused on that foul shoulder a moment before dropping Murdac before us once again, then climbing down the slippery hundred foot or so of sheer cliff to the ground – mercifully, without being seen by the sentries on the castle's western battlements – all the while trying to make minimal contact with the evil-smelling, slimy sandstone cliff wall. My mind, however, on that noisome descent was split between two equally pressing questions: would the men-at-arms in the castle break into Murdac's chamber and cut the rope that held us? And what had Murdac meant when he said, 'I received orders from someone, a very powerful man, a man you cannot refuse.'

Praise be to God: they did not cut the rope, and we reached the ground in safety. All three of us were well befouled, though, by the time we had made it to the bottom. And as we hurried away from the black bulk of the castle, circling round the fish pond and heading north-west towards the King's pavilion in the deer park with Murdac slung like a sack of turnips over Hanno's shoulder, I wondered whether it might not be better to bathe and change our clothing before presenting our trussed prize to Richard. But, as it turned out, we were given no choice in the matter. We were stopped by a couple of sentries in the park and shown directly, stinking, into the King's presence.

Though it must have been nearly three o'clock in the morning, our sovereign was still awake, poring over his plans for the next day's artillery assault which were set up on a trestle table in the centre of the pavilion. The King shouted for wine, and hot water and towels, and we made a hasty toilet in front of our sovereign lord as he rubbed his hands together with satisfaction and looked down at the bound and helpless Sir Ralph Murdac trussed up like a pedlar's package in front of him.

'Well done, Blondel – oh, that was bravely done!' said the King. 'You have saved me time, effort, and the lives of many good men by your actions tonight, and I salute you. I won't forget this, Alan. I am in your debt once more.'

But while the King was fizzing and crackling with energy, after the first cup of wine my eyelids began to droop – it had been a long and exhausting night's work. And I wanted some peace to ponder Murdac's cryptic words again. I had tried, briefly, to interrogate him as we made our way across the park to the King's tent, but groggy and bouncing uncomfortably on Hanno's broad shoulder, he had remained sullenly silent. Tomorrow, I thought, tomorrow I would ask him again about the man who he claimed had ordered my father's death – and if he still remained stubborn . . . well, there were less gentlemanly methods that I would not be too shy to employ. I might well ask Sir Aymeric de St Maur for a few suggestions about the persuasive use of hot irons.

I took my leave of the King – he was elated and chatting

404

nineteen to the dozen with his tired-looking household knights, and with the sergeants who had been charged with keeping Sir Ralph Murdac secured – and went to find Thomas, who was curled up in a mound of straw, sleeping peacefully among the King's horses. I woke him and gave him my weapons and armour, including Rix's beautiful sword, to care for: they were still encrusted with gore from the fight in Murdac's chamber and worse from our escape down the cliff. Then I rolled myself in an old cloak, and lay down next to Hanno in the warm straw. As I drifted off into a deep, satisfied sleep, my last thoughts were: had Murdac been lying? Had he spun me a tale about my father solely to save his neck? It was entirely possible, I thought. But I would surely find out the next day. Tomorrow.

And then Dame Sleep pulled me down into her vast comforting bosom.

I awoke in broad daylight, to the distant sound of snarling saws and ringing hammers. Hanno was snoring gently beside me, and I lay for a few moments in my cosy straw bed and looked up at the blue sky above. It seemed so empty and clean: untroubled by the bloody affairs of men. It was a perfect spring day: I knew I had performed great deeds the night before, and my King had acknowledged them, and now my enemies were dead, or captured, while I was whole. Life was very good, I mused. And then my thoughts turned to Goody, as they often did first thing in the morning. We would be betrothed soon and she would be wholly mine, and that notion gave me a wonderful feeling of warmth and joy.

I noticed that the hammering and sawing had stopped and idly thought about getting to my feet, but there seemed to be no hurry. I was unlikely to be called upon to fight today after my efforts of the night before – there would be negotiations between the heralds and whomever was now in command of the castle – and if they broke down, Richard would begin the long, slow process of bombarding the castle into submission. I might not be called upon for weeks and I felt I deserved a long, lazy rest. In a little while, I thought, I will rise, wash, seize a bite of bread and a mouthful of ale and pay Ralph Murdac a visit to see if I can get any sense from him about my father's death.

I remained there, watching the white fluffy clouds chasing each other over the vast blue heavens until, finally, a full bladder forced me to rise, brush the straw from my clothes, and seek out a latrine. As I made my way over to the big ditch that had been dug as a midden on the edge of the King's encampment, I noticed that there were very few people about the place. And those that were in the park seemed to be making their way over to the east. Something was going on in the northern part of the outer bailey, I guessed, and for the first time that morning my curiosity stirred.

When I got back to the horse lines, Thomas was there and he had brought with him a bowl of hot water for me to wash in, and a clean linen chemise. I shook Hanno awake and, as soon as he had completed his morning ritual of yawning, farting, spitting and cursing foully in German, the three of us set off eastwards to see what we could see.

It was a hanging – or, to be more accurate, several hangings. An enormous gibbet had been erected to the north of the castle, well out of crossbow range from the battlements. And two black figures were already dangling from the crossbar as

Hanno, Thomas and I hurried towards them, slowed by the crowd that had gathered to watch this gruesome spectacle. To my right, I could see that the battlements of the middle bailey were thick with heads as the defenders of the castle came out in their hundreds to watch the executions of their comrades – for I could see by their dress that the two men swinging from the gibbet were both Murdac's men; most likely ones we had captured in the fight for the outer bailey the previous day.

As we approached the gibbet, a cold hand gripped my heart. I saw a third prisoner being set on a horse cart under the half-filled gallows, with his hands tied behind his back and a noose around his neck. A priest was gabbling inaudible words of prayer for the condemned man's soul and the victim had his eyes tightly shut. A signal from a knight, standing by, and a whip lashed down on the cart horse's rump and, as the beast started forward, the cart was pulled away from under the man's legs and he dropped a foot or so, the noose tightening around his neck, strangling him slowly to death.

The hanged man's feet were still kicking wildly, as if he were indulging in a particularly joyful dance, when the cart was wheeled back into position for the next victim. This one was a small man, dressed entirely in expensive black, though rather bedraggled and with, I noticed, his left shoulder wedged high against his neck. It was Sir Ralph Murdac.

My stomach lurched; I was still fifty yards from the gibbet, with a throng of men-at-arms and townspeople from Nottingham between me and the gallows; nonetheless, I shouted out to the knight in command of the hangings as loud as I could.

'Stop, stop. Hold there, sir. He is my prisoner!' I yelled desperately, trying to force my way through the crush of bodies.

Murdac was on the tail of the cart by now, the priest was already halfway through his prayers. And I was stopped by a burly man-at-arms, part of a ring of Richard's men who were keeping the crowds back from the gallows.

'Wait, wait,' I shouted. 'That is Sir Ralph Murdac!'

'We know who he is, lad,' said the man-at-arms, barring my way with shield and spear; by his accent I could tell that he was a local man. 'And no one deserves death more richly than he,' the big man continued. 'He dies on the King's personal orders.'

Murdac, eyes red with weeping, the noose already around his neck, noticed my face in the crowd. He opened his mouth to say something, and just as he was about to speak, the whip cracked down on the horse's rump, the cart lurched forward, and Murdac was left dangling from his neck in space, his face reddening and bulging, slowly choking to death. His bright blue eyes were on mine, pleading, and I honestly tried to go forward, but the big man-at-arms shoved me roughly back, cursing my eagerness. As I watched helplessly, my eyes fixed on his purpling face, Murdac was slowly strangled by the rough hempen rope. His feet kicked and wriggled, his tongue protruded, impossibly huge in that small face, his bladder and bowels released themselves, and I was transported back ten years or more to an old oak tree in a small village, now destroyed, but which had been only a few short miles away from where I stood now. There, ten years before, as a small and frightened boy, I had watched my father hanged – on the orders of this very man now thrashing away his life before me.

I stood still for a long while and watched Murdac slowly die: it was fitting, I told myself.

And as I watched, I offered up a prayer for the soul of my father.

*　　*　　*

408

I took no further part in the siege that day. Hanno, Thomas and I found ourselves a cosy tavern in the English part of Nottingham town and drank ale until it was almost coming out of our ears. Meanwhile, King Richard's stone-throwing machines smashed at the defenders' walls from a small hill to the north of the castle, and our drinking was punctuated by the sound of smashing masonry. The ale seemed to have little effect on me, I felt merely numb. I spoke little to Hanno, and he had the sense to be quiet and order a continual stream of pots of ale from the alewife, with whom he had already struck up a great friendship. After a pot or two, Thomas disappeared on his own business. I did not even ask him where he was bound. I was thinking of my father, of his kindness to me, of the music that as a family we had made together, and of his death . . . mostly about his awful death.

Robin joined us for a while, informed by Thomas of our whereabouts, I supposed, and he congratulated me on the success of my mission the night before. We raised a mug of ale to Murdac's slow, painful death, but in truth I could take no joy from it. Strangely, Robin seemed to understand my flat, empty feeling at my enemy's demise.

'Revenge,' he said, fixing me with his silver eyes, which seemed to be glowing more brightly than ever in the haze of ale, 'is a duty. It is not a pleasure. We take vengeance because we owe it to those who have been wronged. But, in itself, it is not something that can make us whole. We take revenge because we must pay our debts to the dead – and so that people will fear to do us, and those we love, a wrong. But we should not look to it as a balm to the soul.'

But I was in no mood to discuss his peculiar philosophies

and Robin, sensing my mood, soon made his excuses and, after quietly ordering Hanno to see that I came to no harm, left me to my ale jug.

The next day, under a flag of truce, two knights emerged from the battered castle, and on their knees before a stern King Richard began the negotiations for the surrender of Nottingham Castle.

I was in the King's pavilion, still feeling out of sorts with the world, when they arrived. Richard was just explaining to me – I will not say apologizing; kings do not admit it when they are wrong – why it was necessary for Murdac to be publicly hanged.

'They must know that I am serious,' Richard said. 'They must understand that if they do not surrender the castle to me now, when I eventually take it I will slaughter every last mother's son inside its walls.'

Evidently, as usual, King Richard's brutal tactics had worked. A delegation from the castle was here, and surrender was in the air. The two knights who came to parley with him were William de Wenneval, the deputy constable of the castle who had assumed command after Murdac's sudden disappearance – and Sir Nicholas de Scras.

There was a good deal of mummery and show about the parley. The King pretended to be in a towering rage that his royal authority had been defied. The knights, on their knees, begged for his forgiveness, Sir William de Wenneval sticking to Murdac's feeble story that they had not realized who was besieging them. The business did not take long to conclude: the King demanded that twelve noble hostages, including the

410

two knights before him, should surrender themselves to him, throwing themselves on the King's mercy, but he grudgingly conceded that the rest of the garrison – mostly common English men-at-arms and a few undistinguished knights, and the surviving Flemish crossbowmen, of course – would be at liberty to depart Nottingham for their homes without molestation.

As the two humiliated knights were leaving the pavilion to take the King's offer back to the beleaguered castle, Sir Nicholas caught my eye and I went over to greet him.

'It would seem, Alan, that you were right. You evidently backed the right man,' said my friend sadly. He scrubbed at his short-cropped grey hair in frustration. 'And it must be faced manfully that I rolled the dice – and lost!'

'I am sure the King will be merciful,' I said, although I was not sure at all: the five hanged prisoners of yesterday, especially Ralph Murdac, loomed large in my thoughts.

At noon, the twelve knights emerged from the castle. According to the agreement, they were all unarmed, wearing only the linen shift of a penitent and each with a hempen noose around his neck to demonstrate that the King had the right to hang him if he chose. While the rest of the garrison streamed away into Nottingham town, grateful for their lives, the twelve knights were herded by Richard's jeering soldiers to the gallows in the outer bailey.

There were five corpses still hanging there like ripe fruit on a tree of death, including the body of Sir Ralph Murdac. The King, splendid in his finest armour and towering above them on horseback, looked sternly at the twelve men, his face a cold mask of royal justice.

'You have defied your lawful King, and so committed treason

411

– and for that the punishment must be death,' Richard began. Then he continued: 'But one of my most valiant knights, Sir Alan of Westbury, has pleaded for the life of one of your number.'

I was startled by my King's words. I had pleaded with him, of course, but what did he mean by Sir Alan of Westbury? I was no knight. Did he think I was? Was he confused in the head by the battle?

'After listening to the counsel of Sir Alan, my trusty and well-beloved knight,' the King went on, his words having a strange emphasis on the work *knight*, 'I have decided that one man, Sir Nicholas de Scras, shall receive a full pardon for his crimes against my person, and shall not, on this occasion, receive the penalty he so justly deserves.

I caught Sir Nicholas's eye and he smiled ruefully at me, nodding his thanks, but with more than a little relief in his careworn face. I was thinking of the friendship he had shown me in Outremer, his tender nursing of me in Acre when I was sick, of the time he saved my life outside the Blue Boar tavern in Westminster, and the advice about Milo's weak left leg that he had whispered to me before the wrestling match. He owed me nothing, by my reckoning.

The King was still speaking: 'The rest of you' – he paused for a long moment and then pointed at the eleven other linen-clad knights, penitent and pathetic – 'shall also escape death today and shall be set free upon agreement of a suitable ransom from each of you.'

And the King smiled. There were cheers, and shouts of joy, and not only from the eleven knights who had cheated death. Hoods and helmets were thrown into the air and all of a sudden that grim place, in the shadow of five dangling bodies, took on the atmosphere of a holy day. Some people shouted: 'God save the King!' Others cheered the reprieved knights. A group of travelling musicians – not real *trouvères* but lowly market jongleurs – struck up a jaunty tune, and I saw people beginning to tap their feet. Before long there would be dancing. England had been racked by violence and uncertainty for too long. But now the King was back and, with the capture of Nottingham Castle, he was fully the master of his kingdom once more.

I walked over to King Richard's horse. 'Sire,' I said, my heart beating fast, 'I thank you for your clemency to my friend Sir Nicholas de Scras. But I must say one thing . . . I am no knight. I fear you are mistaken in that. I am merely a lowly captain under the Earl of Locksley.'

King Richard smiled down at me: 'Not a knight, you say?' His blue eyes were twinkling at me. 'You think that I do not know that, Blondel? You are no knight, that is true, but you have shown more courage and resource and skill in battle than many a man of more illustrious parentage. You are not a knight at this hour – but by God's legs you shall be before the hour is up. Get down on your knees!'

I goggled at my sovereign, my knees folded under me, and while the King dismounted, I stared at him, and watched while he beckoned over a household knight who handed him a package wrapped in black silk.

'Give me your sword,' said the King. He stood looming over me, tall and proud, the spring sunlight glinting off his red and gold hair. I fumbled with my plain sword hilt, but just then young Thomas ran forward out of the crowd and held out Rix's beautiful blade. I noticed that my hard-working squire had somehow found the time to clean the blood and filth from it.

The King took the weapon from Thomas and admired it for a moment. 'A fine blade, and worthy of you, Blondel,' he said quietly. He looked at the word engraved in gold on the shining blade. It read 'Fidelity'. The King nodded and said: 'And a most fitting inscription!' Then quickly, smoothly, he tapped me three times on the shoulders with the sword, and said: 'In the name of Almighty God and St George, I make thee a knight. Arise, Sir Alan of Westbury.'

My heart was so full that I felt it must burst with joy. I climbed to my feet, and the King handed me Rix's blade – my blade – and then he passed me the black silk package. A breath of wind caught the flimsy covering, blowing it back, and I saw that it contained a fine pair of ornate silver spurs – their value being, I guessed, about one pound. It did not now seem such a paltry sum.

'Sir Alan of Westbury,' the King said, and then stopped. 'That is not right – Westbury is too small a fief for a man of your quality . . . but we shall attend to that presently. Sir Alan of Westbury, may you always serve God, protect the weak, and fulfil your knightly duties as well as you have served me.'

And he smiled at me again, and I had to blink away the hot tears that were filling my eyes, as my King remounted his horse and, quietly humming a snatch of 'My Joy Summons Me' under his breath, he rode away.

On a crisp, clear day in the first week of April, in a green field outside what remained of the burnt-out castle of Kirkton, I became betrothed to Godifa, daughter of Thangbrand of Sherwood. It was one of the happiest moments of my long life – even now, forty years later, the memory of that glorious day

414

warms my old bones. Goody wore a simple gown in blue – the colour of purity – and a white veil. Her plain dress was adorned with a great ruby hanging from a golden chain around her neck. I had been persuaded by Marie-Anne to spend some silver on a new suit of clothes – hose, tunic, hat and mantle – all dyed a deep rich purple-red, and embroidered with wonderful spidery black needlework: I felt like a prince of the royal blood.

I gave Goody a golden ring, engraved with both of our names, and she gave me one of the detachable sleeves from her blue dress as a token, and we both made a solemn oath, similar to the marriage vow but talking of the future: 'I will take you to be my wife,' I said to Goody, and smiled into her lovely violet eyes, and she too vowed that she would soon be mine.

Father Tuck bound our right hands together with a silken rope as a sign of our intention to marry, and then he held a solemn Mass to celebrate the event and to ask Almighty God to bless our lives together. Marie-Anne, as Goody's guardian, was insistent that we do the correct thing, even though Goody had almost no property to speak of, and the Countess had me sign a document of betrothal that gave a formal status to the engagement.

It was a happy day: Robin had had the great hall of Kirkton swiftly rebuilt during the past month, and while the rest of the castle was still scarred by the fire that had destroyed it, at least we had somewhere to hold the betrothal feast. And Robin had determined that it should be a lavish affair with more than fifty honoured guests, friends of his and mine from across the country – and hundreds of people from the surrounding villages, and from all over Sherwood, were invited too to partake of the festivities in the open air. He ordered twenty oxen to be slaughtered and roasted for the village folk; and a dozen of the King's venison appeared from somewhere, nobody liked to ask where, to be added to the tables set up in the fields around Kirkton that were already groaning with pigeon pies and lamprey stews, big bowls of sweet frumenty, whole round yellow cheeses and warm loaves of fresh bread, and fruit and puddings and leafy sallets. Ale was served by the tun, a constant stream of foaming flagons was relayed by Robin's servants to the long tables set out on the grass, and fine wines too were freely poured for the chosen guests who were dining in the newly rebuilt hall.

I was much impressed by Robin's generosity – but I also knew that he could well afford it. After the siege of Nottingham, the King had granted him a slew of lands and honours in Normandy and England that made him one of the most powerful men in both the Duchy and at home. He no longer needed the income that his frankincense trade had brought him; his loyalty to the King in the dark times of his imprisonment had paid a far richer dividend. And I could not complain either: the King had been as good as his word when he said that Westbury was too mean a fief for a man of my quality. I had been given Burford, Stroud and Edington – the manors that Prince John had granted me, and then stripped away when I was exposed as Robin's spy. Richard also made me the lord of Clermont-sur-Andelle, a large and potentially very rich manor to the east of Rouen in Normandy. Sir Alan Dale now had sufficient lands, on either side of the English Channel, to support the dignity of his new rank.

To mark the occasion of my betrothal, Robin had presented

me with a full suit of finest chain-mail armour: full mail leggings or chausses that would guard me from thigh to toe, a knee-length mail coat, split front and back for ease of riding, with full armoured sleeves and mittens, and a head-covering mail coif attached – it was a very costly gift, and one that would, he said, keep me a good deal safer in battle than my battered old hauberk. Marie-Anne gave me a horse: and not just any horse – a destrier, a warhorse, tall, fierce and jet-black and trained for battle. 'He is called Shaitan,' Marie-Anne told me when we admired him in the horse corral behind the castle, 'which I believe is the Saracen word for the Devil. He is certainly full of sin.' Then she looked at the stallion doubtfully. 'You will be careful on him, Alan, won't you? He looks as if he would like to eat you for breakfast, given half a chance.'

But I was barely listening: I was entranced by Shaitan – you might say I had already given him my soul. The dark horse looked at me with his tarry eyes, and I looked at him, and we seemed to come to some sort of understanding. 'We will do great things together, Shaitan,' I said, feeding him a dried apple from my pouch and extending my hand to stroke his long black nose. And he submitted to my caresses with only a slight baring of his big yellow teeth to show me that I should not presume too much on our new friendship. I looked beyond Shaitan's long dark nose to Ghost, who was watching us from the far side of the corral. If horses can feel jealousy, then my grey gelding was green with it. 'Never fear, Ghost, I have not forgotten you,' I said to my faithful friend. And as I moved over towards him, I reached into my pouch and fished for a second apple.

As a gift, Thomas, my squire, had fashioned me a

wood-and-leather scabbard for Rix's beautiful sword: Fidelity. And Hanno had made a matching sheath for my misericorde, too, which would now hang on the right side of my belt. Little John's gift to me, the big man told me gruffly, was the gift of Forgiveness. He had decided to overlook my rough-handling of his wounded arse cheek, 'but, by Christ's floppy foreskin, Alan, if you ever do anything like that again . . .' he paused and poked me hard in the chest with a massive finger to make sure I grasped his point, 'I will rip both of your legs off and beat you to death with them. I swear it on the holy sphincter of the Holy Spirit!'

I believe he meant it, too; although he was not in a condition to make good his threat just then. He was still recovering from the quarrel wound in his backside and could only walk stiffly, with the aid of a stout blackthorn staff. I regretted hurting him, and I was glad to be friends with him once more. And I was not the only one – Little John seemed to have struck up a friendly acquaintance with Roger of Chichester, and they were often seen chatting amiably together. A more unlikely pair, it would be difficult to imagine: the slim, elegant son of a nobleman, and the massive, muscled, limping former outlaw, with a face that looked as if a herd of cattle had danced on it all night. All they had in common, it seemed, was the yellow colour of their hair.

I had apologized to Roger for my rudeness to him that day in Wakefield Inn, and he had been most charming about the whole affair. In fact, I was beginning to like him, and I was glad that he'd been invited by Goody to the betrothal feast.

Beginning not long after noon, the feast was a long, slow business, with much talking and joking between the many courses. Bernard de Sezanne entertained us by performing his latest music and then amused many of the guests by playing parodies of songs that I had written but with new, salacious words that mocked my love life, and mine and Goody's future together – in the bedchamber and out of it. I had to put up with this sort of ribaldry, despite my new rank as a knight, and while it was not very clever, the guests seemed to find it far more amusing than it truly was.

By the time Bernard had finished mocking me and making the most of his applause, it had grown dark. I rose to my feet, a silver wine cup in my hand: 'My lords, ladies and gentlemen,' I began, 'I beg that you will all now join me in drinking a toast to my beautiful betrothed. A woman whose supreme loveliness shines . . .'

The door of the great hall flew open with a loud crash, and a dark figure – a woman clutching a huge round pot – strode into the hall. The figure let out a piercing shriek, a high, eerie howl of rage and fear and madness that stopped every heart in the hall for an instant. I sat down in surprise, as if my legs had been cut from beneath me. Everybody turned to the doorway to look and the Norman healer Elise, who was seated at one of the lower tables in the hall, screamed: 'It is the Hag, the Hag of Hallamshire! God save us all!' Then she clapped both hands over her mouth as if to stop any more sound emerging.

The black-clad woman held the pot high, and I saw that it was painted white and decorated with stars and crescent moons and strange deformed animals and weird symbols in green and black. She screamed: 'A betrothal gift!' The pot, held up in the flickering torchlight, was then dashed to the ground with another shriek of unbearable, unearthly pain. It exploded on the rush-strewn packed-earth floor, and out of the wrecked shards, dozens of small black-winged creatures shot into the air, squeaking bundles of black fur and leathery skin that flapped past our heads, causing many folk to visibly pale and duck before them. And the bats were not the only living things to crawl from the smashed shards: half a dozen poisonous adders slithered out, making for the darkness at the edges of the hall; beetles, lizards and two rats were also liberated by the crashing pot, and these beasts scurried under the tables.

The woman – I could clearly see now that it was Nur – was emitting rhythmical eerie shrieks, like some hellish music that sent shivers running down all our spines. Every eye in the hall was on her, and this night she looked truly terrifying. Her face had been whitened with some kind of paste, but black circles had been painted under her eyes to give her even more of a skull-like look. Her mutilated, glistening nose had been reddened, and her cropped ears and grinning lipless mouth all added to the vision of horror.

Then she began to dance; capering and still screaming from time to time, gibbering and prancing madly in the shards of the broken pot, her rat-tail hair bobbing and swaying about her ruined face. We were all frozen to our benches, not a man could move. I could not drag my eyes away from the awful spectacle; it was as if I was deep in some devilish enchantment, and I was not alone. No one spoke a word, no one moved a muscle while Nur danced her mad dance and sang her awful music in the centre of Kirkton's newly built hall.

We were spellbound.

Finally she let out one final eerie screech, and came to a halt in front of the high table where I was sitting with Goody at my side, with Robin and Marie-Anne and Little John and Tuck. Nur thrust out her hand at me and I saw with a shudder that it held a human thighbone: 'I curse you, Alan Dale,' said Nur, in a low voice bubbling with hatred. 'I curse you and your milky whore!' And she pointed the bone at Goody. I was frozen with shock and terror at this unholy visitation; I could not move my arms or my legs, I could only stare in horrified fascination at Nur's snarling, ravaged white-daubed face, and listen to her hate-filled voice, and the poison that spewed from her lipless mouth: 'Your sour-cream bride will die a year and a day after you take her to your marriage bed – and her first-born child shall die, too, in screaming agony. But your days, my love, my lover' – Nur slurred these words in a hideously lascivious manner – 'your days will be many, your life long, yet filled with humiliation and ultimately despair. You will lose your mind before you lose your life – that is my curse. For you promised yourself to me, and . . .'

'No!' A girl's voice, low but vibrant with passion and loud enough to reach the edges of the hall. I turned my head, the muscles seeming to creak with the strain, and saw that it was Goody speaking. 'No,' she said again, more loudly this time. 'You will not come into this hall, on the day of my betrothal, with your tricks and your jealousy and your malice. No!'

Goody stood. She was staring directly at Nur, her blue eyes crackling with anger. 'Get you gone from here!' said my lovely girl. And Nur seemed to be as surprised as the rest of us at Goody's fiery courage. The woman in black lifted her thighbone, pointed it at Goody and began to speak. But my beautiful betrothed was faster than the witch. She grabbed Little John's staff that was leaning beside her against the table, and smashed the thighbone from Nur's hands. Then she launched herself over the table, seeming to almost fly through the air – directly at the woman in black.

Goody's first blow with the blackthorn caught Nur around the side of the head, jolting it to one side with a splash of red droplets. 'You fucking *bitch*!' said Goody, her voice beginning to rise. 'He belongs to *me*.' Her second blow smashed into Nur's mouth, splintering teeth and dropping the appalled creature to the floor. 'Listen carefully to this, *bitch*. He's my man.' The staff slammed down on to her shoulder. 'And if you ever come near us again, *bitch* . . .' Goody dealt Nur a double-handed lateral blow across the spine that landed with a sickening thump. 'If you come near us once more, *bitch*, I will make you really suffer.' A smash across the back of the neck sprawled Nur among the rushes.

The blood-streaked witch began to scramble towards the doorway, crawling awkwardly with one hand held protectively above her head.

Goody's staff whistled down again, connecting with her forearm, and I heard the crack of bone. Still nobody else in the hall moved a muscle. Nobody else *could* move. We just goggled at the spectacle of a slight girl of no more than sixteen summers taking on the forces of the Devil single-handed and armed only with a stick.

'And you, you bitch . . .' Smash! 'killed . . .' Smash! 'my . . .' Smash! '*kitten*!' Goody screamed the last word at the top of her lungs, and the heavy staff crashed down once more on Nur's back. Goody saved her breath then, to concentrate on giving her enemy a beating she would not forget. The blows rained down with the rhythm of the threshing-room floor, thudding into her enemy's skinny frame; and I could see that Nur's ravaged face was by now mashed, torn and bloody, and one arm seemed to be broken. Finally the battered black-clad woman reached the door; scrabbling on hands and knees in front of the opening, and Goody screamed: 'Get out, *bitch*!' The staff pounded down once more on the crawling witch's skinny rump. 'And don't come back!' Again a massive blow to the buttocks. And Nur shot out of the hall and into the darkness – and was gone.

Finally the whole hall began to come back to life, people moving and talking, many crossing themselves, and nervous laughter broke out at the far end of the high table. Some folk began to cheer Goody, and from across the room, I caught the eye of my beloved, my brave and beautiful girl. Her face was white as bone, knotted and tense, and her thistle-blue eyes still shone with fury. But she locked eyes with me and, as I smiled at her, loving her, so very proud of her courage, I saw that the muscles in her jaw were beginning to relax, and the mad gleam was draining from her eyes. Then she smiled back at me, a look of love, more pure and powerful than anything on earth; and I knew that all would be well with us.

Little John leaned over to me and, in a voice that was filled with awe, he said: 'Alan – little bit of advice: once you're wed, do not *ever* do anything to upset that lass!'

Epilogue

My daughter-in-law Marie is quite right: I am a foolish old man, a dotard. When I had set down these last words of my tale of Robin and King Richard, and Goody and Nur, I fell into a deep and dreamless sleep on top of my bed. I awoke with the day half gone, but feeling refreshed and strangely calm. Marie and I sat down with Osric at the long table in the great hall, and we discussed all of my fears in broad summer daylight. And I have been a fool; it is true. Marie and Osric have been concerned for me. They know that I have not been sleeping well, and my behaviour – my habit of following Osric about the countryside, of watching him constantly, worst of all of leaping out on him from concealment – has been strange and worrying to them. Marie and Osric have both been deeply concerned about me for weeks now. The white powder? It was a medicine, a balm for careworn hearts and an aid to sound sleep, purchased in secret from the apothecary – who much resented having to make midnight assignations to sell his wares – and slipped discreetly into my food so that I could not object and raise a rumpus.

It was a deception that Marie and Osric used which was kindly meant: a lie of love. And yet I feel that I have been betrayed – not by Osric, my mole-ish bailiff, nor by my bustling daughter-in-law, but by my own fogged and aged mind. Perhaps Nur's curse has come true, at last, and I am in truth losing my mind. I see the past so clearly now, I can remember so well the days when I was young Sir Alan of Westbury, a knight of great prowess and courage. But the present? What am I now? A confused old man who leaps out at his servants from behind doors to catch them in imaginary crimes. A dotard.

I remember my glorious past so clearly, and my head is there for most of the day while I write. And where better to spend my last few years on this earth than with my younger, stronger self – with that young man so full of light and love and hope? The indignities of age come to all men who live long enough – but not all men can say that they had the friendship of kings and outlaws and heroes in their prime; that they walked proud and tall, without fear – before the weight and care of years bowed their backs. But I can. I can say, I can swear before God, that I have played my part on the world's stage. And played it to the fullest.

Perhaps I am a silly old fool now, perhaps Nur's malice has reached out to me from beyond the grave. I know that some might say that the black Hag of Hallamshire's other prophecies also came true: my lovely wife Goody is dead; and my son Rob, too. But I tell myself that I do not believe in curses: that they are no more than idle talk to frighten children. And I was a warrior, once, a knight of England – and so I will fight; I will fight her witch's curse – as Goody fought her in the hall at Kirkton on the day of

425

our betrothal; I will fight with all my strength to keep my mind hale and whole. I will struggle to keep my foolish fears at bay. For I can see now that Osric never had the intention of doing me harm. Nor Marie neither. We are reconciled, my loyal, harmless, mole-ish bailiff and I, and I have humbly begged his pardon for my foolishness.

But I still do not like him.

Historical note

King Richard the Lionheart left the Holy Land in the second week of October 1192. The Third Crusade had been only a partial success and, after three years of fighting the Saracens, the Christian warriors were exhausted and their numbers were much depleted by disease, desertion and death in battle. Richard finally agreed a three-year truce with Saladin, the great Muslim general, under which the Christians were to keep a thin strip of land on the Mediterranean coast and several important strongholds, and pilgrims were to be allowed to visit Jerusalem unmolested.

This face-saving temporary agreement allowed King Richard to make plans for his return home, something that he badly needed to do. In his absence, King Philip Augustus of France had been encroaching on his lands in Normandy, and his ambitious younger brother Prince John had been steadily increasing his power in England, illegally taking and garrisoning castles with his own men and constantly undermining the authority of the officials put in place by King Richard to govern the country in his absence. King Richard fully intended to return to the Holy Land, once he had settled matters in Europe and seen off the threat to his throne from his brother, but events were to conspire against him.

Unfortunately, the Lionheart's forthright character meant that he had made many powerful enemies during the course of the Crusade. He had fallen out with Philip of France, a close boyhood friend, and had insulted Duke Leopold of Austria, the leader of the German contingent of the crusaders. He had even alienated Henry VI, the Holy Roman Emperor, by supporting King Tancred of Sicily against him. The Emperor controlled most of Germany and much of the Italian peninsula, southern Spain was in Muslim hands, corsairs infested the North African coast, and France was barred to him by King Philip – so Richard knew that he would have a problem getting home by land. Furthermore, the naval technology of the day did not allow ships to overcome the powerful currents flowing through the strait of Gibraltar and pass westward into the Atlantic, thus preventing Richard from taking the long way back to England by sea.

The whole story of Richard's return is not entirely clear; the facts are fragmentary, and sometimes seem contradictory, but most scholars agree that Richard decided to attempt a clandestine eastern land route homeward. After sending his wife Berengaria by fast ship to Rome where she would be protected by the Pope, he made a feint westward towards Sicily, then doubled back, entered the Adriatic and sailed north. It was the end of the shipping season, the weather was stormy, and after a couple of stops Richard ultimately landed on the northern Adriatic coast at Aquileia, near Trieste in north-eastern Italy – although some scholars suggest that this landing wasn't planned and he was shipwrecked there after bad weather. Either way, that's where the King found himself on or about the 10th December 1192, ashore with only a few companions and hundreds of miles from friendly lands.

Disguised as a Templar knight, or possibly as a merchant, Richard headed north into the heart of Europe, making for safe territory controlled by his brother-in-law Henry the Lion, Duke of Saxony. However, after an icy, gruelling, dangerous journey on poor roads, the King was apprehended by Duke Leopold of Austria's men. It was only a few days before Christmas, the weather was awful and the King was apparently sheltering in a 'disreputable house' or brothel on the outskirts of Vienna. Some stories suggest that it was his aristocratic habit of demanding roast chicken for dinner, rather than humbler fare, that led to his discovery; other tales say that it was his companions' practice of calling him 'Sire' that somehow gave away his royal identity. Neither Richard nor his companions had much talent for clandestine operations, it would seem.

Duke Leopold must have been delighted to have his great enemy the King of England in his clutches, and he promptly locked Richard up in Dürnstein Castle, a stronghold on the Danube fifty miles to the west of Vienna. He also informed his overlord, Henry VI, the Holy Roman Emperor, of his windfall, and a letter still exists (read out by Walter de Coutances in my story) from Henry VI to Philip Augustus of France, which has the Holy Roman Emperor gloating shamelessly about the capture of this returning royal pilgrim. Seizing King Richard was considered an illegal act, as Pope Celestine III had decreed that knights who took part in the Crusade were not to be molested as they travelled to and from the Holy Land. Both Emperor Henry and Duke Leopold were subsequently excommunicated for Richard's detention.

As was the custom of the day, Richard was passed from stronghold to stronghold in the German-speaking lands controlled by Henry and Leopold until he wound up at Ochsenfurt in mid-March 1193. It was there that English emissaries, in the shape of the abbots of Boxley and Robertsbridge, caught up with their captive King and began the long negotiations for his ransom and eventual release.

I should mention here that I have no idea what these two worthy abbots looked like, and absolutely no evidence that they resembled each other in the slightest. My portrayal of them as near-identical was mere whimsy and was inspired by Thomson and Thompson, the wonderfully bumbling detectives who appear in the Tintin books. A homage to Hergé, you might call it.

Negotiations for Richard's release took the best part of a year – and King Philip and Prince John really did make a counter-offer of eighty thousand marks to the Emperor to keep Richard imprisoned until Michaelmas 1194. But after strenuous diplomatic efforts by Queen Eleanor of Aquitaine, the payment of 100,000 marks – an enormous sum, perhaps twice the gross domestic product of the whole of England at the time – and the handing over of hostages, the King was released in early February 1194. One little-known fact about the wheeling and dealing that preceded his release is that one of the conditions for his freedom entailed King Richard doing homage for

England to the Emperor, making Henry VI his feudal overlord. Richard submitted to this ceremony but, as this was viewed as rather shameful, great efforts were made to keep it a secret.

Sadly, there is no historical basis for the legend of Blondel and his role in locating his captive king. But the legend goes like this: after King Richard's imprisonment in Europe, his loyal friend and faithful *trouvère* Blondel – a nickname for anyone with blond hair – searched high and low for him, playing his lute outside the walls of castles all over Germany in an attempt to find his lord. While singing a song under the walls of Dürnstein Castle, a song he had written with King Richard during the Crusade, Blondel was rewarded by a familiar voice singing the second verse from a small cell in a tower high above him. The loyal *trouvère* had found his King, and all would now be well.

Although this charming legend has many highly improbable elements, there really was a Blondel, a famous *trouvère* from Nestlé in France who was a contemporary of the Lionheart and, if he didn't actually seek out King Richard by playing music under castle walls in Austria, at least he has been immortalized in another way, as some thirty of his songs have been preserved in French museums and libraries – including one that begins 'Ma joi me semont . . .' on which I have loosely based Alan Dale's song 'My Joy Summons Me'. In reality, the Emperor and Duke Leopold would have gained little advantage in hiding King Richard's whereabouts from Richard's followers. They wanted the ransom money, and they needed to be in touch with the King's subjects if they were to negotiate a price. I have to admit that because I like the legend of Blondel, and wanted to include it as a key element of the story, I have made slightly more of the importance of finding King Richard than would bear close historical scrutiny. If anyone is interested in reading in more depth about the real history of Blondel de Nestlé, *trouvère* culture in general and King Richard's capture, imprisonment and ransom, I'd recommend David Boyle's excellent book *Blondel's Song* (Penguin Viking, 2005).

The Siege of Nottingham: 25th to 28th March 1194

On King Richard's return to England in early March 1194, he found that the popular tide had turned against Prince John. Indeed his treacherous brother had already fled to France, leaving the men still loyal to him to hold the castles in England that he had snatched from the King. Within a few weeks almost all the major fortresses in England had surrendered to Richard's men – and the castellan of St Michael's Mount in Cornwall really is reported by contemporaries to have died of fright at the news of the King's return. The last castle to hold out was Nottingham, perhaps the best-fortified stronghold in England at that time (see map at the front of the book) and considered practically impregnable.

After landing at Sandwich on March 13th, King Richard paused only to give thanks for his release at Canterbury Cathedral before surging north towards Nottingham, gathering troops as he went. On his arrival, the castle defied Richard and, despite the King riding around the walls in plain view wearing a light crusader's mail coat with his personal standard prominently on display, the constables of Nottingham (Sir Ralph Murdac and Sir William de Wenneval) claimed that they did not believe it was the Lionheart himself but merely enemies of Prince John who were trying to eject them from the castle by tricking them into thinking it was the King.

And so battle commenced.

On the first day of the siege, after a particularly bloody assault, King Richard's men captured the outer bailey of the castle, and later in the day the barbican of the middle bailey was attacked, but the fall of night meant they had to leave the barbican in enemy hands. The gatehouse that Alan of Westbury attacks in this book would have stood on the spot where the later, stone-built gatehouse now guards the entrance to Nottingham Castle. I imagined Alan and his brave men attacking the wooden castle walls roughly where the bronze statue of Robin Hood now stands. During the course of the battle, towards the end of the first day, the palisade of the outer bailey was burnt down, either torched by King Richard's troops or by the defenders.

On the second day, Richard erected a gallows in the outer bailey just out of crossbow range and hanged several sergeants and men-at-arms he had captured the day before as a warning of what would befall the defenders if they did not surrender. I have to confess here that Sir Ralph Murdac was *not* among those unfortunate men who were hanged – the historical Murdac was indeed once the sheriff of Nottinghamshire, and then a loyal follower of Prince John; he married Eve de Grey of Standlake Manor, and he was also constable of Nottingham Castle at the time of the siege, but it was not until about two years later that he was to die in unknown circumstances. My defence for this bending of the truth is that I think of myself as a storyteller, not a historian – and for the purposes of this story, and my future Robin Hood stories, my fictional version of the real Ralph Murdac had to die.

On the third day of the siege, after a severe battering from Richard's newly constructed artillery, negotiations began for the surrender of the castle. The King was merciful and the knights of the garrison were all allowed to go free after suitable ransoms had been arranged. England was once again securely in King Richard's hands.

Mortimer's Hole

When I was researching and plotting this book, I found myself – or rather Alan Dale – in a bit of a jam. I wanted to have my hero locked up in the bowels of Nottingham Castle, awaiting certain death, and then for him to be miraculously rescued by Robin Hood; but I couldn't for the life of me think how this could realistically be accomplished. So I went to Nottingham to have another look at what little remains of the castle and seek inspiration; and while I was there I came across, and took a guided tour of, Mortimer's Hole. Problem solved.

Beneath Nottingham Castle is a network of tunnels dug into the relatively soft sandstone rock that the fortress is built on that dates back to at least the twelfth century and possibly much earlier. One of these tunnels, known as Mortimer's Hole, leads from the southern part of the castle, where the upper bailey once stood, down through the rock to emerge at Brewhouse Yard, next to The Old Trip to Jerusalem pub outside the castle walls. This tunnel was normally only used by the servants to transport butts or tuns of ale from the brewhouse, where this staple part of the medieval diet was made, up to the castle butteries and storerooms. On the 19th October 1330, Prince John's great-grandson, a seventeen-year-old boy who would soon become King Edward III, accompanied by a handful of men, used this passageway to sneak into Nottingham Castle undetected and stage a *coup d'état*. Once inside the upper bailey, young Edward kidnapped Roger Mortimer, the Earl of March – who with Edward's French mother Isabella had usurped the throne of England – and managed to spirit the captured earl away through the tunnels to ignominious imprisonment and death.

Once I had heard this story, and visited Mortimer's Hole, I knew that Robin and Alan could use this secret tunnel to great effect. And I would urge any reader who visits Nottingham to take the tour of these spooky passages – and to have a pint in The Old Trip to Jerusalem afterwards.

Episcopal inquisition
In 1184, Pope Lucius III issued the Papal Bull known as *Ad abolendam*, in which he exhorted all Christian bishops, archbishops and patriarchs to actively seek out heretics and bring them to trial. If they could not prove their innocence, the Pope decreed, people accused of heresy were to be handed over to the lay authorities for their 'due penalty', which in the most serious cases could mean a fiery death at the stake. This bull was a response to the growing popularity of the Cathar movement (and others), and was an attempt to curb what the Church saw as an extremely dangerous heresy.

There is, of course, no record of anyone known as Robin Hood or the Earl of Locksley being tried for heresy at Temple Church, and indeed episcopal inquisitions, more common in the southern Christian lands, were seldom held in northern Europe. But this heretic-hunting institution did exist at that early date and I hope I may therefore be forgiven for inventing a trial, specially sanctioned by the Pope, that brings my pagan Robin Hood into conflict with the Church authorities and his enemies the Knights Templar.

It must be said that the episcopal inquisitions (an inquisition can refer to an individual court case or the investigative institution) as a method of curbing heresy were largely a failure: and one of the main reasons for this, or so Church militants claimed, was that, as Robin points out to the Master of the Templars, a confession made under torture was not admissible in court. It was not until 1252, and the *Ad extirpanda* bull issued by Pope Innocent IV, that torture was officially sanctioned as part of the inquisition process.

Angus Donald
Kent, February 2011

Acknowledgements

Bringing a book from the vague-idea stage to the physical object you are holding in your hand is a team effort; and, although I get to have my name on the front cover, there are dozens of people who have helped me bring this story alive and into the form you have just read. I will only mention a few of them but any others that I have left out, either by design – such as the former member of the Greek special forces who coached me in certain alarming methods of silent killing – or whom I have simply forgotten to thank, should know that they also have my deep gratitude.

Firstly I would like to thank my brilliant and hard-working agents at Sheil Land Associates, Ian Drury and Gaia Banks; and also my kind, patient and meticulous editors at Little, Brown: Daniel Mallory, Thalia Proctor and Anne O'Brien. My former *Times* colleague Dr Martyn Lobley has been full of encouragement and gave generously of his extensive medical knowledge; while Frank O'Reilly and Tez and Dave Tanner of Hadlow in Kent have all provided me with their friendship – and, in Frank's case, occasionally, overnight accommodation – and each has also helped me to work out some of the intricacies of the fight scenes.

I am deeply indebted to Professor John Gillingham, whose magisterial book *Richard I* was my guiding historical light in this fictional story. And my wife Mary has also been a tower of familial strength – and has given up many hours of her free time to go over the book with an eagle proofreader's eye.

Finally, I'd like to thank my brother John for driving me on a research trip to Ochsenfurt after a beery night on the tiles in Frankfurt, when I had quite possibly the worst hangover of my life. If I have made any mistakes in the German part of this book, I am afraid they may be due to my weakness for sausages, sauerkraut and huge steins of Pilsner. For any other errors in the book, my apologies, and I really have no excuses whatsoever.